What reviewers are say

Rebecca Hagan Lee

"Rebecca Hagan Lee warms my heart and touches my soul with her delightful and beautifully written romances. "
—*New York Times* bestselling author Teresa Medeiros

"Spirited and entertaining . . . a delectable treat. "
—*Booklist*

Alicia Rasley

"Excellent . . . Alicia Rasley has an impeccable writing style. Her word choices and turns of phrase are near-perfect, and she has a knack for evoking just the right mood in a given scene, whether it be adventurous, humorous or passionate. "
—*TheNonesuch.com*

"This is an engaging regional family drama in which keeping secrets cause more harm than revealing them would have done. "
—*5 stars,* Harriet Klausner

Lynn Kerstan

"Kerstan's writing is as powerful as ever, richly emotional, exquisitely focused on resonant details . . . "
—*Contra Costa Times*

"Lynn Kerstan's talents continue to reach new heights as she explores all aspects of the human heart . . . "
—*Romantic Times*

Allison Lane

"It's innovative plot, vivid characters, and tender romance mark *The Rake and the Wallflower* as one of the outstanding Regencies of the year. This is Allison Lane at her finest, and a story no Regency lover should miss. "
—*The Romance Reader*

"Ms. Lane writes with a blistering intensity that involves the reader with her very human characters."
—*Romantic Times*

A Regency Holiday

A Christmas Regency Anthology
With novellas by

Lynn Kerstan
Rebecca Hagan Lee
Allison Lane
Alicia Rasley

Bell Bridge Books

Bell Bridge Books
PO BOX 300921
Memphis, TN 38130
ISBN: 978-1-61194-057-2

Bell Bridge Books is an Imprint of BelleBooks, Inc.

Printed and bound in the United States of America.

We at BelleBooks enjoy hearing from readers.
Visit our websites – www.BelleBooks.com and www.BellBridgeBooks.com.

10 9 8 7 6 5 4 3 2 1

Cover design: Debra Dixon
Interior design: Hank Smith
Photo credits:
Girl © Jaguarwoman Designs
Scene © Unholyvault | Dreamstime.com

:Lrah:01:

For those who keep the faith. With love and gratitude.

COVENTRY'S CHRISTMAS

Rebecca Hagan Lee

Chapter One

Suffolk, England
21 December 1813

"Are you sure about this, Miss?"

Amabel Thurston stood shivering on the side of the post road that ran through the small village of Finchley. Dark and damp, it was long before the sun broke the horizon, and she was so cold her teeth chattered and her fingers and toes were numb. But she had made up her mind to leave and nothing would keep her from doing so—not even the coachman's concern. She'd been born in Finchley and had lived there all of her twenty years. She knew and loved every inch of it. It was home. But with Papa gone, everything had changed.

The whispers about Squire Lakewood paying calls upon Lady Thurston with seven months left in the lady's mourning period had begun weeks ago. When Amy mentioned the impropriety of her stepmother's actions, the woman made it quite clear that she was ill-suited for widowhood and intended to remedy that unfortunate situation by becoming the next Lady Lakewood as quickly as possible. Lucilla also explained Squire Lakewood's terms and made it quite clear that she could ill afford a stepdaughter so near her own age as competition for the squire's affection. The village wasn't large enough for the both of them.

It was time for Amy to make her own way in the world.

Amy glanced back at Hawthorne Abbey. She would miss the house with its gray stone walls, tall windows, and cheery fireplaces. She would miss the smell of bread baking in the kitchen, her father's study with its wonderful nooks and crannies, the bookshelves filled with lovely old books and ancient parchment scrolls, and her cozy little bedroom tucked beneath the eaves with its window seat overlooking the back garden. Her heart broke at the thought of abandoning to her stepmother's care the house in which Amy had been born—especially during her favorite time of year, but her father's house belonged to his widow now and his widow had ordered her out of it. There was nothing Amy could do except leave her home and everything she'd ever known and loved behind and move on. She must find another home, another place to belong.

She finally answered the driver's question. "Quite sure, Mr. Hervey."

Alfred Hervey, who had been driving The Royal Post Stagecoach since Amy was a girl, glanced around. "What about Lady Thurston?"

"She won't be accompanying me." Amy straightened her shoulders and lifted her chin a notch higher.

Mr. Hervey drew back at that, surprised that a well-bred young lady, daughter of a renowned King's College scholar, would venture out without maid or chaperone. "I knew your father, Miss. I carried him back and to from Finchley to Cambridge more times than I can count, and I don't like the idea of Sir Gregory's daughter traveling alone."

"It's all right, Mr. Hervey," Amy said, firmly. "I'm going to spend Christmas with my guardian."

Mr. Hervey looked alarmed. "You won't be home for the holidays?"

Amy shook her head.

"Who's going to be the Virgin Mary?"

Amy fought to keep from giving in to the fit of hysteria rising in her chest. While she was worrying about her future, Mr. Hervey was worrying about the Christmas pageant. She did her best to hide the fact that she was scared to death of leaving Finchley and striking out on her own, headed for the unknown. The only thing keeping panic at bay was the knowledge that her Papa had complete trust in the man he'd chosen for her guardian—a good man with a wife and family who had promised to welcome Amy with open arms and provide for her as his own in the event of her father's death. Taking a deep breath to steady her nerves, Amy answered, "I suggested Janet Beasley have the honor."

"Janet Beasley is twelve."

"I was only a little older when I took on the role," Amy pointed out. "And I couldn't be the Virgin Mary forever." She had helped the vicar of St. Luke's Church organize the Christmas Eve nativity play and had acted the role of the Virgin Mary in it for the past six years.

Mr. Hervey nodded in understanding. "That's true, but Janet will take some getting used to. And the idea of you traveling without chaperone or companion doesn't sit well with me, Miss."

"It can't be helped." She sighed. "And in any case, I don't think Papa would object . . . "

"Oh?"

"I'll be traveling with you. So I shan't be alone. You'll be driving. And even if no one else takes passage, there will still be two of us. We shall serve as each other's companion and travel together."

"How far do you intend to go, Miss?"

"To Buckinghamshire."

"That's a long way. A day and a half. Maybe two. And it won't be comfortable. The weather's miserable. The rain's liable to turn to sleet by afternoon, and I'll be collecting passengers in the next village. Every seat is taken. The best I can offer you is a place up here beside me."

Grabbing her valise, Amy hefted it up and thrust it toward the driver. "I'll take it."

Chapter Two

Coventry Court
Buckinghamshire, England

"My lord, the staff have asked if they might make preparations and display candles and greenery this year. Or perhaps, a log for the fire . . ."

Deverel Brookfield, eighth Marquess of Coventry, looked up from the annual account books, fixed his gaze on Seton, who stood in front of the massive oak desk dominating the study and frowned. "You disturbed me to ask about greenery?"

Dev despised the annual review of the estate accounts. He considered the chore a necessary evil because deciphering his land steward's spidery handwriting and checking the sums took his utmost concentration. But only a fool allowed his man of business—even a trusted man of business—to operate unchecked.

"I'm afraid so, my lord." Seton tried to look apologetic, but failed in the attempt and maintained his usual impassive mien. "The staff asked me to intercede with you on their behalf."

Dev gave his butler a sharp look. "And the purpose of this intercession?"

"It's Christmas, my lord."

"Again?"

Seton nodded. "It generally occurs this time of year. Every year, my lord."

Dev lost count of the sums he was adding and slapped his palm against the account book in frustration. Once again, he had let the season slip up on him unawares. He should have remembered that he'd been reviewing the account books this time last year when Christmastide intruded. "Blister it!"

"My lord, the staff here at Coventry Court are composed of mostly country folk."

"Your point?"

"Country folk celebrate Christmas."

"I do not."

"Understood, my lord."

"Which is why you took it upon yourself to intercede on behalf of the staff of Coventry Court . . . " Deverel glanced at the mantel clock, then fixed his stare on his butler's unreadable expression. " . . . at a quarter to eleven in the morning."

"I am the head of the staff, my lord. It's my duty to bring staff concerns to your attention once again. And I daren't wait any longer, as it is the shortest day of the year and the staff must have time to prepare."

"How long have you been in service, Seton?"

The butler thought for a moment. "Thirty-two years, my lord."

Deverel frowned. "How long have you been in my service?"

"Five years this past April, my lord. I assumed the role after the passing of your previous butler . . . Pendleton."

"*Pendry*," Deverel corrected.

Pendry had been with the Brookfield family for as long as Deverel had been alive. Even longer. He'd begun as a young man in service to Deverel's grandfather, had stayed to serve Deverel's father, and extended his service to Dev. Pendry had been as much a part of Coventry Court and Brookfield Manor as Deverel himself and had given him loyal service and unwavering support until his dying day. After five years, Deverel still missed him.

"Pendry," Seton repeated. "I beg your pardon, my lord."

Deverel nodded. "In the five years you've been in my service, have you ever known me to pay any heed to the folderol made over Christmas?"

"No, my lord."

"Have I given you any reason to think I've changed my opinion?"

"Indeed not, my lord."

"But you inquired just the same."

"I owe it to the staff, my lord. They look forward to the season's festivities."

Deverel closed the account book and locked the padlock attached to the buckle at the end of the leather tabs before dropping the key into his waistcoat pocket. He pushed his chair away from his desk and stood up. "No greenery or candles this year or any year and no Yule log." He looked Seton in the eyes. "Understood?"

"Yes, Lord Coventry."

Deverel picked up the account book and secured it in the wall safe behind a Gainsborough landscape his father had talked the artist into selling. Removing a leather pouch full of gold and silver coins, he weighed it in his hand, and offered it to Seton. "Here. Consider this reimbursement."

"For what, my lord?"

"For the coins I know you've been squirreling away from . . ."

Glancing at the locked, leather-bound ledger Lord Coventry shoved into the safe, Seton drew himself up to his full height. "My lord, I would never presume to borrow from household accounts—"

Deverel cut him off with a wave of his hand. "I never suggested you would. Or you would not remain in my employ. But I've no doubt that you *would* borrow from your own personal wages in order to provide the staff with gifts for Boxing Day."

Seton looked affronted. "My wages are mine to do with as I see fit, my lord."

"Yes, they are," Deverel agreed. "Now, take the pouch."

Seton accepted Lord Coventry's offering. "Thank you, my lord."

Deverel ignored his butler's thanks. "Have you enough boxes?"

"Of course, my lord."

Deverel gave a quick nod of his head. "Keep some coin for yourself, then double the usual amount and furlough the staff until the end of the holiday."

"I don't understand, my lord."

"Close the house and send everyone home for the duration. Let them display their greenery and candles and light Yule logs elsewhere. The staff cannot be disappointed by the lack of greenery and candles or puddings and cakes and punch and sweetmeats if I supply them with paid leave to celebrate somewhere other than Coventry Court." Having already sent his valet, Kennedy, to the Lake District for his annual holiday, Deverel did his best to convince his butler and the rest of the staff to do likewise. "Surely, you and Mrs. Trent and Cook would appreciate some time off." Deverel named the two other primary members of his household, the housekeeper and cook.

"Of course, my lord. I have a brother in Cornwall I've been meaning to visit, and just the other day, Mrs. Trent remarked that she would enjoy seeing her daughter and grandchildren in Brighton. And Cook has a sister in the next village . . . "

Seton might have rambled on, but Deverel interrupted. "Then it's settled."

Seton frowned. "But, my lord, what about you? What will you do for help during the holidays?"

"Don't worry about me." Deverel shot his butler a wicked grin. "I've a standing appointment to keep at a certain house in London, and Kennedy's already packed my bags."

Chapter Three

Two days later

"Halt! Who goes there?" a man challenged from the second floor window of the stone gatehouse attached to the gate guarding the entrance to the county seat of the Marquess of Coventry.

"Alfred Hervey, driver of The Royal Post Stagecoach. Service from Cambridge to London. Who are you?"

"Shadrack Mincey, gatekeeper to the Marquess of Coventry at Coventry Court."

Mr. Hervey drew the coach as close as possible to the gatehouse. "Well, Mr. Mincey," he announced to the wizened little man poking his head through the open casement, "I've a passenger here who has come to call on your marquess."

"Do you see his standard flying?" The gatekeeper demanded.

"I didn't know the marquess flew a standard," Mr. Hervey retorted. "So I didn't know to look. And it wouldn't have done me any good if I had known." He glared at the gatekeeper. "Who can see a standard in this muck at this distance?"

The gatekeeper considered the question before replying. "No matter. His lordship is not in residence."

"The gentleman is not at home." Mr. Hervey turned to Amy and repeated the gatekeeper's pronouncement even though she was seated beside him atop the coach and was clearly able to hear the exchange. She was a young lady, and young ladies did not speak to strangers—even gatekeepers—when a male companion was available to intercede on her behalf.

Accepting the coachman's role as intermediary, Amy asked, "When does he expect the marquess to return?"

"When do you expect the marquess to return?" Mr. Hervey inquired.

"Not until after the holidays."

Amy bit back a groan.

Mr. Hervey frowned at her. "I thought he was expecting you."

Hiding her crossed fingers in the folds of her traveling cape, Amy looked the kindly coachman in the eye and prayed he'd believe her harmless fib. "I thought so, too, Mr. Hervey. I can't think what might have gone wrong, unless the letter announcing my visit and the intended date of my arrival went awry." She stiffened her spine and raised her chin a notch higher. "But, I've arrived nonetheless, and I see no reason why I should go back when I can simply wait here for his return."

Mr. Hervey nodded. As much as he liked Miss Thurston and appreciated her company, he was relieved at the prospect of delivering her safely to her destination. "The young miss is expected. Open the gates. She's decided to wait at the house for the marquess's return."

"She can't wait at the house," the gatekeeper protested. "It's closed. Ain't nobody there to make her welcome."

"What?" Amy gasped.

"The house is closed. The staff are on holiday. Ain't nobody here but me, the head groom, and a couple of stable boys who come in to tend the horses twice a day. Nobody else in residence."

"But it's Christmas." Amy dispensed with propriety and directed her words to the gatekeeper instead of Mr. Hervey.

"Not at Coventry Court. His lordship don't keep the old traditions."

"At all?" Amy couldn't hide her disappointment or shock. Christmas was old-fashioned, and she had heard that the Prince Regent's friends and a great many members of the *ton* considered the traditions surrounding the holiday too unsophisticated and rustic for modern life, but she found the idea of ignoring Christmas and all its lovely old customs appalling.

The gatekeeper shrugged. "I ain't privy to whether or not his lordship observes the holiday in London. That ain't my concern. I'm only privy to what goes on at Coventry Court, and I tell you that you cannot stay in an empty house without the staff or his lordship to look out for you."

Mr. Hervey nodded in agreement, furrowed his forehead in concern, and looked down at Amy. "We'll change horses and put up at the coaching inn in Northfell for a bit before we head home to Finchley."

"I'm not going home."

"You can't stay here, Miss," Mr. Hervey told her.

"Nor can I go home," Amy countered. "Not with my stepmother keeping company with Squire Lakewood."

"What do you plan to do?"

"After we change horses and put up at the coaching inn in Northfell, we'll travel on to London."

"London?" Mr. Hervey said the name as if he'd never heard it before and began shaking his head. "Oh no, Miss. I can't take you to

London."

Amy gave him a reassuring smile. "Of course you can, Mr. Hervey. We'll get a change of horses and in a few hours we'll follow the post road right through the city gates.

"To where, Miss?" Mr. Hervey demanded. "'Cause I ain't leaving you alone in no inn in London."

She looked up at the gatekeeper. "I'm sure Lord Coventry must have a residence in London . . . "

Mincey nodded. "That he does, Miss. The gatekeeper nodded. I'm told he has a right fine townhouse just off Park Lane."

Amy beamed. "Wonderful. I'll stay there."

Mincey shook his head. "Can't."

"Why not?" She asked.

"It's closed."

"Closed?"

The gatekeeper nodded. "Until Parliament opens and the Season begins. Ain't no reason to keep it open when his lordship always retires to Coventry Court at the end of the Season. Except for the Christmas holidays when he returns to London."

"And stays where?" She inquired.

"With friends, Miss."

"Good." Amy rubbed her hands together. "If you'll give me the address, I'll contact him there."

"Can't," Mincey said. "I don't know the address or the name of his lordship's London friends."

Mr. Hervey cleared his throat. "That settles it, Miss. We're going back to Finchley."

"You may go back to Finchley," Amy said. "I am going on to London."

"But, Miss," the driver protested. "I can't leave you in London by yourself. It wouldn't be proper."

"No need to worry, Mr. Hervey. I've my own connections in London and a place to stay which I'm told is in a most respectable neighborhood. I can stay there until I locate the marquess."

"Which neighborhood, Miss?" Mr. Hervey asked.

Amy gave him the street name.

Mr. Hervey heaved a sigh. "All right, Miss. So long as it's a respectable place with respectable folks to look out for you."

Chapter Four

The air surrounding the tidy ivy-covered red brick townhouse located at Number Forty-seven Portman Square in London was charged with excitement. The red front door sported a wreath made of fresh evergreen branches. An evergreen garland wrapped the lamp post beside the walk and was tied with a large red satin bow. The halls inside the house were decked with holly boughs and balls of mistletoe, and the rooms were lit with tapers scented with bayberry and spice. It was Christmas Eve, and the "Devil of Coventry" had come for his traditional twelve nights of revelry.

The sound of pianoforte music drifted upstairs along with a chorus of male and female voices and the occasional burst of raucous laughter. Upstairs, Lord Devil lay sprawled upon Madame Theodora's elegant four-poster, bare-chested, but with the covers pulled modestly up to his waist.

"I left Buckinghamshire to get away from all the Christmas foolery. Why didn't you tell me you were having a party?"

Seated at her dressing table, Theodora met his gaze in the mirror. "You left Buckinghamshire so you wouldn't be alone."

She studied the young lord before applying a light dusting of powder on her face and across the tops of her breasts. At six and twenty, Deverel Brookfield was the epitome of young male beauty—sleek, long-limbed muscles, broad shoulders, sculpted chest and torso—reclining lazily among the pillows. Michelangelo would have wept at the sight of him. He was at once beautiful and completely masculine. Theo would have liked nothing better than to spend an hour or two enjoying her randy young Adonis, but she had a business to run and guests to welcome. She wove a ruby-red ribbon through her pale blond hair, then stood up and paraded across the room to retrieve her clothing.

"And you know I always give a party on Christmas Eve. It's tradition."

He watched as Theodora walked from dressing table to screen and back again. She wasn't a young woman any more, but she was still a beautiful one and she knew how to use her body. "I don't recall your other parties having so many guests or being this loud."

Theo glanced over her shoulder. "We usually have hours to spend together *before* my guests arrive. We usually couple, then drink and dine, and couple some more—"

"And sleep and eat and . . ." He considered using the vernacular instead of the euphemism because he knew she liked the way he said it, but Dev changed his mind. "*Couple* some more. We haven't *coupled* at all."

Theo laughed. "The price you pay for arriving late."

He shrugged his shoulders. "I had account books to review before I could depart. And for the price I pay, you should make an exception and skip the party downstairs."

"I could, but I won't."

"Even for me?"

"Even for you." She might have felt self-conscious with any other young buck a dozen years her junior, but not Lord Coventry. He didn't notice her flaws—the flesh that sagged the tiniest bit, the little laugh lines at the corners of her eyes and lips. He still found her beautiful and swore that she would always be beautiful to him.

She wanted to believe him, but time had a way of changing things. Theodora knew she wouldn't hold his affection much longer.

A dozen years ago, the young lord's butler, Mr. Pendry, had brought him to her for tutelage. He had heard, he said, that hers was the place where gentlemen of discretion found suitable female companionship, where a young marquess might acquire the tender skills necessary to woo a bride and beget an heir. Theo tousled her short blond curls. She'd been teaching him the art of seduction ever since.

Over the years he'd become an expert at it. A true student of the art. There was no rushing Lord Coventry. He was a man who liked to take his time. Her young ladies adored him, naming him Lord Devil because he was so devilishly clever and inventive in bed. They all wanted to entertain him. So much so that they argued over who would grace his bed first every time he visited, even though they knew that, eventually, he would make time for all of them. He was the finest, most considerate lover any of them had ever had, and Theo was quite proud of having taught him the myriad ways to pleasure a woman.

Still, she worried about him. He gave and received it, but he gave far more than he seemed to get. He possessed remarkable control in the bedchamber. Theo had yet to see him lose it.

She knew he was fond of her and of the other girls, but no one had ever touched his heart. And after years of practicing the art of lovemaking, the young Marquess of Coventry had yet to woo a bride. Not that he would ever find one here in a house of pleasure. But he enjoyed practicing his skills—especially during the Yuletide season—

and Theodora usually enjoyed indulging him.

But not tonight.

She was his first and favorite bedmate, but she'd learned to put business before pleasure, and the party downstairs was business.

"Now, be a gentleman and let me get dressed. I'm pressed for time as it is."

He gave a dramatic sigh. "If you're not going to join me in bed, how about feeding me? I'm hungry."

Theodora stepped into a crimson silk evening gown trimmed in white ermine, pulled it onto her shoulders, and fastened the bodice that displayed her bosom to perfection. She slid her feet into matching slippers, pulled on her gloves, and picked up her lace fan. Ruby drop earrings played peek-a-boo with her curls, but she refrained from wearing other jewelry. It was Christmas. The season of giving. There was no need to discourage her admirers from lavishing her with expensive trinkets by exhibiting previous gifts from her extensive collection. Men always liked to think they were first. And Theo saw no reason to disabuse them of the idea that her naked bosom should be adorned by precious and semi-precious gems.

She blew him a kiss and reached for the doorknob. "I'll bring your supper to you as soon as I can."

"How long will that take?" he grumbled, knowing he sounded like a spoiled child. But Theodora only allotted him one night in her bed, and he preferred not to waste a moment of it.

She shrugged her shoulders and her bosom came dangerously close to spilling out of her dress. "I daren't hazard a guess." She hesitated. "But there's a sumptuous repast downstairs if you'd care to escort me."

He shook his head.

"You might enjoy it."

He recognized the spark of hope in her eyes and hated to disappoint her, but there were some things he just couldn't do. Even for her. Christmas gatherings were one of them. "No."

The spark he'd seen in her eyes flickered and disappeared as Theodora gave a nod of acceptance.

Feeling like an ungrateful lout for dashing her hope, Deverel suggested an alternative. "If you want to stay and entertain your guests, you can always send one of the girls up with my supper."

Theo shook her head. "And have you coax her into my bed? Not on your life, my lord."

"As you wish." He shifted his weight in order to call her bluff and roll out of bed. "I'll go to mine."

"We agreed you'd spend one full night in mine."

"You can have all twelve of them as far as I'm concerned," he offered, honoring their agreement by settling back against the pillows once again. "Variety can't compare with you."

It was very gallant of him to say so, and Theo knew he meant it. But she'd not forgotten the damage unwittingly inflicted upon her business three Christmases before when she'd indulged Lord Coventry's desire for unrestricted access to her for the duration of the holiday season.

Her regular clients had been upset and insulted by the amount of time she'd devoted to the young lord. They had resented her lack of attention to them, and her girls had been sullen and indignant throughout the twelve-day period. It had taken her weeks to soothe injured feelings and set things to rights.

Theodora had learned her lesson. She would never again engage in any activity that might endanger her livelihood like that. She didn't open her doors to everyone. Her clientele was wealthy *and* highly exclusive. They paid as much for discretion as for pleasure, and she could not afford to alienate them.

Business before pleasure. No exceptions.

Not even for her finest pupil, the devilishly handsome, wickedly talented Marquess of Coventry. No matter how flattered or how tempted she was. No matter how much he offered.

"You agreed to the conditions, my lord, and rules are rules."

He gave her a sinful grin. "You made the rules, Theo. You can alter them."

"Not without upsetting the girls and the routine upon which my business depends." She made a face at him. "You obviously don't remember what happened the last time."

"T-h-e-o-d-o-r-a . . . " He enunciated each letter of her name, imparting deeper meaning to each one.

Theo was unmoved. "I can't change the rules at this late date. The girls have already drawn lots for you."

Deverel clamped his jaw shut and sunk his fist in one of Theo's fine goose down pillows. Three Christmases ago he'd believed Theo cared more for him than she cared for her business. Tonight, she'd made sure he knew better.

Chapter Five

"Wake-up, my lord. You have a visitor."

Deverel opened his eyes, focused his bleary gaze on the elaborate monogram decorating Theo's pillowslip and groaned. "Go away."

He had nearly given up on supper when Theo brought it to him, along with a bottle of wine and one of port, a little after midnight. He'd devoured the roast beef and Yorkshire pudding, green beans, and spiced beets, then downed the wine and half of the port while waiting for her to reappear. At half past two, finally succumbing to exhaustion, he'd rolled over and gone to sleep without her. He should still be sleeping. And unless it was midmorning, everyone else in the house should be, too.

"My house. My room. My bed, my lord." Theo leaned across the bed and shook his shoulder. "Rise and shine."

"I'll rise, but I refuse to shine." He muttered the double entendre then glanced over at the window overlooking the back garden. The heavy velvet drapes were drawn, and he couldn't tell if it was night or day. "What time is it?"

"Nearly half-past six." Theo covered a yawn. "In the morning."

"What the devil are you doing up so early?"

"Not early," she informed him. "Late. I haven't been to sleep yet."

"Then, it's long past your bedtime." Flipping back the coverlet and the sheet, Dev moved over to make room for her. "Crawl in. We have time."

The other ladies in the house wouldn't stir before nine at the earliest. He could spend a few hours with Theo before heading to his room to greet the lottery winner—even if all they did was sleep.

Deverel heaved a sigh. He had enjoyed his arrangement with Theo the first few years they'd done it. He relished spending Christmas Eve with her and entertaining a different girl every night for the next eleven nights. But the novelty had worn off. He realized he'd rather spend every night with Theo than be obliged to perform for eleven other women.

Perhaps it was time to end their arrangement. It had served its purpose. As soon as the holidays were done, he'd give up his room at Theo's. His twelve nights of debauchery weren't as enjoyable as they'd once been.

"No, we don't have time," Theo interrupted, musing. "I need my beauty sleep and you need to get dressed. There's a girl downstairs waiting for you."

Deverel sat up. "Blister it! Don't tell me it's time for the lottery winner! I'm not ready yet."

"I beg to differ, my lord," Theo teased.

"I'm not ready to leave your company and go elsewhere."

"I'm flattered, but you can't keep the girl waiting indefinitely."

He grunted. "Who won?"

"Charity."

His grunt turned into another long-suffering groan. Charity was a hot little minx. Endlessly inventive and completely insatiable. A tigress in bed, she was every man's dream companion—unless the man was weary of endlessly inventive sex with insatiable strangers and wanted something else. Something more meaningful.

"It's not Charity," Theo told him. "You've a guest."

"I can't have a guest," Dev insisted. "No one knows I'm here."

"Half the House of Lords know you're here."

"Their daughters don't."

"Then it must be a bloomin' Christmas miracle!" Theo exclaimed in exaggerated Cockney, venting a bit of her exhaustion and frustration on Deverel for looking so young and comfortable and cozy in her bed when she was dead on her feet and afraid she was showing every one of her thirty-nine years. "Because this one does."

"The only way anyone could possibly know I'm here is if they followed me. And on a nasty day like yesterday, that's highly unlikely. Unless one of your girls mentioned it."

"I suppose it's possible," Theo admitted. "But I don't know how she could have heard it. She's new in town. Came to the door and presented one of my calling cards."

He sat up a bit straighter and frowned deep enough to draw his brows together. "How did she get your card?"

"If she is who she says she is, I sent it to her five months ago."

"Five months ago? You promised you'd cease your recruiting efforts at the start of the Season."

Theo had been in the practice of scouring obituaries printed in the newspapers and sending cards bearing the name and address of Miss Jones's Home for Displaced Women to orphaned young women as a means of soliciting new girls to work in her establishment.

"I promised I would stop sending the cards, and I did. As soon as I exhausted my supply. Three months ago."

"If you sent this girl a card five months ago, why has it taken her so long to come here?"

"She didn't say. But in my experience, it takes a while to work up the courage to leave home and set out for London. Country girls and young ladies suddenly bereft of means generally find the idea of braving the city in search of shelter and sustenance a daunting prospect."

"Not nearly as daunting as the prospect of the workhouse or starving to death, I imagine," he retorted.

"True. But most females have other options. Relatives willing to take them in, or employment in shops or farms or country houses— provided their town or village is large enough to have those things. And there's always the prospect of marriage. Unless a girl is high born or too well-educated for the local men to consider." She glanced at Deverel and sighed. "At any rate, a girl would have to be desperate to come to Miss Jones's Home for Displaced Women in London."

"How desperate were you when you came to London?"

"Very."

"Too high born and well-educated?" he guessed.

"High enough to have received an excellent education," Theo told him. "But without suitable prospects. Probably like the girl downstairs." She fixed him with a sharp look. "Who arrived this morning seeking temporary lodging until she can locate her guardian."

"You know half the House of Lords and most every other gentleman in London. Find him and send her on her way."

"I know all the House of Lords," Theo corrected, "and most every other gentleman in London, though only a select few are allowed within my doors. This girl's spent two days riding a stagecoach from some little village in Suffolk. Alone. She's half frozen and looks as exhausted as I feel. I can be hard-hearted upon on occasion, but not that hard-hearted." Theo pulled herself up to her full height, straightened her shoulders, and lifted her chin to a position between noble and regal. "I took her to the kitchen for a pot of hot tea and some breakfast."

"After she breaks her fast, send word of her arrival to her guardian. Let him take care of her."

"If you'll get out of bed and make yourself presentable, you can do just that. I assumed you wouldn't want to receive her in your current state. And I'm certain she'd be shocked if you did."

Deverel frowned. "Me? What have I got to do with it? Surely, you aren't suggesting that I go about London looking for her guardian?"

"That won't be necessary," Theo replied. "I told her I would arrange to notify her guardian while she ate, and she's in the kitchen eating." Theo managed an ironic smile. "She probably thinks I sent a footman around to a townhouse with a note. She has no idea her guardian was upstairs sleeping in my bed."

Dev shot to his feet, then grabbed his aching head and moaned. "Don't look at me like that. I'm not her guardian."

Theo reached for the half empty bottle of port, walked around her private bar, grabbed a glass, and poured him a measure. "Are you or are you not the Marquess of Coventry?"

"I am." Deverel took the hair of the dog Theo offered and drained the glass in one swallow.

"Then you're the man she's seeking."

"That's impossible! I don't have a ward."

"Apparently, the previous Marquess of Coventry did. You inherited responsibilities along with the title."

"I've held the title for almost fifteen years. My solicitor has never brought it to my attention."

Theo shrugged. "Guardianships are like that. One doesn't need a guardian unless disaster strikes." She pinned Deverel with her ice blue gaze. "One day all is right with your world, and then a father dies and your situation changes, and suddenly you're in need of a guardian. It happens all the time."

He raked his fingers through his hair. "To whom did it happen this time?"

"She says her name is Amabel Thurston. Her father was Sir Gregory Thurston. He died five months ago. Now, she's in need of her guardian and a place to go."

Deverel thought back, to a distant memory from the time before he'd inherited the title. He'd accompanied his father on a journey to a village in Suffolk once to visit one of his father's friends. That man had something to do with Bibles and had a daughter who looked to be about three or four. A few months later, the man had sent Deverel a note of condolence on his loss. Deverel had written him back. He'd been eleven at the time.

Reaching for his clothes, Dev pulled his shirt on over his head, grabbed his buff trousers and stepped into them. "How presentable should I be?"

Theo rolled her eyes at him. "That's up to you, but she's an innocent if ever I've seen one."

Shoving his shirttails into his skin-tight breeches, he buttoned himself in, then sat back down on the edge of the bed, located his stockings, put them on, and pulled his boots on over them. His cravat lay in a heap on the Turkey rug, wrinkled beyond redemption. "What the devil is the daughter of a baronet doing here?"

Theo took a neatly pressed and folded cravat from a tall chest of drawers and offered it to him. "Looking for a savior, I should think."

Deverel took the length of linen from her and draped it around his neck. "She's not likely to find one here."

"I wouldn't be so sure." Theo cocked a single elegantly-arched eyebrow at him.

He ran his hand over the stubble along his jaw and chin. "I should shave."

Theo gasped in mock horror, trying to recall the last time she'd seen him make an effort to impress anyone, much less an unknown girl. "Is it possible? Could Lord Devil of Coventry care about making a good impression?"

Chapter Six

"Miss Thurston?"

Seated at the table in Miss Jones's warm, cozy kitchen, savoring a steaming cup of tea along with her breakfast, Amy was taken unawares by the sound of the deep, smooth baritone speaking her name. Her hand shook as she set the delicate rose-patterned china cup down. It clattered against the saucer and wobbled precariously. Hurrying to right it, she succeeded in splashing droplets of hot tea on her fingers and the back of her hand.

She sucked in a breath, gritted her teeth against the sting, and fought to calm the rapid thudding of her heart and the sudden onslaught of jitters. Turning, she caught sight of the man standing in the kitchen doorway and gasped. "Y-yes."

"I'm Coventry," he offered. "And I apologize for giving you a fright."

Amy stared at him. He hadn't given her a fright exactly. Not in the usual way. Not in the way Squire Lakewood frightened her. The tiny hairs on the back of her neck hadn't prickled in alarm, and she wasn't afraid or wary. But she'd been expecting the cook or Miss Jones to return, not a man. Certainly not a young man.

She'd expected her guardian to be older. More fatherly. Less lover-like. And nothing could have prepared her for the sight of him.

This man set her skin tingling with an unexpected sense of awareness. She felt as if she'd been struck by lightning and lived to tell the tale. He was dressed in snowy white linen, a dark blue coat and matching waistcoat, his long, well-muscled legs encased in snug fitting buff-colored breeches. Coventry quite literally took her breath away.

Amy cleared her throat twice before being able to acknowledge his introduction and apology. "You're Lord Coventry?"

Deverel studied her.

She wasn't beautiful by the standards of the day. In fact, he wasn't certain she'd be considered beautiful by any standards. Her looks were much too arresting and too unconventional for that.

He wasn't quite sure what he'd expected—someone plain or pale, perhaps, or reticent. Or a waif desperately in need of rescue. Whatever his nebulous expectations, Amabel Thurston exceeded them. She was quite attractive, far from reticent, and more woman than waif. Her situation might be desperate, but beyond her momentary attack of nerves, she gave no sign of it. And he took full responsibility for her show of nerves because his sudden appearance had startled her.

Watching as she reached up and tucked a stray lock of hair behind her ear, Deverel found himself trying to describe the color of it. It wasn't flaxen blond or silvery blond like Theo's, and it wasn't brown, but something in between. It was a mix of blond and brown, the color of toffee or dark rum, long and thick and straight without a hint of curl.

He studied the way she'd anchored it into place at the nape of her neck and wondered what it would take to loosen it, and how it would look unbound.

Pulling his attention from her hair, he turned it to her face and discovered her hair wasn't her most striking feature. Her eyes were. Expressive, almost too big for her face, a shade of blue so dark they looked almost black—a man could drown in her eyes and still wonder at the secrets hidden in them. Her nose was a shade too small and her mouth a bit too generous, while her chin was a little too pointed. None of her features fit the pattern of a classic beauty. And yet, she had the sort of captivating face that sent artists and poets into raptures.

"The *Marquess* of Coventry?"

Dev blinked, realizing that while he'd been staring, she'd been waiting for his response. Taking her hand in his, he lifted it to his mouth and brushed his lips across the back, where droplets of hot tea had blistered her.

"Deverel Brookfield, Marquess of Coventry, at your service."

His voice sent a thrill through her, and her skin tingled at the touch of his lips against her flesh. Amy couldn't tell if it was caused by the burn, or by him.

"And you are Miss Amabel Thurston, lately arrived from Suffolk."

He gave her a rueful half-smile, noticing as he did so that her hand was small and delicate, fine-boned, pale and cold against his much larger, darker, warmer one.

She was indeed, half-frozen. Her hand was like ice in his. Her nose was red with cold, her cheeks and lips chapped a rosy pink, and the almost transparent skin beneath her eyes was purple with exhaustion.

His sudden urge to protect her took him by surprise. "Is there another Lord Coventry?" She asked, wondering if Miss Jones had somehow misunderstood her and sent for the wrong lord.

"Not in England. One at a time is the rule." He let go of her hand and executed a courtly bow.

"There must be," she insisted, still unconvinced he was the

marquess she was seeking. "Perhaps an earl or viscount or baron with the same surname . . . "

"I fear not." His smile was meant to put her at ease.

Amy wrinkled her brow in confusion. "But the Marquess of Coventry is my father's age. They were friends at school together. He came to visit us when I was a little girl, and Papa told me that if anything ever happened to him I should seek out the Marquess of Coventry. He made me repeat the name so I didn't forget it."

"The seventh Marquess of Coventry was your father's friend and contemporary," Deverel said simply. "I'm the eighth."

"The eighth Marquess . . . " Her frown deepened. "That means the seventh Marquess . . . "

"Was my father. He rests beside my mother in the family crypt at Coventry Court where they've been for the past fifteen years." He tried to sound matter-of-fact, but his tone wavered slightly, revealing the raw emotion beneath his smooth delivery.

She appeared as stricken as he felt. Deverel thought she might faint, but she surprised him.

"I'm so sorry, my lord. Had I known, I would have paid my respects when we were at Coventry Court." She spoke as if his bereavement was as recent as her own.

He looked down at her. "No need to be sorry, Miss Thurston."

"Amy," she told him. "My friends call me Amy."

"It happened a long time ago, Amy."

"It happened, my lord. I can't imagine why Papa didn't tell me."

"Judging from your looks, I'd say you were still in leading strings at the time. I doubt the notion occurred to him."

"There were plenty of opportunities in the intervening years," she said, neither confirming nor denying Deverel's judgment. "And judging from your looks, you couldn't have been much older."

"I was eleven."

"Eleven isn't much older, and losing one's parents and assuming a title at such a young age had to be monstrously painful for you. I can only imagine the difficulty and the challenges you must have had to face."

Deverel stared at her, taken aback once again by the compassion he heard in her voice, the pain he saw mirrored in the depths of her extraordinary eyes.

Her reaction surprised him, and he wasn't a man given to surprise. He'd spent his entire life among the members of the *ton,* and few of them had ever offered genuine condolences for his loss. One or two acquaintances over the years may have inquired, but he couldn't remember anyone doing so since he'd reached his majority.

As far as society was concerned, the loss of his parents was ancient history. No one expected the heir to a noble title or a vast fortune to care about his predecessor or his siblings, and most of his peers would be stunned by the notion that Deverel had adored his. In his rarefied world, parents died. Heirs succeeded to titles and fortunes, and circumstances greatly improved. His acquaintances who had yet to inherit envied him, and the marriageable young ladies of the *ton* who might have once caught his eye looked at him as a prize to be won.

Amy Thurston was the first young lady in recent memory to express genuine regret at his loss, and the look in her eyes was humbling.

Dev took a deep, steadying breath, then slowly released it and changed the subject. "When were you at Coventry Court?"

Her days had run together into one long, cold, bone-jarring journey, forcing her to stop and think. "Yesterday. According to Mr. Mincey, we arrived shortly after your departure."

"We?" He glanced around the kitchen, looking for a companion, a maid or chaperone who might have accompanied Miss Thurston from Suffolk to Buckinghamshire to London.

Amy nodded. "I rode with Mr. Hervey, the driver of the Cambridge to Oxford Royal Post, from Finchley to Coventry Court."

"That took two days in a mail coach?"

"It took one and a half days," she corrected. "In the rain. Despite its name, Mr. Hervey's Royal Post isn't a mail coach but a stagecoach. It stops in all the villages along the way to deliver goods and let off or take on passengers. And Mr. Hervey had a full coach of passengers, so I had to ride atop with him."

No wonder she looked half-frozen and at the point of collapse. She'd trailed him across the better part of five counties while traveling without chaperone, and on top of a stagecoach in the rain and cold.

Theo was right about the girl being alone, but he wasn't convinced that Miss Thurston had not known he was upstairs. "How did you know where to find me?"

Amy gave him a quizzical look. "Mr. Mincey told us you were on your way to London and that you owned a townhouse just off Park Lane."

"My townhouse is Number Eight South Audley Street, and it's closed."

"I know." She nodded. "Mr. Mincey told us."

"Mincey seems rather forthcoming, as he appears to have told you quite a bit about my private life."

"I think he's rather lonely in the gatehouse away from everyone else." Amy rushed to the old gatekeeper's defense. "He's quite proud of you, and protective, as well. He didn't mean to betray any confidences, but saw no point in allowing me to go looking for you at another empty house, or in letting me to think that I might take shelter there." She lifted her teacup and took a sip, then grimaced at the cold liquid. She reached for the teapot, but Deverel beat her to it. Lifting it from the warming plate, he leaned over and deftly refilled her cup. "Thank you."

"You're welcome." Deverel hadn't considered Mincey might be lonely in the gatehouse. Always sickly, Mrs. Mincey had died the previous winter, leaving her husband by himself. He should have realized her loss would leave a huge void in his gatekeeper's life. Ashamed that it had taken a slip of a girl—an outsider—to bring Mincey's plight to his attention, he said, "Please, continue," then waited while Amy added a drop of honey to her tea and took a swallow.

"Mr. Mincey told us that you always spend the holidays with friends."

"So you followed me to my friends' house." Collecting a cup and saucer from the sideboard, Deverel poured himself a cup of tea despite the fact that he preferred coffee.

Amy shook her head. "Oh, no, I don't know who your friends are or where they live."

"Mincey didn't tell you?"

"He didn't give any particulars. Not your street name or house number or where you were staying while your house is closed. Only that you stayed with friends in town." She hesitated. "I gave him a Christmas box. I hope you don't mind."

Dev frowned, making a mental note to find out how much and reimburse her later. "How did you know about this place?"

Amy's face brightened. "When Papa died, Miss Jones sent me a note along with her calling card inviting me to stay with her here if I ever found myself in London and in need of food and lodging." She paused long enough to take another sip of tea before placing her teacup on its saucer. "And since Mr. Hervey was eager to be on his way home and I was in need of food and lodging, I asked him to bring me here." She looked up at him, saw the frown on his face and rushed to add, "I can't believe you arrived so quickly. Not that I was expecting you. I was expecting a much older man. Miss Jones promised she would fetch the Marquess of Coventry while I broke my fast. And she did. I think it most kind of her, don't you?"

Deverel lifted his teacup to his lips and nodded to keep from disagreeing. He wasn't sure it was kind of Theo at all. He wasn't sure she wasn't being entirely self-serving and opportunistic, prepared to take advantage of this girl's misfortune. But he saw no reason to disillusion Miss Thurston just yet. Not unless she proved herself to be something other than what she seemed to be—an innocent country miss come to town.

"How long do you plan to stay in London, Miss Thurston?"

"I hadn't planned to stay in London at all, Lord Coventry."

"Oh?" He arched his right eyebrow.

"I had planned to live in Buckinghamshire at Coventry Court with you."

Chapter Seven

Deverel nearly choked on his mouthful of tea. He swallowed hard and took a moment or two to compose himself. "You cannot live with me."

"Why not?"

"I'm a bachelor."

Amy hadn't considered that her guardian might be young or a bachelor. She had believed him to be a gentleman her father's age with a wife and family.

The fact that he wasn't shouldn't matter. "I'm the legal ward of the Marquess of Coventry. Bachelor or not, you're my guardian."

"That remains to be seen."

Amy bristled at his contradiction. "What do you mean, that remains to be seen?"

"It means that I'll need to speak with my solicitor."

"I have papers. Legal papers detailing the arrangement between Papa and the Marquess of Coventry. In them, in the event of his death, Papa names Lord Coventry as my legal guardian until I marry or reach the age of majority." She stared at him, almost daring him to contradict her, despite the fact that he was a marquess and she the daughter of a mere baronet. "Whichever comes first."

"A circumstance that, if true, will be confirmed by my solicitor," he attempted to mollify her and succeeded in casting doubt on her veracity. "And while you may have planned to stay with me in Buckinghamshire, the fact is that I am not *in* Buckinghamshire. I'm in London."

"Obviously. As am I."

"Indeed," he pronounced. "You're in London, and with my house closed, I've nowhere to put you until we can sort this out."

Amy smarted at his choice of words, but did her best to remain reasonable and accommodating. "You needn't worry about *putting* me anywhere, my lord. I've no wish to be a burden to you or your friends. Nor do I wish to impose upon their hospitality. I'll remain here with Miss Jones until you've satisfied your concerns about my claim."

"No." His objection was instantaneous and came across much harsher than Dev intended. "Miss Thurston, you will not."

"Why not?" Amy demanded.

"Yes, Lord Coventry." Theo chose that moment to return to the kitchen. "Why not?"

Deverel glared at her, noting as he did so that Theo had changed out of her crimson evening gown and into a smart looking day dress. He wasn't sure what she wore when he wasn't in residence, but since he'd never seen her in anything more substantial than a sheer dressing gown this early in the morning, Deverel assumed the day dress was part of Theo's guise as Miss Jones. "You know why not."

Amy glanced down at her simple traveling ensemble and back at the lines of Miss Jones's dress. The jaconet muslin fabric made the older woman's garment of finer stuff than anything Finchley's drapers stocked, thus more fashionable than any village seamstress could offer.

"I have an empty room," Theo said. "If you've no place to put her, I'd be glad to have Miss Thurston stay here. Besides, it's Christmas. Or have you forgotten, my lord?"

"That's very kind of you, Miss Jones," Amy told her. "I would be happy to accept your invitation."

The only room Theo kept unoccupied was his, and Dev wouldn't dream of allowing Theo to put Amy Thurston up in it. And Theo knew it. Just as she knew reminding him it was Christmas Day would irritate him. The holiday presented obstacles, but nothing that couldn't be overcome with a little blunt. She would be open for business as usual this evening, and other businesses would be open today, too.

He might not care for Christmas or all the folderol that accompanied it, but he wasn't blind to the wistful expression on Amy Thurston's face at the mention of it or the longing glances she gave to Theo's dress.

"Thank you, Miss Jones, for your kind offer," he said. "But it won't be necessary. As my ward, Miss Thurston will naturally accompany me to my townhouse."

"That remains to be seen." Amy reminded him, using the phrase he'd used moments earlier.

He whirled around and threw Amy a stern look. "I beg your pardon?"

"You said my being your ward remains to be seen."

"You said you had proof," he pointed out.

"And you said you needed to confer with your solicitor in order to verify my proof." Amy stood her ground. "Besides, your townhouse is closed."

"I'll reopen it," he pronounced, sounding like a man accustomed to overcoming obstacles and getting his way.

"Without a staff?" Theo inquired sweetly.

"Not without *a* staff. Without my *customary* staff. I'll make arrangements to hire a temporary staff and have them sent around."

"In London? On Christmas Day?" Theo gave a little laugh. "Are you mad?" She pinned him with a sharp gaze. "Of course Miss Thurston is welcome to be my guest until the holiday is past. I'll see no harm comes to her person."

Deverel returned Theo's sharp look with one of his own. "Do you propose that I continue my visit with my *friends* and allow Miss Thurston to stay here? And can you guarantee no harm will come to her reputation if she does?"

Theo shook her head.

"Exactly."

"You can't take her to an empty townhouse," Theo stated, placing her hands on her hips. "And securing staff to open it today will be next to impossible."

"Unless her position as my ward is firmly established, escorting her to an inn or hotel without benefit of a chaperone is tantamount to destroying her reputation," Deverel argued. "It would be more public and bear the same fruit as leaving her with you."

"Have you a better idea?" Theo asked.

"I have an idea," Amy announced.

Theo and Deverel turned to look at her.

"Stop talking around me. I'm in the room and perfectly capable of hearing and understanding what goes on around me."

Deverel snorted. He admired her pluckiness, but Amy Thurston hadn't the foggiest notion of what went on in Theodora's house.

"His lordship is looking out for your good name."

"Is there a reason staying here should damage my good name?" Amy asked. "Because Mr. Hervey would not have left me off if we had not been assured Portman Square is a respectable neighborhood."

"It is quite respectable," Theo agreed.

"But your establishment is not?" Amy wondered how the neighbors felt about a Home for Displaced Women situated in their midst. If London was anything like Finchley, there were those who were heartily against such a charity, no matter how well-intentioned. The loudest protests typically came from the town matrons seeking to better their stations by climbing the social ladder, and the ploughmen and laborers fearing mass desertion as their wives and daughters left their bed and board in search of better living arrangements.

"Oh, but it is," Theo was quick to protest. "As respectable as is possible for a home for displaced women in a city that thrives on cruel gossip-mongering."

Theo's clever prevarication had Deveral gritting his teeth. Number Forty-seven Portman Square was in a highly respectable residential neighborhood only a few streets away from his own highly respectable neighborhood. Theo's establishment was one of the most exclusive, if not *the* most exclusive, and discriminating houses of pleasure in London. But when all was said and done, a house of pleasure was a polite term for a brothel, and Theodora was a highly educated and exquisitely-refined madam, rather than the respectable proprietress of a privately funded charity.

Amy Thurston was entirely ignorant of the nature of Theodora's establishment, and he meant to keep it that way.

For his sake and well as for hers.

His reputation wouldn't be damaged by his association with Madam Theodora's house. He was a man of the world and a bachelor. His discerning taste and discretion would be admired in most circles and envied in others. No scandal would be attached to his name if word of his residence there got out.

But Amabel Thurston would be ruined by the slightest association with Theo and her "home for displaced women." Amy's reputation would be tainted beyond repair by the mere fact that she'd stepped foot inside. Her prospects for a good marriage would be diminished, her relationships destroyed, and her character, if not her person, assaulted.

He must tread carefully to avoid a mistake.

Amy turned to Miss Jones, genuinely dismayed at the prospect of committing a big city *faux pas*. "But you invited me to stay. You sent me a note indicating I would be welcomed if I ever found myself in the city and in need of food and lodging."

"You are welcome," Theo assured her. "But I feel it only fair to inform you that any young woman who comes to town and stays here is liable to suffer some damage to her reputation by association. For most desperate, displaced women, that's a small price to pay for food and lodging, but you are a young lady of some standing, Miss Thurston, and held to a higher social standard than most."

"I'd no idea." Amy struggled to make sense of Miss Jones's concern.

"I am sure you understand my position. When I sent the note issuing the invitation, I did not know you had a guardian. Now, I do, and he has raised an objection to my offer of hospitality. While I am happy to extend the offer to you, I've no wish to upset Lord Coventry by doing so. Running a home for displaced women is not an easy task.

I solicit help from many quarters, including young ladies of good family, but I daren't tread on the toes of the generous benefactors who help support my efforts. And I wouldn't wish to be responsible should town gossip damage your good name."

"I would never hold you responsible," Amy said.

"I realize there are times and situations where young ladies like yourself need assistance," Theo continued smoothly, "but members of the *ton* are not as broadminded as I. To their way of thinking, there is a vast difference between calling at a charitable foundation in order to determine whether one might wish to offer one's services, and seeking refuge." She shrugged. "And as I'm always looking for well-bred ladies, my invitation was meant to encourage the former rather than the latter."

Amy frowned. "I assumed your establishment was a temporary lodging house for women without escort. I did not realize you were soliciting *volunteers.*"

Deverel shot Theo another warning glance before turning the full force of his smile on Amy. "Miss Jones was *soliciting* . . . " he paused for effect, "help. And she's been known to lay a gentleman's pockets bare in pursuit of enough coin to keep her establishment running."

"Including yours?" Amy knew it was too personal a question to ask, but the image of him laid bare, pockets or otherwise, was intriguing. The words were out of her mouth before she could stop them.

"Including mine. Miss Jones has managed to wheedle a small fortune out of me over the years in support of this house. That's how we became acquainted." He hadn't meant to volunteer the last tidbit, and he wasn't surprised when Amy seized on his slip of the tongue.

"She sent you a note?"

Deverel shook his head. "We were introduced by a mutual friend."

Turning away from Lord Coventry, Amy reached for the coin purse concealed in a hidden pocket of her walking dress. She looked at Miss Jones, then opened the purse, extracted several coins and offered them to her. "I am not destitute. I have the means to secure accommodation at an inn, compensate you for my breakfast, and make a small contribution to your efforts to help other unfortunate women."

Theodora inhaled sharply and took a step back. "Oh, no, Miss Thurston. I appreciate your thoughtful generosity, but I couldn't accept repayment for your meal or your contribution."

Deverel closed his hand over Amy's and gently guided it back to her purse. "Keep your coin, Miss Thurston, and allow me."

Amy started at the contact, enjoying the feel of his hand on hers. "I couldn't ask you to do that, my lord."

"You aren't asking, I'm volunteering." He waited until she returned the money to her purse then reached into his coat, pulled out his wallet and removed several large bank notes. Folding the notes, he handed them to Theo. "For you and your displaced women, Miss Jones, on behalf of Miss Thurston and me. Happy Christmas."

Theo accepted the bills and carefully tucked them in her bodice. "Thank you, your lordship, for being a great supporter of charity and a most generous benefactor."

Deverel winced at the double meaning in Theo's words. He recognized the glint in her eye. She was baiting him, playing word games and enjoying his predicament even as she pretended to offer assistance. He looked at her. If he didn't know better, he'd think Theo . . . Deverel shook his head. She wouldn't . . .

He turned back to Amy. "Miss Thurston, if you'll be good enough to collect your belongings, we'll be on our way."

"Now?" She didn't mean to sound churlish or ungrateful, but it had taken her a half hour to get warm and dry and overcome the queasy feeling produced by two days of traveling atop a coach. She'd just eaten and regained her equilibrium and didn't relish the thought of climbing aboard another coach again any time soon.

"No time like the present." Deverel recognized the source of her protest. "Rest assured that I have a well-sprung coach and an excellent driver. We will be the only occupants, so you won't be required to ride atop. I promise you'll find the interior quite comfortable."

"What about your holiday? And what about your friends? Won't they be disappointed?" Amy gathered her traveling cape from the peg and her valise from beneath the table.

"Immensely," Deverel answered, gazing over her head to look Theo in the eye. He wasn't quite sure what had happened or why he'd done what he'd done, but he'd just forfeited twelve nights of sin. No, not forfeited, tossed aside. No doubt this year's lottery winners were going to be disappointed. "But they'll survive without me."

Chapter Eight

Three-quarters of an hour later, Amy was seated inside the Marquess of Coventry's luxurious coach. The cold drizzle had turned into a fine sheen of ice crystals. The damp chill penetrated the interior of the coach, but Lord Coventry's coachman had seen to her comfort by providing her with a thick warm blanket, a flagon of hot chocolate, and hot bricks wrapped in flannel at her feet.

Lord Coventry sat on the opposite seat, his back against the front of the coach, gallantly taking the gentleman's position while allowing her to ride facing forward. He'd removed his top hat but kept his great coat and gloves on, eschewing the offer of a blanket and bricks for himself, but gratefully accepting the silver flask his coachman handed him.

An interior lamp glowed above his right shoulder, and Amy was able to see his handsome face quite clearly.

"Have you the papers?" He asked almost as soon as he settled onto his seat and stretched out his long legs.

"Papers, my lord?"

"The papers proving your claim to be my ward."

Amy blinked at the change in his tone. Back in Miss Jones's kitchen, he'd seemed more than eager to take her word that she had the necessary proof, rushing her out of the house and into his coach. Now that she was out of Miss Jones's house and into his vehicle, he sounded almost angry when demanding confirmation.

Amy nodded at the lump beneath the blanket on the seat to the left of her. "They're in my valise."

"Would you mind producing them?"

She couldn't tell if his anger was directed at her, at himself, or at Miss Jones. But, as they shared a closed coach, she decided it was best to ignore his brusque manner and placate him. "Not at all, my lord."

Deverel waited patiently while she loosened the blanket tucked around her, lifted her valise and pulled it onto her lap. Unfastening the battered leather satchel, she rummaged inside until she located a sheepskin pouch filled with folded documents. Carefully closing the satchel, she set it aside then handed him the sheaf of papers.

Deverel studied them closely. "The seal's been broken."

Amy stared at the dark blue wax seal her father had used to secure the document. "It's Papa's. His solicitor, Mr. Chawson, gave me the papers after the funeral. I broke the seal and read the document at his request."

Deverel nodded as he scanned the legal text naming James Robert Edward Brookfield, seventh Marquess of Coventry, legal guardian of Amabel Mary Ophelia Thurston, minor female child of Gregory Harwell Thurston, Baronet Thurston, and the late Mary Ophelia Jane Thurston nee Finch, of the village of Finchley, Suffolk, Great Britain in the event of Sir Gregory's death. In the event that James Robert Edward Brookfield, seventh Marquess of Coventry should predecease Sir Gregory, the legal guardianship of the minor female would become the responsibility of the eighth Marquess of Coventry, or his legal heir, until such time as the minor female should marry or reach her majority.

It was just as she said. All there in black and white. Signed, dated, witnessed, and as far as Deverel could tell, quite legal. Just as he'd known it would be. Amy Thurston wouldn't have traveled all the way from Finchley if the papers hadn't been in order.

He finished reading the document, refolded it and tucked it in the inner pocket of his coat. "Any prospects?"

"I beg your pardon?"

"Have you any immediate prospects for marriage?" Deverel didn't know why he asked, as he knew the answer. If she'd had any prospects, she'd have gone to her intended. She would not have gone looking for her guardian and wound up at Theo's.

Amy blushed scarlet. "None immediate or otherwise, my lord."

She spoke so softly Deverel barely heard her over the sound of the coach wheels. He hadn't meant to embarrass her. "You've no suitors back home in Finchley? No young gentlemen knocking on your cottage door?"

"No young gentlemen at all."

There had been one unwelcome middle-aged suitor in Squire Lakewood, but she'd escaped his attentions and left him to his pursuit of Lucilla. As she'd been mourning since her father's death, no one else had dared approach her. Not that she held out any real hope that anyone would.

Still Coventry's question pricked her pride. Amy straightened her shoulders, raised her chin a notch, and did her best to look down her nose at him. "And no need to make sport or mock me, my lord."

"Mock you?" He sounded outraged at the idea. "I'm not mocking you. I'm wondering at the intellect of the eligible men in your village."

Despite her unconventional looks, Amy Thurston was quite lovely. In the right clothes and the right circles, she would have any number of eligible bachelors in the *ton* queuing up to pay court to her.

Amy released a heavy sigh. "Intellect has been the bane of my existence, my lord."

"Oh?" He lifted an eyebrow in query.

"Most of the men in our village are married. And those who aren't are simple men. Farmers, laborers, and clerks. My father was a baronet."

"Simple men like farmers, laborers, and clerks would naturally deem you above their station," Deverel concluded. "A problem, but not necessarily an insurmountable one. Ladies have been known to successfully marry below their stations."

"Not in Finchley. But it's more than that."

"No dowry?" He guessed.

Amy shook her head. "I have a dowry. I'll come into my mother's portion of three thousand pounds per annum on my twenty-fifth birthday."

"Not a fortune, but a respectable sum." One he would be happy to increase should the right suitor come her way. "I cannot contend that a dowry of three thousand per annum would present a problem."

She gave a heavy sigh. "Neither can I, my lord. The problem is that I *read* and *write*."

He raised his eyebrow in query once again. "You cannot tell me that Finchley men prefer *illiterate* wives."

"In Greek and Latin. Hebrew, some Egyptian, and a bit of ancient Aramaic, as well as French, Italian, German, Spanish, and English, of course."

"Of course," he replied, dryly. "I suppose you speak those languages as well?"

She nodded. "Mostly. Ancient Aramaic is no longer spoken, and I only speak a bit of its modern form."

Deverel was thoughtful. That much education might present a problem. A good many would-be suitors would find intimidating a female who'd received a better classical education than most men. "I'll wager your talents are well-known around Finchley and Cambridge."

"I didn't boast about it," she told him. "Although I suspect my father might have done so at one time. He was a Biblical scholar, and I assisted him with his work from the time I was old enough to comprehend its importance." She grimaced. "Everything was fine while I was in the schoolroom. Having Papa see to my education seemed quite natural, and there didn't seem to be any harm in my helping him with his work. Once I left the schoolroom, however, it was almost impossible to keep secret the fact that I was his assistant. I'm afraid his friends and colleagues were aware of it."

Her smart little mouth probably hadn't helped the situation, either. Deverel shifted in his seat and did his best not to smile at her look of dismay at the fact her proud Papa had not only taught her about his work and made her his equal, but refused to hide it from his learned colleagues. "I fail to see how a superior education and a talent for languages is a liability."

The frown creasing her brow grew deeper. "It isn't in a man. But in a woman, it's practically a sin."

He surprised himself by thinking about engaging in a bit of sinning with her—maybe stealing a kiss or two and seeing where it led.

"It made me a bluestocking," she continued, oblivious to the fact that he was doing his damnedest not to kiss her. "And none of the eligible men in Finchley cared to offer for a bluestocking wife they feared had been taught history and philosophy and mathematics and literature and economics and languages. They were only interested in the traditional wifely arts."

Deverel couldn't help smiling at that. "Any deficiencies you have in the traditional wifely arts can be overcome with books and tutors. If you can read, you can learn how to sew a seam and run a household."

"Yeomen don't seem to know that," Amy complained. "Besides, I don't need to learn wifely arts. My father may have paid more attention to the ancient world and the Holy Land than to everyday life in rural England, but my education was complete. In addition to scholarly lessons, I received a normal female education. I sing passably well, play the harp and pianoforte, am able to sketch and do watercolors and sew an exquisite seam." She paused. "Cook taught me to run a kitchen, and our housekeeper, Mrs. Elmshaw, taught me to run a household."

Deverel shook his head. The bachelors in Finchley were true village idiots. This girl was an intelligent man's dream of a helpmate–lovely, smart, conversant in several languages on a variety of subjects, refined, able to manage a household and oversee the smooth running of an estate. She would make some MP, government leader, or diplomat a remarkable hostess and an exceptional wife. Even a high churchman, a bishop or archbishop, would value such a helpmate, although a churchman wouldn't make the top of his list of possible suitors. "I don't suppose anyone bothered to find out if you knew how to take care of a house and family."

She shook her head once again. "Everyone knows. I managed my father's household from the age of eight until he remarried when I was fifteen. And even then, I saw to it everything at Hawthorne Abbey continued to run smoothly."

"I don't follow why the local gents wouldn't see you as a prize."

She exhaled her exasperation and looked at him as if demanding he keep up. "Everyone in Finchley knows the value of Father's work, but none of the men who might have offered for me want a wife obligated to continue it."

"Are you obligated to finish it?"

"Someone should and my stepmother is incapable. The research is never-ending, and at times, all consuming. Most men are naturally concerned that important scholarly work would take precedence over a husband and a family." She shrugged. "My bluestocking reputation hounds me."

It doomed her to certain spinsterhood in a village as small and unimportant as Finchley, unless the vicar or some gentleman other than Squire Lakewood found himself widowed and in sudden need of a well-educated wife.

"Your father remarried?" Deverel found that bit of information surprising. Biblical scholars who cared more about ancient texts and the Holy Land than they did day-to-day life in rural England didn't seem likely to take on the yoke of matrimony a second time.

Amy managed a mirthless little laugh. Out of all she'd just told him, Lord Coventry seized on the fact of her father's remarrying. "Incredible as it seems, Biblical scholars aren't as different from other men as one might think. Papa hired Lucilla as my companion when she was two and twenty and I was fifteen. Her responsibility was to prepare me for my London Season and presentation at Court since she'd experienced both, and to teach me the things Cook and Mrs. E. knew nothing about. Papa turned out to be more impressed by her credentials than anticipated."

"How old was your father?"

"Three and fifty."

"A vulnerable time in a man's life when many have foolishly fallen for ladies less than half their ages."

She knitted her brow again, pursing her lips in concentration. "For an exceptional man, Papa was no exception. He always told me I was the perfect daughter and that he never regretted the lack of a son. But he changed his mind after he met Lucilla. Suddenly, having a son and heir became paramount. Two months after Lucilla came to live with us as my companion, she became my stepmother."

"How long after your father's marriage did you make your curtsey at Court?" Deverel wondered how long before the new Lady Thurston fulfilled her end of the bargain and began preparing her stepdaughter for her first London campaign. How many seasons had Amy Thurston been a part of the marriage mart? Why was she still on the market? And why hadn't he ever seen her?

"I haven't," Amy replied.

He was stunned. "You haven't been presented at Court?"

"Don't say it like it's the end of the world," she admonished. "Until this morning, I'd never been to London."

"Why not?" he demanded.

"After Papa and Lucilla wed, he went on a lecture tour about the Holy Land and the early Christians. Going to churches and universities all over Great Britain gave him the chance to examine several ancient manuscripts. He took Lucilla with him. She required a more extensive wardrobe than her wedding trousseau, and when they returned from the speaking tour, she began redecorating the abbey, readying the nursery and schoolrooms."

Amy shrugged. "I'm sure Papa didn't mean to neglect something as important as my introduction into Society, but he began working harder than ever, lecturing at Cambridge and deciphering their libraries' manuscripts. There just never seemed to be enough time or money to spend on my season."

"I see." Deverel was silent a moment. Her lack of prospects wasn't simply a matter of intellect, but also lack of opportunity. Her London Season had been sacrificed on the altar of her father's second marriage. And his obsession with the Holy Land. "Is that why you're traveling with a valise, not a trunk and lady's maid? Your stepmother got a new wardrobe, and you made do with castoffs?"

Amy couldn't answer. Biting her lower lip to keep it from trembling, she turned to gaze out the coach window, pretending to study the scenery even though it was impossible to see through the layer of ice crystals clinging to the windows.

She hadn't realized she looked like such a rustic and supposed it was too much to ask of a man as smartly dressed as Lord Coventry not to notice her clothes after seeing Miss Jones's. But Amy wished he hadn't mentioned it.

Ever since Papa hired Lucilla to be her companion, she'd spent hours on her knees praying for guidance and help in overcoming her feelings. Envy was one of the Seven Deadly Sins, and she had tried hard not to be guilty of it. But she envied Lucilla her wardrobe, especially her trousseau. As hard as it was to admit, fine clothes were her Achilles' heel. She loved nothing better than to spend leisure time poring over the illustrations in *Ackermann's Repository, La Belle Assemblée, The Gallery of Fashion,* and other fashionable magazines she borrowed from the lending library inside Sloan's Linen Drapers.

Unfortunately, Papa viewed fine clothes as unnecessary expense and the perusal of fashionable magazines and newspapers a colossal waste of scholarly time. Until he met Lucilla, he'd never cared a whit about the cut of his coat, or pristine neckwear. The only linen he'd valued was covered in ancient writing and the dust of the ages.

Amy had learned to be satisfied with the clothes her mother had left and one or two new dresses a year. She'd refashioned her mother's garments so many times the fabric and notions had grown shiny and threadbare with age and wear. But she had a few rather fashionable dresses to show for her efforts and had brought them with her—a serviceable dress for day wear, one for church, and the one she was traveling in. Nothing nearly as lovely or smart as the two gowns she'd seen Miss Jones wearing. Certainly nothing that would require a trunk or a ladies maid. Amy bit her lip a little harder. No need to bore Lord Coventry with that bit of information. He'd seen her cloak and traveling dress, and he'd see the others soon enough.

"I haven't a trunk or a lady's maid," she said.

Looking at her, Deverel felt a strange pang in his chest. Not exactly a physical pain, but not imagined, either. The ache was real, and it scared him.

He hadn't felt much of anything since Pendry died. No ache. No pain. No deep emotion. And he preferred it that way.

Though he liked a few of Theo's girls and was genuinely fond of her, he didn't miss them when he left. He didn't think about them during the day or dream about them at night or wish they were with him at Coventry Court. He didn't count the days or weeks or months until he saw them again. He felt nothing beyond normal male arousal when he was with them or physical relief and gratification when their sexual congress reached its inevitable conclusion.

He didn't lose his head over any woman, and his heart remained untouched, so what was it about this girl that created that troublesome pang? Was it the fact that no matter how she tried to hide her feelings they were written all over her lovely face? There for everyone to see? Was it because she was so utterly defenseless in a city full of predators waiting to pounce on weaker mortals? Or because she struggled so mightily to appear otherwise?

He didn't know and didn't care to probe the matter too deeply.

So, his next words took him by surprise.

Chapter Nine

"I'll wager you're dreadful at chess."

Grateful for the change of topic, she shot him a saucy look. "You would lose that wager. I'm rather good at chess. And card games of chance."

He snorted. "Playing against your father, perhaps."

"And the vicar."

"A Biblical scholar and a man of the cloth." He baited her deliberately.

"Your point?"

"Not the most ruthless of men or of chess and card players," he replied. "Turn the other cheek. The meek shall inherit, etcetera . . . "

This time she snorted. "You obviously have little understanding of Biblical history or church politics. Chess is child's play compared to that."

"I'm rather good at chess myself," he drawled.

"That remains to be seen," she countered.

It did indeed. Dev gave a little half-smile. The woeful look was gone from her face and the color had returned to her cheeks. "How old are you?"

"Nineteen." She paused a moment to listen as church bells began to toll throughout the city. "No, twenty."

"Which is it?" He wondered how long he'd have to worry about the odd twinge in his chest. If she didn't marry soon, would his legal responsibility to her end in two or three years?

"Twenty," she said. "Today, my lord."

"Today?"

"Yes." Looking down at her lap, Amy began toying with the nap of the wool blanket. "December twenty-fifth."

"Please allow me to offer my sincerest felicitations on your birthday," he told her.

"Thank you, Lord Coventry." Her eyes shimmered with unshed tears, and her voice vibrated with emotion.

He cleared his throat, swallowing the lump lodged in it. He could practically read her thoughts, and his sudden clairvoyance was as annoying as it was disconcerting. He didn't want or need the burden of discerning her emotions any more than he wanted or needed the responsibility of caring for her.

"Tell me, Miss Thurston, what do you normally do to celebrate your birthday?"

"When Papa was alive, I would wake up to find a gift on my counterpane and a smaller gift every day thereafter until Twelfth Night. When I was small, it would be a plaything or trinket." She smiled at the memory. "I used to love shiny beads, and Papa would scour the marketplace for them—the brighter and shinier the better. I'm afraid I was scandalously gaudy. He always teased me about being part Gypsy. Once I learned to read, it was books. He'd give me interesting books on obscure subjects to improve my mind." She grimaced. "I got books for years, until I finally told Papa I'd like something else for my birthday. I think it broke his heart, but he started giving me other gifts to go with whatever interesting book he planned to give me. A packet of handkerchiefs to embroider. Ribbons. A sewing kit or a sketchpad, sometimes a new pen and an inkwell. When I was thirteen, it was a tortoiseshell brush, comb and mirror set. At fourteen, a bar of attar of roses soap and a bottle of scent. A gold locket when I turned fifteen. . ."

She took a deep breath. "After I opened my gift from Papa, I'd go downstairs and Cook would make me my favorite breakfast of griddlecakes with sausages and hot chocolate, and Mrs. E. would present me with her gift—a needlepoint pincushion with new pins, a chatelaine for my keys, a new apron, packets of tea, sachets for the linen cupboard or seeds for the kitchen garden. Thoughtful little gifts of housekeeping items she knew I wanted. I always had such wonderful birthdays until—" She broke off abruptly and shrugged.

She spoke lovingly of the gifts she'd received over the years and Deverel could tell that the memory of waking up to find them on her counterpane was as much a treasure as the gifts themselves. "What did you do after your birthday breakfast? Did you sit and read the interesting book meant to improve your mind, or was it business as usual?"

She smiled. "We went to church. It was my birthday, but it was also Christmas. Papa, Mrs. E., Cook and I would take the boxes we prepared for the poor to St. Luke's." Amy looked at him. "We went to Christmas Eve services and to Christmas morning services."

Deverel grimaced. "You sat through two sermons in a row?"

"Of course." Her look became a curious stare. "Didn't you?"

He shook his head.

"What do you do on Christmas Eve and Christmas morning, Lord Coventry?"

Deverel gave a brief thought to explaining how he spent them making love to the woman she knew as Miss Jones. He wondered how she'd react to his spending the twelve days of Christmas with a different woman every night or learning that his holiday was one long carnal adventure.

Fortunately, he retained his good sense and gentlemanly discretion. Amy Thurston was an innocent who could never comprehend the appeal of his Christmas celebrations, just as he couldn't quite understand the appeal of the more traditional form of celebrating the holiday.

All he remembered of his boyhood church experiences was the sermons were deadly dull and the pews extremely uncomfortable. The only thing he liked about church was the music, and there never seemed to be enough of that to keep the boredom at bay. "I celebrate Christmas by entertaining and being entertained by friends."

She made a face. "But what do you do?"

"We dine, play games and enjoy each other's company. We have fun."

"You don't go to church?"

He shook his head.

"Ever?"

Her expression was so incredulous, Deverel couldn't help smiling. "I have been known to darken the doors of a church a time or two over the years, but not recently."

"Why not?"

"Some men are religious. I'm not one of them."

"Papa wasn't especially religious, but he *was* a Biblical scholar. And a baronet. We were expected to attend services every Sunday and every holiday in order to set a good example for the other families." She smiled at him. "But I didn't actually sit through the Christmas Eve service."

He gave her his most innocent schoolboy look, but his tone was anything but innocent. "Do tell."

"On Christmas Eve, St. Luke's hosts a traditional Christmas pageant, with live animals and everything. I play the part of Mary."

"Mary?" He repeated the name as if he'd never heard it before.

"The Virgin Mary." Amy frowned. She'd started out teasing, but her voice suddenly wavered. "I've played the part every year since I was thirteen. Except this year. Last night, Janet Beasley played the Virgin Mary."

He had done his share of role-playing on Christmas Eve, but the similarities ended there. His performances were private, intimate and confined to a bedchamber. He'd never contemplated a role in a Christmas pageant. "Tell me you didn't leave Finchley because you competed and Janet Beasley won the coveted role of Mary."

"I didn't."

He glanced skyward, pressed his palms together, and pretended to utter a prayer of thanks.

His irreverence made her smile. "I suggested Janet take on the role *because* I was leaving."

"And what's a Christmas pageant without the mother of the Christ Child?"

"Exactly."

"And the rest of it?"

"I beg your pardon?"

"You said you didn't run away from home because Janet Beasley usurped your role as Finchley's Virgin Mary."

"I didn't."

He gentled his voice when he asked the question they both knew wasn't a question at all. "But you did run away from home?"

"It's not my home now. It's Lucilla's."

He was thoughtful. "She doesn't want you running the abbey any longer."

"She plans to marry Squire Lakewood."

Deverel let out breath. He was doing his utmost to be patient and understanding, but pulling information from her was like pulling hen's teeth. He ventured a guess. "Squire Lakewood is opposed to having you live with them after he marries your stepmother, but you can't remain at the abbey by yourself."

"Not at all. Squire Lakewood offered us a private family arrangement. He's more than willing to offer both of us a home with him and to marry Lucilla provided she conceives his heir before I do."

"The bas—blackguard wants both of you!" Deverel sputtered, outraged.

It was one thing to have a Cyprian every night at a high class house of pleasure. Gentlemen, himself included, did that every day. It was quite another to suggest the same arrangement to a lady—especially an innocent lady. Deverel considered paying a visit to Squire Lakewood in Finchley and administering a sound thrashing. But the ensuing scandal would do Amy more harm than good and blight her father's good name and his widow's reputation.

"It's a small village with few eligible men," Amy reminded him. "I'm sure the squire would contend that I should be honored by the offer." She frowned. "But I've no wish to become part of a private *family* arrangement to conceive the Lakewood heir, and Lucilla didn't care for the idea either, so . . . " She shrugged in a gesture that would have been purely Gallic if Amy Thurston wasn't so thoroughly, refreshingly English.

"So, you left."

She nodded. "As you say, I ran away from home in search of my guardian."

"What did you expect to find?"

"What my father promised I'd find."

"Which is?"

"A place to belong."

Her answer sucked the breath from his chest, and Deverel felt that pang once again. For the longest time, neither of them spoke as they sat in companionable silence listening to Christmas bells toll throughout the city.

"I'm a bachelor," he finally said. "I can offer you a big, empty country house and an equally empty townhouse, but not much of a home. And there are . . . " He searched for the right word. "*Complications* inherent even in that inadequate offer. You deserve better, and if I were . . . " Older. Wiser. ". . . *different* I might do better." He raked his fingers through his hair in a rare show of frustration. "I can't ease your hurt at losing your role as the Virgin Mary in Finchley's Nativity reenactment, and I'm quite certain anything I offer will be a poor substitute, but I'm willing to try." He looked at her and found himself drowning in her deep blue eyes.

"All a body can do is try," Amy whispered.

Another pang hit him, this one in a region well below his chest, a pain with which he was most familiar. He was in danger, but she was in greater danger. He wanted her. And there was no one to protect her from him.

"I'm willing to help you celebrate today," he said, at last. "So tell me, Miss Thurston, other than playing the Virgin Mary, is there anything in particular you'd like to do for your twentieth birthday?"

Amy gave a wistful sigh. "I haven't seen much of London."

"It's early. And one of the few times of the year when we're likely to find most everything closed," he warned.

"Are the parks closed? Or the gardens?"

Deverel inhaled a lungful of cold air and slowly expelled it. It was pouring rain outside and freezing cold, and he was trapped in a closed coach with a girl who wanted a tour of London's parks and gardens.

He squeezed his eyes shut. He should be back at Number Forty-seven Portman Square rolling around in a big comfortable bed entertaining and being entertained by Charity. He should be there where he felt safe. Where he could be Lord Devil. Where no one expected more of him than a good ride. Where he could tease and torment and pleasure, and be teased and tormented and pleasured, and engage in a satisfying romp between the sheets without fear of anyone getting hurt. He should be back there at Theo's where he knew what to expect and how much to give.

Instead he was riding around in his coach with his ward feeling like a fox guarding the hen house. Or a wolf tending the sheep. Or the proverbial lion longing to lie down with the lamb. He had to get her out of his coach before he ruined her beyond redemption.

"What would you like to do after the Town tour?"

She stared up at him with her big, blue eyes. "Some men are religious. You are not one of them. Yet I would like to see London's churches."

"Have you a preference or shall I do the honors?"

"That one," she answered, listening to the toll of a particularly melodic set of bells.

Deverel focused on the direction of the sound, then rapped his cane against the roof of the coach and issued instructions to the driver. "St. Michael's it is."

Chapter Ten

On their whirlwind tour of London, he drove her to Piccadilly, into the western end of Hyde Park, along a drenched, deserted Rotten Row, past the Serpentine and the gates of Kensington Palace. They followed the bells as Deverel took Amy to see the great churches—St. Paul's, St. George's, Hanover, and Westminster Abbey. They rode down Pall Mall to view the beautiful façade of the Prince Regent's palace, Carlton House, then wound their way through Mayfair and the smaller parks and squares to Haymarket, and the theaters of Covent Garden and Theater Royal, Drury Lane. Avoiding the exclusively male environs of St. James, Deverel showed her the fashionable areas around Berkley Square and Old Bond and New Bond Streets until they finally emerged near St. Michael's Church on St. Michael's Square.

"It's perfect!" Amy glanced out the window as the marquess's coach rolled to a stop alongside other coaches lining the street that marked the entrance to the square. "It looks exactly the way a church should look on Christmas morning."

The exterior of St. Michael's and the square surrounding it were decorated with evergreen wreaths festooned with red ribbons. Lamp posts and handrails on either side of the steps leading up to the entrance were done up in the same fashion, with long evergreen garlands tied with matching greenery and ribbons. Even the benches lining the square sported evergreen wreaths. And to add to the picture, the icy drizzle had become a mix of ice and fat, heavy snow that cast both church and square into a perfect blend of stately and festive.

Deverel found the lack of coaches bearing coats of arms perfect. The cold, inclement weather and the date on the calendar had apparently combined to keep a number of the more fashionable members of the *ton* who would normally be in attendance on Christmas morning at home, either in London or in the country.

"Can we go inside?"

He glanced over at Amy and bit back a groan. He'd rather be drawn and quartered on Tyburn Hill than enter a church on Christmas morning. But she had that wistful look, and a church offered better protection for her from the weather—and from him—than the coach, so Deverel snatched up his hat and cloak and alighted from the vehicle before he changed his mind.

The young footman riding on the back grabbed an umbrella from the leather boot and hurried forward to shield him from the worst of the sleet and snow as Amy prepared to exit the coach. Dev reached out and helped her down the step and onto the pavement, then taking the umbrella, held it above their heads as he escorted Amy up the steps and into St. Michael's narthex.

He gave serious thought to seating her in the pew closest to the door then escaping to the coach and driving about town until the service ended, but couldn't bring himself to do it. There weren't a great many members of the *ton* in attendance, but there was a good chance the ones who were there knew him and would be scandalized by his ungentlemanly behavior.

Like any other man, he had moments of knavish behavior, but he'd never abandoned a female to the mercy of a church full of strangers—certainly not a lady in his care—as the documents she carried suggested she was. He might be called the devil in some quarters, but he wasn't that cold-blooded.

Deverel decided that if he was going to break a five-year personal record of avoiding church by attending the Christmas-morning service, he wasn't going to skulk in and sit on the back pew. He was going to walk in, put a generous amount of cash in the poor box, and sit where generations of Brookfields had sat before him, right where the bishop could keep an eye on him. In for a penny, in for a pound.

Depositing the umbrella in the stand just inside the massive doorway, Deverel guided Amy to the poor boxes where he left a sizeable contribution. Amy smiled her approval as he dropped in the coins, so Dev added another guinea to each box for good measure. Then he ushered her through the narthex, into the nave, and up the aisle. They moved past the back pews to the one at the front close to the high altar and dedicated to Michael James William Brookfield, first Marquess of Coventry in the Year of Our Lord seventeen hundred and twelve.

Following the Christmas service, which Dev survived intact, the bishop greeted the parishioners at the door. He reached for Deverel's hand, and there was no avoiding him.

"Happy Christmas and welcome back to St. Michael's. I'm Bishop Manwaring, and you must be the young Marquess of Coventry all grown up."

"Yes." He politely shook the bishop's hand. "I'm Deverel Brookfield."

"I would have known you anywhere, my lord," the bishop offered. "Even if you hadn't chosen to sit on your family's pew. If I may say so, you are almost an exact likeness of your late father except for the color of your eyes. I believe his were darker."

The bishop's comment surprised him. Very few people mentioned his father these days, and no one in recent memory had remarked on a paternal likeness. Logically, he knew it was there, but when Deverel thought of his father he remembered him as a parent and himself as a child. He recalled him as tall, broad-shouldered, and exceptionally handsome, with a ready smile and a deep, soothing voice. He never thought of himself that way.

"I'm pleased to hear it, sir."

The bishop leaned closer. "I appreciate your coming today, and hope you'll consider coming again, my lord."

Deverel swallowed a lump in his throat, then gave the bishop a brisk nod of acknowledgement.

Bishop Manwaring paused long enough for Deverel to recover his power of speech, then politely turned to Amy. "Is this your lady, my lord?"

His voice sounded gruff when he spoke, and Deverel carefully avoided hints of a relationship as he introduced her. "This is Miss Thurston. Sir Gregory's daughter."

Amy offered her hand. "I'm most pleased to meet you, Bishop Manwaring. I so enjoyed your sermon."

On a warm, welcoming smile, he took her hand in his and patted it as he spoke. "Ah, yes, Miss Thurston. I'm delighted to meet you again. Please accept my deepest condolences on the loss of your father. He and I enjoyed a long friendship and an equally enduring and lively correspondence. I was gratified to learn you are continuing his work."

"Thank you, Bishop."

Cupping her elbow with his hand, Deverel gently urged Amy toward the exit as an attractive, smartly dressed matron approached them. Other members of the congregation were moving closer, eager to speak with the bishop.

But Manwaring hadn't finished his conversation. Motioning for the matron to join them, he said, "You're most welcome, Miss Thurston. If you have a moment, I know my wife will want to join me in wishing you many happy returns of the day."

Amy halted in her tracks. "How did you know?"

Deverel watched Amy as the older woman approached. Too polite to ask about her appearance, or to compliment her on it, she studied it covertly, memorizing the details of her costume the way she'd studied Theo's gown before they'd left the house on Portman Square.

Bishop Manwaring greeted his wife warmly. "Ah, there you are, my dear. Come meet Lord Coventry and Miss Thurston. I couldn't let them get away without introducing you." He smiled. "Miss Thurston, Lord Coventry, may I present my wife, Lady Manwaring?"

Deverel bowed. "A pleasure to make your acquaintance, Lady Manwaring."

The lady glanced at Deverel, but her attention was focused on Amy. "Thurston? Is she Sir Gregory's little Amy?"

"Indeed, she is," the bishop confirmed. "Little Amy. And, if you remember, today is her special day."

Amy gave the ecclesiastical couple a quizzical look.

"We know all about you." Lady Manwaring hugged Amy to her bosom then held her at arms' length. "Your father shared so much of his life with us through his letters. We were always so thrilled to get them. He filled each with news of his work and his travels and you."

The bishop met Amy's look with a smile broader than before, then looked up at Deverel. "I daresay Gregory was as proud of his Christmas child as Mary and Joseph were of theirs." He bowed to them, a twinkle in his eye. "I'm sorry to have to desert you, Miss Thurston and Lord Coventry, but I'm leaving you in the best of hands until I return." With that, he turned to greet the other members of the congregation who had patiently waited to speak with him.

The bishop's wife gave Amy another quick hug, then released her and launched into conversation.

"My dear girl, it's so good to see you. The bishop and I feel we know you as if you were ours, yet we only met you once, when you were barely three. After your mother died. Sir Gregory brought you with him when he came to consult with the bishop on some early manuscripts we'd discovered hidden away. You stayed with me while the curate, the bishop, and Sir Gregory pored over those dusty old books. After that, your father always included a few words about you in his correspondence." Glancing around at the crowd of worshippers, Lady Manwaring continued, "He wrote to us that he had remarried. Did Lady Thurston come with you? I confess to being curious about the woman who captured Sir Gregory's heart after so many years."

"I came alone," Amy replied. "My stepmother decided to remain in Finchley."

Considering all that had happened to bring her to this place, Deverel found Amy's tact extraordinary.

"I suppose that's understandable," Lady Manwaring concluded. "As she's only a few months into her widowhood and still mourning the great loss that's befallen her."

"In her fashion," Amy managed.

"Well," Lady Manwaring patted Amy's arm once again. "Everyone mourns in his or her own way. There is no time limit on grief."

"Apparently not," Amy agreed.

A sudden thought occurred to Lady Manwaring. "Don't tell me you traveled all the way from that little hamlet alone. Without chaperone."

Amy shook her head and gave Lady Manwaring a reassuring smile. "No, Ma'am. Mr. Hervey escorted me from Finchley to London in the company of three other ladies and their families. It was quite proper. I was well-chaperoned all the way to town, and Lord Coventry met me immediately upon my arrival, so I've been well protected."

Lady Manwaring pinned Deverel with a sharp gaze. "Where did Lord Coventry meet you?"

"At Miss Jones's—"

"Hush, child." Lady Manwaring quickly shushed Amy. Looking about, she checked to see if any of the other church-goers had overheard before continuing. "Don't tell me that *female* sent you her calling card."

Amy bobbed her head up and down in mute confirmation.

The bishop's wife let out a rush of air. "That *female's* calling cards are turning up everywhere." She glared at the marquess. "Don't tell me *you* let a young lady go there."

"I—" he began, but Amy didn't let him finish.

"Lord Coventry was not expecting me to arrive on Christmas Day, but he graciously collected me from Portman Square and escorted me here."

The bishop's wife nearly leveled Deverel with another withering glance. "I don't imagine he had to come far."

"As a matter of fact, I didn't." Deverel withstood Lady Manwaring's attack. "I have a townhouse around the corner at Number Eight, South Audley Street."

"Which is closed until the start of the Season," the lady retorted. "Or that is what I was given to understand."

Deverel glanced over the woman's head, to where the bishop stood in rapt conversation with a parishioner. He didn't know where the bishop's wife got her information, but it was right on the mark.

Lady Manwaring took a step closer. "The bishop doesn't reveal what he learns in the confessional. He doesn't have to. As a woman and a clergyman's wife, I'm often called upon to witness, and people tend to take me into their confidence. I've heard quite a few tales in my time and come in contact with a variety of Cyp—"

"*Madam.*" This time, Deverel cut her off, reminding Lady Manwaring that, while she had some experience of the world, she was in the company of a young woman who did not.

"*City* residents," she amended. "And I read the '*Ton* Tidbits' column in the *Morning Chronicle.*"

That explained where she got her information. There was no escaping the gossips who contributed to that dastardly column. Although not surprised, he expected better of a bishop's wife than to indulge in gossip. Everyone who was anyone in the *ton* read the *Morning Chronicle*. He read it himself, if only to find out what everyone else was reading. "You cannot believe all you read in gossip columns."

"I can believe the *Chronicle* more than I can believe that a reputable coachman would drop a lady off there," Lady Manwaring continued in a low, furious voice.

"It's a perfectly respectable Mayfair address," Amy protested.

Her protest didn't mollify Lady Manwaring. "Only to the unsuspecting."

"Mr. Hervey was unsuspecting. And so was I. We don't take the London papers." Amy made a face. "Papa wasn't interested in London news unless it took place during the early Christian era or the Roman occupation, so I didn't realize that particular residence wasn't quite up to snuff until I got there."

Lady Manwaring opened her mouth to speak, but Dev's upheld hand forestalled her. "She arrived at six this morning and was there less than an hour. The—" He caught himself before committing a major indiscretion. "The mistress of the house fed her breakfast and sent for me. Miss Thurston was exhausted after the journey from Coventry Court."

"You went all the way to Buckinghamshire before coming here? Oh, you poor child." Lady Manwaring's maternal instinct came to the fore.

"It's not that far from Finchley," Amy hedged.

"In this weather? Why, it's a day's journey at least!"

It was a day and half's journey in weather worse than today's, but Amy wasn't foolish enough to point that out.

"Oh, my dear girl, anything could have happened to you."

"It didn't. I arrived safe and sound."

"And I collected her within the hour," Deverel added.

Lady Manwaring narrowed her gaze at him once again. "And took her where? If your townhouse is closed and you were spending the holidays with *friends* as was reported, where has she been since seven o'clock this morning?"

Deverel took a deep breath and answered, "Touring the town with me."

"Oh, good heavens," Lady Manwaring muttered. "Don't tell me you took her riding all over London in a closed coach at seven in the morning?" She glared at the young lord. "Have you no shame? Or regard for her reputation?"

"Would you rather I had taken her touring in an open barouche or my phaeton?" Deverel was rapidly reaching the end of his patience. He had done everything in his power to protect Amy from scandal and from his baser instincts, and he didn't appreciate the bishop's wife—a lady he'd only just met—ringing a peal over his head on today of all days. "I brought her to *church*, Lady Manwaring. She's as pure now as the Virgin Mary she was supposed to play last night in the Finchley nativity. I haven't touched her. Nor will I so long as she is under my protection."

"I appreciate your honesty and your resolve, my lord," the bishop's wife said, "but being seen alone in your company at that hour of the morning is enough to ruin her."

"Is there anything scandalous or disreputable about my being seen alone in the company of a legal guardian?"

"No, of course not," Lady Manwaring replied.

"Then we've no cause for worry." Amy smiled. "Lord Coventry is my legal guardian."

Lady Manwaring whirled on Dev. "Is that true?"

He nodded. "According to the legal documents Miss Thurston brought to prove her claim."

"What was Sir Gregory thinking?"

"Papa was thinking the seventh Marquess of Coventry would become my legal guardian in the event of his death," Amy explained.

"But your father has been . . . "

Deverel nodded. "And as the eighth marquess, I inherited my father's legal obligations along with his property and title when he died."

Lady Manwaring frowned. "I don't understand why he didn't name someone else during the past fifteen years."

"On that we are in accord," Deverel told her.

"No matter," Lady Manwaring pronounced. "What's done is done." Pinning on a bright smile, she turned to Amy. "We'll think of something. In the meantime, it would give me great pleasure and comfort to have you assist the bishop and me in assembling the poor boxes this afternoon for distribution tomorrow. As soon as the bishop finishes here, we'll repair to the house for a light repast, then spend the afternoon assembling boxes. Afterwards, we'll enjoy Christmas dinner and entertainment. We'll have a lovely time, and it will give us a chance to get to know one another."

"Thank you, my lady," Amy said, "I would like that very much. But Lord Coventry and I are returning to Coventry Court."

"Leaving? On Christmas Day?" The bishop's wife gave Deverel an incredulous look. "Nonsense. You can't travel on to Buckinghamshire today."

"What else am I to do?" Deverel demanded. "If her reputation is to remain unblemished, the best thing is remove her from the gossipmongers to the country until she's ready to make her curtsey."

"Or you can allow her to stay here," Lady Manwaring pronounced. "With us. Where she and her reputation will be safe. We've a Christmas dinner already prepared, and we'd be delighted to have Amy as our guest—with your permission, of course. And you, too, Lord Coventry." She hesitated. "Unless you'd rather return to your friends."

Deverel met Lady Manwaring's knowing gaze and saw the challenge in her eyes. She was offering him a way out. He could go back to Portman Square or accept her invitation and see where it led.

Amy placed a hand on his sleeve. "I know my unexpected arrival interrupted your holiday. I would be pleased to accept Lady Manwaring's invitation. You won't have to worry about me, and you'll be able to stay in London, visit your solicitor and conduct business without disappointing your friends."

"Are you so eager to be rid of me?"

"Not in the least." Amy held his unwavering gaze for a long moment, then abruptly turned her attention to the toes of her half-boots.

"I'm pleased to hear it." He waited until she looked up at him, then gave her his most devastating grin before turning it on the bishop's wife. "I accept your kind invitation, Lady Manwaring, and your challenge."

"Challenge?" She feigned surprise.

"Yes, ma'am." He bowed low, lifted her hand, and brushed his lips against the glove covering her knuckles. "And if you'd be kind enough to entertain Amy while I'm away, I've a few errands to attend to before dinner."

"Of course," she said. "We dine at eight."

"One more thing, Lady Manwaring."

"Yes, Lord Coventry?"

Deverel leaned close to her ear, lowering his voice to a whisper. "You should know that I don't care for Christmas celebrations."

"Oh?"

"No. But I would like to honor Miss Thurston's birthday."

"Admirable."

"As such," he continued in his low, husky whisper, "I would appreciate the name of the best mantua maker in town. Preferably one who won't spare any expense and who has an exceptional assortment of garments and accessories readily available."

"Madame Racine," she whispered back, "on Conduit Street."

Chapter Eleven

Deverel knocked on his solicitor's a half hour after leaving Amy in Lady Manwaring's care, interrupting Mr. Travers's Christmas gathering to show him the document Amy had brought.

"It's all in order, my lord." The solicitor took off his spectacles and handed the papers back to Deverel. "You are Miss Thurston's legal guardian."

"Why didn't you tell me I had a ward before the young lady traveled from Suffolk and showed up upon my doorstep?" Deverel demanded, pacing the confines of the small study where Howard Travers practiced law.

"Because I was unaware of this arrangement, my lord. As you can see this document was drawn up by Sir Gregory Thurston's solicitor, Samuel Chawson."

"Surely, my father had a copy of it."

"Most likely."

"You were my father's solicitor, yet you have no knowledge of it."

"This is the first I've seen or heard of this arrangement between the previous Lord Coventry—"

"My father," Deverel interrupted.

"Your father," the solicitor acknowledged his mistake, "and Sir Gregory Thurston. Had I known of it, I would have informed you of the situation as soon as I learned of Sir Gregory's death." He looked at the young marquess. "It's possible your father had a copy of the agreement in his study at Brookfield Manor. It's dated a short time before he died. Quite possibly, he may not have had time to send a copy to me for safekeeping and it was destroyed when—"

Deverel held up a hand. "I know. What I don't understand is why he didn't name someone else in the years since my father died."

Mr. Travers gave Deverel a sympathetic nod. "You might call upon Samuel Chawson and inquire about it there."

"Yes, of course." Deverel retrieved his hat and gloves from the side table near the door.

"Is there anything else you require of me, my lord? Arrangements to be made on behalf of the young lady?"

"No," Deverel began, then changed his mind. "Yes. I would appreciate it if you would contact my London staff and arrange to have the Audley Street house opened as soon as possible. In the meantime, you can reach me at—"

"Portman Square," Mr. Travers concluded. "Yes, Lord Coventry, I know."

Deverel gave the solicitor an enigmatic smile. "At Number Four, St. Michael's Square."

The solicitor frowned. "Number Four? That's the—"

"The Bishop's Palace." Deverel nodded. "Yes, Mr. Travers, *I* know."

Travers frowned. "If there's nothing more, my lord, my family is waiting."

"Of course." Deverel gave the slightest of nods, then turned and walked through the study door, through the foyer, and out the front door.

His next call was on Samuel Chawson, Sir Gregory's solicitor, where he again interrupted Christmas festivities.

He showed him the document, and Chawson led him to his office. There, Chawson informed him that he had kept one copy of the agreement in his office for Sir Gregory and sent the second copy to the late Lord Coventry at Brookfield Manor shortly before the lord's untimely death. He had carried his copy, the one Lord Coventry had in his possession, to Miss Thurston following Sir Gregory's death five months before.

"I see," Deverel said.

"I'm sorry I cannot be of further help, your lordship," Chawson apologized. "But I have no explanation as to why the agreement was not among your late father's things."

"I think I know what became of his copy. What I want to know is why Sir Gregory didn't destroy the agreement when my father died?" This question had been weighing on his mind since Amy showed up on Theo's doorstep.

"There was no reason to destroy it," the solicitor replied. "As long as the previous Lord Coventry had an heir the agreement was valid. I included a provision to provide for that unfortunate eventuality." He pointed to the paragraph, then handed the papers to Deverel to review.

He gave it a cursory glance before folding the document and tucking it inside his coat pocket.

Chawson crossed to his desk to dig through one of several stacks of unfiled papers littering the surface. "Perhaps, this will explain. Sir Gregory sent it to me some time ago, and I came across it whilst tidying my desk. When I gathered the other documents to give to Miss Thurston, I noticed it and meant to send it on to you." He pulled out an envelope and handed it to Deverel.

The back of it bore the same blue seal as the other documents. Deverel's name and address were written in a neat hand on the front.

"I can't imagine how I mislaid it," the solicitor continued. "I do apologize if its lack has caused you any inconvenience."

Deverel gave him a wry look. Chawson's desk hadn't been tidied in weeks, if not months. How he'd mislaid it was not a mystery. How he'd come across it was. "Not to worry. It hasn't caused me the slightest inconvenience." Opening his coat, he added the envelope to the other papers in his pocket.

"Aren't you going to read it?"

"I prefer to read it in private."

"Oh, well then, if there's nothing else I can do for you, my lord, it's Christmastide and my family is waiting."

"Yes, of course." Deverel bowed.

Christmastide was a constant reminder. Everyone had a family waiting. Everyone except him.

He left Samuel Chawson's office and drove to his last errand of the afternoon, a visit to Madame Racine's Dressmaking Shop on Conduit Street. There he proceeded to purchase every suitable finished garment she had on hand as well as place orders for a dozen more, including all the usual undergarments and accoutrements. Morning dresses, day dresses, walking dresses, riding habits, pelisses, pelisse robes, redingotes, spencers, evening gowns, and ball gowns, all in colors to compliment Amy's eyes and hair and skin tone. Last, he selected an ermine-lined cloak with a matching muff and fur-lined boots to keep her warm.

He made arrangements for one dress to be delivered early each morning for the next eleven days. The rest were to follow when completed.

Satisfied, and with his errands done, he climbed into his coach and heaved a huge sigh of relief. It was Christmas Day, and he'd done two things he hadn't done in years—attended church and shopped for someone other than himself. Shopped for gifts. And although it was Christmas Day, the shopkeepers upon whose doors he knocked had gladly opened up for a marquess willing to part with his blunt.

Settling into his coach's plush seat, Deverel called out directions to St. Michael's Square, arriving in time to find the Manwarings and Amy helping unload the offerings that would go into the poor boxes.

"Come, Lord Coventry, you must join us." The bishop beckoned him to the covered wagon as Deverel alighted from his coach.

"Misery loves company?" He called back to the bishop.

Manwaring laughed. "Half the fun of assembling boxes is unloading the wagon ourselves and selecting items for each family."

Dev thought it would be more fun to allow the footmen to unload the wagon and tried once more to beg off, but Amy would have none of it.

"Please, Lord Coventry, it's Christmas." She pursed her lips and pretended to pout most prettily.

"It's cold and wet and miserable," he replied, but he wasn't thinking about weather. He was thinking how kissable her rosy lips looked when she pursed them like that.

She laughed up at him. "Cold and wet and miserable or not, it's my birthday."

That odd pang vibrated in his chest. "And you want us to catch our deaths on your birthday?"

"You're in no danger."

He wasn't so sure.

"Besides," she continued, "it's our duty to give to those less fortunate than ourselves."

He'd left his hat on the seat in his coach and realized the dampness he felt on his head was snow. "My darling girl, it's positively freezing and getting colder by the minute. Would you say it's our duty to catch our deaths of cold *and* give to the less fortunate on your birthday?"

Amy's breath caught in her throat at his use of an endearment, but Lord Coventry didn't seem to notice. "I'd say it's our duty to give to the less fortunate every day in whatever way we can."

"Spoken like a true churchman's daughter," he teased. "You are being very generous with my coin. If you recall, I've already contributed rather heavily to several charitable causes on your birthday."

"Spoken like a true benefactor. And I promise to do the same on yours." She crossed her heart. "When is it?"

"The sixth of January," he confided.

"Twelfth Night."

"Indeed."

"How marvelous! I am Christmas and you are Twelfth Night."

He devoured her with his gaze, unable to look away from her laughing eyes and rosy lips. "The Alpha and the Omega."

"The beginning and the end." She stared back, drinking in the sight of him, enjoying the way snowflakes clung to his dark hair. "We go together."

"We're *going in* now," the bishop called. "For hot chocolate. Amy, Lord Coventry, are you coming?"

Deverel tore his gaze away from Amy and discovered Bishop Manwaring had come to his senses and decided to let the footmen finish unloading the wagon, and that he and Lady Manwaring were no longer supervising the operation.

Amy held out her hand.

Deverel reached out and took it. "Indeed."

Once inside the house, the Manwarings retired upstairs to change into dry clothing. Amy and Lord Coventry followed a footman up the stairs and into their assigned bedchambers to do the same. Amy changed to a dress from her valise, and Dev sent the footman back out into the weather to retrieve his luggage from the boot of his coach.

When they were dry and dressed for dinner, the four gathered in the drawing room to enjoy hot chocolate while arranging gifts for the poor boxes. Once the boxes were completed, Bishop Manwaring offered his elbow to Amy, and Deverel escorted Lady Manwaring into the dining room for a dinner of roast turkey and potato stuffing, beets, carrots, and celery soup with gingerbread, plum pudding, and marzipan for dessert.

After dinner, Lady Manwaring led Amy back to the drawing room while Bishop Manwaring and Dev retired to the bishop's study to enjoy a glass of port.

The ladies were engaged in embroidery and conversation when the gentlemen rejoined them in drawing room. Lady Manwaring laid her needlework aside, and the four of them paired up for a rubber of whist. Amy played an excellent game of whist, but the bishop did not. No matter what strategy she tried, he seemed fated to ruin it. Deverel and Lady Manwaring took trick after trick, declaring themselves the winners three games later.

The evening was one of the most enjoyable Deverel had spent out of bed in years. The way it should have been for him. Could have been. And could still be if Amy . . . If Amy didn't decide she liked it better with the Manwarings than with him.

She was in her element, enjoying herself. What if the bishop and his wife took it upon themselves to fight him for custody of her? Manwaring was powerful enough, and he had a sterling reputation.

What if Amy chose to stay with them?

Dev caught himself. Why not let her stay with the Manwarings? Why not let them assume responsibility for her? Let them bring her out into society and find her a husband.

Because. . . Because he would miss her. Because he would be alone. He'd have no one to care about and nothing to look forward to except the time he spent at Theo's. And he didn't want that any more. He didn't want to be known as the Devil of Coventry any longer. He wanted to be the kind of marquess his father had been, the kind of husband and father.

Deverel took a deep breath. Listening to his heart as well as his head, he admitted what he'd known since he'd entered Theo's kitchen and seen Amy sitting at the table that morning.

He wanted Amy. But more importantly, he wanted a life with her.

And he would have found a few private moments to tell her of his feelings if Lady Manwaring hadn't invited Amy to walk about the room with her.

Listening with half an ear as the Bishop extolled the virtues of something or other, Deverel watched the two women stroll the perimeter of the drawing room.

While their hostess was intent on pointing out the architectural features of the residence and the advantages of living on St. Michael's Square, Amy admired the holiday decorations.

"The Christmas greenery and the Yule log are quite spectacular, Lady Manwaring. Thank you so much for inviting us to share it with you."

"Thank you for accepting." Lady Manwaring gave a wistful smile. "Christmas is all about celebrating with family and friends. The people we are blessed to know and serve." She halted beside her husband's chair. "The bishop and I weren't blessed with family of our own, but we still do our best to observe the old ways and keep Christmas."

Bishop Manwaring reached for his wife's hand and covered it with his own. "People in Town don't keep the old traditions as much as country folk. But we in the clergy are in the business of keeping Christmas, so we do our best to set a good example and make everyone feel welcome."

"I've always loved Christmas." Amy paused to enjoy the fire. "Even if it weren't my birthday. I love the chill in the air. Christmas bells. Church services and the Nativity. The scents of meat roasting and of gingerbread baking. Hot chocolate and Wassail and cider and Christmas punch, the fragrances of oranges and bayberry candles and fresh greenery. And the roaring fire. What would Christmas be without the warm, lovely fires?" Turning from the fireplace, Amy looked at Deverel.

The sight of him tugged at her heartstrings. Though he appeared attentive to the bishop, he was distant, absorbed in his own thoughts. Watchful and wary, he was removed from their host and hostess and out of the reach of the fire's warmth. Lonely, his expression filled with longing.

In a strange sort of way, he reminded her of a stray dog. A regal stray, but a stray nonetheless, sitting outside a cottage, hoping for companionship and scraps of food and affection. But too proud and too wary, too afraid of rejection to scratch on the door.

Reaching out a hand, Amy invited him in. "Lord Coventry, won't you join me by the Yule fire?"

"I'm comfortable here, thank you," he replied stiffly. "Why don't you join me?"

"You don't look comfortable," Amy chided. "You look cold." She smiled to soften her scolding tone, but Deverel refused to play along. "You could catch your death."

"I am warm enough." Deverel stared at the orange and blue flames licking the underside and ends of the massive oak log, snaking their way high up the chimney's walls. He shuddered. Cold sweat beaded his brow and dotted his upper lip as Amy moved closer to the fire, her skirts swaying dangerously near the flames. The delicious dinner he'd eaten roiled in his stomach, threatening to reappear, and his voice cracked when he spoke. "I cannot admire a Yule log or greenery or the things that cost a body so much without worrying."

"Nonsense," she pronounced, adopting Lady Manwaring's favorite protest. "The cost is negligible compared to the joy those things inspire."

"Nonsense? The only nonsense I hear is that spoken by a foolish young woman who has never lost everything and everyone she ever loved to a damned bunch of fresh greenery, too much Christmas punch, and a spectacular Yule log!"

Deverel sprang to his feet only to discover his knees barely supported him. He fought for the strength to get out before he disgraced himself further. "Thank you for dinner. Good night."

Amy stood open-mouthed, watching as he left the room, not to go upstairs, but out the front door and into the snowy night. She jumped at the sound of the front door slamming, then turned to the bishop and Lady Manwaring. "What did I do wrong?"

Lord Manwaring sighed. "Nothing, my dear."

"But I upset him and made him angry enough to leave."

"That's true," the churchman agreed, "but the circumstances lent more weight to your words than they would normally warrant."

"What are the circumstances?"

"It's Christmas," Lady Manwaring offered gently.

"Lord Coventry has made it quite clear that he dislikes Christmas." Amy lifted her chin a notch and straightened her spine. "And that he thinks I'm a foolish young woman because I enjoy it so much."

"Words spoken in haste, my dear," the bishop said. "Because Christmas is a constant reminder of the loss he suffered, he must find it difficult to reconcile holiday cheer with his sadness. I think he feels terribly alone."

Amy was thoughtful. "But he told me he always celebrates the holiday with his friends."

Lady Manwaring gave a loud harrumph. "That's one word for them."

"Now, Freda, you shouldn't pass judgment or give credence to rumors," the bishop admonished.

"They aren't rumors if they're true," his wife replied. "You know how Coventry spends his Christmas."

Manwaring looked his wife in the eye. "Indulging in a pastime guaranteed to help him forget."

"Forget what?" What had caused Lord Coventry so much anger and pain. What had hurt him so deeply?

The bishop took a deep breath, gathering his thoughts. "Fifteen years ago, his mother, father, younger sister, and their entire household staff perished when Brookfield Manor burned to the ground on the twenty-first of December."

The air rushed out of Amy's lungs.

"Their butler had been sent to fetch Lord Coventry home from school. They arrived at the country house to find it a blackened pile of smoldering ash and stone. It took three days to recover Lord and Lady Coventry's and Lady Elise's remains." The bishop paused, remembering. "We buried them in the family crypt at Coventry Court on Christmas Day." When his voice cracked a bit beneath the strain of recounting the tragedy, he paused to regain composure.

"Except for five years ago when he attended the family butler's funeral, Lord Coventry hasn't been seen in church since then. Until today."

"When I insisted he bring me." Amy's knees gave way. She sank down onto the nearest chair and covered her face with her hands for a moment before looking up at the bishop. "No wonder he hates Christmas. He has no family with whom to share it."

"He has *you*, my dear," Lady Manwaring reminded her.

"A foolish young woman who showed up at his house without warning, tracked him to London, threw herself on his mercy, and couldn't cease prattling about the joys of the Yuletide holiday." Amy's words were bitterly ironic. "Who ignorantly belittled his pain." She squeezed her eyes shut as her words came hurtling back to haunt her. *Nonsense! The cost is negligible compared to the joy those things inspire.* "I hurt him. I don't know how he endured my company for as long as he did."

The bishop clucked his tongue in sympathy. "You cannot blame yourself for not knowing of a tragedy that happened years before you were old enough to understand it. And I'm quite sure Lord Coventry doesn't blame you for it either."

"But the look on his face. . ." Amy sighed. "I hate that I'm the one who put it there. What if he does blame me? What if he can't forgive me for my thoughtlessness? What if he decides he's better off without me?" She looked at the ecclesiastical couple, fixing her gaze on one and then the other. "I can't stand to think of him separating himself from the people—from the person—who loves him. I can't stand the thought of him holding himself apart from the rest of the world for the rest of his life, afraid to care about people—afraid to love for fear of losing everything and getting hurt once again."

Lady Manwaring was silent for a moment before she pinned Amy with her sharp gaze. "How is it that you think you know those things about him on such short acquaintance? What happened between the two of you this morning?"

Amy inhaled deeply then slowly expelled the breath. "I don't know if anything happened *between* us, Lady Manwaring. I only know what happened to me."

The bishop's wife leaned closer, apparently prepared to be outraged. "And what was that?"

Amy managed a tremulous smile. "I lost my heart." *To a man who may not want it.*

Chapter Twelve

"Is she all right?"

Amy followed the sound of conversation as she made her way from her bedchamber down the stairs to the morning room. She was about to enter and greet her hosts when she realized they were deep in discussion, and she was the topic.

She hesitated then stepped carefully away from the doorway and back against the concealment offered by the heavy, winter draperies. She didn't mean to eavesdrop, but couldn't stop herself once she'd heard the concern in Lord and Lady Manwaring's voices.

"She was still in bed when I came downstairs," Lady Manwaring replied. "And since I suspect she cried herself to sleep, I was loathe to disturb her. What of Lord Coventry? Has he returned?"

"He hadn't when I retired for the night, and he's not in his bedchamber," the bishop answered sadly. "I knocked on the door before I came downstairs. There was no answer."

"I beg your pardon, my lord, my lady." Danbury, the butler, placed the silver coffee pot on the table. "But the maids and the footmen, and I'm told even the grooms, have been buzzing about it all morning."

"About what?" Lady Manwaring refilled her husband's coffee cup before warming up her own.

"The Christmas boxes?" the bishop asked.

It was Boxing Day and tradition dictated that after breakfast, in appreciation for service throughout the year, the staff of the Palace of the Bishop of St. Michael's be given double wages in blue boxes, as well as the afternoon off. Tradesmen who came to call would also receive monetary gifts in blue boxes. It was the most exciting day of the year for maids and footmen and grooms who eagerly anticipated a free afternoon with coin to spend.

"Not the Christmas boxes, my lord. The buzz has been about Lord Coventry and the boxes arriving since early morning for Miss Thurston and for you and Lady Manwaring."

Bishop Manwaring looked at Lady Manwaring who shook her head. "I know nothing of this."

"I had yours sent to your sitting room, my lady," Danbury told her. "Bishop Manwaring's are in his study. And I instructed one of the maids to take the boxes from Madame Racine's for Miss Thurston up to her bedchamber. She arranged the garments upon the counterpane at the foot of the bed according to Madame Racine's instructions."

Amy quietly smoothed the fabric of her new dress with one hand and inhaled the soft fragrance of the long-stemmed rose she held in her other hand. She'd found it lying atop the dress laid out across the foot of the bed when she'd awakened.

"Did Lord Coventry return with the boxes?" The bishop inquired.

"No, my lord. Lord Coventry returned a little after midnight. The boxes arrived later."

Amy's heart leapt in her chest at the news. He'd not only gifted her with beautiful dresses and a hothouse rose, but he'd returned as well. And with his return came hope that he would find it in his heart to forgive her.

Bishop Manwaring didn't sound nearly as thrilled by Danbury's answer as she was. "The house was locked. How did he get in?"

"Through the service entrance, my lord," Danbury replied reluctantly.

"Good heavens!" Lady Manwaring exclaimed. "What if he'd been a footpad?"

The bishop ignored his wife's exclamation and concentrated on his butler. "If Coventry's returned, where is he? And why didn't he answer when I knocked on his door?"

"He isn't in his bedchamber," Danbury told them. "He's outside asleep in his coach."

"Is he foxed?"

"No, Ma'am. Merely tired. According to the first footman on duty this morning, Lord Coventry kept watch throughout the night while the rest of us slept."

"Kept watch for what?" Lady Manwaring asked.

"Fire. Lord Coventry rang a peal over the footman's head for leaving the Christmas fire unattended. Apparently, his lordship will not sleep in a house where a Yule log is left burning through the night."

The bishop sucked in a breath. "I didn't think . . . I should have realized. I knew his outburst last night was uncharacteristic."

"How could you have known?" his wife demanded. "We haven't seen him since he was nine or ten or years old—"

"Eleven," the bishop recalled. "He's his father made over, my dear. Did you ever see the previous Lord Coventry lose his composure?"

Lady Manwaring thought for a moment. "Only once. After services that morning when the little one darted out in front of Lord

Linton's phaeton. But, my dear, he was frightened half out of his wits at the thought—"

"Exactly, my dear."

"Good heavens, because of our thoughtlessness, we've had a marquess sleep *outside* in a coach rather than inside our house."

"He didn't sleep, my dear, not a wink," the bishop said. "He watched over us—or rather, he watched over her—while we slept." Directing another question at Danbury, the bishop asked, "Did the footman say where the marquess kept watch?"

"In the drawing room, Sir. In the blue wing chair by the fire."

Remembering all that had taken place there last night, Amy glanced over her shoulder in the direction of the drawing room. Hope flared again. He'd kept watch over them all. She hugged that thought to herself as the bishop asked another question.

"When did he leave to go outside?"

"When the house began stirring." Danbury was thoughtful. "That's the thing, Sir. The second parlor maid swears she saw him slip out of Miss Thurston's bedchamber when she went in to light the fire. The girl reports that there was a pink rose lying atop the clothing she laid out on the foot of the bed. She said Lord Coventry left Miss Thurston sleeping, then crept downstairs and out of the house. One of the grooms reported that His Lordship is now sound asleep in his coach."

"Make sure he's warmly wrapped," Bishop Manwaring instructed. "And don't wake him. Let him sleep."

"Let him sleep? Danbury, do nothing of the kind," Lady Manwaring corrected. "Wake him. We've arrangements to make."

"Now, Freda, what's done is done, and it won't hurt to let the lad get a bit of sleep."

"Titus, he compromised that girl under our roof, and you want to let 'The Devil of Coventry' sleep undisturbed in his coach outside our house on Boxing Day?" She paused long enough to take a breath before continuing, "You know how people love to gossip. What will the servants and the tradesmen say? It's your duty to see that Lord Coventry doesn't shirk his—"

"There's no danger of that."

Lady Manwaring was momentarily speechless. "How can you be so sure?"

"Haven't you noticed the way he looks at Amy? Freda, my dear, he can't take his eyes off her."

"He's young and healthy and *male*. She's young, pretty and female. Birds and bees, Titus."

The bishop laughed. "He's her guardian. He sat up all night to watch over her. I can't believe he means to do her or her reputation any harm."

"And the bit of skullduggery with the rose?"

"No skullduggery, my dear. He simply wanted to surprise her, so he slipped into her room and left a rose on her bed."

"Pray that's all he did," Lady Manwaring murmured. "But the damage is done nonetheless."

"He's only spent one day in her company."

"Sometimes a day is all it takes," Lady Manwaring pronounced. "But his being her guardian should work to our advantage."

"What are you going to do?"

"Not me. *You. You're* going to give him something to think about."

The bishop sighed. "It might be better if we stayed out of it and let them work it out."

"You heard her," his wife reminded him. "She's already lost her heart to him. Would you have her heart get broken? Or have her lose her virtue to him without benefit of marriage lines? You're a bishop. It's your duty to help things along."

"All right," he acquiesced. "I'll do what I can."

"That's all I ask."

Amy silently thanked the lady and tiptoed away.

Deverel awoke with a start to find his neck crooked at a hugely uncomfortable angle. He stretched his arms and banged his fist against the inside wall of his coach.

Blister it, but he'd been sleeping in it.

Pushing himself upright, he remembered he'd first awakened in the bishop's drawing room in an uncomfortable wing chair. Dev shook his head. Yesterday, he woke in Theo's luxurious bed. Today . . . a chair and a vehicle. His world had been turned upside down in the space of a day. Remembering the reason for it, he exited the coach and headed for the palace.

"I want to see the bishop," he announced as soon as the footman opened the front door.

"He's in the morning room, my lord, with Lady Manwaring."

Brushing past the servant, Deverel strode into the morning room without so much as a passing glance. "I've come to get Amy."

"Good morning, Lord Coventry." The bishop greeted him warmly. "Would you care for some coffee?"

Deverel ignored the offer. "I would care to see Miss Thurston."

"She hasn't come downstairs yet. Why don't you have some coffee and some breakfast while you wait? You look tired."

Deverel fixed him with a hard gaze. "If so, it's because I spent the night watching over your Christmas fire after you failed to assign someone to attend to it."

"Oh?"

"The door was unlocked," Deverel added, for good measure as he began to pace the confines of the morning room. "The door to the service entrance was left unlocked, and the fire unattended last night. Miss Thurston is not safe here. I shudder to think what might have happened had I not returned from my drive around the park."

"You know all too well what might have happened," the bishop said.

"I do," Dev retorted, raking his hand through his already disheveled hair. "I do know what can happen. That Yule log everyone loves so much could have burned the place down along with everyone in it." He glared at the churchman. "I know what it's like to come home and find that the house and everyone you love is gone."

He stopped pacing long enough to grab the silver coffee pot and pour himself a cup, which he swallowed in three big gulps. "You don't. That's why I've come to get Amy—"

"Lady Manwaring and I have decided to offer Amy a home with us. She can continue her father's work under the auspices of St. Michael's. And my wife will sponsor her into society. If she chooses to marry, she can have her pick of suitors. If she doesn't, she can remain with us. We'll give her a good home."

Deverel snorted. "You'll have to fight me to do so. Amy is my responsibility. Her father gave her to me fifteen years ago, and I intend to keep her."

Bishop Manwaring was stunned. "How do you mean?"

From his coat pocket, Dev pulled the envelope Samuel Chawson had given him. He handed it to the bishop.

Manwaring opened it and read:

16 January 1798
Dear Sir Gregory,

I thank you for your sincere condolences on my loss. A loss so great I am not sure I will be able to bear it. But Pendry (our butler) assures me it will get better with time. It's especially hard here at school, since, as you know, Etonians and Marquesses don't cry.

During our journey home from Suffolk, Papa told me of the arrangement you made with him. He explained that if anything happens to you, your little girl will be part of our family. I will, of course, honor the arrangement as I will honor all of Papa's business agreements. But now that Papa is gone and I have become the Marquess of Coventry, I think it only fair that I should ask you to reconsider.

I am not yet a man and can only pray that I may become half as good a man as Papa was without him here to guide me.

I do not seek to shirk my responsibilities or foist them off on someone else, but I would not want to bring shame or dishonor to my family name or my father's memory by not being good enough to take care of your little girl.

So, until I reach my majority and you can take my measure and know for certain whether or not I am the man you wish to have in charge of your daughter's future, I ask that you please reconsider the arrangement. For her sake.

I remain, Your Devoted Friend's son and heir, Brookfield

P.S. I would deem it a very great favor if you would hug her and kiss her at night and tell her that she is in my prayers. That way she will know she is part of my family and won't feel alone if something should happen to take you away.

The letter was yellowed with age and written in a childish hand, ink-smeared and tear-blotched, and contained one or two misspelled words. The bishop swallowed the lump in his throat, then looked up from the letter and met Deverel's gaze. "This doesn't prove he didn't grant your request."

"This does." Deverel handed him the note Sir Gregory had written in reply fourteen years later.

> *21 May 1812*
> *My Dear Lord Coventry,*
>
> *A mutual friend on Portman Square assures me that you have grown into a fine, young man, a credit to your family and your father's memory. I would be honored to have you take care of my daughter should it ever become necessary.*
> *If not, I hope you have the opportunity to meet her socially one day soon and discover for yourself that she is unique among women and a match for you in every possible way.*
> *I gave her into your care some fourteen years ago, and you have given me no reason to change my opinion.*
> *I remain Your Devoted Friend,*
> *G. Thurston*
>
> *P.S. I have done as you asked and made certain that she knows she is loved and never alone.*

The bishop cleared his throat a second time. "This makes it clearer. But what of Amy? What is best for her? You are a bachelor and as such, having her under your protection will give rise to gossip and innuendo. You say she's your responsibility, but how do we know you can be trusted with her?"

"I give you my word as a gentleman."

"Your word as a gentleman isn't worth anything when emotions run high and the urge to mate overcomes good intentions. I was a young man once. I know."

Lady Manwaring gasped.

"If I were to compromise her, I would marry her."

"If my staff is to be believed, you have already compromised her beneath my roof."

"I didn't touch her. I checked to make certain all was well and left a rose on her bed." Deverel met the bishop's unwavering gaze. "I've never even kissed her."

"Why not?"

Dev turned in the doorway to find Amy standing there in one of the new dresses from Madame Racine's, clutching the pink rose he'd placed on her bed. She stared up at him, her blue eyes dark and huge in her face.

"Amy."

"Why didn't you?"

"You were sleeping," he said simply. "A gentleman does not take advantage of an innocent young lady when she's sleeping."

Bishop Manwaring cleared his throat again, but for a different reason.

Deverel smiled down at Amy. "He doesn't kiss a lady without her consent. You weren't awake to give it."

"Did you want to kiss me?"

"Endlessly." *Every day for as long as I live.*

"Is that why you came into my room?"

He quirked an eyebrow at her.

"I saw you smiling down at me. I thought I'd dreamed it."

He shook his head. "No. I was there."

"Why?"

He took a deep breath. "I was worried about you."

"Why?"

"You know why."

"Tell me," she ordered. "So, I'll know for certain."

"Because I hurt you."

"No more than I hurt you," she whispered.

He stood before her, refusing to allow her to excuse his ungentlemanly behavior. "I lashed out. You were unaware of the circumstances. You didn't mean your words to hurt. I did. I insulted you. I meant to inflict pain."

Tears stung her eyes. "You called me foolish."

He nodded again. "I don't know what to say except that I hope you'll forgive me. I didn't mean it. And I promise never to do it again. I lost my family in a terrible fire."

"I know," she whispered, not trusting herself to speak aloud. "The bishop told me."

"It was winter solstice. They were celebrating—decorating the house with greenery and candles, and drinking Christmas punch. Lighting the Yule log. My father and mother and four-year-old sister went to sleep with the fire burning. Brookfield Manor burned to the ground, and everyone in it died."

Fighting to control his emotions, he took another deep,

shuddering breath. "I shall never forget how they looked. I buried my family on Christmas Day." He moved close, reached out and touched Amy's hair.

She wrapped her hand around his wrist and brought it to her lips. "Which is why you don't celebrate Christmas." She kissed his wrist where his pulse beat, then pressed a kiss to his palm. "Why did you watch over me last night?"

Dev felt the pang in his chest, recognized it for what it was, and took the plunge, drowning himself in her eyes. "Because I couldn't stand the thought of losing you."

"You can never lose me," Amy said. "Even if I were to die, I would still be your ward. I would still be part of your family. You would carry me in your heart, the way you carry all those you lost."

"You are *all* of my family." Dev gazed into her eyes, memorizing the unconventional features that made her so beautiful and so beloved. "I already carry you in my heart. I don't want you for my ward, Amy. I love you. I want you for my wife."

She gasped. "You only met me yesterday."

He shook his head. "I only knew you yesterday. I met you fifteen years ago. But I'll give you time, all the time you need to decide if you could love me. If you could find it in your heart to marry me. However long it takes."

"I'll take until Twelfth Night," she told him, wrapping her arms around his neck and pressing close. "Now, kiss me endlessly and tell me again that you love me. Because I've loved you since I was five years old."

"How?"

"You're young Dee Brookfield."

Dev smiled. "That was my father's pet name for me. Dee. Short for Deverel. "

"Every night, Papa would give me three hugs and three kisses. A hug and a kiss from Mama in Heaven. A hug and a kiss from him. And a hug and a kiss from young Dee Brookfield who was waiting for me to grow up and marry him."

"He was right," Dev said. "Only I didn't know it until yesterday."

"Papa was exceptional."

"Not as exceptional as his daughter," Dev assured her.

"Prove it," she challenged.

"I love you, Amabel Mary Ophelia Thurston," he told her and because she was exceptional, he said it again in Latin and Greek and French and Spanish and Italian and German.

Amy arched an eyebrow at him. "I love a man with a classical education."

"Lucky for you, because unlike the idiots in Finchley, I like a challenge. I look forward to having a bluestocking wife."

Amy laughed.

Then, because she was standing under the kissing bough and because they were practically engaged, he kissed her endlessly, and nobody said a word.

Epilogue

They were officially engaged on Twelfth Night after eleven days of courtship when Deverel presented Amy with a sapphire and diamond ring to go with the eleven other gifts he'd given her.

She accepted his proposal of marriage and gave him a miniature with her likeness so he'd never be alone again.

Although Dev purchased a special license, the Bishop insisted on reading the banns in church.

The wedding took place three weeks to the day after the last banns were read. The bride wore an exquisite pale blue gown from Madame Racine's, the groom knee breeches and buckles. Bishop Manwaring walked the bride down the aisle, and the vicar of St. Luke's officiated.

They breakfasted at the Palace of the Bishops of St. Michael's and spent the night in the townhouse at Number Eight, South Audley Street before leaving for an extended honeymoon at Coventry Court.

The wedding announcement appeared in the *Morning Chronicle* the following day, and in her house at Number Forty-seven Portman Square, Theodora Jones read the announcement with a broad smile on her face, and then crossed another name off her client list.

The Devil of Coventry had surrendered to a Christmas angel.

"For my intrepid travel buddy, Pat Potter. We'll always have Montenegro!"

STAR OF WONDER

Lynn Kerstan

Chapter One

North Yorkshire Dales, 1819

"Wretched holly!"

Stella shifted the overstuffed burlap sack from her right shoulder to her left and winced as it found new territory to torture. Woolen undergarments under a woolen dress under a woolen cape were no protection, not with breads and cold meats and tins of biscuits, nuts and cheeses juggling around the bag and pressing the holly prickles into her back.

Where were Magi with camels when she needed them?

Nowhere to be seen this night. But there were sheep, chomping a few last bites of grass or hunkering down against the storm sweeping in from the southwest. A bank of clouds lay dead ahead and was moving fast. It would surely beat her to the house.

She'd make faster time without the Christmas supplies, but they were sorely needed. Bertha's knees were paining her, and the packets of food meant less work for her in the kitchen. When she asked, Mrs. Rondale added a bagful of medicinal salts for soaking Bertha's arthritic hands and creating hot compresses for John's knee. There was something for Annie as well. Stella didn't know what it was, but Mrs. Rondale had smiled and winked when she slipped it into the sack. Leaving anything behind was unthinkable. If she abandoned so much as the holly on Rondale land, they might discover it and be offended that their generosity had meant so little.

Stella picked up her pace, dodging sheep as she sped by, until the burst of speed fizzled out. Panting, she dropped the sack and sucked in long breaths of icy air. Overhead, stars blazed against the clear black sky. Her last chance to see them for several nights, most like, if the storm settled in. With her luck, it would last until April.

Lifting her head, she traced the winter constellations as her father had taught her. *Orion. Gemini. Taurus. Perseus. Casseopeia.* She loved Papa's stories about the constellations. They brimmed over with violence and passion, vengeance and sacrifice and heartbreak. Gods and goddesses were invariably up to no good in the myths, but at least they had adventures. Challenges. Excitement.

"If ever you wander astray," Papa always said, "look to the golden star. It will guide you where you need to go." She knew where to find Capella, the goat star, far to the north, but because she'd never had an adventure that could possibly have led her astray, she'd had no need of a guiding star.

Sometimes she'd longed for a different life, though, one with fewer sheep, closer neighbors, and friends her own age. If she sold the property, she could rent a small townhouse in York, where there were museums and musical evenings and dancing. Perhaps meet a gentleman who would see something fine in her. But that was only an air dream. Years of isolated country living and making do had worn her to a nub and ground her girlhood hopes to powder. She had obligations as well, and was glad of them. Nothing would change. Not here in the moorlands. Nor would she abandon the loyal servants who had helped care for her father and seen her through her darkest days. They were her family now, and she loved them.

Papa had also assured her that stars could grant wishes if they chose, and if they got around to it. They needed to be regularly reminded. And sometimes, they didn't quite understand what you meant. "Choose a star carefully," he'd told her. "Kiss the wish onto your fingertip and point it at the star. Then speak your wish three times in simple words, and imagine you have pinned it to the star. Someday, when you're not expecting it, your wish will come true."

From experience, she knew better. For a long time, she'd wished for enough money to escape the moors and set up a townhouse large enough for all of them, until she realized they loved the country life and would be unhappy there. So she wished instead to provide Bertha and John a fortnight in Buxton or Bath to take the waters. But life shuffled on, and not even her smallest wishes were granted. She'd long ago given up on the stars, except to delight in their beauty.

Still, it was Christmas Eve, and in the absence of angels announcing good news to shepherds, she might as well send a holiday message of her own. Maybe some of the sheep had magical powers. Scanning Orion, the doomed hunter, she found the pale star at the tip of his sword and pinned her wish to it. "Don't let her come home," she called three times, imagining Orion slashing his sword into action. "You know who I mean."

Just thinking about her stepmother made her want to stomp on something. Instead, she hoisted up the burlap sack, muttering un-Christmassy oaths as the holly had at her again, and set her feet into a steady lope. In her experience, anger was reliably energizing.

Almost immediately, the first white flakes wafted down. Clouds scudded overhead, grey and black, roiling as they smothered the stars. By the time she reached the low stone wall and located the stile, the snow was falling in earnest, encrusting her lashes and numbing her lips. She clambered to the other side and wiped her eyes, seeking lights from the house to guide her.

A narrow path led from the stile to the barn and from there to the scraggly kitchen garden, two small sheds, the chicken house, and a carriage house leased to the Rondales for storage. Beyond it sprawled Moor Mansion, her name for the creaky old building, part stone, part wood, all in need of repair. Built two centuries earlier, it had served as a rich sheep farmer's residence, a school, a makeshift orphanage, a poor man's home, and was now become a refuge for four lost souls.

To save oil and wood and coal, no lights or fire showed at the rear of the house. Grumbling, she trudged along the carriage road, head down against the blowing snow, hoping John would see her from a window and come out to help her with the sack.

No such luck. But as she drew closer to the front corner, a glimmer of light—no, two lights—caught her attention. They were about six feet apart and high off the ground, taller than any man. Lanterns, perhaps, attached to poles. And they were moving in her direction.

Then a dark shadow, large and swaying, passed through ambient light from the windows at the front of the house.

A carriage.

A driverless carriage.

She dropped the sack and sidled along the wall of the house, one thought thumping in her head. The witch had come home. Edging closer, silently cursing Orion, Stella tasted bitterness in her mouth. So much for her wish!

When she reached the corner, a blast of wind blew back her hood and lifted her cape behind her like one great wing. Peering through the whirling snow, she saw the carriage pull up to face the house about twenty yards away. From this perspective, she could make out a lump huddled over the back of the left-position horse. A postilion, showing no signs of dismounting to open the carriage door for Her Greediness. Stella couldn't see his face, but she thought it might be Tom Basker. He would be in no hurry to help That Woman.

It opened anyway, and two black-booted feet—large feet—hit the ground. The rest followed swiftly, clothed in black from head to toe save for a bit of forehead and eyes above a thick woolen scarf wrapped around his throat and over his mouth and nose. The capes and skirts of his greatcoat flapped in the wind.

Male. Tall. Hatless. Had Her Odiousness found herself another victim to exploit?

He strode purposefully in the direction of the front door, white snow settling on his overlong black hair, gloved hands clenching and unclenching as if he was angry. Or his hands might be cold, she had to admit in fairness. Hers certainly were. Wind, whistling through the eaves and bare-limbed trees, set her cape to fluttering wildly. She pressed her back against the wall, but not in time.

He swung around to face her.

She could barely distinguish his features, the bits she was able to see. When he fixed his gaze on her, she lifted her chin and tried to meet his eyes.

No point standing in place like a hitching post. If he meant harm, she couldn't outrun him. And if John had seen him arrive, he'd be loading his rifle by now. Not that he could hit a woodshed, given his poor eyesight, but perhaps the threat would be enough.

Meantime, she might as well find out what the stranger wanted. Likely something perfectly natural, perhaps directions to where he'd intended to go. It couldn't possibly be here, unless Her Nastiness was stewing in the coach, waiting for a covered palanquin with four bearers to carry her inside.

Besides, the postilion still hadn't moved. Could he be in need of help?

Stiffening her spine, she set herself on a course that would put her face to face with the stranger in a rectangle of light cast from an upper window. She stopped dead center and lifted her chin. "Are you lost, sir?"

He glanced at the lump of postilion, who lifted his head long enough to shake it. "It seems not," the man said in a smooth, educated, slightly accented voice. "I have come to speak with Sir Edwin Bryar on a matter of urgency."

At the sound of her father's name, her stomach clenched. "That won't be possible. He is not here."

The man's shoulders lifted as he sucked in a deep breath. "You speak the truth? Be sure I will not leave without seeing for myself."

She heard a click and the squeal of hinges as the front door opened behind her. A shadow advanced across the snow ahead of John, who took up a position at her side, his rifle cradled in his arms. The stranger, she was sure, could down him with one swat of a powerful hand before John got the gun pointed the right direction. "Search the house, you mean? On what authority?"

"My own. I intend no harm, but my business with Sir Edwin is of surpassing importance."

"To you, perhaps. But Sir Edwin is not to be found here." She glanced at John. "If the gentleman makes a move to approach the house, shoot him."

John raised the rifle in shaky hands and tried to look intimidating.

The man ignored the rifle, his gaze now focused on the window directly behind Stella. She looked over her shoulder to see Annie and Bertha staring at them from the window, their mouths rounded into O's.

"Will you tell me, then, where he can be found?"

"Oh, yes." With deliberation, she sounded chirpy. "He is at St. Mary-in-the-Moors church, just outside of Hawes. It is a long way, though. You'd better get started before the storm makes the roads, such as they are, impassable."

"He went so great a distance to attend Christmas services?"

"Oh, no. Actually, he's not in the church itself. He's in the churchyard. I'm not sure it's worth the journey. You won't be able to speak with him. Or, you could, but he won't reply."

His head jerked back as if he'd taken a blow. "Sir Edwin is dead, then?"

"He was when we buried him."

As the stranger searched her face intently, a cold knot of fear lodged in her stomach. Without realizing it, he had opened an unhealed wound, and she'd responded like a shrew. Her sharp tongue never failed to land her in the soup. Even so, her lips tightened against the apology she ought to be making. Instinct whispered that he was dangerous. Perhaps her father had offended him in some way. But if so, there was precious little anyone could do about it now.

He turned and stalked to the horse bearing the lump. "Why didn't you tell me? Why did you bring me here?"

"C-cuz," the postilion wheezed, "you said you wanted to go to Sir

Edwin's house. Nuthin' 'bout seein' 'im. I reckoned you knewed he weren't 'ere."

"You should have asked."

Stella had heard enough. "Stop scolding the boy. I know him. His name is Tom Basker. He's eager and reliable, and he wouldn't have dared question your orders."

"Unlike you." He held out a hand to the postilion. "I'll pay you what we agreed. Come down now."

"Can't. M'gloves is freezed to the reins."

The man turned to her. "Scissors and warm water, if you will."

"No scissors." The boy's tone rose an octave. "I needs gloves to work."

"I'll buy you new ones."

From his tone, she could tell his short lease on patience had run out.

"John," she said, "stay here and make sure the gentleman does the same. And while I am gone, you, sir, must decide if you can make your own way to your next stop. If not, you may shelter the horses and yourself in the barn. The boy can't possibly travel any farther tonight, and the horses ought not."

"You expect me to spend the night in a *barn*?"

"Why not?" She turned toward the house. "Mary and Joseph did," she added over her shoulder. "There's even a manger in there."

Chapter Two

At the trestle table in the kitchen, Stella and Annie shelled walnuts for the Christmas bread while Bertha chopped potatoes, turnips, and carrots for a stew. Perched on a footstool near the fire, Tom soaked his hands and feet in pots of warm water, his gaze fixed on Annie's freckled face.

Stella suppressed a smile. Since their first encounter at a church fair, the two of them had been flirting in the way of shy youngsters, which meant an abundance of blushing and grinning while keeping a safe distance. Rejection would come hard, and neither was prepared to risk it. They had not spoken or looked directly at each other since John carried Tom into the house.

John had fetched the burlap sack as well, and Bertha wept as she unpacked the Rondales' princely Christmas offerings.

"They are good people," she kept saying. "So good to us."

Annie was wide-eyed when she opened the little felt bag and discovered a small glass bottle of fragrance. The light scent of citrus and honey suited her exactly. She was also in alt about the holly and wished to decorate banisters and mantelpieces with it straightaway.

Stella wanted to fling it into the fire.

From the brick steps outside the kitchen, she heard the stamping of boots and felt a spark of panic. The stranger unsettled her, like vibrations of electricity in the air before a lightning storm. She looked around for a weapon and spotted a cast-iron skillet near the end of the table. She tugged it closer as Bertha went to open the door.

It was only John, carrying a bucket filled with coals and an armload of firewood clutched to his chest.

Stella released the breath she'd been holding. "Is he settled?"

"As well as may be." John set the coals beside the stove and placed the wood in a tin box near the hearth. "We'll be needin' more."

"Use the sack." She gestured to the pile of burlap spread over a rocking chair. "It's nearly dry. But first, have some tea. And biscuits, before Tom eats them all."

The boy, chomping on a biscuit with another in each hand, went red as holly berries. Annie covered a smile before he could see it.

Love. So silly. So . . . sweet. So long ago. Stella's heart felt like a chunk of ice in her chest. When she was Annie's age, she and her father lived in York. Surrounded by young men eager to catch her eye, she hadn't been the least bit shy about flirting in return. How else was she to discover if one of them could give her what she wanted most in her life—a joy-filled marriage like her parents had created. Her parents' only sorrow had been her mother's failure to bear another child. As the lone daughter she'd been cherished from birth and a little spoiled, but she never did anything to cause them displeasure or pain. Years later, when her widowed father took a second wife, she saw the other side of the coin—a marriage gone frightfully wrong.

Even so, for a long time she continued to dream of meeting a man who would shower her with love, a man she could love in return. She would settle for nothing less. Nor had she.

Instead, she'd settled for nothing at all.

John took up his usual place at the end of the table, hands wrapped around a mug of steaming tea. "It be uncommon cold out there, Miss. We oughtn't to leave 'im in the barn."

"Where, then? I won't have him in the house."

"Can't think why," he murmured, staring into the cup.

Tom stopped chewing. Annie stopped cracking walnuts. Bertha stopped stirring the stew. John never spoke out like that, even under his breath. All save John pinned her with astonished and then speculative looks.

She winced as she realized they agreed with John. "Because I . . . oh, I don't know. He's angry. He wants something he can't have. He'll make trouble. I feel it in my bones. I think he's dangerous."

"We could lock him in a room," Annie said, head lowered as her cheeks went fiery.

"We may as well," Bertha agreed. "What's to stop him from breaking in through a window tonight?"

All of them, lined up against her. It needed only Tom Basker to chime in.

"*I* will stop him," she said, not the least sure she could manage him at all. But feeling powerless, which she had so often been in her life, exacted a great price of its own. After Papa married the witch, Stella had taken to reading myths and legends about women who knew no fear. Amazon women who took up arms and fought in battles, like Androdameia, whose name meant Subduer of Men. Until the stranger had gone on his way, she would be Androdameia.

"I have papa's pistol," she declared, "and I know how to use it." She turned to John. "Did he say anything while you were in the barn?"

"When I said they was good nags, he said they was 'is."

No surprise there. A matched pair of such quality couldn't be hired at a country posthouse. "That's all?"

"The locks are strong," Annie said, still fixed on lodgings for the stranger.

She was right about the locks. They were about the only things in the house that worked well. The old ones had been replaced when Her Despicableness demanded to search the house for anything she might have left behind, doubtless in hopes of stealing more items of value to sell. As if she hadn't packed up nearly everything in sight when she departed for York. She'd even threatened to take her case for plundering to the magistrate.

Stella turned back to John. "He didn't tell you his name?"

"Didn't ask."

Talk about locked doors. John was more impervious than the Tower of London. "Anything to add, Tom?"

"No, ma'am. 'Cept," he said in a shy squeak, "I 'ope he don't leave afore payin' me."

She swallowed hard. The last thing she wanted was to go out there and face the tall stranger again. He agitated her in ways she couldn't explain. She had never encountered anyone like him. Masterful, wealthy, exotic gentlemen did not frequent the back roads of north Yorkshire. Even so, it wasn't fair to ask John to become a collection agent, and Tom, plucky though he was, shriveled in the presence of quality.

At least she had an excuse to appear at the barn. And if the man handed over Tom's wage, she would see to it he got some supper. "Very well, then." She came briskly to her feet. "I shall speak with him myself. If he behaves, perhaps I'll lock him in the attic room."

"Not if he don't want you to," John said with exceptional clarity.

Lantern in hand, pushing against the forceful wind, Stella slogged along the snow-covered path to the barn. Snow was already piling up around its edges. Guided by pale light flickering from the cracks between the window shutters, she made her way to the entrance, set down the lantern, and lifted the heavy bar from the latch. In a fashion, he was locked in. But that did not mean the barn could contain him.

She took up her lantern, stepped inside, and pulled the door closed behind her. Even without the wind, the air in the barn was bitter cold. From the stalls to her right, the horses whickered a welcome. Or a warning. On a table outside the tack room, she saw the blankets and pillow John had provided for the stranger.

Of him, there was no sign. Uncertainty, the legacy of helplessness, slithered in. She tossed it out. Androdameia would be calm and casual until the adversary showed himself. Visit with the horses, she decided, and do it with a display of insouciance. Let *him* make the first move.

Abandoning her lantern on the gravel just inside the door, she ambled over to the stalls, clasped her hands behind her back, and gazed into a pair of dark eyes almost as black as the rest of him. *I'm no threat*, her posture told the horse while quite different thoughts raced through her head. She was behaving just as she had done when flirting with potential mates years earlier in York. Confidence, indifference, and mild interest, all sauced with "Give me a reason to pay attention to you."

"Miss Bryar, is it not?" said a voice from overhead.

Spinning around, she gazed up at the hayloft. On the edge near the ladder, his long legs dangling down, sat the potential troublemaker. He wasn't wearing his greatcoat.

"You aren't wearing your coat," she advised him, knitting her hands behind her back to keep them from shaking.

"Did you wish to borrow it? I don't feel the cold so much as you English, although I admit that Yorkshire is far colder than London, where I have been living. Or have you come to make sure I am still here?"

By nature quick with a retort, she was having trouble rallying her wits. If nothing else, the man was dangerously attractive. "Indeed, I was rather hoping you were not. But since you are, I am come to collect Tom's wage for guiding you here. He fears you will depart without paying him."

"Ah. So cynical at so young an age. Wait a moment and I'll fetch what I owe him."

"Also the price of new gloves. Good ones."

"To be sure."

He didn't smile, but she felt certain that behind that indifferent pose, he was laughing at her. Feeling defensive, she watched him swing gracefully onto the ladder and reach the ground before gravity could have pulled him there. Dangerous indeed, she reflected for about the fiftieth time.

Passing by her without a glance, he strode to the rear of his carriage, opened the boot, and pulled out a small portmanteau. She watched as he rifled through the contents and came up with a flat leather case. From it he removed what looked like a bank note and returned the case to where it had been.

"I don't think Tom will abide payment with paper," she advised him. "Most shopkeepers in this area won't accept it, except from selected customers."

"Well, I gave the last of my coins to the stable master at the post house in exchange for a postilion. He was supposed to pay the boy on his return, and perhaps he will. Meantime, let me give him this. If need be, you can help him exchange it for coins."

Reasonable, if true. Even generous, if he meant it. She stared at the ground, unable to look at his face. She didn't like him doing things that tempted her to rethink her first impressions. *He has a silver tongue on him*, she decided. *That's how he draws people into his web.* She wondered what flummery he had laid on John to win him over.

When she looked up again, he was directly in front of her, holding out a banknote. "Money is not my concern," he said quietly. "Believe that much, if nothing else."

His carriage, horses and clothing supported that claim, but she wasn't ready to concede. Not yet. Not until he told her why he'd come here in the first place.

"May I inquire your name, sir?"

The slightest pause, as if considering her simple question. "I am Kiro Viscardi," he finally said. "Have you heard this name before?"

"I have not. You said you knew my father."

"No." He dropped his arm to his side. "We never met. I said only that I'd come to speak with him."

"On a matter of urgency."

"Just so. And with every day that passes, the situation becomes more pressing." His expression darkened. "I mean no harm. If you will permit me, I shall explain why I have come here. And possibly beg for your assistance."

A shiver ran down her back, but she met him eye to eye. "If we are to speak, let us find a place in the house for you. Should you freeze to death in the barn, I'd have a great deal of trouble explaining your demise to the authorities."

"Oh, they are unlikely to care, me not being born an Englishman. And I believe I can survive one night wrapped in blankets and sleeping on straw." His head tilted, his gaze indecipherable. "If I may inquire, what changed your mind?"

"Nothing. My mind is precisely where it has been since first I saw you. But others feel it would be uncharitable to exile you to a stable on a stormy Christmas Eve. A vote was taken, and I lost."

The ghost of a smile flitted across his lips. "I am indebted to your comrades, then. For their sakes, I will try not to prove a nuisance."

"Oh, you won't. We will provide for your needs. It is perhaps an excess of caution, but when no one in the house is free to provide supervision, you will be kept to your room. We are isolated here, and from time to time have experienced . . . difficulties. When the weather lifts, I expect you to take yourself elsewhere."

"Harsh terms, milady." He looked amused. "But I accept. Unless circumstances change, of course. They usually do."

This, she understood, was a warning. "Come along then, before the snow is knee-deep."

Kiro, bemused, retrieved his portmanteau from the carriage and followed her into the swirling snow just as a blast of wind caught the stable door, wrenched it from her hand, and swung it open wide. Dropping the luggage, he put his back to the door and, inch by inch, pressed it closed.

"No!" she screamed. "Noooo!"

He saw her take off running across the field, away from the direction of the house. Releasing the door, he sped after her and quickly caught her up. Ahead, moving even faster, he spotted two shapes in the snow. The closer one appeared to be a fox, but the creature it was chasing was too far ahead for him to tell. He did know that pursuing them was futile.

"Stop," he shouted, his voice barely audible through the skirling wind. When she failed to slow, he seized her arm, encircled her waist, and pulled her tight against him. For a few seconds, she fought him like a madwoman. Then, like a marionette with its strings suddenly cut, she went limp.

He let her hang there, pressed against his chest, supported by his arms, until she lifted her head and gazed into his eyes. He saw tears freezing on her cheeks. "What is it?" he said.

"The c-cat," she said, choking on the word. "The fox will kill her."

A cat? All this over a *cat*?

"It is the way of nature," he said, turning her so that his body sheltered her from the worst of the wind. "The fox may have cubs to feed."

"Not this time of year. But Molly does. Kittens, I mean. Did you see them? Did the fox eat them?"

The wind was making it difficult to hear. "Come," he said. "We can't leave the barn door open with horses, a cow, and maybe cats inside."

It would have been faster and easier if he carried her, but even overset as she was, he didn't think she would welcome the offer. As she struggled beside him through the snow, she kept babbling about the cat and the flap door John had fixed for it to come and go, the one that must have let in the fox as well. She intended to nail it shut the moment they got there.

But first they had to pull the heavy door closed, which required all his strength and a gallant effort from the girl as well.

She went instantly to a toolbox and pulled out a hammer and nails.

"Not now," he said, gently removing them from her hands. "The cat may escape the fox. Cats can climb, you know. And she'll need a way back in. Perhaps I should remain here for the night."

Eyes wide, she gazed up at him in apparent surprise. "Thank you. But whether she escapes or not, the fox could creep back for the kittens. I'll take them to the house, where they can be kept warm and fed. But first, I have to find them. Molly invariably moves them after someone enters the barn. Even John. And we need something to carry them in. They're very small, barely two weeks old. Will you locate a pail or something and line it with straw and rags?"

He nodded. "They're not in the loft. Nor the stalls where the horses and cow are stabled. I've been nowhere else."

As she headed for the stalls on the left side of the barn, he went to the tack room for a pail and found a pile of clean rags as well. He lined the pail with hay for insulation, added the softest of the rags, and set out to explore the right side of the barn. Bypassing horses and cow, he examined the two end stalls. Both were stacked with hay, piled taller than he was, which appeared to rule them out.

He was about to try elsewhere when he heard the tiniest of sounds from the gateless stall he'd first rejected. Probably nothing, possibly a mouse. He stood outside and listened.

It came again, like a soft note played on a harpsichord, but he was unable to tell the direction. Moving silently inside, he looked back to make sure Miss Bryar was not in the vicinity. Coast being clear, he squatted down and emitted what he hoped sounded like a cat's meow. No response. Remembering that Molly was a female, he tried again in a higher pitch.

This time he detected a slight rustling sound on his left and low down. He dropped onto hands and knees and crawled to where the banked hay met the wooden stall enclosure. Nothing appeared out of the ordinary.

Feeling ridiculous and oddly desperate, he tried another meow.

This time, the response was slight but unmistakable. With care, he began to pluck strands of hay from the bottom corner of the stack, and before he'd removed a good-sized handful, he detected the small, dark cave that lay beyond.

Clever cat. The deception would fool a human. But not, he was certain, an animal with a keen sense of smell. Like a fox. So when confronted, Molly had made a run for it to draw the fox away. Good strategy all around, so long as she escaped or someone discovered the kittens in time to save them.

Was that even possible? And how was it he had become so invested in the fate of foreign felines?

God, he was tired. Nearly asleep on hands and knees. He struggled to his feet, intending to fetch Miss Bryar, when he heard something that sounded like a snort. Followed by a laugh that would have sounded musical if not directed at him.

"How long have you been here?" he said, feeling heat rise up his neck.

"Long enough," she managed to say before laughter overtook her again.

"I'm pleased to have amused you."

"You sounded nothing like a cat."

"Is that so? The kittens beg to differ. They told me where they were."

"Yes." Her laughter vanished as quickly as it had erupted. "I am astonished, is all. I wouldn't have thought you had it in you."

"Nor did I." Rising, he passed her the bucket. "You should take command now. I don't know how to safely pick them up."

"Then nail the flap door closed, if you will. Should Molly return and find she cannot enter the barn, she'll come to the house. Let us meet at the door when you are done."

He bowed consent, imagining how silly that must look on top of his previous behavior. At least he had probably undercut her fear of him, although in her own self-interest, she'd probably do better to maintain and strengthen it. If nothing else, he'd managed to infiltrate the house, and the storm would keep him there for several days.

Chapter Three

Stella, cradling a kitten against her waist, looked around the company gathered in the kitchen. Six kittens, six people. Sometimes the stars aligned.

Better if Molly came home, to be sure. The cat had been a gift from her father when he returned, for the last time, from his travels. Like everything else he brought or had shipped home during what he called his "marriage exile," she treasured the cat and had kept her safe at Moor Mansion.

"She adopted me," he'd told her. "I couldn't leave her behind."

Nor could Stella abandon the kittens. They were the only litter Molly had ever birthed, and as such, her own last living link to her father if Molly was gone forever.

"Very well," she said, addressing the silent, reluctant kitty godparents. "Each of you has a fleecy rag to contain the kitten and a small piece of cotton cloth with the tip rolled into a point and tied off. Bertha has warmed some sheep's milk. I shall provide each of you with a small container of the milk. Dip the rolled tip of the cloth into it and bring it to the kitten's mouth. If it suckles, well and good. If not, you must squeeze milk into its mouth while taking care that the kitten does not choke."

John, who understood animals, looked calm as a dozing cat. The rest pinned her with panicked gazes.

Bertha spoke up. "Have you done this before?"

"No. But a school-friend did, and she told me all about it. Well, maybe not all. I'm going by what I learned, and we must hope it is enough. Above everything else, let us hope that Molly returns. She'll come to the kitchen door and scratch for admission. Yowl, if need be. Tom, will you sleep on a pallet near the door for tonight?"

He nodded, clearly glad to be of use. And he flushed when Annie sent him a warm smile.

"Here's the difficult part," Stella continued with a rueful shrug. "We must feed them every two or three hours. Isn't that right, John?"

"Aye," he said. "Dunno the time for kitn's, but most all newborns needs feedin' through the day and through the night."

"B-but how will we all stay awake?" Tom, wide-eyed, was blushing nearly as fiercely as Annie.

"I will see to that." Stella said, smiling. "If Molly gave her life by drawing off the fox, we must honor her memory by saving her babies.

Let us remember that it is Christmas Eve, when angels sang to shepherds as they tended their sheep. Like them, we shall keep vigil here with the small creatures given into our charge and do our best. After each feeding, place your kitten into the bedding that Annie fixed for them and get what sleep you can until I knock on your doors again. Are we agreed?"

"Aye," said John, echoed by the others. Even Mister Viscardi.

I should stand for Parliament, Stella thought as she ladled small helpings of warm sheep's milk into the cups set out before each foster parent.

Kiro, feet hanging over the end of a too-short bed, woke to a blade of light spearing from the tattered curtains directly onto his face. Startled, he sat up too fast and thumped his head against the low-slanted ceiling of the attic dormer room. How could it be light? He fumbled on the rickety night table for his pocket watch.

Ten and eighteen? He'd practically slept the clock around. Stumbling to his feet, he heard the sound of clanking metal directly outside the door. The *locked-from-the-outside* door. Why was he still here, hours later? Why had he not been awakened to feed his kitten? *A kitten.* They all looked alike to him.

"Sir?" A light rap on the door. "Be you awake, sir?"

Not Miss Bryar. "Yes," he called. "Give me a moment, please." He located his banyan and shrugged it on over his smallclothes. Flicked a glance at the mirror and winced. Tangled hair, stubbled chin, the face of a sinister ruffian.

Shrugging, he crossed to the door and grasped the unyielding knob. A *stupid* ruffian, locked in an attic. And to dissipate Miss Bryar's concerns, if not outright suspicions, he had let them do it. No great matter. It wasn't as if he couldn't get himself out if need be. More clattering, which sounded like a tray being set on the floor, and the sounds of a key inserted into the lock, and another key into the second lock. Why the devil did a remote old house have a small attic room with two locks on the door? He'd fallen asleep on that thought.

Moving to the window, he looked outside. Still snowing, but the wind was not so fierce. "You may enter," he called.

The door cracked open. "I've brought you warm water, sir, and towels, and soap."

A heavy burden for a tiny lass, carried up two flights of uneven stairs. He went to the door and took hold of the tray when it came into view. "Thank you."

She glanced at his face and went white, save for her freckles. Her gaze dropped and rooted itself on the floor. "Shall I fetch you a pot of tea, sir? Boiled eggs and toast? There be breakfast in the kitchen, too, if you want it."

It was the red-haired girl he'd seen through the window when he first arrived, and later in the kitchen. He felt rather silly inquiring, but he wanted to know. "What became of the kittens?"

She brightened like a summer sunrise. "Oh, sir! Molly come home last night. We was all in bed, and Tom 'eard 'er scratchin' like she always do, exceptin' Tom never 'eard that afore and thought it were the wind. But 'e opened the door to be sure, and in she come. Like a queen, Tom says. It were just after midnight. She come home for Christmas."

The girl, for all her shyness, knew how to embellish a story.

"I'm glad," he told her, surprised that he meant it. "Thank you for the tray. I'll be down shortly."

She looked worried. "I'm not supposed to leave lessn' you be locked in."

There was no point arguing with her. Miss Bryar held all the authority in this house. "Then come back in fifteen minutes, if you will."

"Yes, sir." With a curtsy, she withdrew and closed the door.

He heard the locks click into place. At some point during the day, he must bring to the house a bag he'd left in the carriage, the one containing, in a hidden compartment, his toolkit. For the moment, using supplies from his personal kit, he shaved, washed his hair and face, and dried himself with a small, threadbare towel from the tray. Best he could do, although he donned clean smallclothes in honor of the day. By his tradition, Christmas wouldn't be celebrated until the seventh of January, but he'd been long enough in England to ignore cultural differences.

He spent the remaining time staring out the window, contemplating the intricate locks. Did suspicious-looking strangers regularly wander by in search of shelter? Not likely, considering how difficult it was to even find this place. So far he'd spotted nothing worth stealing, but he'd seen only the kitchen, the staircase, and this sparsely furnished room. Perhaps it once housed a crazy uncle. Were the locks meant to keep people in, or keep them out?

What if he wished to protect one item of great value but had little money to spare? Would he install double locks on the doors of *all* the rooms? A few, to misdirect a thief? A single room with double locks would practically advertise where the treasure was stored.

Ah, well. Whatever Miss Bryar was trying to accomplish, she would give him no opportunity to search the house. There had been trouble in the past, she'd said. What self-respecting thief would fix on this ramshackle house? He had a good deal more to learn before he could make progress on his own search.

She wouldn't make it easy for him. And to further antagonize her would set her back up even higher than it was. Perhaps he should wait until tomorrow, when Christmas was done with, at least the better part of it. The delay gnawed at him, but he required more information about the lady before trying to winkle out her father's secret. If the holiday was spoiled for everyone, she'd likely close like a clam. At any rate, he could not leave here until the weather let up and the roads were cleared. He'd already lost too much time. Sweat beaded his forehead.

A deadline without a date. It might already be over.

Outside his door, the floor creaked. Moments later, he heard the keys in the locks. Belatedly, a knock. "Are you ready to come downstairs, sir?"

Not a servant this time. Miss Bryar.

With a grimace, he crossed to the door. She was, too often, one step ahead of his expectations. "If I may," he said, hoping he didn't sound as desperate as he felt.

"Go directly to the kitchen. Bertha is preparing your breakfast."

When he opened the door, the officious Miss Bryar was already on her way down the stairs. He trailed behind her like an unwelcome puppy, wishing he had met her in better circumstances. He sensed, beneath that armor of anger she wore for protection, a generous and loving spirit. Had he not stopped her, she'd have chased that fox all the way to Scotland. The lady took care of her own.

Which didn't bode well for his mission. If she disliked him now, and she clearly did, she would almost certainly come to despise him before he was done.

No waiting, he decided on the instant. The more time he spent with these kindly people and their astonishing field marshall of a leader, the harder it would be to cause them pain. He didn't want it to come to that.

But to fail was unthinkable. Lives hung in the balance, and only he could set things right. Christmas or not, before the day was ended, they would come to terms.

Along the way he passed the freckled girl and Tom attaching holly branches to the banister while stealing glances at one another. They did not appear to notice him.

Miss Bryar was standing outside the kitchen door when he arrived, gazing at him from narrowed eyes. "The storm has let up a bit," she said, "although I fear the situation is temporary. Tonight is like to be much the same as last night."

"Are you suggesting I leave while I still can?"

"My fondest wish. But no. Tom will need transport to the posthouse where he works, and I am reluctant to send him into a storm on Christmas Day. Of course, we cannot hold you here against your will."

"Notwithstanding imprisonment in the attic."

"Just so. Kindly partake of breakfast straightaway. Bertha wishes to start on Christmas dinner, so it's best if you take yourself out of her kitchen."

"If I am to stay," he said, "I shall need to collect a few items from my carriage."

"John is there now, milking the cow. Perhaps you can help him by gathering eggs from the chicken house."

"It will be my pleasure." He bowed. "Anything else, Miss Bryar?"

"Yes. Thank you for finding the kittens. They mean a good deal to all of us."

Surprised, he stepped aside, and she moved past him as if he were a tree stump. A fair field marshall, it appeared, one who gave credit where credit was due, even if it rankled her to do so. He realized he was grinning after her.

When he arrived at the kitchen, Bertha looked up at him with a smile. "Good morning, sir. Happy Christmas." She pointed a serving spoon toward the place laid out for him at the trestle table. "How do you likes your eggs? Rashers or sausages? Potatoes? Toast or baps?"

"Eggs fried in butter," he said, suddenly ravenous. When was the last time he'd sat to a home-cooked meal? Years. "Everything else you said. And coffee, if there's any to be had. With sugar and cream. And Happy Christmas to you as well."

Her smile widened. "I likes a man what enjoys his food. No coffee, but the Rondales sent a tin of cocoa. That's me applesauce in the saucer. It be good for you."

No resentment from Bertha, but she hadn't been close enough to hear what transpired when he first arrived. "Where are the cats?"

"In the pantry for now, what with all the doings in the kitchen. It be through that door, if you wants to see."

To his own amazement, he did. The pantry was dim, but when his eyes adjusted, he located the straw-lined crate in a corner. Molly, white with silver and black markings, lifted her head as he approached. She lay on her side, and lined up like tiny bowling pins between her four legs, six kittens suckled contentedly. Resilient cat, utterly relaxed after a terrible night. He should take the lesson and apply it. The more relaxed he was, the more relaxed the others in the house would be.

Stella, standing by a window in her bedchamber, watched the unwelcome guest clear the knee-high snow from the path with a shovel as he made his way to the barn. He didn't strike her as a man accustomed to common labor, or as one who ever bothered to make a good impression. He'd made no effort to explain why he wished to speak with her father, a man he'd never met. What possible business could have brought him here?

With an exasperated sigh, she donned an apron, pulled back her hair, and tied it with a faded ribbon. The good china, good being a relative word, required dusting, and the candlesticks needed polishing for Christmas dinner. She'd work out her temper on the tableware. Then she'd unearth the small Boxing Day gifts she'd been gathering for John, Bertha, and Annie at local fairs and town markets. Imagination and good luck couldn't compensate for her lack of funds, but she thought she'd done well. And they, being kind-natured, would appreciate whatever they received.

She headed down to the dining room, wondering for the millionth time what she would do without them.

"Miss Stella?" Annie was standing on the bottom step, looking up. "I weren't supposed to tell you, but a footman from Mister Rondale's house come here with a ham and a joint. Said Mr. Rondale meant us to have them, but they was too heavy for you to carry last night, and you didn't bring the pony trap."

"He doesn't know I sold the trap." And the pony as well. "Why weren't you supposed to tell? Did they think I'd imagine a ham and a joint had materialized out of thin air?"

Annie grinned. "You means like a Christmas miracle?"

"To be sure. That would explain it." Guilt and indebtedness gnawed at Stella's insides. At least Mister Rondale's sheep were thriving on the land he'd bought from her father, because there was precious little she could do to repay him for his many kindnesses.

"Can we sing tonight, Miss Stella? For Christmas. Tom and I been practicing."

Annie had taught herself to play an old lute salvaged by Sir Edwin on one of his trips, but Stella had never heard her sing. In fact, new strings were one of her Boxing Day gifts. It seemed those ought to be presented early. "If you wish," she said. "After supper, perhaps. We'll light candles in the sitting room and open a bottle or two of Bertha's cloudberry wine."

Annie's face lit up. "Thank you, Miss." She bobbed a curtsey and sped away.

Against her will, Stella found herself caught in the swirl of a celebration for which she had no appetite. But she couldn't deny it to the others, and they'd be hurt if she failed to play her part. "I am *not* in the mood for this," she told Molly, who was gazing at her from the kitchen doorway. "Taking a break from nursing duty, are you?"

Without so much as a meow of sympathy, Molly ambled off in the other direction.

"Fair weather cat," Stella muttered. But Molly could always decipher her moods. No great achievement there. She'd been in a bad mood for the last six years.

Now, where had she been going? A sleepless night was playing havoc with her concentration. Dusting and polishing. Perhaps she ought to assign the stranger to that task in exchange for an invitation to Christmas dinner. It would keep him out of trouble for the afternoon in a place where she could keep an eye on him.

Or, she could take him to a place of privacy and ask him to explain why he had come in search of her father. A matter of urgency, he'd said. *Urgency* never meant anything good, or even tolerable. She wanted answers, but fear of them hung over her head like the sword of Damocles.

Better that she wait a little time longer. If what he had to tell her was as troubling as she imagined, the others would sense her distress, and that would spoil their Christmas Eve celebration. Later, then, when they'd gone to their beds, she would hear what the gentleman had to say.

Chapter Four

It was mid-afternoon before Kiro returned to the house with a large traveling case and a basket of eggs. While John spent much of his time stuffing gluey hay and woodchips into small spaces open to the cold, Kiro had mucked out the stalls, rubbed down his horses and the ancient spotted nag in a back stall, checked their hooves, provided a treat of oats, and supplied fresh water from the well. More water then, fetched for a makeshift bath in an empty stall with a stiff sponge and all-but-petrified bar of soap. No matter the cold and discomfort. When he confronted Miss Bryar at long last, he preferred not to reek.

Entering by the kitchen door to leave off the eggs, he felt as if he'd stepped into an oven. Heat rose from the hearth where a large pan caught drippings from an enormous joint of beef, with Tom turning the spit. Heat rolled out from the oven as well. He smelled bread. Crusted pies sat on the table, waiting their turn. Lidded pots crowded the top of the stove, cooking invisible contents.

The maid, Annie, was seated at the trestle table, intently studding a ham with cloves and dried cherries. In a corner beside a window slightly open against the heat, Bertha waved a fan at her gleaming face and smiled at him. He felt the tightness in his chest, which had clamped down like steel bands when he read the letter a fortnight earlier, loosen the slightest bit. Life went on, it seemed, at least for some.

He bowed to her and held out the eggs, looking a question.

"In the pantry," she told him. "Miss Stella would like to speak with you in the dining room."

"Indeed." This could not be good.

He left his case by the stairs and backtracked to the dining room, where he glimpsed Miss Bryar through the barely open door. She was vigorously rubbing a candlestick as if set on reducing it to a toothpick.

Widening the opening, he stuck his head inside. "You wished to see me, Miss Bryar?"

"Several hours ago," she snapped. "I assumed you'd taken your leave after all."

"Only to be disappointed." Suppressing a smile, he stepped inside and made a proper bow. Sometimes the lady reminded him of his temperamental mother, apprentice level. "My apologies for keeping you waiting. I had thought you wished me out of your sight."

"As soon as may be. But while you are here in the house, with no one free to supervise you—"

He broke out laughing.

"This amuses you?"

"Apparently so, although I can't think why. You intend to lock me in my room, yes?"

"John says that when womenfolk are cooking and cleaning, men should take themselves elsewhere."

"He told me the same thing, which is why I stayed so long in the barn and the chicken house. Allegedly, we get underfoot and make nuisances of ourselves."

"Exactly."

"Then for your peace of mind, by all means secure me in the attic." Just as he wished. He had work to do there. "Might I first select a book from the library?"

"No!" She looked, for a moment, shocked, as if the word had erupted of its own accord. "The library is securely locked. It was my father's refuge and now mine. I dust it myself. No one else is permitted to enter. But there are books in the sitting room. During the day, so long as you remain on the main floor, you are free to make use of that room, and the parlor, and any other where you won't be in the way."

A concession! Precisely when he didn't want one. If he were to mount a search in the night, he had to best those locks. That required time to work when the rest of the house was paying him no mind. But her offer gave him an opportunity to appear gracious and harmless. "That's very kind of you," he said. "At another time, I would enjoy reading by a window. But for now, if it is permitted, I will take a book to my room. I feel a nap coming on."

"Very well. When you are settled, I shall secure the locks. Someone will call you in time for dinner. "

He lifted a brow. "I am invited?"

"There was another vote."

"And you lost."

"Even Molly and the kittens voted for you."

The glint of humor astonished him. "An important constituency, cats. I must cultivate their support."

For a silent moment, they gazed at each other without challenge or rancor.

Then she frowned, and he shook off an unwelcome impulse to prolong the truce. He had, after all, got what he wanted.

"I bid you good afternoon." He bowed, but she had already turned away.

He ducked into the sitting room, took up the first book he saw and carried it, along with his large traveling case, to the attic. A few minutes after he arrived, the door was double locked behind him.

By then he had already extricated his toolkit. When reasonably certain his jailer had left the attic, he set to work on the upper lock.

Twenty minutes later, sweating with effort and frustrated beyond tolerance, he flopped onto the bed and stared at the slanted ceiling eight inches above his head. Excellent locks. Superb, really, and of a design he had not encountered before. They must have come dear. And on his way upstairs, risking a quick look down the passageways, he'd seen shiny double locks on nearly every door. Which implied, of course, that she was hoarding something of great value and disguising that reality by flaunting an ostentatiously frugal life. One replete with a large ham and a joint of beef. He hoped he was right about her intentions. He needed his suspicions to be true.

Meantime, he hadn't given up on the locks. His picks, hand-crafted, were the best, as were the flat tension wrenches. He'd practiced with them and could now break into half the clubs and hotels in London. So far, these locks had proved impervious, which was a shame. He preferred to escape the room without leaving evidence that he'd done so. He could then enter other rooms with equal stealth and no one the wiser. But if he failed to out-master the locks, he'd use the quite different tools he'd filched from the barn to bypass them altogether.

His greatest problem, so far as he could tell, was determining which room had been Sir Edwin's library. Miss Bryar, defending that territory like a lioness, had given too much away. Or she had been trying to throw him off course. He relied on his judgment of people. In the business of international trade, at which he was notably successful, he'd learned to take swift measure of his trading partners, his competitors, and the politicians who had influence where he needed it.

Of course, they were all men. And as his father once advised him, "A man is a simple creature, predictable and self-absorbed. But a woman of intelligence and spirit is a puzzle that no discerning man can decipher. Or live without."

Miss Bryar's nature and intentions continued to elude him. She was clearly intelligent, organized, and kind to her servants. She would naturally be suspicious of a stranger descending on her household on Christmas Eve, and his behavior at the time was uncalled for. Learning of her father's death had hit him hard, and he reacted badly. Quite reasonably, she had taken him in dislike. He was also fairly certain that she was unhappy, if not resentful, at the circumstances of her life. In his youth, a stranger in a strange land, he'd profoundly felt that way. If she possessed what he'd come for, he wasn't altogether sure he could compel her to relinquish it.

If it came down to it, how far would he go? Take a hostage? Close them all in the barn while he ransacked the house?

No good options. Again, the steel bands were making it hard to breathe. Somehow, by whatever means, he must find a solution. Rising, pillow in hand to place under his knees, he went to resume his battle with the locks.

Two hours later, as the pale winter day yielded to the press of night, Kiro rose on aching legs and used a tinderbox to light the small lantern perched on a side table. He could not have persisted in any case. His hands kept cramping up, and numbed fingertips had made it impossible to feel any response in the mechanism. Failure burned low in his throat. He sat on a rickety wooden chair, leaned forward, and buried his face in folded arms. So much time wasted. Lives ticking away.

Now there was Christmas supper to get through. He gave a moment's thought to pleading off, if only to escape the humbug of fake civility and good humor. He hadn't a jot of either to serve up, and he did not want to spoil the festival for the others. But if that meant playacting, he'd developed a talent for it. As Shakespeare wrote, one could smile, and smile, and be a villain.

A poorly dressed villain, he realized as he pawed through his luggage for a clean, unwrinkled shirt. Probably just as well. He would seem less threatening in rumpled clothes. He'd packed only a traveler's sparse wardrobe and had been on the road for nearly a week. The sidetrack to York, where he'd been told Sir Edwin was living, had eaten several days. He managed to locate the house owned by his quarry, but the tenants had never heard of him. They'd resided there only a few months and paid their rent to a leasing agent. When he tracked down the agent, he was told the house now belonged to a lady who preferred to live in the south. Five years earlier, she had turned over management of the property to him. He knew nothing of its previous owner.

When questioning the neighbors, he inquired only about Sir Edwin and where he might be found. Several remembered him, but they could not say where he'd gone.

"Travelin', most like," one man speculated with a look of disapproval. "Always rattlin' off to some heathen place, like York weren't good enuf for 'im. Guess it weren't, after 'is wife went to the angels. She were a fine woman. Anyway, 'e never come back 'ere after she were gone." He hadn't appeared to know Sir Edwin had died, and Kiro hadn't thought to ask.

It was a sullen fellow behind the taps in a nearby pub who said he couldn't be sure, but he thought he remembered that Sir Edwin, who'd stopped by for a pint now and again, had bought a property in the north Yorkshire dales.

Now he was here and knew little more than when he began, except that Sir Edwin could never tell him what became of the knife poised at his parents' throats. That's how he'd come to think of it, anyway. His father could provide only a description and a drawing, but said that by this time, it had likely been altered. That's what he'd have done, anyway.

After stashing his ineffective tools out of sight, Kiro laid his prospective dinner attire across the bed and used the full pitcher of water and bowl provided him to wash up. Then he cleaned his boots, the only footwear he'd brought, with the damp towel. When he'd set out, he never thought to wind up a prisoner of the weather in the back of beyond.

He was dressed, his small, specially designed pistol secured in a leather holster under his left arm, when the knock came. He ran a comb through his hair, pasted a pleasant expression on his face, and faced the door. "Come."

Chapter Five

Annie's passion for decorations had gone a little mad, Stella was thinking as she lavished praise over the shy girl and the shyer young man beaming at their masterpiece. Holly, ivy, and mistletoe were draped over every flat surface in the dining room, save only the sideboard and table. The centerpiece they'd arranged had been relocated to the sitting room, making space for Bertha's bowls and platters.

"Food enough for a regiment," John muttered as he took in the scene, his good arm wrapped around Bertha's waist. In honor of the celebration, he'd donned his faded uniform, the one he wore on the Peninsula in Wellington's army.

Annie, red hair and freckles ablaze like autumn leaves above a simple forest-green dress, stood beside her rag-tag beau, still wearing the trousers, shirt, and jacket he'd arrived in. Laundered, thanks to Bertha, going without her apron for the first time since early morning. Annie had washed Bertha's hair, pinned it up, and pressed the same blue homespun dress she wore at every celebration.

Stella wanted to hug each of them, but understood an emotional display would embarrass them. Yorkshire born and bred, they nearly always kept their feelings to themselves, especially in the presence of strangers. Tonight seemed a little different, though. Even with the intruder standing a little out of the way, aloof but watching everyone with dark, intent eyes, her makeshift family was knitting itself together in equally mysterious ways.

Handsome as sin, he cast a shadow she could all but feel weighing down on her. "Shall we take our usual places?" she said in the chipper tones of the headmistress at York Academy for Young Ladies. "You will be at the foot of the table, sir." As far away from her as possible. But as he sat, after everyone else had done so, she realized the mirror over the mantelpiece made it possible for her to see both sides of him at the same time. A double helping of temptation for a female far beyond the reach of snagging a prize. The day was long past when a gentleman would mercifully offer for a penniless, sharp-tongued spinster firmly ensconced on the shelf. Miss Stella Bryar was practically swaddled in cobwebs.

As John said grace in his quiet voice, she saw Mister Viscardi make a small backward sign of the cross. Christian, then, but not a sort she was familiar with.

"Help me carry in the supper, Tom," John said. He turned to Viscardi, who was already coming to his feet. "Be ye able to carve the 'am? Me arm is no' steady, and Tom's no use with a blade."

"My pleasure," he said, smiling as if he meant it.

She swallowed a sigh. This was certain to be a tense night, at least for her. To distract herself, she complimented Annie on her appearance and thanked Bertha yet again for her devoted work in the kitchen, wishing she could carry a tray to her room and leave the others to enjoy themselves.

After a short time, laughter erupted from the kitchen, John's deep bass voice and Tom's clear tenor. Bertha and Annie looked at her with surprised expressions.

Still laughing, Tom came in with a tureen of creamy corn soup.

"What's be goin' on in me kitchen?" Bertha said, frowning. "I best go see."

"You best not," Tom said, astonishing them all. "No 'arm done. Mister Viscardi were tellin' us 'bout the bear and, well, good thing 'e'd put on the apron."

With effort, Stella pasted a mildly interested expression on her face.

"Bear?" Annie piped, eyes wide with fascination.

"'E tole us some, but then the 'am slid off an' 'e catched it."

Bertha shook her head. "Men in me kitchen. I be cleanin' all this night."

"But 'e *caught* it. Now 'e be cuttin' it, and John takin' at the joint."

Stella sighed. In less than twenty-four hours, Mister Viscardi had them in the palms of his long-fingered hands. "While we wait," she said, "perhaps you and Annie should begin serving."

With Tom holding the tureen and Annie ladling the soup, they were at the last bowl, Stella's, when John entered with the joint and set the platter on the sideboard. The ham followed, looking somewhat the worse for wear, and was gingerly placed beside the beef.

Mister Viscardi turned to Annie with a remorseful smile. "I must beg your pardon, Ma'am, for the sad fate of the cherries you had so delectably arranged. The ham was a thing of true beauty before I took a knife to it. Alas, most of the cloves and cherries wound up in Bertha's apron, which is now soaking in a pail of soapy water."

Annie's face, gone bright pink, tilted to his with a smile.

Stella wondered if anyone not in this little household had ever issued the girl an apology. Whenever they were in company, she made herself small and rarely expressed an opinion or asserted herself. A haunted girl, Annie Litton, orphaned at age six when her parents and two older sisters died of typhoid. John and Bertha had taken her in. It was kind of Mister Viscardi to pay notice to her feelings. Her father had been like that, observant and generous with praise.

For a time, all attention turned to the soup. Then, one by one, they served themselves from the bowls and platters on the sideboard and settled again around the table. The men, as expected, piled their plates with ham and beef and shamelessly returned for second helpings.

Accustomed to the silence, she wondered what Mister Viscardi thought of it. There was so little to be said, really, among naturally reserved people who rarely went anywhere or did anything unusual. Her nature was quite different. She yearned for travel, new experiences, good conversation, music, and all the pleasures of society. It had required years for her to cobble a truce with the quiet landscape and her quieter companions. Things could change a bit, she supposed, if Tom became part of the household. He, at least, had employment that took him on the road, if never very far. Sometimes she felt entrapped in a bottle, able to see out, unable to escape its boundaries.

"Sir?"

Stella nearly dropped her fork. That was Annie, addressing the stranger.

"Yes, Miss Annie? May I fetch you something from the sideboard?"

"I were hoping, sir, you would tell us about the bear."

His gaze flicked to Stella, as if seeking permission. "By all means," she said as everyone regarded Annie with startled expressions. Everyone but Mister Viscardi, whose dark eyes, fixed on hers, looked amused.

"Well, Lord Byron and I became friends, after a fashion, when he taught me to spar at Harrow, where I was regularly bullied on account of being a foreigner. He then taught me to play cricket, and because I helped our team prevail over Eton, the other boys began to accept me. Byron adopted me in great part because I was marginally exotic and relatively uncivilized. He, of course, was madly exotic and unabashedly barbarian whenever he chose to be. At Cambridge, that was nearly always. And for much the same reasons, I suspect, he acquired a bear."

Bertha's eyebrows shot up. "A real one?"

"Indeed. He always preferred animals to people, especially dogs. But by Cambridge regulations, no student was permitted to possess a dog or bring one into his lodgings. So, adhering to the letter of the law, he went out and got himself a bear."

Stella, unwillingly entranced by his acquaintance with a celebrated poet, could not resist joining in. "And how, precisely, does one come by a bear?"

"Very carefully, as a rule. But in this case, he purchased a retired dancing bear, named it Bruin, and kept it in the stable with his horses. Of course, it was invited to our drinking parties, so we saw rather a lot of Bruin. A nice bear, all-in-all, and far tamer than the rest of us."

From then on, as pies and custards, cheeses and nuts were brought out, everyone but John and herself plied him with questions. He replied with apparent good humor, but she saw in his eyes a darkening mood. He wanted to be elsewhere, she suspected, doing something other than telling outlandish stories. She wondered if he intended to join them in the sitting room for wine and music, and was surprised to find herself hoping that he would.

"Cloudberry wine?" Mister Viscardi examined the glass he'd just taken from the tray, his expression patently dubious.

"Bertha can wring wine from just about everything that grows," Stella advised him in a low voice. "Often, it is very good. And if not it is, at the least, exceedingly strong." She gestured to a wingback chair across from the one she had chosen for herself.

Near the fireplace, silhouetted with flickering light, Annie and Tom sat on a pair of low stools. John and Bertha, his arm around her waist, relaxed on the settee, wine glasses in hand. Everyone looked tired, so likely the evening wouldn't stretch on much longer. Just as well.

After a few tuning adjustments on the restrung lute, Annie grinned at Stella and began to play.

"*Deck the halls with boughs of holly,*" sang Tom in a true, clear tenor voice, and everyone glanced over at the centerpiece covering most of a low table in front of the settee. When he waved his hands during the fa-la-la's, they obediently fa'd and la'd with him. Even John, who sounded like he was singing from the cellar.

More of the old songs followed, one after the other, with Tom and Annie on the verses and the rest chiming in for the choruses. *Hark! the Herald Angels Sing. Oh Come, All Ye Faithful. Joy to the World.*

Stella, lost in her own world, dutifully complied, her mind roiling with plans and anxiety. Tonight, nearly twenty-four hours after his arrival, she would finally learn why Mister Viscardi had come to her home. She was relieved when Tom announced that he and Annie would sing two songs by themselves, but as they began *Bring a Torch, Jeanette Isabella*, the beauty of their voices in close harmony snapped her to attention. Even at services in York Minster, she had rarely heard so simple and beautiful a sound. And when they followed with *Lo, How a Rose*, tears burned in her eyes.

After that, in something of a daze, she heard applause and watched everyone, even Mister Viscardi, surround the glowing singers with applause and praise. Almost, she could not bear to ruin this beautiful night.

Quietly, she drew John aside, watching to make sure her quarry did not leave the room before the others while she gave John his instructions. "And when everyone else has retired," she concluded, "bring him to me."

Chapter Six

The summons came as Kiro was laying out his tools for another go at the locks.

"Sir?" John said from the passageway. "Miss Stella be wantin' to speak with you in the library."

"Certainly." His heart started pounding like the thump of hooves on a racing track. While John unsecured the door, he stowed the tools under the mattress and pulled on his jacket, covering the pistol he hadn't yet removed.

In silence, they descended one flight of stairs and turned in to a long passageway illuminated by a lone flickering oil lamp on the wall beside a door.

After knocking, John turned the knob and stepped aside to let him enter.

Acutely aware of Miss Bryar seated behind a large desk to his left, Kiro paused with his back to the closing door and took stock of the room. It was smaller and plainer than he'd expected, if this was indeed Sir Edwin's library. Bookshelves lined three of the walls from floor to ceiling, including the one behind the desk. But directly ahead, a large, polished worktable extended the length of the wall, three stands of small drawers on wheels beneath it and two armed chairs, also on wheels, nearby.

Finally, he turned to Miss Bryar and bowed, noting a bottle of what looked like brandy and a glass, one only, on the desk near where he'd be expected to sit.

She looked over at the bottle. "John provided this. He fancies you will need it."

"Or you fancy that drinking it on top of the cloudberry wine will leave me witless."

"Is that likely?"

"No." Moving to the desk, he filled the glass and took a long swallow. "In Byron's circle, drinking is a competitive sport."

"Was it all true, then, what you told us at supper?"

"Why do you doubt it?" So far, the confrontation he'd both dreaded and required was playing out like the warm-up before a tennis match, both players lobbing the ball back and forth, watching keenly for weaknesses to exploit. "Mind you, with ladies present, I omitted the shocking details."

She nodded toward the chair. "Pray be seated, sir."

Her tone had hardened, as had her eyes. Still holding the glass, he slumped onto the chair and took another drink, leaving her to make the first move.

"I believe," she said, "that before we begin, you should know these things. John is directly outside the door, his rifle at the ready, and will enter if I call for him or if he hears anything that might indicate trouble."

Despite his own somewhat nefarious intentions, he couldn't help wondering what the devil she expected him to do.

"Also"—she lifted her right arm, at the end of which was a small, sleek pistol—"you will at all times keep both hands above the desk where I can see them."

"Anything else?" So much for intimidating a lonely country spinster to draw out the information he needed. "I take it these are your terms of war."

"Are we at war, sir?"

He couldn't miss the glint of anticipation in her eyes. "It appears so. You have chosen the battlefield, provided yourself with a bodyguard, and threatened me with a gun. Whereas I had the misfortune to descend upon your house in darkness and the insolence to react poorly when told Sir Edwin was not to be found here. For that, I apologize. Oh, and I carelessly permitted the Christmas ham to slide off the platter and onto my lap. I believe that encompasses the extent of my crimes. Can you, Miss Bryar, explain precisely what else I have done to offend you?"

"No," she said, chiseling the word out of stone. "I am merely anticipating what you might intend to do. Given reason enough, I would not hesitate to pull this trigger."

Her hand on the pistol, her arm, and all the rest of her he could see were perfectly poised to do exactly that. He'd already considered an advance strike, flinging brandy in her eyes with one hand as he knocked the pistol away with the bottle and launching himself across the desk to cover her mouth before she could scream. He'd been training for war, one way or another, since he was a boy. He could take down John as well, long before he managed to sight the rifle. But he didn't want to do any of those things.

"If you say so. However, I doubt your conscience would permit you to kill me in cold blood."

"Probably not." Her smile would have curdled milk. "But I have no aversion to wounding in cold blood."

Despite the tension wringing him out like a rag, he nearly laughed.

A remarkable woman, this country wench. Were the stakes not so high, he could fancy—

He sucked in a deep breath. For the present they were at war, and he had to win. "Do you know, I quite believe it," he said. "And now that the opening feints and posturings have been flaunted, shall we converse like two adults with a serious problem to address? And allow John to take to his bed?"

A long hesitation, followed by a nearly imperceptible sigh. "Although I, too, wish that were possible, he must stay. But sitting in one of those chairs, perhaps. Will you see to it?"

She had lowered the pistol without him noticing. Neither hand was visible, but when he rose, he saw she'd opened the desk drawer and rested the hand with the pistol atop a book she must have placed there before he arrived. Her other hand held a small brass bell. Her tactics were first rate.

When he opened the door and rolled the chair into the passageway, John gave him an inquisitive look. By way of answer, he shrugged, grinned, and rolled his eyes.

"Thank you, Mister Viscardi," Miss Bryar said stiffly when he settled again on his own chair and took up his glass of brandy. "Are you, by birth, Italian?"

"Does it matter?" he replied with equal stiffness. "Kiro is my given name. I am, as were my ancestors from centuries past, a native of Montenegro."

When she went pale at the last word, he leapt to seize the moment. "Viscardi is my mother's family name. My surname is Radanovic. I am Kiro Radanovic of Montenegro."

"Ra-*dan*-ovic," she murmured slowly, as if testing it on her tongue. "Radanovic," she said, more firmly. "I have never heard that name. But I have read it many times."

He'd been sure she would have encountered it by some means. It was why he had concealed his full identity. Now he waited. Let her make the next move.

She did. Pistol still in her grip, she went to the door and asked John to step inside.

With two guns ready to cut him down, although he doubted John would pull the trigger, he watched Miss Bryar pull one of the wheeled cabinets from under the side table and open the bottom drawer. Crouching, she flipped through the contents and emerged with a thick packet of folded papers tied with a black ribbon. Letters, he was fairly certain, written by her father.

Back at the desk, she signaled John to withdraw and set down her pistol within easy reach. Of his reach as well, although he didn't point that out. Instead, he applied himself to the brandy and watched her gingerly open letter after letter, skim what was inscribed there, and refold each with care. As impatience began to dig claws into him, he wanted to rip the letters from her hands and read them for himself. Surely they contained the answer he sought.

After a year or two, she restacked the letters, tied them together with the ribbon, and stowed them in the desk, he couldn't see precisely where. Then, laying her hand atop the pistol, she lifted her gaze to meet his.

"It appears that my father resided with your family for nearly a year. Do you still claim you never met him?"

"If that year followed 1803, I could not possibly have done so. I have lived in England from that time until now. But I do know that my father met yours, discovered they shared many interests, and invited him to stay at our home in Kotor."

"Did you know that while there, he took ill?"

Patience, never his long suit, began to fray. Time to start laying his own cards on the table. "I weary of this inquisition. Of your father, I knew absolutely nothing until a fortnight ago. All of what I now know was contained in a letter from my own father."

"Then what is it you wanted to ask him? Or tell him?"

He wasn't ready to disclose that. Not yet. He feared he'd choose the wrong words. Give more hurt than she could bear. And truth be told, he feared her answer. Worse, she might close down altogether, and he would learn nothing more from her. Best to begin slowly, feed her the few bits of information that were his to offer, and gauge her reaction.

"The letter said your father, after living at the palazzo for several months, became ill. The physician believed it was his heart. Sir Edwin had planned to return to England within a few weeks, in great part because my parents intended to spend the spring in Venice. They agreed Sir Edwin should remain in Kotor until his health improved. When they returned, he was no longer there."

For a time, head lowered, she did not respond. He let the silence stretch out, in great part because he couldn't think what to say. To give himself something to do, he topped off his glass with brandy.

"He shouldn't have made the journey so soon," she said in a tight voice. "When he arrived, he could scarcely walk more than a few minutes without gasping for air. He said he would have crossed all the world's oceans to see me again, and that no price was too great for him to pay. He said that last part many times, often murmuring it to himself during his final illness. Two months after his return, he died."

And she had not ceased mourning for him, Kiro understood. He wondered if she held herself responsible, as if her very existence had hastened his death.

"Before his return," she said, sounding more like the confident Miss Bryar he had come to expect, "crates and parcels, shipped from Montenegro, began to arrive. There were a great many of them. He brought some with him as well, and others were delivered much later. He'd always posted the things he collected on his travels, broken tiles and sculptures, fabrics and laces, all manner of items he considered of historical or cultural interest. Indeed, anything that caught his fancy. 'What's the use of a big old house,' he'd insist, 'if we don't fill it with the people and things we love?' I cannot blame him for taking himself away from England, but sometimes I find it hard to forgive him."

Just as he could not blame his parents for sending him into exile, Kiro acknowledged with the same bitterness he'd harbored for sixteen years. Nor was he permitted to return home now. Not empty-handed.

"Is that why you installed the locks? To protect the things he collected?"

"In a manner of speaking. There is nothing of significant value, and most pieces have no financial value at all. Although I cannot convince his wife of that. She believes I am hoarding treasures that properly belong to her, though the marriage settlement left her with the lion's share of his holdings, including the house in York where I was born and grew up. There are no boundaries to her greed, nor her talent for spending, and she never ceases to plague us. This house, such as it is, and its contents, were willed to me. I have forbidden her to enter. But I put nothing past her, so I protect the things that meant a great deal to my father. In his memory, I intend to preserve them all."

Elation fizzed inside him. She'd kept everything. It must be here. All he had to do was find it, or compel her to hand it over. He required more information, though, as much as he could elicit, before she became resistant. "Did he say why he'd been invited to stay at the palazzo? Before his illness, I mean."

"They had met by chance at some sort of festival. Does it signify?"

"I am merely curious. To welcome a stranger as a houseguest for nearly a year is surely out of the ordinary."

"Yes. But when he arrived in Kotor, it was crowded with visitors and he could find no lodging. Your father invited him for supper and offered a room until he found a suitable place of his own. During that week they discovered a mutual passion for music boxes and automatons. The consummate blending of art and science, he told me in a letter."

It had been impossible, Kiro remembered, to walk through the palazzo without hearing the tinkling of a music box or tripping over a mechanical soldier or bird. "Yes. Those were my father's obsession as well. He purchased nearly every one he came across and devoted himself to repairing and restoring them. After which, a place had to be found, and La Principessa, as he called my mother whenever they had a dispute, complained that the palazzo was grossly overpopulated with his toys."

The ghost of a smile played on her lips. "Papa wrote me about that. He said your father was delighted to have a partner in crime, although the alliance produced even more clutter. As a compromise, your parents agreed to reward him with as many music boxes and automatons as he wished, save those of historical value and your father's personal favorites. He had only to remove them from the premises. So he began shipping them here, and brought several with him on his return."

"And nothing else?"

"Very little from Montenegro. He was also interested in classical antiquities and weaponry, but could not afford to purchase articles of quality. Instead, he settled for common items, broken or shabby relics, bits and pieces."

"No gemstones? No jewelry?"

He shouldn't have asked. Eyes flashing with anger, she put her hand on the pistol. "I told you. Nothing of value. A few tarnished silver medallions, a brooch of woven copper and silver wires, and a belt buckle studded with chunks of onyx. I remember those because they were unlike his usual interests. And now I am done inventorying for you my father's souvenirs. Let us return to the reason I brought you here. What is it you wanted to ask or tell my father?"

Instinct told him he'd learn nothing more by indirection, and he doubted she would permit another private meeting. It had to be now.

He fixed his gaze on her face, watching for the slightest reaction as he spoke. "As you will, Miss Bryar. When he left Montenegro, your father took with him something of great value and importance. It must be returned. I came here to retrieve it."

She frowned, as if she didn't understand what he'd said. Watching her eyes, he saw the moment when the implications sank in. "You accuse my father of *theft*? On what grounds? What is it you think he stole?"

"A large and perfect diamond of unusual cut and color. It was shown him by my father soon after he took residence in the palazzo, and when my parents returned from Venice, it had gone missing. Only your father had access to the private rooms where family records, jewelry, antiquities, and other valuables were stored. He had seen the cast-iron safe where it was kept and apparently took note of where my father stored the keys."

On her feet now, white-faced, right hand closed around the pistol, she fixed him with a look of pure hatred. "In all his life, my father never told a lie of consequence or stole so much as a daffodil. Nor did my mother. Their honor, their integrity, guided everything they said or did."

"It is not my intention to insult your family. But for mine, the stakes are very high." This was the moment. He took a deep breath and met her burning gaze. "Unless the diamond is returned without further delay, my parents will pay for it with their lives."

She blinked. Then, head canted, she cast him a wary look. "If any word of this fantastical tale is true, you should be looking elsewhere. I catalogued everything my father collected during the last years of his life. I could not have failed to notice an enormous diamond."

"In some lights, at some angles, it appears golden. It was cut to resemble a sta—"

"Enough! He would *not* steal from a friend, from a stranger who granted him hospitality. From anyone. Even if I granted the possibility, what you seek is not here. If it were, on my word, I would give it you." She was already at the door. "John will escort you to your room. In the morning, whatever the weather, you will take your leave."

Rising, choked with failure, Kiro turned to her and bowed.

Chapter Seven

John made no objections when Kiro carried the brandy and glass to his room.

As the locks clicked into place behind him, he sat on the edge of the bed, face buried in his hands. What next? Dear God, what next?

He could by no means walk away from this. But to find the diamond, he required Miss Bryar's cooperation, and she had all but thrown him out. By early morning, every door of this house would be locked against him. What was left for him to do?

Nothing that wouldn't bring harm to people he had come to like and respect. He wondered if his own life, should he return to Montenegro to offer it, would be accepted as compensation. Most likely not. What was an expatriate son, compared to the daughter of a Venetian princess and the Montenegran equivalent of a prime minister? Shkoder Pasha, whose pride outdistanced even his ruthlessness in battle, would cheerfully strike down the lot of them.

What was left, then? He'd wager Miss Bryar knew nothing of the *Harika Altin Yildiz,* as the Ottoman had named the diamond. The Great Golden Star. But he felt certain it was in this place. His father would never make such an allegation against a friend without evidence. Neither could he fault Miss Bryar for believing in her own father's integrity and defending his reputation. But what had she to lose by permitting a search? Pride was no justification, and she had not even permitted him to explain the consequences of her decision.

It followed that by whatever means, he must search the house. Tear it apart if need be. That could require him to secure five people, two of them armed with guns, in a place where they could not obstruct him. Given a chance, the others would defend themselves with knives or whatever they could put their hands on. He'd have to be swift and, very likely, merciless.

It could be done, though. It *would* be done.

Confidence and desperation made strange bedfellows, but they also provided excellent fuel. He would first target Miss Bryar. Once she was in his power, he thought—hoped—that to protect her, the others would surrender.

He doubted she would appear in the morning to see him off. How to gain access to her? A feint? Make it appear he'd absconded during the night? Not in the carriage, though. He'd nowhere to safely leave it while he returned to the house. One missing horse and the battered old saddle he'd spotted in the barn would do it. After setting hoof prints as far as the road, he'd circle around, conceal the horse in one of the buildings behind the house, and decide where to lie in wait. When he spotted a member of the household alone, he'd seize a hostage and improvise from there.

That's what he ought to have done in the beginning, he supposed, when he learned Sir Edwin was dead and while the residents were strangers to him. But as in all matters of importance, he'd chosen to first evaluate his potential adversaries or allies. Now he knew the lay of the land and the opposition he faced, and found himself with no stomach for violence against these people.

Miss Bryar's outrage was genuine, he was sure, as was her pain. He no longer suspected her of concealing the diamond. Even so, it might be stashed among the collection of things Sir Edwin had sent home. She hadn't come across it, most likely because it no longer resembled a diamond. Now, whatever it required him to do, she must consent to letting him search for it.

The immediate challenge was to exit the room and get himself downstairs without being detected.

It required effort to pull himself to his feet and begin preparations. From the secret compartment in his bag, he took a sheathed stiletto and slipped it inside his boot. Another blade, smaller, was strapped to his forearm. The pistol remained where it was, holstered under his arm.

With regret, he returned the lock picks to the case and unearthed the tools he'd taken from the barn and hidden under the bed. When reasonably sure everyone had retired, he'd use them to dismantle the door.

"Sir?"

He was coming to his feet when he heard John's voice, followed by a rap on the door. He stuffed the tools between the sheets, straightened his jacket, and crossed to the window. "What is it?"

A pause as John cleared his throat. "Miss Stella wants to speak wi' you."

Kiro's heartbeat kicked into doubletime. Did she mean to toss him out in the middle of the night? Did it matter? A brief time alone with her, even with John nearby, would drop her into his hands like a ripe peach. Was his luck turning at last?

"I shall be glad to oblige her," he said, inserting a tone of mild grievance. It wouldn't serve to sound as eager as he felt. Swiftly, he moved the pistol from his shoulder sling and stuffed it behind him in

the waistband of his breeches, easier to reach. Before she knew what
was happening, the lady would be in his power.

John was turning away when the door swung open, and he said
nothing as they descended stairs, all of them, until they reached the
ground level. There, he stepped aside and gestured to the right. "She
be in the sittin' room."

Before Kiro could reply, John was headed the other direction.

More puzzled than ever, he sifted explanations and possibilities,
wanting to be ready for whatever he faced when he went through the
door. Then, blood pulsing at his temples, he made a silent entrance.

She was standing with her back to the fireplace, silhouetted by
light from the glowing red coals and looking as if she'd just emerged
from a portal to hell. She stood straight as an arrow, eyes dark with
sorrow, her arms at her sides.

Of a sudden uncertain, he approached her and stopped a polite
distance away. Bowed. Silence shrouded the room, save for only the
ticking of the long-case clock. He glanced at the face. It was still
Christmas.

"Thank you for coming," she said with evident restraint. "I
expected you to refuse. Now I hope you will be kind enough to answer
a question."

"By all means."

"When last we spoke, at the end you were trying to explain
something. I refused to listen, cut you off, and sent you away."

"I distinctly recall the event."

"What were you trying to say?" The words came tumbling out.
"When you described the diamond, you began a word but failed to
complete it. 'Cut to resemble a sta—' you said."

"Star. The word is 'star.'"

Silence. Then, her gaze fixed on the floor, she murmured, "I
thought it might be."

Hope rose in him like a bird taking flight. "Have you remembered
seeing something of the kind?"

"I am sure I have not. Nor can I believe my father would ever
steal, especially from a gentleman who had become his friend and
extended him many kindnesses."

Time for a concession, Kiro understood. "I'm not sure Sir Edwin
thought of it as stealing. Not in the way of a common thief. He
believed he had a higher purpose for the star, something better then
leaving it hidden in a private collection. My father holds himself in part
responsible because he permitted Sir Edwin to see the diamond. Until

then, no one but he himself knew it was in his possession. While certain Sir Edwin took the diamond, he does not consider him a thief and said so in his letter. Your father must have known he was dying. What would he *not* have done to secure the future of his daughter?"

She was looking beyond him when he finished, one tear sliding down her cheek. "Nothing," she whispered. "Except stay with me. But she made him so unhappy. No one could have endured it. If he'd not found an escape, neither of us would have been happy."

The second wife. "Why, if she is a harpy, did he marry her?"

"Because he had found perfect happiness with my mother, I have always thought. And knowing my grief matched his own, he wished to create a new family for us both, like the one we had lost. But he understood little about opportunistic women. His first experience of love, instant and enduring, left him unprepared for the likes of Eliza Bligh. She swept him off like a butterfly caught in a cyclone, but once the marriage was sealed, she began milking him like a cow." A grim chuckle. "I beg your pardon. I am wallowing in bad analogies."

He'd been so caught up in her story, he had nearly forgotten his purpose. "The love match you describe," he said carefully, "is like the one I grew up with, if you factor in high-drama temperaments and a nation encompassed by war. Although I have not seen my parents for sixteen years, I am bound to them by affection and loyalty. May I explain to you why recovering the diamond is of surpassing urgency?"

Her eyes had widened when he named the years of his exile. Encouraged, but fearful of making a wrong move, he cast about for a narrative she could accept. One that would wring from her permission to examine every room and every item in this house. But it was too late to manufacture a plausible lie, leaving him with the cold, harsh, and to a young and sheltered Englishwoman, fantastical tale.

"Please," she said. "But shall we draw chairs to what remains of the fire?"

"I'll see to it." It gave him something to do while ordering his thoughts. He towed the wingback chairs to the hearth, added a few small chunks of wood to the firedog and placed tinder underneath. A slender stick, ignited by a determined little flame among the dying coals, served to set the tinder ablaze. He remembered campfires in the mountains, and wrestling with his brothers, and the night he defeated them both to applause from his parents. Later, he'd realized they had given him the victory, but only because he fought well and refused to accept defeat.

Nor would he accept it now. Angling his chair to better see her reactions, he began a tale on which, he feared, everything would depend.

"Being a place of great beauty and strategic position, Montenegro has been the target of invaders for many centuries. Most recently the French, but in my lifetime, and my parents', the greatest struggle has been with the Ottomans. When they invaded, we fought them off. When they attacked our neighbors, we fought them there as well. Not I, of course. I was a late child and declared too young for battle. Father, a leader held in high esteem, found himself relegated to strategy, arms, and supplies. Neither of us took our situations well." He gave her an apologetic shrug. "I am rabbiting on about matters that cannot interest you, but I must lay the groundwork for my father's crime."

"I don't mind," she said earnestly. "This is important to us both, is it not?"

"So I believe. But difficult. I have never spoken of these things to anyone."

She was frowning. Something he'd said must have finally registered. "Crime?"

"Just so. But first, more explanation. In part by way of justification, I suppose, but without it, none of this would be credible." The difficult words, for him at least, had arrived. "I had two brothers, Luka and Danilo, eight and ten years older than I. Both were killed in battles outside of Montenegro at different times and places, but they fought against the same foe, a fierce and mobile army of Ottomans led by a flamboyant Turk known as Shkoder Pasha. To flaunt his victories and threaten Montenegro, he subsequently built an extravagant fortress on the side of a mountain just outside our borders, overlooking the Bay of Kotor. 'I am coming,' he proclaimed, 'when I will.'

"But when other battles drew him away, he kept only a small contingent of soldiers and servants to protect the fortress. On one such occasion, my father decided without authorization to mount a raid. His band of attackers met with little opposition and looted everything of value, most of it used to supply arms and provisions to our soldiers." Kiro took a deep breath. "It was my father who discovered the diamond, attached to a gaudy turban on a shelf in Shkoder Pasha's bedchamber. He squirreled it away and, I am sorry to say, kept it for himself."

"He *stole* it?" She nearly came off her chair. "Your father was a *thief?*"

"At that time, in that moment, yes. It was Shkoder Pasha's raids that took both his warrior sons. My father took a souvenir. In his mind, it was a gesture of tribute to Luka and Danilo. But his conscience always ate at him, and he could not, practically speaking, return it. Nor was he willing to do so."

"You knew about this?"

"No. Nor did my mother. He disguised the diamond and concealed it."

"Yet he showed it to my father. For what reason?"

"His letter did not explain. But I suspect he had long been wishing to tell the tale to *someone*, and he'd made a friend who had no stake in the turmoil afflicting the Dalmatian Coast. Your father was sworn to silence."

"He kept that oath." She clasped her hands together. "So we have come to why I asked to speak with you. I had not thought of this before tonight. After his return, he would often say to me, 'Look to the star, My Treasure.' That had used to be his pet name for me. 'Whenever you are in need, look to the star.' But he'd always said that, from the time I was a child. He loved the night sky and would take me to a dark place and name the stars and the constellations and tell me stories about them. He taught me how to choose a star and pin a wish on it. So I imagined no significance to his words, except they had always been *our* words, and the stars a bond between us. When he grew fragile during the last few days, it became 'Look to the golden star.'"

Because he was trying to tell her about the diamond, Kiro was certain, without strictly breaking his word. It *was* here. The sheer relief of certainty made it hard to think clearly.

"But he'd always said that as well," she told him, gaze still fixed on her white-knuckled hands. "The golden star in the north was his favorite, and mine as well."

"Capella."

She looked up, eyes ineffably sad. "I thought so, until you told me about the diamond and its color. It seemed purely a coincidence, but now you have confirmed its shape as well. Nonetheless, in his delirium, he may simply have reverted to a time when we believed that good things could happen if only we wished hard enough. And the fact remains that no such diamond has been found here. If he wished me to have it, it stands to reason he'd provide a clue to its location."

"He may have done. You'll likely recognize what it was when the diamond is found."

"Perhaps." She appeared to brace herself. "I apprehend you wish to mount a search."

"Above all things, if you will permit me."

"I will not prevent you. Nor will any doors be closed to you. If you wish, select a bedchamber where you will be more comfortable."

"Thank you, but I expect there will be little opportunity for sleeping. Will you mind if I begin straightaway?"

"I rather thought you would." The briefest flash of a smile. "The sooner you find it, or accept that it is not here, the sooner you will be gone. And to that end, I believe an organized approach is required. Would you take offense if I suggested a course of action?"

He leaned back in his chair, almost dizzy with relief. "I would be grateful beyond measure. Where should I begin?"

"With a plan. I expect the other members of this household will be eager to help, but we must decide how best to employ them. Can you provide a precise description of what we seek?"

"My father sent a sketch of how the diamond looked when he acquired it, and another of its appearance after he added a disguise. Given Sir Edwin's talent for craft and restoration, we may assume the form has been radically changed."

"Cut, you mean? That seems unlikely on many counts. If he'd acquired the skill to do so, I have no knowledge of it. And he had always devoted his talents to *preserving* things of beauty."

"I cannot think it an easy matter to sell a diamond so large and unique without drawing unwelcome attention. He may have wished to make it easier for you. In one of his homeward ports of call, he may have found someone to cut it or, at the least, reshape it. We should allow for that possibility."

"But he also said, 'Look to the golden star.'"

"And that possibility as well." He took a slim leather case from his breast pocket and withdrew the drawings his father had sent. The letter, he'd decided, was too personal to reveal. "The sketches of the star without disguise, front and side views, are to size. The back is identical to the front." He passed them to her.

"Ah. I'd been thinking of the usual five-pointed star. This is four-pointed, like those often placed over the stable in a crèche. A strange design, I should think, for an Ottoman to choose."

"To loot, I daresay. The diamond is surely one of the spoils of war. There is no telling where he got it, or how long he held it."

She looked over at him. "My father, you believe, possessed the diamond for a few months, and he has been dead for three years. How long did your father have it?"

He regarded her warily, trying to decipher the question at the heart of this interrogation. "Nothing in his letter specifies the date," he finally said. "But I concluded his raid on the fortress took place around the time of the battle of Piperi in 1811, when Shkoder Pasha had allied himself with the French."

"And only now have your parents' lives been threatened?"

"Just so. Two of Shkoder Pasha's sons were dispatched to reclaim the diamond. A matter of family honor, they told my father. When he said it was not in his possession, they laid down an ultimatum. Should he fail to return it before the day celebrating their father's birth, the family would exact retribution. I will spare you the details."

"And you don't know when that is?"

He closed his eyes. "They didn't say. Instilling uncertainty and dread is a common tactic. But it remains that every day that passes is a day lost. A day closer to their slaughter."

"Then we have no time to waste." Her no-nonsense voice again. "Come along to the library. While you examine the catalogue I made of my father's collections, I shall read again the letters he sent from Kotor. Perhaps he embedded a clue."

Shaking with relief, he rose, turned, and bowed deeply. "From my heart, Miss Bryar, I am sorry for causing you distress."

"Very well, then. Deception will cease, doors will remain open, and if the diamond is here, we shall find it. Together."

Stella's mind was spinning with plans as she mounted the stairs. For now they must work together in the interest of their common goal, and he was about to find out how difficult achieving it would be. First a tour, she decided, to show him what lay ahead.

He came up beside her when they reached the library and waited while she took the master keys, a small chapbook, and a pencil from the desk.

"Why have you decided to trust me?" he said as they returned to the passageway. "I gave you little reason."

"Because, I suppose, no one could make up such a tale and tell it so earnestly. I have been at fault as well. I wished to protect my father, or perhaps my memories of him. And I have been angry, I think, for a very long time. Everything I cared about was lost, and while I came to love John and his family, I remain dissatisfied with my life. Which is selfish indeed, because so many others have far less than I do." She paused in front of a door and gazed up into his dark eyes.

"I have felt the same," he said quietly. "When my parents sent me away, the world came to an end. Or so I believed, until people began to welcome me into the world of England. Despair is often a self-inflicted wound, and I have the scars to prove it. Things can change for the better. Never stop believing that. Hope and determination are powerful forces."

"Thank you. I shall take your words to heart. But time speeds by, and we must find the diamond. For now, I mean to show you the rooms where the collections sent from Montenegro are stored, outline my plans for the search, and answer any questions you may have."

She opened the door and stepped aside to let him enter. "Here, in boxes, drawers, and cabinets, are tiles, bits of mosaics, marble pieces from columns, statues, and friezes. The large ones are on the shelves. Several boxes contain unusually colored or shaped stones, some of them painted and some bearing carved or painted images. There is another room with similar items. I thought to let Annie and Tom sort through them and select possible candidates for a more thorough inspection. Bertha has a steady hand and a good eye, so I will ask her to make copies of the drawings for reference."

"How many rooms are in this house?"

"Eighteen altogether, not counting the kitchen and cellar. For the Montenegro collection, three. It is far larger than the other collections, which are gathered in one room."

"Your father might have stashed it anywhere." He ran his fingers through his hair. " A thorough search will take—"

"As long as necessary. Perhaps we should postpone the rest of the survey until morning. The automatons and music boxes will require particularly close examination, and you should not attempt them without sleep."

"What of the letters? May I read them? I might spot a clue."

"As you wish." It was time he met her father, the only way he could. "I'll collect them for you when we return to the library."

"And we'll make an early start in the morning. Yes?"

"That is my intention. But do not stay awake all night reading." The course now set, that flutter in her chest might possibly be eagerness to get on with it.

Chapter Eight

Kiro woke to silence, an aching head, and pale winter light sifting through the curtains. In the north, morning light came late. That much he knew. The rest was pretty much a blur.

He swung his legs over the side of the bed and cast around for his pocket watch. Found a stack of letters and a near-empty brandy bottle. That would explain his headache and a night of restless dreams. Saw on the floor his boots, breeches and shoes. His jacket was draped over the chair back. Stumbling that direction, he spotted his pocket watch under the chair. What the devil had happened to him?

The time, he saw, was well after ten o'clock. He had meant to rise early for the diamond hunt. Why had no one awakened him?

The door was unlocked, he discovered when he gave it a try.

Unshaven, raggedly clothed, and, he was certain, no fit company for decent people, he pelted down the stairs, pausing at each landing to listen for activity of some sort. Silence everywhere, until he reached the kitchen and saw Miss Bryar pouring steaming water from a kettle into a teapot.

"Good morning, sir," she said, not looking up. "Did you sleep well?"

"I slept too long. Was no one willing to call me?"

"To what purpose? I assumed you would not rest until reading my father's letters. Without sleep, and with five of us busy organizing the search and getting underway, you would only have been underfoot. When you've had breakfast, a cold one, I'm afraid, I will show you the procedures and you can begin examining the automatons."

He scraped up enough dignity to accept, in large part because his stomach was rumbling, and dug into a large helping of ham, cheese, slices of boiled eggs, and mustard piled atop a thick slice of Bertha's chewy bread.

"Did you discover any clues in Papa's letters?" Miss Bryar sounded reluctant to ask as she added milk to a mug of tea and passed it to him.

He vaguely remembered something that had caught his interest, but mostly he'd become absorbed in Sir Edwin's elegant, often witty narrative about his adventures and trials in Montenegro, and in particular, about his impressions of Kiro's father and mother. In many ways, he seemed to know them better than their last remaining son. "Something about Beatrice and a dancing star," he said. "It sounded familiar."

A soft laugh, belied by sad eyes. "Shakespeare," she said. "*Much Ado about Nothing*. Before my birth, my mother miscarried two children and another was stillborn. Papa decided that I, like Beatrice, had been born under a dancing star and wanted to name me for her. My mother disliked the name, so they eventually compromised with Stella. But he often called me Beatrice, sometimes to tease my mother, but mostly because to him, I was star-born. A miracle child. Nothing to do with a diamond shaped like a star."

When Mister Radanovic had downed his breakfast and several mugs of strong tea, Stella towed him upstairs and showed him what the others were about. Silence reigned as Annie, Tom, and Bertha contemplated the shape and size of every item they examined, requesting a second opinion when uncertain. John's poor eyesight consigned him to other tasks, and from all she could tell, everything was proceeding as she'd directed them over oatmeal and sliced ham well before dawn.

Now, with some pride, she led him to a room lined with shelves and crowded with tables, all of them covered with self-operating mechanical devices, most of them key-wound— dogs and devils, cats and clerics, birds and bawds, strutting Turks and whirling dervishes.

"I remember this," he said now and again as he wove around the tables, lifting pieces in his hands and setting most of them down on their sides. "Too light to contain the diamond," he added when she looked a question, "or too small. I'll come back to investigate the others. You said there was another roomful of automatons?"

"The larger ones, yes, and all the music boxes. They're next door. Come along."

He began with a general inspection, as he had done before. "I'll need time with many of these," he soon decided. "And better light. Which room is brightest this time of day?"

Late morning. She riffled through her mind. "The parlor, I expect. It faces south. If you will indicate those you wish to examine, John will bring them down."

"And those still standing upright in the prior room."

Repressing a wish to salute, she went off to make arrangements and monitor the progress of Bertha, Annie, and Tom. Never mind standing for Parliament. Given the chance, she could efficiently manage a small country.

An hour or so later, she joined Mister Radanovic in the sun-drenched parlor and quietly followed his instructions as the afternoon wore on. His focus was absolute, and she dared not break it.

Until the banging at the front door. Even from a floor down, it resounded like thunder. They both leapt to their feet.

"Expecting someone, Miss Bryar?"

She rushed to the window, looked down to the stoop, and let out a squeal. "It's her! The Witch. Come back, I daresay, to make off with anything she can get her claws on. I knew it. I knew she would!"

Mr. Radanovic joined her at the window. "Do not be concerned," he said, turning her to face him. "And do not, on any account, come into the entrance hall. If you must watch and listen, find a place where you cannot be observed. Above all, do not interfere."

"You must continue with the search. I can manage her. I've done it many times before."

"I am sure of it. But kindly permit me the pleasure of dispatching the lady this once. I've been sitting too long, and I need some fresh air. Will I require a key?"

She saw in his eyes the look of a man who would not be denied. And they didn't have time to quarrel about it. "Go on, then," she said, handing him the master keys. "And be careful. She scratches."

As Stella followed him down the stairs, which he took two at a time, she felt uncharacteristically relieved to have the matter lifted from her hands. Ducking into the dining room, she left the door open a crack and took up a position where she could see and hear the eviction. She wondered if Her Malevolence would be able to hear the pounding of her heart.

Kiro, who was looking forward to dispensing with the bane of Sir Edwin's existence and the tormenter of his daughter, let her beat at the door a while longer before keying the locks, pulling it open, and planting himself dead center of the frame.

A gloved fist nearly landed on his chest. The woman stopped it in time, mouth open as she stared up at his face. An attractive woman, he had to concede, with blond hair that owed some of its color to chemicals, cheek rouge and redder lip rouge, and brows plucked into high arches.

She was evaluating him as well, her gaze running down the length of him and back up again.

"Who the blazes are you?" she demanded.

He made a slight bow. "The butler, Madam."

Frowning, she waved at his shirt and breeches. "A proper butler dresses in accord with his profession."

"Indeed. But we are presently dealing with an infestation of spiders, so you will understand that Miss Bryar is not welcoming company until the house is purged of them."

"Never mind that. I am not company. I am family, and I am come to collect what belongs to me."

He glanced past her brittle hair and wide-brimmed bonnet to a small coach and its bored driver pulled up near where his own coach had stood. Was it only two days ago? "That will not be possible."

"Who are *you* to say? What is your name?"

"Peeves, Madam."

"Step aside, Peeves. I intend to speak with my stepdaughter."

"I think not."

With both hands, she pushed against his chest. He failed to budge, so she slapped him across the face and was setting up to kick him when he grabbed her around the waist, tossed her over his shoulder, and stilled her flailing legs with one arm. The other pressed her against his shoulder, and he seized a handful of hair. All she could do was pound his back with her fists while he carried her like a sack of turnips out to the coach.

"You there," he called to the driver. "Come down and open the door."

"Stop this brute," she screeched. "Hit him with your whip."

With a shrug, the driver jumped to ground and held the door ajar while Kiro tossed her onto the bench and held her there. She stared up at him with spiteful eyes and pursed her lips to spit.

He slammed a hand over her mouth. "Listen carefully. You will never return to this house. All communications between you and Miss Bryar will cease. You will not level false accusations against Miss Bryar or say anything to injure her reputation. If I learn you have done so, or if I wake up one morning imagining that you have done so, I shall rip your tongue from your mouth. Do you understand?"

She was squirming now, trying to bite his hand. He transferred the hand back to her hair.

"How dare you threaten me? For what you have already done, I will bring charges of assault, battery, and unlawful confinement. You will be tried and, at the very least, transported."

"My connections with the diplomatic community and the Prince Regent, who has kindly provided me immunity, will toss a spanner in your plans. Better you sever your brief, unhappy association with the Bryar family and seek new opportunities for yourself. If compelled, I will make certain that you do."

"Who *are* you?" she demanded. "What the devil have you to do with Stella Bryar?"

"Did I not say?" He bent a little closer and looked directly into her eyes. "I intend to marry her. To love, honor, and *protect* her." He rose and stepped back from the coach. "Don't let me see you again, or hear your name."

He slammed the door, signaled the coachman to drive off, and turned back to the house. His bride—When had he decided that?—was standing in the open doorway, looking worried. He understood only that when he said the words, they sounded exactly right, as if he'd known something in his heart that had only just now made its way to his brainbox.

"Back to work," he said, passing by her, not altogether rid of the fury that had possessed him.

She scurried behind him. "Aren't you going to tell me what happened? I mean the details. When you were with her in the carriage."

"Later. I promise. But for now, the diamond. We must use the daylight while it lasts."

She couldn't argue with that.

Curiosity squirmed inside, but when he was settled, she took the chair beside him, passed tools to him when he gestured, and felt the heat from his body wash over her. After a time, the ice that had encased her for years began to soften. Melt, at least a little. For one day, she'd had a champion, a shining knight to protect her.

Not that she needed one. She was Androdameia, Subduer of Men and Wicked Stepmothers. But only bad men, like the grocer who tried to cheat her. This was a good man. Her ally. Moving slowly so as not to distract him, she brushed away an escaping tear. Above all things, he must find the diamond and arrive home in time to save his mother and father. If the sky was clear tonight, she would pin a wish to Capella.

Chapter Nine

"I've brought you some supper," Stella said from the parlor doorway.

It was well past nine o'clock, and she had sent Tom and Annie to bed. Disappointment curled in her chest. They had sorted through everything in one room and made progress in the other, scraping paint from tiles and stones to see what it hid, comparing size and shape to the drawings. She'd told them the reasons for the search, and they had thrown their hearts into it. Meantime, in silence save for the occasional instruction or question, she had worked with Mr. Radanovic to disassemble automatons that might have concealed the diamond and stored the pieces away to deal with later.

He had barely glanced at her when she spoke, so she set the tray in a cleared spot on the table. "Only five to go," she said. "Do you mean to finish with them tonight?"

He set down the strutting duck he'd been working with and reached for a cold roast beef sandwich. "What do you think? That will leave only the music boxes."

She sat across from him, elbows propped on the table, and rested her chin on her hands. "If the diamond was broken up, I can't imagine how we'd find all the pieces. And would the owner accept them as compensation for what was stolen?"

"I shouldn't think so. But I'd have to try."

"You will go there yourself? Will your father permit it?"

"This one time, yes. Even without the diamond I will go, and do everything in my power to keep them safe."

She took a deep breath. "Is it permitted to ask why he sent you away?"

A swift smile came and went. "Not for anything I did, but for what he expected me to do. He had lost two sons, and only I remained to carry on the family name. He knew that I, too, would go to war, by one means or another. And I would have done."

"How old were you?"

"Twelve. I'd have attached myself to any group of Montenegrins heading to any battlefield. If they wouldn't have me, I'd have gone into the mountains and fought Ottomans with the resistance. He told me, when I departed under guard on the ship, that I should not count the days of my exile, because he would never permit me to return."

She was horrified. "What kind of father could send his son away forever?"

"One who wanted his son to live. For that matter, what kind of father goes traveling and leaves his daughter in the clutches of a monstrous stepmother?"

"One who wanted to preserve his sanity," she said. "I have sometimes been angry about it. I know he betrayed me, but I was only ten-and-six when he left. He had little money, not enough to care for me on his travels. I was very hurt, but I've never blamed him."

"Nor have I blamed my father. I was a reckless, fearless boy who would likely have been cut down like a weed. And my death would have broken my mother's heart. He made a hard choice, and I respect him for it."

"Thank you for telling me," she said, resolved not to ply him with all the other questions burning on her tongue. There was no time for them now. "Do finish your supper, please, while I dismantle this duck."

The next morning, Kiro was called early as promised. He stopped by the kitchen, wolfed the breakfast laid out for him, and went upstairs to find the others already hard at work. Tom and Annie were huddled over bits of marble and stones, John and Bertha searched the spare bedchambers, and Miss Bryar was dusting the music boxes he was about to take apart.

Molly, padding behind him, scooted into the room and twined around Miss Bryar's legs. She glanced up. "What is that you are carrying?"

"My good luck charms. Six thriving kittens, born of a mother who outfoxed a fox."

She laughed. "How unexpectedly sentimental. Set their box near the fire. This room was an ice house when I first arrived, and it will take awhile for it to warm up."

She would take awhile to warm up as well, he reckoned, when time came and opportunity permitted him to speak from his heart. "Where shall I begin?"

"Near the fire." She sounded exasperated. "Where I laid out your tools."

He'd finally found a good use for his lock-picking devices. But by taking apart these beautiful creations, which meant a great deal to her, he was also silencing their music. Regret hummed low at the back of his mind. One day he would have them all put into good working order. And if she accepted him, or at the very least this one idea of his, he would establish a small museum to exhibit Sir Edwin's collections and keep his memory alive.

There were thirty-eight music boxes, and by noon, he'd worked through twenty-one of them. The larger, more intricate ones loomed ahead. He rose, stretched, and went to pet the kittens. Molly obligingly sprang out of the box and began to groom herself, watching closely as he knelt beside the box. Four pairs of blue eyes regarded him curiously. The other two kittens continued to snooze. He decided he would like six children, if Stella was up to it. He realized that he now thought of her as Stella.

"Only seventeen to go, kittens," he murmured. "If angels speak cat-language, ask them to help us."

Where the smaller boxes had featured music and intricate decorations, the larger ones added objects or characters moving to the music. Two sailors saluting to *Heart of Oak*. A paunchy cleric strutting about to *Vicar of Bray*. Italian folk songs like *Carettiera*, featuring a wagon driver snapping a whip, which had gone missing.

Edging closer to despair, he turned the key of the largest of them all, and when he raised the lid, heard a melody he remembered because his mother, who loved opera, often hummed it around the house. On a shiny wooden platform rigged out like a baroque stage, a ballet dancer began to twirl. Her skirts, formed of starched tulle and netting, pale gold in color, nearly overwhelmed her slender body.

His heart began to pound. "Stella," he said. "Come look at this."

She leaned over his shoulder. "Her costume seems out of proportion. And she's not in rhythm with the music."

"Because the skirts are too heavy." He hoped that was true. "I need scissors, small ones if you have them."

With effort, he resisted the urge to rip the dancer off the box and strip her with his own hands, and by the time he had scissors in hand, the music and dancer were stilled. With care, he cut out a triangle of skirting and felt something hard underneath, although he couldn't yet see what it was. Some of the tulle appeared to be glued to its base. He took up a lock-picking tool, one with a razor-thin blade at its tip, and worked it into a barely visible crack at the dancer's waist. After some maneuvering, the top of her body popped off. He leaned over the box. At the juncture where her waist had been, he saw the cradle that had held it.

When he chiseled that loose as well, he saw a small portion of the diamond. Or glass, it might be, but he wouldn't let himself believe that.

Another several minutes of work exposed the entire foundation of the skirt, the exact size and shape of the diamond, the spaces between the four points filled in with hardened clay. His heart was pounding like a battle drum. Victory!

"Shall I tell the others?" Stella said in a shaky voice.

"By all means, General Bryar. And bring them to see it." He leaned back in his chair, breathing heavily. "Tell them a star danced. Just as your father told you."

Chapter Ten

After a celebration featuring cloudberry wine, treats from the Rondales' Christmas sack, songs from Tom and Annie, and a ceremonial naming of the kittens—one called after each of the treasure hunters—Kiro and Stella sat alone by the fire in the sitting room.

A dozen questions bubbled in her head, but she hadn't worked up the courage to ask them. It felt as if putting her fears into words would make them all become true. As they must, she understood. His departure. The end of the only adventure she'd ever have. The death of hopes that had been seeded without her knowing it and blossomed into . . . she didn't know what. It didn't matter. Tomorrow morning, she would see him for the last time.

"How long will it take you to pack?" he said out of nowhere.

"I beg your pardon?" Lack of sleep must be catching up with her. "Pack what?"

"Sorry." He ran his fingers through his hair. "I didn't mean to start there. I don't know how to say any of this. And it should not be rushed, but it is." His gaze became intense. "I must leave tomorrow. You understand why. I wish you to accompany me."

"What do you mean?" She seized a shallow breath. "To where?"

"York, first. Then Southampton, and a ship, and finally, Kotor."

"Are you addled? Good heavens. I cannot leave here."

"And I cannot stay. Addled, probably. But in the best of ways. I have fallen in love with you, Stella Bryar. I want to marry you, if you will have me, as soon as may be. But I don't want to stampede you. If you'd rather, you could wait and think it over while I'm gone, and I'll come back and say it again. In better fashion. Many times, if need be. But I wish to present you to my parents, and this may be our only opportunity. Do breathe, my love."

She kept forgetting. Lightheaded, she sucked in a deep draught of air.

"I know this is like asking you to jump off a cliff. I understand that. It came to me the same way. I told myself I had to be sure. I had to consider. Know that it was exactly right before I spoke to you. But however I twisted and turned, the answer never changed. I already knew. Last night I made that jump from the cliff, my love, and I feel perfectly safe where I landed. Will you join me where I am, and where I must go?"

"I—but how can I leave these people? I love them. They depend on me. They are my only friends. I will not abandon them."

"I know, Stella. I would not ask that of you. Nor will I abandon them, even if you decline my offer of marriage. Nor will I abandon hope. On my return, I will court you and languish on your doorstep and wish on every star in the heavens. Decisions must be made, to be sure, and we have a long voyage to Montenegro and a long return as well to plan the future. But only if we are to share our future, and that decision is now yours alone. Mine is made for eternity."

A gentle smile on his lips now, touched with sadness. "We have known each other for, what, two days and nights? A trifle longer? Your mind is telling you, quite reasonably, 'no.' I am asking you to listen to your heart."

"I don't know where it is," she said with fearful honesty. Years of unfulfilled hopes and dreams had left a great desert where her heart should be. But she loved her family and Molly and the kittens, so perhaps it wasn't too far away. And this man, so beyond anything she had ever dared to imagine, loved her?

Maybe that's why the stars had never granted any of her wishes. They'd been saving this impossible wish, this man, for when the two of them needed each other. Even so, uncertainty thrummed in her veins. How could such a remarkable man love a female gone suspicious and sour? That's all he'd ever seen of her. Was she more than that? Better than that? Perhaps his startling proposal was fueled by relief and exhilaration on finding the diamond and his lack of sleep. In fairness, before she could answer him, she must come to terms with herself. "I have misplaced it," she finally said. "May I have this night to look for it?"

"To be sure, if that is your wish. You must take all the time you require. But I can be very persistent, my love. Think of that as you consider my offer. And remember, I must leave at dawn. For York, if we are to secure a Special License and be married. For Southampton, if you are not willing to have me. Yet."

"Shall I wake you early?"

"That won't be necessary." He swallowed the last of his wine and came to his feet. "I'll not sleep, I am sure, until I have your answer."

Only a few hours passed before the sky began to lighten, but to Kiro, the night had seemed eternal. After shaving, dressing, and packing, he'd stared blankly out the window into grey-white nothingness, no stars to be seen, as if all the brightness in the universe had hidden itself from his eyes. She would be awake as well, he knew, her remarkable mind clicking away, totting up a thousand perfectly good reasons to reject him. And if any arguments on his behalf chanced to filter through, she would likely talk herself out of them. She'd lost her mother, been abandoned by her father, and was bullied by her stepmother. She'd lived too many years without trust and now, even with all her skills and intelligence and confidence, she did not trust herself.

He couldn't fault her for being cautious. Better she come to terms with fears before placing her life in his hands. All the time she needed would be hers. There would be another offer, and another, and another after that. Radanovic men were famous for never giving up. His father, who had courted his mother for two years before she stooped to have him, said it was the most important battle of his life. And the most rewarding.

He checked his watch. Bertha and John at the least would be stirring by now, and the walls of his attic bedchamber were closing in. He pulled on his greatcoat, stuffed gloves in his pocket, and attached to his belt the small lead-lined container Stella had devised to hold the diamond. His pistol was holstered under his arm.

With a travel case in each hand, he descended two flights of stairs and paused to listen. No signs of life, no sounds. Just as well, he supposed. Perhaps a quiet leave would be best for everyone. Tom and John had promised to ready the coach, so likely they were in the barn, and Bertha in the kitchen, as usual. Perhaps Stella had managed to fall asleep. Better that way, if a meeting would distress her. He'd write a letter of farewell, one that emphasized his intention to return, and post it along the way.

But she was there, he saw from the next landing, wearing a forest-green dress, her light brown hair unbound, looking up at him from the entrance hall. He could not decipher her expression. Nor could he move. He fixed her image in his mind, something to carry with him, and cast about for something to say.

She made a slight, graceful curtsey and stepped to one side, exposing what her skirts had concealed. A small, battered portmanteau.

With a whoop, he dropped his own cases where he stood, pounded down the stairs, seized her by the waist and swung her around and around. The portmanteau toppled over and she laughed until, both of them breathless, he set her down.

"Is this what I am to expect from you?" she demanded, eyes sparkling. "Maulings?"

"Frequent maulings, of the lover-ly sort."

"Mind the children, sir." She gestured to a point behind him.

He turned to see John, Bertha, and Annie, faces flushed and smiling. At their feet, Molly groomed herself while six kittens gazed up from their crate. His new family. The first installment, anyway.

"I be tellin' Tom to bring around the carriage," John said. "Th'orses oughtn't be kept to stand."

The others melted away as well, except the kittens. He stroked each one on the head, sad to realize they'd be grown by the time he saw them again.

When he turned back to Stella, she was fastening a pelisse over her dress. "I didn't expect this," he said. "What persuaded you to accept me?"

"Well, for a time I dithered. I imagined you were in the room with me. Then I counted out all the reasons I didn't deserve you. There were a great many, but you didn't seem to mind."

"There aren't. I don't."

She ignored him. "Then I totted up my excellent qualities, and they were few. But this time, *I* didn't seem to mind. You have seen my flaws. Suffered my distorted and inappropriately timed sense of humor. Endured me at my worst. And still you wish to marry me."

"Above all things," he said quietly.

"It's the accepting of love I need to learn. And the trust I must place in myself. You have already begun to teach me these things. But the key that opened my locked heart was the one I always carry with me. I am my mother's daughter. She knew how to love with all her heart, and her spirit lives in me. I did not understand that until you awakened it."

Her eyes glistened with unshed tears, but she was smiling. Then, even as he watched, she gazed up at him and her smile turned wicked. "But mostly, I decided to be practical."

"Yes?" He stepped closer. "How so?"

"I am seven-and-twenty, and in the Yorkshire dales, swains are not exactly thick on the ground. You are probably my last and only chance. So I shut my eyes, clenched my teeth, and leapt off the cliff."

Laughing, he placed his hands on her shoulders. "And how did it feel?"

"Glorious. As if I were flying."

Time stopped for a long kiss that spoke truer than words.

"And fly is what we must do," he said when he came up for air, "if we are to reach York in good time."

"But what if the archbishop isn't there to provide a special license?"

"You worry too much. Come along, beloved. All will be well. If we must, we'll track down the Archbishop of Canterbury. And if you don't object, anticipate our vows along the way."

Winter's route to Montenegro took the newly married couple through Lisbon, Seville, Cadiz, Gibraltar, and Malta. Stella, giddy with excitement, explored the sights in the invisible tracks of her father. And shopped as well, when it dawned on her that three ancient, threadbare dresses and scuffed half-boots rendered her unfit for civilized company. By the time they docked in Dubrovnik, north of Montenegro on the Adriatic coast, she was kitted out in style and beginning to panic.

"I shall wait on the ship while you hand over the diamond," she said as they boarded the yacht Stefan Radanovic, Kiro's father, had sent to carry them into the Bay of Kotor. Only a few hours now.

Her toes curled inside her soft leather half-boots. The nearest she'd come to Society were Assembly dances in York long years ago. Her father's knighthood had been the surprising consequence of an antique vase he'd presented to the Prince Regent, along with a book he'd written about the prince's art collections. By blood, she was common as grass.

"You'll do nothing of the kind," Kiro told her. As always, he remained maddeningly unruffled. "My parents are expecting you, and they will welcome you."

"Do you *never* worry?" He could be the most exasperating man. "What if Shkoder Pasha's sons take the diamond and murder your parents anyway?"

They were on the foredeck, watching the seamen cast off. "About that I am indeed concerned, although less so after reading the letter waiting for us in Dubrovnik. Have you forgotten? It appears the sons who issued the threat are pleased to end this feud in a civilized manner. And my father, of course, is taking every precaution." He wrapped his arm around her. "Put away bad thoughts, love. You are about to see one of the most beautiful places on God's earth."

And it was true. Under a cloudless sky, the sapphire-blue water was banked by tall rising hills lush with greenery and studded with pale stone houses. As the fjord-like bay narrowed, she saw two small islands topped with churches, and then the chain at the narrowest point was lowered to let their vessel pass through.

Ahead, high stone walls and turrets nestled against a mountain rimmed with the ruins of a fortress and a monastery. Kiro described it all, what she was seeing, but nothing could explain what she felt. A long hoped-for homecoming for him. The last place her father had been healthy and happy. A place she feared her husband would want to stay after the reunion with his family.

The boat drew up near the iron gates at the high city walls, open to allow a throng of elegantly clad people to stream out behind a man and woman she knew immediately must be her husband's parents. Tall, slim, elegant, they stopped a short distance from the gangplank and were immediately flanked by uniformed men wearing swords and carrying rifles.

"Time for the grand entrance, love," Kiro said, taking her arm.

As she drew nearer, she saw that Stefan and Bianca Radanovic were considerably older than she had imagined, but splendid nonetheless. Kiro led her to a spot directly in front of them, where he bowed and she curtsied. They had practiced that. Then an exchange in a language she did not understand.

"The return of the diamond is to be now, in public, by agreement," Kiro whispered as the guardsmen reconfigured themselves to create a path. Along it came two young men with bronze skin and short, pointed black beards. Shkoder Pasha's sons, she realized, armed with long, curved swords. Kiro tugged her to one side, creating a triangle of three pairs. The Ottomans bowed.

"They will speak in French," Kiro told her in a low voice. "I will translate for you."

She knew French, but not well enough to trust it. Mostly she watched the faces and tracked what was happening. Stefan Radanovic made a formal apology to the sons and to Shkoder Pasha for having dishonored his family. The Ottomans expressed regret for the loss in war of Stefan's sons under their father's command, about which they had not known when first they made their demands.

Kiro, now holding the box with the diamond, said nothing as he passed it to his father, who held it in his opened hands and offered it to the two young men. They took it and bowed again.

"Honor is satisfied," Kiro whispered as the Ottomans spoke in unison. "Our father nears death, and the return of his treasure will ease his passing, Allah be praised. Peace be upon you and your family."

"And so it ends," he said softly, taking her hand as they watched the enemies bow and withdraw. "Next we will follow my parents to the

Palazzo. You are not to be concerned. If you cannot believe they will come to love you as I do, keep this thought. Whenever they look at you, they are seeing grandchildren."

Small comfort, but it helped. Especially when La Principessa looked back at her and smiled. But she couldn't help voicing her deepest fear. "Do you wish to live here?"

He drew her aside, lifted her chin with his forefinger, and looked deeply into her eyes. "I wish my exile lifted, yes. I wish to visit here as often as may be. But despite my heritage, England has been my home for most of my life. My business is there. People we care about are there. We have cats. And always, we will make important decisions together. Come along now. And think about learning Italian. That's the second-best way of winning my mother's blessing."

As they passed through the gates and came into the city square, she couldn't help noticing wreaths and ornaments on the buildings and a large crèche display featuring a live donkey and three unruly lambs. "Whatever does this signify? Christmas is long over. It is the middle of January, for heaven's sake."

"Orthodox Christians observe the nativity on January 7th and celebrate until the Feast of the Three Kings. The ones who followed the star." He grinned at her. "How lucky we are, my own precious star. We have a chance to live Christmas all over again."

"For all the members of the Beau Monde who selflessly share their research."

A CHRISTMAS HOMECOMING

Allison Lane

Chapter One

December 22, 1814

You must obey, Alex. You have no choice. You are not of age!

Echoes of their last argument assaulted Captain Alex Northcote, now the new viscount, the moment he entered the bedchamber that had once been his father's.

I've done nothing wrong!

Liar! You spent the summer in wasteful idleness, ending in Brighton, of all places. Consorting with that popinjay will ruin you.

One soiree at the Marine Pavilion is hardly consorting. Everyone in town was there. Refusing a royal command is an insult that could harm me for yea—

Silence!

A quarter hour of complaints had followed, all of them variations on the dishonor Alex heaped upon his family by cultivating bad companions and embracing worse vices. The man finally concluded with an order that Alex remain at Northcote Manor until he learned proper respect.

But compliance would have driven him mad. Alex had departed immediately, joining the 95th so he could help dispatch Napoleon. Since he already faced endless battles, he might as well engage in useful ones.

It had been a childish reaction, he admitted now, shaking his head. He'd seen worse reasons for buying colors, but that didn't excuse him. Leaving had surrendered any chance of rapprochement. He would go to his grave with that fight ringing in his ears.

"Your wash water, Captain." Wilson's arrival shoved the memories aside.

Alex nodded to his batman. "I'd best have the dress uniform. I may not have a chance to change again before dinner." He'd arrived home half an hour earlier, shocked to find a house party in progress.

"Why the crowd?" he asked now as he washed. "The Manor should still be in mourning."

Wilson shrugged. "Your mother remains secluded, but you are no longer restricted. Nor is the dowager. She invited the entire family for Christmas in honor of your return."

"Everyone?"

"Out to third cousins. Plus others."

Alex groaned. "Not young ladies."

"Half a dozen of the appropriate age and station."

He grimaced. After more than six years' absence, he must reacquaint himself with his inheritance before considering the future. Choosing a bride too quickly risked making another mistake—his last fiancée had jilted him.

"The dowager is determined," continued Wilson, briskly brushing Alex's green uniform pants. "Your cousin Harold has overseen the estate since your father died, but she distrusts him and wants the succession assured now."

Alex swore. Harold might be his nearest cousin, but they had never liked each other. "Is anyone here besides family and females?"

"Two of your schoolmates—Mister Holcombe and Mister Craft." Wilson handed over the pants, then attacked the green jacket.

If his grandmother thought they could convince him to wed, she'd miscalculated. He might never consider marriage again. Returning home was cracking the walls he'd built around his heart, resurrecting so many memories of his betrothal that his fingers shook. With pain. With agony. With a fury hotter than her cruelty had triggered when she had married another without warning. If he ever got his hands on the wench . . .

He forced his mind back to the present as he fastened his jacket. "Grandmother is rushing her fences. I've been in England barely a week and have no idea what condition the estate is in. I don't have time for a house party."

"In her defense, she expected us shortly after your last letter."

Alex bit back a sigh. November was a terrible time for an ocean crossing. It had been stormy to the point of near-disaster, emphasizing how little control he had over his life. But he must control his grandmother if he wanted a peaceful future. It would take time to find a female he could live with. First, he must discover if his judgment remained flawed—Sarah was the last person he'd thought could betray him, proving that he'd misjudged her badly. He could not let it happen again.

Sarah Heflin leaned closer to the bed, straining to understand Harbaugh.

"-ah-ark—"

"Do you need to speak with Larkins?" she asked patiently, naming the estate steward. Harbaugh had been Lord Northcote's secretary before suffering an apoplexy. Tragically, his mind operated normally though his right side refused to move. Having lost his left arm a decade earlier, he was now helpless. But long practice let her recognize most of his words and the ideas behind them.

Harbaugh moved his left foot in the signal that meant *yes*. "Pla-ant."

"Are you concerned about the spring planting?"

Again he signaled *yes*.

"I will ask him to visit," she promised, though she knew Larkins would refuse. He'd ignored Harbaugh since the day the viscount died. Females were even lower in his eyes.

"Har-ld."

"Did Harold call on you again?"

Yes.

And had likely upset him. Since assuming Harbaugh's duties, Harold took unholy glee in taunting the man. Harbaugh couldn't avoid him, and Harold's derision made enduring his infirmity even harder. If only she could bar Harold . . .

"Wan shangsh ro-ta-shu—" His eyes blazed with fury and helplessness.

"Harold wants to change the planting rotation?"

Yes.

"It doesn't matter. Lord Northcote will return soon and bar him from further interference."

The reminder calmed Harbaugh, though she didn't believe her own words. Alex was behaving abominably. The letter announcing his return had arrived in October, but he had yet to make an appearance. She'd expected more from him despite some youthful bouts of selfish behavior.

Harbaugh's eyes closed with fatigue. Every day the effort to communicate tired him faster.

She bade him farewell, then headed for her daughters' room. They should have finished dinner by now. Despite the influx of visiting playmates, they still expected a bedtime story.

But she'd barely closed Harbaugh's door when a ferocious apparition blocked the hallway.

Alex.

"What the devil are you doing in my house?" he demanded. "I can't believe you would flaunt your family in my face after betraying me so brutally. Wasn't using me to test your wiles enough?"

Terror choked her. This wasn't the gentle boy she'd known since childhood. This man exuded power, displaying broad shoulders and muscular thighs. Scars slashed a leathery face fringed with sun-bleached hair and dominated by icy gray eyes. Danger radiated from every pore.

Heart hammering, she tried to move around him.

"Well? Cat got your tongue?"

He slapped a palm against the wall, forming a barricade that blocked her escape. Fury thickened the air until she could barely breathe.

"I— I—" She tried to back the other way, but a table trapped her. Cringing against it, she fought off the spots whirling before her eyes. Fainting would leave her at his mercy.

"Don't think you can smile your way back into my good graces," he continued harshly. "I will never forget what a schemer you are—"

"I'm not—" Her throat locked. His face leaned closer, weakening her knees. Larger spots battered her consciousness. *The girls—*

"—so pack up your husband and remove your lying, cheating self from my property. I barely survived your last scheme. You won't get a chance to repeat it."

The reminder of her girls conquered terror long enough that she could shove at his chest. When he backed up a pace, she escaped around the table.

"War has unhinged your mind," she gasped before jerking open a panel to reach the servant stairs.

When he didn't follow, she sank onto a step and let shudders overwhelm her. Alex was back, but not the Alex she'd loved since age fourteen. The uniform accentuated new strength. His harsh voice cut her to ribbons. Fury twisted his face into a demon fiercer than Heflin.

Poor Lady Northcote. Could she cope with the imposing stranger who now owned the Manor? Not that Sarah would know. Alex had ordered her to leave. The harshest lesson she'd learned from her marriage was who wielded power. And it wasn't females.

She had to find a new position. Immediately.

By the time the red cleared from Alex's eyes, Sarah was gone. His behavior appalled him. Even a deliberate attempt to destroy him did not warrant such a tirade, and he had no evidence that it had been deliberate. Could he blame her for falling in love with another? His only valid complaint was her failure to tell him she'd changed her mind. If he'd expected this meeting, he could have controlled the pain and fury already stirred up by coming home. But he hadn't known she was here . . .

His knees turned to water as he catalogued her appearance. The youthful promise of adult beauty was more than fulfilled by womanly curves and a full bosom. Her hair had darkened to sable silk that intensified her blue eyes. But her shabby gown belied a wealthy husband, so it had to have been love.

New pain stabbed his heart, for he'd never fully accepted that her vows of eternal love had arisen from a youthful infatuation. Seeing proof of how wrongly he'd judged her revived the agony of her jilt tenfold, overwhelming his anger.

As it faded, he frowned. Her face had blanched at his first blistering word. Tremors had followed. And panic. The reaction seemed extreme, even when faced with his fury. Sarah had always remained calm in any crisis. Now she'd fled as if hellhounds were slavering at her heels.

Something was wrong.

He'd known her since birth, for her father's estate bounded Northcote Manor. They'd been friends forever. And more. He'd fallen in love with her at eighteen, though she'd been barely fifteen at the time. Two years later, she'd accepted his proposal.

Yet he should have suspected trouble when she'd insisted that they keep their betrothal secret on grounds that her father would refuse her a London come-out if he could settle her in the country. Squire Potter was a renowned nipfarthing.

Awash in love, Alex had agreed, for experience with London society would make moving to Town easier for her after they wed.

To avoid raising conjecture by living in her pocket, Alex had joined his friends on their summer rounds. When he'd bade her farewell after breaking with his father, her support for his new plans let him relax, confident that he would defeat Napoleon and return within the year. Her letters had eased the discomfort of the battlefield. But not one had hinted that she might jilt him. The pain remained to this day.

Thrusting his memories and questions aside, he headed for his mother's new suite. She would be chafing at the bit by now.

Sarah drew in a deep breath as the dowager bade her enter. Only Alex's grandmother could find her a post quickly enough to satisfy his demands. The last thing she wanted was to return to Potter House, her childhood home. Asking Great-aunt Beatrice to take them in would be nearly as bad. The girls deserved better. It would have to be another position.

"Is there a problem, dear?" asked the dowager, motioning her to a chair.

"I must find a new employer, my lady. Immediately. I cannot share a roof with dangerous men."

"Nonsense. No one here will harm you."

"On the contrary, my lady. I barely escaped Lord Northcote just now. I cannot risk another confrontation."

The dowager frowned. "What happened?"

"He backed me into a corner, shouting accusations and glaring until I feared he would strike. His fury terrified me. Then he ordered me to leave his house, so I have no choice." She hated to bear tales, especially to a doting grandmother, but her safety and that of her girls must come first. Angry men were dangerous.

"That is not like him."

Sarah scowled. "Since buying colors, he has endured more than six years of violence and deprivation. We cannot know the effect of such experiences." His one letter after her marriage had bristled with threats and recrimination, which proved that even a few months of war had destroyed his manners. What had subsequent years wrought?

"Perhaps." The dowager sighed. "But you cannot leave immediately, no matter what he said. It will take time to find an employer who accepts your daughters. Returning to Potter House would destroy you. That woman could lock you away until people forget you exist."

Sarah sagged. Her brother's wife, Caroline, loathed her with an antagonism that bordered on madness and had made it easy to accept the post of companion to Alex's mother. While she personally could have endured life as a poor relation, for she'd had much practice adhering to even ridiculous demands, she could not subject her daughters to Caroline's abuse. If she went back, escaping a second time would be difficult.

Yet how could she share a roof with Alex? Would he allow it even if his grandmother demanded that she remain? Males wielded all the power. Defying them never worked. After years as a military officer, Alex would expect instant obedience.

The dowager smiled. "I will remind Alex of his duty. Sending you away would cause his mother considerable distress. So hold your head high and join the company for dinner."

"I can't."

"You will. An earl's granddaughter does not hide from society. No matter what your future holds, you will occasionally mingle with others. So practice."

Sarah nodded, accepting defeat. Finding a new post required a reference. If dining with the guests was now part of her duties, she must comply.

It need not be wholly unpleasant, she decided as she again headed for the nursery. No one would notice an unobtrusive companion. Even during her Season, she had stayed on the fringes to avoid drawing censure. And with so many more important ladies present, she could easily avoid a male escort to dinner.

Her heart lightened when she reached the girls' room.

"Mommy, Mommy!" They rushed into her arms for hugs.

"Dragon story," demanded Emily.

"With a princess," added Alice. "And knights. And a tournament!"

Sarah smiled, the last of her fear draining away. "I haven't time for a complicated tale tonight. Would you settle for one about a brave little dog?" When they nodded, she sank into a chair, a girl tucked under each arm. "Once upon a time, there lived a scruffy scrap of black fur named Timothy . . ."

The moment Alex reached his mother's sitting room, she flung herself into his arms, a smile splitting her face. "Alex! You're home! When did you arrive?"

"An hour ago. Weren't you informed?" Her surprise was obvious.

"I've been napping." She stepped back to look at him. "Goodness, but you look imposing. Downright fierce. Haven't you something else to wear?"

"None of my old clothes fit. I ordered new in London, but they won't arrive for another week." He shrugged. An imposing appearance might hold eligible females at bay.

She resumed a seat on her Grecian couch, sagging into a weariness that added years to her face. Mourning appeared to have taken a greater toll than Wilson had reported. To avoid distressing her, he kept his narrative light as they exchanged news.

"Did Grandmother have to fill the house with people?" he finally asked.

"She insisted on celebrating the season." She waved the topic away.

His need to understand recent events trumped his concern for his mother's fragility. "Estate business will prevent me from entertaining guests. I'm told Harbaugh remains abed and Cousin Harold has been managing things. Why is he in charge?"

She shrugged. "His father is dying, so Harold can't leave. He needed occupation. And someone has to deal with Larkins. The man hates females."

"Uncle Charles is dying?"

"He collapsed at George's funeral." Tears glistened. "He can barely swallow and shows no awareness of his surroundings, so he had to stay here, of course. We couldn't ask Harold to leave under the circumstances."

Alex cursed himself for reminding her of funerals, but he still needed answers. "I passed Sarah in the hall just now. Why is *she* here? Her husband isn't related to us." He hoped. He couldn't recall the fellow's name.

Eyes wide, Lady Northcote stiffened. "He died two years ago. Surely you heard about it. The tale dominated gossip for weeks."

"No." One of several letters he'd penned in a drunken rage after Sarah jilted him had ordered his mother to never mention the Potters again. "What happened?"

She relaxed. "Sarah and the girls returned to Potter House the moment he died. She was left with nothing, of course. But once her brother wed that harpy Caroline—her father runs an inn in Stafford, of all things—How a man so aware of his consequence would even consider such a mésalliance—Now Caroline is trying to use Potter's connections to push into even higher circles. And he lets her!" She paused to draw in a deep breath. "Anyway, Caroline's antagonism put Sarah in an untenable position, so when things fell apart here, I asked for her help and let her bring the girls. We've plenty of space, and I needed her to keep my wits intact. She has been invaluable with

Harbaugh, too. No one else can understand a word the man says."

Alex was reeling. Sarah's mother was an earl's daughter, which was why she'd claimed that bedamned Season, but—

"How could Norbert's wife drive Sarah out? Surely her parents supported her."

"They are long gone. I know I wrote about the squire. He died just after Sarah's marriage. Mrs. Potter passed a year later." Her voiced faded as exhaustion claimed her.

Alex took his leave, again castigating himself. The news about the squire would have been in the letter that announced Sarah's marriage—the one he'd consigned to the fire the moment he'd read the first sentence. Did Potter's death explain Sarah's marriage? Faced with his imminent demise, she might have chosen security over the uncertainty of being dependent on a younger brother she didn't know well and didn't much like. Norbert had too often criticized her interests and activities.

Yet that didn't explain why she now cringed from Alex in horror. Something else was very wrong. The Sarah he'd loved was a ray of sunshine. He'd rarely seen her without a smile.

Whatever the truth of her marriage, he owed her an apology for losing his temper. It was highly improper to dress her down like a disobedient soldier. Learning that she was now his mother's companion made his attack even worse.

Yet how could he live with her under his roof? The daily reminders would destroy him.

Chapter Two

Sarah paused outside the drawing room to settle her nerves, then followed three girls inside and slipped into a corner. Joining the guests at Northcote Manor was harder than making her first appearance in London had been. Back then, her status as a squire's daughter had kept her on society's fringes, though she'd had the support of her maternal grandmother and the security of her betrothal to sustain her.

Now her status as an employee placed an even bigger gulf between her and the others. Too many gentlemen might consider her prey. All she could do was hope they would leave her alone and that Alex would not punish her apparent defiance. He and the dowager were across the room. With luck, they would stay there.

No one disturbed her for a quarter hour, then the dowager swooped into her corner, a lady in tow. "I believe you know Mrs. Harris," she announced. "Formerly Diana Martin."

"Of course," Sarah managed through her shock. "We met in London."

"What a delightful surprise." Diana's smile was wholly natural.

"Most unexpected. Wasn't Lord Ware courting you when I left town?"

Diana laughed. "What a bore he is, but I managed to deflect him long enough that Papa finally accepted Mister Harris's offer. Such a relief!"

"Congratulations. How is your family?"

"Wonderful." Diana described her three children. In moments, swapping tales of their children's escapades had them both chuckling.

"What is so funny?" a newcomer asked.

"Agnes?" Sarah was amazed to see another London acquaintance. "I didn't realize you were here."

"It's Lady Fortner now," said Diana, emphasizing the address. Agnes's goal in London had been to snare a wealthy title. She'd obviously succeeded, though Fortner's reputation as a rakehell had prompted most mothers to steer their daughters elsewhere. Diana turned back to Agnes. "Are your boys here? I didn't see them in the nursery."

"Heavens, no." Lady Fortner plied her fan. "Traveling in winter is uncomfortable enough without dragging children along."

Sarah kept her mouth shut. Agnes had always put her own desires first. Apparently that hadn't changed.

Lady Fortner frowned. "Who did you wed, Sarah? I don't think I ever heard."

"Richard Heflin."

"What?" Diana's eyes widened. "I thought you turned him down."

"I did."

"So why did you wed him?"

She shrugged. "Father insisted."

Diana gasped. "So that explains it. I never believed his claim that he'd locked his wife away after discovering her in bed with a neighbor. He lied too often."

Sarah nearly fainted. No wonder the dowager was pressing her to join the guests. The girls would suffer unless she quashed this calumny.

"What lies?" demanded Lady Fortner. "I've never heard that Heflin lied."

"His story about Mister Mann and the one about George Farber were complete fabrications. Most of the others were badly twisted, so it's obvious he schemed to keep Sarah from Town."

Sarah grimaced. "Very true. If he'd allowed me into Society, I would have revealed that he regularly cheated at cards."

"You had proof?" asked Diana eagerly. "Many suspected him, but without evidence, they couldn't bar him from the clubs."

"Just my word. But he often bragged about his skill, both at fleecing gentlemen and at intimidating them so they would remain silent about it," she said bitterly. Heflin's boasts had been a reminder that he did not accept defeat. Ever. Anyone who defied him paid, especially her. To avoid further mention of her husband, she continued, "I've heard little news since leaving Town. What is happening?"

If anyone knew, it would be the gossip-loving Agnes.

Agnes eagerly repeated tales that differed from those bandied about during her Season only in the names of the participants.

Her friends hadn't changed, either. Diana remained sweet and caring, putting the best face on any tale and possessing a heart that embraced the world. Agnes still suspected the worst of others, using those judgments to justify her own actions. Sarah had heard of the notorious Lady Fortner and her growing list of conquests, though without realizing her identity. Having provided the requisite heir, Agnes was now pleasing herself.

But not until Sarah met Alex's gaze did she fully relax. While his eyes remained icy, he made no attempt to have her removed or to approach her, so the dowager must have prevailed.

Alex had escorted his grandmother downstairs, then held his impatience in check while she introduced him to the guests. Her protégées ranged from the simpering to the giggling to the insipid, but the frowns that had kept his troops in line worked on them, too. The moment he escaped, he made a beeline for the corner sheltering his schoolmates. They might be near strangers after all this time, but at least they were safe.

Nearly fifty people were gathered for dinner, with more arriving every minute, Sarah among them. One glimpse re-ignited his old attraction, again raising his temper. Habit, he assured himself. If he avoided her, the feeling would fade. But with his grandmother's scold still ringing in his ears, he must accept her presence for now. He turned to Edward and Michael, grateful for the distraction.

"Welcome home, Northcote." Edward Holcombe clapped him on the back. "Must feel good."

Alex shook his head. "Hard to tell. I just arrived."

"Shocked to find so many of us, I expect," said Michael Craft.

"A bit. How long has everyone been here?"

"Since yesterday." Edward quizzed the lovely Miss Norton with his glass.

Alex turned to Michael. "Don't you usually spend Christmas with your family?"

Michael shrugged. "Too much pressure. Mother is determined to set up my nursery. I leaped at the chance to welcome you home, if truth be told."

"Ah. It seems my grandmother has the same thought. Stay close. While I'm comfortable on a battlefield, I've no practice dodging matchmakers."

Both men nodded.

"What's the latest news?" He didn't care about society scandals or Shelford's latest speed record or who was vying for the most desirable courtesans. He didn't recognize half the names, but listened raptly, nodding and expressing occasional surprise. As long as he seemed deep in conversation, the ladies held back.

When his friends ran down, Alex took charge. "Coming home after so many years presents unexpected problems. I ran into a neighbor upstairs and didn't know how to address her. She married some years ago, but I've no idea to whom."

"Who was she?"

"Sarah Potter. She was planning her Season when I bought colors."

"Ah." Michael shook his head. "Quiet girl cited as a pattern card whenever someone wished to chastise one of the flightier chits. Richard Heflin paid her assiduous court, though she never seemed interested. We were surprised to hear they wed, but no one knows the details, for she never returned to Town."

"Heflin claimed she preferred the country," said Edward. "But rumors hinted that he kept her there because she played him false."

"That doesn't sound like her." The words were out before he could stop them, so he had to explain his comment. "Her father's estate runs with this one, so I've known her since childhood. There were no odd rumors about her, and her behavior always seemed exemplary."

"True. She was never flirtatious or aggressively forward like some chits." Michael glanced at Miss Field, whose avid expression had already warned Alex of potential trouble. "Heflin likely started the tale for some reason of his own. It died immediately, of course. No one knew her well enough to keep it alive. And since Heflin died a week later . . . "

"*That* was a tale worthy of notice," said Edward, chuckling.

"What happened?"

Michael laughed. "Few liked Heflin. He was an arrogant braggart and far too lucky at the tables. So his death was widely toasted."

"He and young Braxton set up a curricle race," put in Edward. "Awkward for the rest of us. Braxton is another obnoxious toad, and both teams were unworthy. Braxton's were all flash, and Heflin's short-chested."

Michael shook his head. "Their course across Hampstead Heath included that narrow track up through the rocks. Heflin was in the lead at one of the choke points, with Braxton breathing down his neck. He topped a rise and came upon a flock of sheep."

"Fools." Alex had little patience for reckless racing or any other childish stunt. He'd lost too many men to such idiocy.

"Worse than fools," Edward agreed. "No one of sense races across that portion of the heath. There are always sheep out there."

"So what happened?"

"What you'd expect," said Michael. "Heflin stopped. Braxton didn't. His horses tried to jump the unexpected obstacle, landing atop it and sending Heflin flying. The sheep trampled him as they scattered. Broke his neck. Braxton was also tossed out, but he only broke a leg."

"Boys." Alex shrugged.

"Braxton was a boy—no more than twenty. But Heflin was in his mid-thirties and should have known better."

"Some people never grow up." Alex tried a new topic. "Miss Field seems rapacious. Is there anyone else who might prove dangerous?"

"She isn't bad on her own account," said Michael. "But her father wants a wealthy son-in-law."

"The safest girl is Miss Norton."

Alex frowned. "Why? Is she already betrothed?"

Edward shook his head. "Spite."

Michael nodded. "Two Seasons ago a schemer spread false rumors to drive her from Town—they were both diamonds, but the schemer hated competition. Miss Norton's court abandoned her. The truth emerged within days, reviving her status, but the experience turned her cynical. Don't compliment her, or she'll bite your head off."

"I hadn't planned to. What about the others?"

Michael rolled his eyes. "Miss Ingleside's father refuses to finance a third Season, so she's desperate."

Edward turned his glass on a girl whose gown sported an excess of ribbons. "Miss Billington is clumsy and prone to hysterics. Her fit when she caught her cloak on her carriage door was bad enough. Then she stumbled entering the breakfast room this morning, wailed loud enough to wake the dead, and accused a footman of pushing her."

"How distasteful."

Edward nodded. "She should have stayed in the schoolroom another year or two. Miss Harper's father is a gamester. He's flush for now, but she fears reversals that might cancel her come-out."

"Miss Eldridge is no problem," said Michael. "She's barely seventeen and while she flirts quite prettily, she won't jeopardize her first Season."

"Lady Fortner is seeking new conquests, but she's not a comfortable bedmate."

The pair described other house parties, revealing the stratagems that ladies used to attract men to their beds and that parents used to bind men to their daughters. Alex had been young enough before buying colors that he'd not been a target. Now he marveled at how alien this world seemed. The military was easier to understand.

Reynolds arrived to announce dinner, sending the gentlemen off to collect their dinner partners. Alex girded his loins as he offered his arm to Miss Harper, praying that he could survive the evening without falling into anyone's trap. Dinner promised to hold as many dangers as any battle.

To accommodate the crowd, the dowager had opened the Tudor

great hall. Alex's position on the raised dais provided a view of everyone, including Sarah. Lust speared him whenever she laughed. This was the Sarah he remembered—relaxed, funny, fascinating. Just so had she laughed as they'd raced their horses across the hills.

Lust was a habit, he assured himself again, shifting to relieve discomfort. But her laughter raised new questions. She'd been laughing in the drawing room, too. So why was she terrified of him? It couldn't be that letter. Granted, he owed her an apology for sending such a diatribe, but she should have long since put it behind her.

Her terror and Michael's description of her Season made it less likely that her marriage had been the love match he'd envisioned. Which again raised the question of why she had jilted him. Before he made his apology, he needed enough facts to avoid making a further cake of himself.

Forcing Sarah from his mind, he focused on deflecting flirtation— thanks to his grandmother's manipulation, he was flanked by Miss Field as well as Miss Harper. His temper was nearing the explosion point when shrieks silenced everyone else in the room.

Miss Billington leaped up, her chair crashing to the floor behind her.

"Look what you've done!" She shook her gown, spraying droplets of wine on Nigel Ingleside as a glass crashed to the floor. "Clumsy Oaf! How could you? It's ruined!"

She burst into tears.

A red-faced Mrs. Billington hurriedly dragged her daughter from the room. The rest of the company exhaled in unison, then resumed their conversations.

Alex stifled an urge to laugh. What a nitwit. His eyes automatically sought Sarah to find her gaze on him, eyes dancing with the smile she kept from her face. The moment of mutual hilarity recalled everything good they'd shared and made him feel eighteen again . . .

Cursing under his breath, he jerked his gaze back to his plate. What was he doing? This was hardly the way to banish lust.

He kept his temper in check during three courses of determined flirtation from his dinner companions, but once the ladies retired to the drawing room, it flared. Half a dozen eligible females meant half a dozen fathers hoping to avoid the expense of a Season. He finally prodded his Uncle Henry into describing the estate's shooting opportunities, then announced an expedition for the following morning, with Henry in charge. Claiming urgent business, he sent the gentlemen to join the ladies and locked himself in the library.

Chapter Three

Alex turned his horse toward home, his head bursting with the information he'd amassed since breakfast. After seeing the shooters off, then sending the ladies into town with the dowager for some last-minute Christmas shopping, he'd set out to survey the estate and call on Squire Potter. Sarah had invaded his dreams last night, daring him to open his mind. He needed to discover the truth.

The first truth was that he must replace Larkins. The steward was clearly incompetent. After six months of minimal supervision, hedgerows were unpruned, broken limbs littered the park, and the wall of a sheepfold had collapsed.

But the meeting with Sarah's brother Norbert, the new Squire Potter, dominated his thoughts, inciting guilt that was already eating at his soul. The boy had not improved with age. His revelations were worse.

"A belated condolence on your parents' passing," Alex had offered, accepting a glass of wine in Norbert's study. "I missed much local news these past years, so I just heard."

"Yes, well—" Norbert frowned. "If Papa were still here, I'd likely strangle him for tarnishing the family name with his idiocy."

"What?"

"Surely they told you he blew his brains out."

"Is that why Sarah wed Heflin?"

Norbert frowned. "No, no. She was already gone."

Alex leaned forward. "Something haunts Sarah. Her *joie de vivre* is missing. I thought the problem arose from her marriage, but your father's death might be responsible. I need details if I'm to help her."

"Why would you care? She's just a servant."

Alex could see why Sarah preferred employment as a companion to living at Potter House. Norbert had become the stuffiest of prigs. Worse even than the old squire. "We were betrothed before I bought colors," he revealed. "That gives me the right to some answers."

"My God!" Norbert paled. "I had no idea."

Alex glared. Had they driven Sarah into Heflin's arms? "She wished to postpone the announcement until after her Season."

He nodded. "Of course. Papa would never have sprung for London if he'd known. No wonder—"

The door burst open. A woman rushed in, her fawning smile aimed at Alex. "Shame on Norbert for hiding you away, my lord. We are delighted that you called here on your first day home. But, of course, you've come for the latest news. You would never believe—"

"We are discussing business." Alex glared, reminding himself that Norbert's wife was not a lady and might not understand the difference between a drawing room and a gentleman's study.

She flinched.

"That is enough, Caroline," said a pink-cheeked Norbert, waving her away. Once the door was firmly shut, he addressed Alex. "My apologies for the interruption."

"Sarah. What happened?"

"I don't know. I was barely down from Eton when they returned from Town. Papa was livid that she'd refused an offer he'd already accepted. Everyone avoided him when he was in a fury, so we didn't speak. He didn't calm down until Heflin showed up two days later."

"Did you talk to Sarah when she returned?"

"Just once. She was furious at what she called Papa's hard-headed idiocy and swore she'd tried to discourage Heflin. Nonsense, of course. Mama knew how often she'd danced with him. Only a tease would let him live in her pocket without intending a wedding." He noted Alex's face and added, "We didn't know about you, of course."

Alex's head was spinning with new uncertainties. If Sarah didn't want Heflin, why hadn't she revealed their betrothal? He was by far the better catch. "What I don't understand is why your father pushed an alliance with a man suspected of cheating."

Norbert paled alarmingly. "People knew he cheated?"

"There was insufficient evidence to bar him from the clubs, but new arrivals always received warnings. Reasonable men refused to play with him."

"But Papa never joined a club. He was so rarely in town that he considered paying membership fees a waste."

So the squire's parsimony had kept him ignorant of London's dangers. The clubs were a primary source of information on gentlemen's habits. Society's matrons kept a close eye on young ladies, but they knew far less about gentlemen. "What happened when Heflin showed up?"

"Sarah's maid swore she was calling on a friend and would not return until the next day. Papa hid his fury and invited Heflin to dinner." Another long pause. "Papa was haggard at breakfast. Three sheets to the wind, if truth be told. Announced Sarah would wed Heflin. No choice. He and Heflin had played cards all night. Heflin held vowels for everything Papa owned, including the estate. He would trade them for Sarah's hand. If she refused, he would toss us out without a penny."

Alex swore, long and luridly. "And no one questioned his honesty? I never knew your father to wager more than penny stakes. Or to drink heavily, either."

Norbert's hand waved off his words. "Papa and I were in shock. Mama fell into hysterics. Her maid dragged Sarah downstairs. When Papa explained, she cursed him up one side and down the other, accusing him of willful stupidity and more. But with Mama wailing and Papa promising disaster if she refused, she had no choice. Heflin returned with the vicar in tow and a special license in his pocket. They were wed before we had time to think. He hustled her into his carriage, tossing Papa's vowels from the window as it pulled away. He wouldn't even wait for her luggage, but ordered that it be sent after them."

Alex was so furious he could barely breathe. Poor Sarah. The truth was nothing like what he'd believed.

Norbert again shrank into his seat. "It was the next morning before Papa looked at the vowels. Only three were in his hand. The rest were forged. That's when he admitted he had little memory of the game. But it was too late. The vicar believed Sarah willing."

"She freezes when shocked, appearing calm."

"Papa fell apart. And when a groom reported seeing Heflin strike his horse, he locked himself in here and put a pistol to his head."

Alex forced one last question past icy lips. "How did Sarah fare with Heflin?"

Norbert shrugged. "The next we heard of her was when she and her brats turned up after Heflin's death. We could hardly bar the door."

But Norbert hadn't welcomed her. He blamed her for drawing Heflin into their lives.

Alex couldn't bear to hear any more. Uttering a curt farewell, he slipped out a side door to avoid Caroline.

No wonder Sarah had accepted a companion's post. Her presence at Potter House had been a constant reminder of her family's selfish behavior. They had forced her onto Heflin to save their own skins without even questioning whether their skins were actually at risk.

But Alex was also to blame. Keeping their betrothal secret had been dishonorable. Once he'd decided to buy colors, he should have spoken to the squire. Sarah would have missed her Season, but she would have been safe.

He must atone by helping her. She'd reacted to yesterday's diatribe like a badly abused horse, hinting that her life had been a worse hell than he'd endured in Spain. Perhaps he could ease her fears and revive her spirits.

Excitement stirred at the thought.

Sarah ignored the scent of mince pies and Christmas puddings as she paused outside the library. Would Alex turn her off after all?

"Enter."

"You sent for me?" She chose a seat as far from the desk as possible. Experience had taught her to hide all fear, so she adopted her best submissive pose, her eyes staring at the hands clasped in her lap. Heflin had considered eye contact an assault on his authority.

"Thank God you didn't accompany the ladies today."

She flinched at his tone, but a glance verified that he remained seated.

In a softer voice, he continued, "I have questions about the estate."

Surprise raised her eyes, and then she couldn't look away. He seemed calmer today. More familiar. More like—She stifled the thought, for trusting him was dangerous. Heflin had often lulled her with charm to increase the pain of his next attack.

"I know nothing of estate matters."

"Harbaugh does. I'm told you are the only one who can understand him."

She relaxed. Even the doctor needed help translating Harbaugh's words. "He suffered an apoplexy shortly before your father died. His mind functions normally, but his infirmities interfere with speech. He frets about estate business, however. Yesterday he asked about the planting. Harold was taunting him again, vowing to institute detrimental changes. The doctor warned us that Harbaugh must not become agitated, so the encounter did him no good."

Alex's eyes blazed with fury, sending her gaze back to her lap. "I will dismiss Larkins and see that Harold does not interfere again. He has no authority now that I am home."

Sarah peeped up, uncurling her fists when she realized that his anger was not directed at her. "So I told him. But it will help him to see you." To protect Harbaugh, she dared to add, "Please stay calm and ask questions that can be answered yes or no. The harder he has to work, the sooner he will tire. And tell him about your planting plans."

"I have none yet, for I first need a new steward." Alex rose, offering his arm.

Ignoring it, she slipped through the door ahead of him. As long as he didn't touch her, she could control the terror men aroused.

He said nothing about her refusal. As she scurried toward Harbaugh's room, he remained at her side, hands clasped safely behind his back. "What do you know about Sneaky Harold—besides his penchant for taunting the weak?" His voice invited confidences.

"He enjoys gaming." She stifled a smile at the name she'd last heard in childhood.

"Interesting." Disapproval laced his voice. "Did he really stay here in support of his father, or is he on a repairing lease?"

Sarah shrugged.

Alex accepted her silence, for he said nothing further.

By the time they reached Harbaugh's room, Sarah's protective instincts again drowned her fear. "My lo— Alex." She paused out of his reach, unsure how he would react to criticism.

"What?"

"Forgive my impertinence, but you are no longer in the army. Harsh tones, barked orders, or anger will intimidate Harbaugh. Precipitating another attack will not help you."

He nodded.

Alex mulled over Sarah's admonition as he entered Harbaugh's room. She was equally susceptible to harshness. He must efface himself if he hoped to set her at ease. Now that truth had diverted his anger to others, his attraction was stronger than ever. Habit, he hoped. Something that would quickly fade. While he was determined to ease her fears, reattaching her affections was likely impossible. So he must banish lust and stop remembering the missing sparkle in her eyes, or her laugh, or the passion she could incite with a glance.

He inhaled deeply, adopting a neutral expression as he approached the bed.

Harbaugh looked more like a corpse than a man. The right side of his face sagged. His skin drooped in papery folds, and had darkened around his deep-sunk eyes. The coverlet molded a skeletal body, accentuating his missing arm.

"Good morning, Harbaugh," said Sarah, turning his head so he could see his visitors.

"Goo orni."

"Lord Northcote has returned at last." She stepped aside,

exposing Alex to view.

"-y or."

"Good to see you again, Harbaugh," said Alex as Sarah shoved the coverlet aside to bare Harbaugh's left foot. "Are they caring for you properly?"

The foot flexed.

"That means *yes*," said Sarah.

"I've not spoken to Larkins, but Sarah says you have questions about the planting."

Yes.

"Should I stick to the usual rotation?"

The foot waved side to side.

Sarah coughed, then spoke when Alex glanced at her. "Your mother mentioned that shortly before his death, your father was reading an agricultural treatise that convinced him to try a new rotation next year."

"Is that right?" Alex looked at Harbaugh.

Yes.

"I will read that treatise myself, and I plan to let Larkins go since he is not fulfilling even basic duties. Is there anyone who can advise me until I find a replacement?"

"Hen-Hen-" His left eye tightened with the effort.

"My Uncle Henry?" he asked.

Yes. Harbaugh's face again relaxed.

He glanced at Sarah.

"Your uncle visits often. He has experimented with agricultural reform at his own estate."

"And he knows this one well, having grown up here." He returned his attention to Harbaugh. "I will look into it, so set your mind at ease. Now about the investments. Do you know why ten thousand in Consols were sold around the time Father died?"

Harbaugh's left eye widened as his foot waved wildly.

"Might Father have sold them without mentioning it? You had just fallen ill."

Again the foot waved.

"What was the date of the sale?" asked Sarah.

"June 22, but the certificates would have been sent several days earlier to Father's man of business in London."

Sarah glanced at Harbaugh. "But if he sold the Consols, the proceeds should be in the accounts, or some mention made of whatever expense they were meant to cover."

Alex nodded. "So Father did not order the sale. But a man on horseback could have reached London before news of Father's death."

"Harl- nee- mon-"

Sarah frowned. "Harold needed money?"

Yes. "Ash- hel. Refoosh. Fi."

Alex touched Harbaugh's shoulder, surprised that others had trouble following his words. It only required a little attention. "Did Harold come to the Manor to ask for money?"

Yes.

"Did Father refuse, leading to a fight?"

Yes.

Sarah spoke up. "Do you recall the date?"

"Shun wen."

"June 10th?"

The foot waved.

"The 20th?"

Yes.

"But you were ill by then. How did you overhear them?"

"In here. Hout coma."

Alex forced his hands to unclench. "They argued across your bed, thinking you were unconscious?"

Yes. "Harl in line sush—"

Sarah's face turned to granite. "Did Harold actually claim he deserved the money because he was in line for the succession?"

Yes.

"I suppose he assured Lord Northcote that Alex was bound to die."

Yes.

"But Napoleon had already abdicated," protested Alex.

"Yet instead of coming home, you sailed for America to continue fighting."

"I—" He shut his mouth. He should have sold out after Napoleon's abdication, but he hadn't wanted to face the ghost of the life he'd planned—the ghost now standing in front of him.

Sarah turned back to Harbaugh. "Do you believe their argument caused Lord Northcote's attack?"

The foot quivered in indecision.

Alex again touched Harbaugh's shoulder. "How many times did Harold strike Father?"

Four flexes.

Sarah's comment about Harold's penchant for gaming echoed in his ears. "Rest, Harbaugh." He turned to Sarah, who was staring as if he'd begun speaking in tongues. "Do you think Harold sold the Consols?"

"I've no idea. I arrived after your father's death and was too occupied with your mother's hysteria to notice who was here or what they were doing. I heard Harold and his father shouting at each other the morning of the funeral, but that was a week later. Only Harold knows what it was about. Charles collapsed at the burial. Harold has been running the estate ever since."

"We will discuss this later." Harbaugh was becoming agitated, so he laid a hand on the man's shoulder. "I am now in charge. As questions arise, I will check with you. Rest for now."

He added a few more soothing words. Harbaugh was much like his wounded troops. Excessive fretting about friends or the war often retarded their recoveries. Not that Harbaugh was likely to heal.

But he kept his voice light as he bade the secretary farewell.

Sarah reluctantly obeyed when Alex directed her back to the library. She needed time alone to think. He was a maze of contradictions it would be safer to avoid.

His gentleness with Harbaugh went far beyond her suggestion that he stay calm. It contradicted her earlier impression of him as a fierce warrior. Not only did he pay enough attention to follow the man's speech, but he'd soothed Harbaugh's agitation, allowing no anger into his voice or face, though she knew he must be furious. Ten thousand pounds was a huge loss—Heflin had destroyed a parlor after losing a fraction as much playing dice. But Alex's sensitivity fit the boy she'd once loved.

Warmth washed over her.

Alex again sat behind the desk. "How could Harold have accrued a ten-thousand-pound debt? Surely Society understands his financial position."

"I can't say. Until your father died, I hadn't seen him since my Season. Back then the gossips decried his reckless gaming, but revealed no details to innocent girls. The problem must have been bad, though, for his father sent him home. I've no idea what he has been doing since."

"Why the devil was he allowed into my accounts if he has a reputation for gaming?"

She cringed.

Alex twisted his face back into calm. It was a skill he'd not previously possessed, but it made discerning his reactions harder. "I'm not angry with you, Sarah. This isn't your fault. But I need information. Did you know Harold was here when Father died?"

She sighed. "No. Today is the first I'd heard of it. And I've no idea when he returned. Your Uncle Charles arrived two days before the funeral. The dowager should know if Harold traveled with him."

"I'd rather not distress her with questions. Reynolds can confirm Harold's movements. How did that sneak wind up in charge?"

"No one actually put him in charge, Alex. You must know that your father avoided most employees. He rarely met with Larkins, using Harbaugh to gather reports and relay his orders."

And to improve them, from what she'd heard. George Northcote had been an arrogant man who rarely sullied his hands with anything he considered beneath him, so Harbaugh had been free to institute efficiencies and ease the tenants' lives, changes he'd dared order because he was George's cousin.

"Harbaugh collapsed in mid-June. Your father had no time to replace him before his own death. The dowager took to her bed in shock. Your mother alternated between hysteria and a melancholia so deep we feared she might take her life. That's when I came to stay."

Alex shuddered. "I had no idea things were that bad."

"We knew it would be at least two months before you could return—"

"An optimistic estimate," he interrupted on a sigh. "My regiment was on the move, so Grandmother's letter took three months to reach me. By the time I extricated myself from the military, the weather was so bad, the crossing took double the usual time."

"But we expected you much sooner. Your Uncle Charles's collapse meant Harold remained here instead of leaving as he'd intended—the doctor's initial diagnosis was imminent death." She sighed. "The day after your father's burial, Larkins tossed your grandmother's orders back in her face. Harold overheard, reminded Larkins of his place, and forced him to show proper respect. Larkins's willingness to obey Harold made using Harold as a go-between reasonable. Again, no one expected the situation to last this long. They thought you would have returned by the harvest."

"So Harold has had access to the estate accounts. Why didn't my Uncle Henry help?"

"He'd already left. He didn't believe his brother was dying. And he was right. Charles remains among the living, at least in body." She fleetingly wished they could insert Harbaugh's mind into Charles's body.

"So Uncle Charles's mind is gone, and Harold has been running things while Uncle Henry went about his own business. What other changes have occurred since Father died?"

"One of your tenants died—old Hardesty. He must have been nearly ninety."

"I'm surprised he lived so long."

"Cook has a new assistant. The old one married the apothecary. And your father's valet is gone, of course."

"Is there anyone who might know what Harold was doing before he moved here?"

She frowned. "Your friends Holcomb and Craft both frequent London. And your cousin Derrick actively avoids Harold, so he has to be keeping track of him. They hate each other."

"But you know nothing of his recent activities."

"No." She rose. "If you will excuse me, I have duties to attend to."

"One more question. How are your daughters?"

She backed up a pace. Did he object to housing them? Even Heflin had hated the girls.

"Relax, Sarah. It was a simple question. I was out of line yesterday and must beg your forgiveness. They are welcome here, as are you."

"They are fine," she choked out, head whirling in confusion. Why was he interested in her daughters? Was his apology setting the scene for some new attack?

"Make sure they join the festivities, especially the decorating excursions tomorrow and the children's activities on Christmas."

"Thank you." She escaped the library, head again reeling. He changed character too often for her to keep up. Who was the real Alex? She could only pray it wasn't the warrior.

Chapter Four

To reach his friends before dinner, Alex again had to run a gauntlet of his grandmother's protégées. Sarah was the only sane female in the room.

"Disinterest offers a challenge and irritates the matchmakers," Michael commented when the dowager glared at him for ignoring the ladies. "Mask it by spending a few minutes with Miss Norton."

"Why bother? I cannot believe Grandmother thinks any of these chits suitable even if I were seeking marriage, which I'm not."

"Take it from someone with too much experience dodging matchmaking relatives. Pick someone who won't trap you, then use her as a shield. Miss Norton is perfect, for she hates men just now and is intelligent enough that you needn't endure a monologue on fashion or a description of this morning's shopping expedition. And she's beautiful, so no one will question your apparent interest."

Alex shrugged. He preferred dark hair to Miss Norton's blonde. And while the girl was brighter than the other eligibles, she couldn't hold a candle to Sarah.

Was that his grandmother's goal? Sarah seemed a paragon next to the brash silliness of the others. Even as a girl, she hadn't been a simpering fool.

She again stood with Mrs. Harris, her unadorned gown more appealing than the over-decorated fashions of others—styles had changed since he was last home. But Sarah's taste remained simple, much like the girl he'd loved.

His groin tightened as longing surged, recalling more of their courtship. Their incendiary kisses had been so much more exciting than anything he'd experienced before or since. He'd had trouble controlling their embraces. Her passion . . . best not to think of that in company.

The respect she accorded Harbaugh increased her appeal. He refused to admit to love, for six years apart had changed them both, and his lust might arise more from anger and guilt than from present reality. But until he knew how he felt and why, he had no interest in others.

Was loving Sarah something he wanted? Could she again care?

To exert control over his body, he focused on business. "I remember my cousin Harold as a very poor card player. Has he improved?" he asked Michael.

"Must have. He frequents the tables, but rarely draws attention, winning as often as he loses and covering any vowels promptly."

Edward frowned. "But that game against Andrews in June was odd. Both players changed afterward."

"How so?"

"They attracted a crowd, for the stakes were high and the hands fairly even. Play continued all night and well into the morning. But the few remaining watchers fell asleep before they called quits, so no one knows how much actually changed hands."

"When I left at four, Harold was down two thousand but had won three hands in a row, halving his losses," said Michael. "Andrews suggested they call it a night, but Harold refused—hardly a surprise after such a turn in luck."

Edward took up the tale. "His luck didn't last. Most agree that the final tally was five thousand, but I've heard estimates as high as ten. The only certainty is that Andrews bought an estate in Kent a week later, then married and retired to the country."

Michael nodded. "Harold gave up his rooms and hasn't returned to Town, either."

"His father fell ill about then. We don't expect him to live much longer." Alex refused to feed gossip, though this confirmed his suspicions. Ten thousand would have set Andrews up nicely. That Harold would wager such a sum when he had nothing—

Reynolds announced dinner.

Dodging the dowager's continued machinations, Alex escorted an elderly aunt to dinner and made sure one of her friends occupied the seat on his other side. Sarah shared a table with his younger cousins, her calm keeping their antics under control.

She had always been a calming influence, able to restrain his occasional recklessness without making him feel hobbled. Their discussions had been the most stimulating he'd ever experienced—far more interesting than any he'd conducted in recent years. Her love of books let her converse on many topics, often pushing his thoughts in new directions. Yet he never felt threatened by her knowledge, even when she convinced him to change his stance. Very unlike his father . . .

Had that changed? Heflin didn't sound the sort to condone reading in a wife. Years of abuse during which Heflin had likely blamed her for her father's suicide would have left deep scars. Her brother blamed her for that death, too. Caroline reportedly despised her, perhaps because she had the breeding Caroline coveted. The only place where she'd found respect was at Northcote Manor.

Earlier that day, when he had returned from Potter House to find the shooters straggling home, Alex had called Edward into the library to ask more questions about Heflin.

"He fleeced one of my cousins, but we couldn't tell anyone while Heflin lived," Edward had admitted.

"Why?"

"Heflin was a vicious cad. Within hours of Drew telling me about his cheating, Heflin beat him senseless. We've no idea how he knew we'd spoken, for I didn't mention it to anyone else, but he told Drew he'd do worse if he ever opened his mouth again, then named others who had flouted his orders. One of them died."

Alex wasn't surprised such bragging had kept victims in line. But if Heflin had been accustomed to violence, what had he done to Sarah? He wasn't a man to forgive that she'd turned him down, and if he knew she'd preferred another . . .

After years under Heflin's thumb, was the Sarah he'd loved still there?

He had to find out. And soon, for his grandmother was right about him needing an heir. He couldn't leave the estate to Harold—he'd already discovered further thefts. Small sums each time, but they totaled two thousand pounds. The tenants would suffer if a gamester inherited, and Alex could not allow that to happen.

After dinner, Sarah checked on Lady Northcote, then retired to consider her future. It didn't matter what the dowager or Lady Northcote wanted or whether Alex agreed. She could not remain at the Manor. *Tête-à-têtes* with him revived too many memories, along with feelings she'd long since buried—it had been disconcerting to discover that their ability to read each other's minds still functioned.

But she could never remarry. Not even him. Heflin had made sure of that. Yet Alex needed an heir. Watching him choose a wife would be more painful than Heflin's fists. So she must leave.

But she couldn't ignore his summons when it came.

"What now?" Sarah asked when she reached the library. "Why aren't you playing charades with your guests? Is Harbaugh worse?"

"No." He shook his head. "They are Grandmother's guests, not mine. I have more pressing matters to address."

"As viscount and head of the family—" She abandoned the admonition. "Why am I here?" Alex looked more hesitant than she'd ever seen him. She nearly reached out to touch him before she stilled her hand.

"I owe you a profound apology," he began, then cut her off when she started to protest. "Not only for snapping at you yesterday, though I regret that, of course. But for that unforgivably rude letter I sent you after your marriage."

Pain stabbed her from head to toe. She opened her mouth, but nothing emerged.

"We were recovering from a skirmish when a letter arrived from Mother. I opened it eagerly, hoping it would help me forget our losses for a time." He shuddered. "But her first words reported your marriage. No details, just the bare fact of it. I thought I would die. It was worse because I hadn't heard the news from you, not even a hint that you might wed another. And since Mother wrote nearly a fortnight after the fact . . ."

"I wrote," she swore. "It was the hardest letter I've ever composed because I knew it would hurt you. I later discovered that Heflin had destroyed all my correspondence. Even my family heard nothing from me." She had stopped writing to anyone after that, for Heflin used the contents of her letters against her.

Alex sighed. "It fits what I know of the man. But at the time, the news nearly drove me mad. The only way to dull the pain was wine. I'd downed too much before I penned that missive. My words were dishonorable even had my assumptions been correct. Now that I know you were forced into the marriage, I cannot live with the memory. So I owe you a deep apology."

Sarah bowed her head, hating that his apology recalled every word of that letter to mind. It was the only one Heflin had let her see. He'd stood over her while she read it, beat her for encouraging other men, then quoted from it often as proof that he was the only man who mattered, the only one who would touch her, the only one who loved her—what a travesty *that* had been. Obsession she would grant him. He took what he wanted, through fair means or foul. Then he guarded his prizes with a passion that bordered madness. But that wasn't love.

"I'll not forgive myself for my cruelty," Alex continued, probably recalling some of his vitriol.

She could quote every word despite having seen his letter only once.

"Not even the next day's injuries were sufficient atonement."

"Injuries?" She met his gaze in surprise.

"I paid for my overindulgence," he admitted with a sigh. "I was

not myself when we ran into another patrol. They nearly killed me."
One hand traced the scars on his face.

"Why didn't you come home to recover?"

"I couldn't face England with the pain of your rejection so fresh
in my mind."

"I didn't—"

"I know that now. I should have known it then." He frowned. "If
Heflin destroyed your correspondence, how did you see my letter?"

She shrugged. "That one made appropriate reading material."
When shock twisted his face, she rose. "Enough of the past, my lord.
You are no longer the youth who lashed out to relieve your pain, and I
am no longer the girl who hurt you. You have my forgiveness, if that's
what you need. But I don't wish to discuss it again."

She fled the library but could not flee the memories. His apology
revived the horror of those dark days before she'd had children to give
purpose to her life. How often had she cursed her love for Alex? It had
caused nothing but trouble.

It also revived the memory of the day her father had informed her
that Heflin would offer. When he'd ignored her initial protests, she'd
revealed her betrothal to Alex. But her father had called her a liar,
swearing Alex was far too young to consider marriage. After she
turned Heflin down, her father had treated her to a two-day tirade as
he dragged her home, accusing her of creating fantasies from whole
cloth to justify a childish *tendre*. Trapped in the carriage, she'd been
unable to escape her father's fury. Their next confrontation had forced
her into marriage. A day later he was dead.

Her fault. Every bit of it was her fault. Alex might regret writing
that letter, but she'd deserved his disdain. Her selfish insistence on
hiding their betrothal so she could enjoy a London Season had
destroyed them all.

Alex stared at the door long after Sarah left. Her words raised images
worse than anything Napoleon had thrown at him. Anyone who
cheated to gain a wife would not tolerate her thinking of another man.
Heflin would have used Alex's words as whips whenever Sarah did
anything he considered disobedient. That childish outburst had handed
the man a weapon capable of breaking her spirit and wearing away her
soul. No wonder she cringed from him.

"Damnation!" He had been too young in those days, so full of his
own importance that he hadn't even recognized his dishonor. He'd

proposed, then used frivolous excuses to leave Sarah behind so he could enjoy idle pleasures like all his friends. Then he'd let the fight with his father justify seeking adventure, postponing the marriage he wanted but wasn't ready to accept. If he'd demonstrated half the maturity he'd claimed to possess, he would have been at hand to protect her. What a fool he'd been.

Chapter Five

"Mister Harris won a fortune last night!" Diana whispered, her head bent close to Sarah and Lady Fortner. "I couldn't believe it. He usually breaks even at cards."

"Men always exaggerate," Lady Fortner scoffed. "Fortner has been in alt more than once over winning a few pounds from a rival."

"It was ten thousand." Diana grinned. "A Christmas miracle! We can buy our own town house! No more rentals with odd rooms and shabby furnishings."

"Congratulations," Sarah said, squeezing Diana's hand.

"What a ridiculous sum to wager at a family house party," complained Lady Fortner. "This isn't a hunting box. Lord Northcote should know better."

Sarah opened her mouth to defend Alex, but Diana beat her to it.

"Lord Northcote retired early. You know that he joins us only for dinner. You've complained about it often enough."

"Proof that he cares nothing for his position," Lady Fortner snapped. "He should make sure his guests are content."

Sarah swallowed a gasp, shocked to realize that Agnes hoped to entice Alex into her bed. Fury raged at the image of them together. And jealousy. She still cared.

She forced her attention back to Diana. "Such stakes do seem odd. What happened?"

"Once the charades ended, most of the men turned to cards. Mister Harris won a hundred pounds from Mister Harold, but when he rose to retire, Mister Harold demanded a chance to recoup his losses. He was drinking heavily and was so belligerent, Mister Harris couldn't refuse."

"Men!" snapped Lady Fortner. "They never learn. That's how Lord Underwood lost half his fortune to Collingwood last month."

"And Mr. Carlson last spring. To say nothing of Brummell. Mister Harold is another noted for poor judgment, though he always pays promptly, so few complain."

Sarah ignored their comparison of gentlemen's reckless play. Harold must have hidden his penury from society, paying recent losses by dipping into the Manor's accounts. With Alex now home, how would he cover this debt?

But Harold's folly wasn't her problem. Excusing herself, she skipped the breakfast room and headed for the garden. Every minute she remained at Northcote Manor would make her inevitable departure harder. Heflin had been right that she still loved Alex. But love was not enough—and it might not even be real, she admitted. Alex was no longer the boy she'd known, and years of exaggerating his character to counter the pain of Heflin's attacks had muddied her memories. Beyond that, her first priority was to protect her daughters.

But in minutes, the rarity of having time alone to enjoy the gardens drove planning her future from her mind. With the guests avoiding the cold until it was time to gather greens, she was free in a way she'd not experienced in years. A stray breeze teased a strand of hair loose to tickle her neck. Another fluttered a lone leaf clinging to a rose bush. The sky arched overhead, surprisingly blue. Days like this were made for riding neck-or-nothing over the hills as she'd done as a girl, often accompanied by Alex . . .

Movement interrupted her memories. She'd been wrong to believe she was alone. A thin spot in the hedge separating the gardens from the estate offices revealed Harold slipping from the carpenter's shop, a saw in one hand.

"What the—" She dodged out of sight as he scanned the gardens. Why would Harold need a saw? He was too accustomed to servants to tackle a job himself.

Peering between two branches, she watched him disappear toward the stable, then followed, staying on the garden side of the hedge.

Before entering the stableyard, he again looked in all directions. Definitely suspicious. If today's behavior related to last night's gaming loss, Alex needed to know.

The moment he disappeared from sight, she picked up her skirts and ran, reaching the stable as he disappeared into the carriage house. One glance through the window ignited her temper. Harold lay under Alex's curricle, sawing on the axle.

Mister Harris would expect his winnings shortly. Harold was penniless. But if Alex died, Harold's father would inherit the title and estate. With Charles helpless, Harold could take charge of the viscountcy.

Turning on her heel, she hurried back to the house. To Alex.

Alex leaned back in his chair as Harold sprawled onto a chair in the library. The dandy's façade had changed little over the years, but inside, a weak character and jealous nature had merged into venality. He had long suspected that Harold's lies had precipitated the final confrontation with his father.

"Is there a problem, Cousin?" Harold's sneer was all too familiar.

"You damaged my old curricle so it would pitch me out when I skirted the ravine. A probable death sentence."

"You jest."

"No!"

Harold jerked to attention.

"Don't bother to lie," Alex continued. "A witness watched you remove a saw from the carpenter's shed, slip into the carriage house, and cut my axle."

"Who?"

"It doesn't matter. This is merely the latest in a long list of crimes. Let's start with last night's card game. Harris remains appalled that he let you talk him into continuing the game. But you were drunk, belligerent, and determined to recoup your losses. Your threats forced him to continue. But your luck did not turn. And now you are in deep trouble, for you haven't got ten thousand."

"I—"

"Don't lie to me. You haven't got the hundred you'd lost before he tried to retire. You haven't a groat to your name, and with me home, you've no chance of stealing the money you need. Did you think I wouldn't check the books?" He tapped the ledger, refusing to let Harold interrupt. "You've already stolen more than twelve thousand from the estate. Ten thousand in Consols the day my father died, and another two thousand in the six months since."

"I had no choice!" Harold surged to his feet and retreated to the window.

"Really?"

"I'd had a run of bad luck. I couldn't go to a moneylender—do you know the interest those fellows charge, or what they do to those who fail to pay? So I approached Uncle George. But the dastard refused me a loan."

"It wasn't a run of bad luck. It was one drunken game against Andrews that was not my father's responsibility. And you are the last person he would have helped in any case. Believing your tale-bearing sent his only son into danger, something he'd hated you for ever since."

Only as he uttered the words did Alex understand their truth. One of Sneaky Harold's letters accusing Alex of myriad misdeeds would explain his father's fury in that last fight. Once he calmed down, he would have considered the source of the tale and discovered the truth from his many other correspondents. But by then it had been too late to change course—and new anger over Alex's flight would have already provided a new grievance. Harold had manipulated both his father and him.

If he'd stayed home instead of running away to the military, they would have made their peace years ago.

Harold sputtered in denial.

"Enough," Alex continued over Harold's protests. "Father knew your weaknesses too well to loan you money. Your father would not have remained quiet about incarcerating you six years ago. You know how close he and Father were."

Harold crumpled back onto the chair.

Alex hardened his voice. "You are a gamester, Harold. Your withdrawals from estate accounts show your habits clearly. You don't play cards for fun or to pass the time or to socialize with your peers. You play because you cannot stop, accepting any opponent, even when your pockets are to let. But Lady Luck always turns her back in the end. Especially when drinking prevents concentration."

"How dare you judge me?" snapped Harold.

"I *am* your judge. If I show this ledger to any magistrate, you'll be on the next ship to Botany Bay. Is that what you want?"

Harold bared his teeth.

"Pay attention," Alex continued. "Before I decide your fate, I want facts—all the facts. And remember that I can learn the truth within days, so do not lie to me. I will check any claims you make."

He waited as Harold slowly unclenched his fists. He continued to wait until Harold drew in several deep breaths, then he softened his tone. "What is the condition of your father's estate?"

"It can support its residents, but produces no extra."

"Is it mortgaged?"

"Father refused. Claimed the estate would never produce enough to pay off a mortgage."

Alex nodded, for his Uncle Charles had always been frugal. "How did he finance his trips to London?"

"He'd invested his second son's portion well, and Mother's dowry included both money and the estate. The man is wealthy as bedamned, but he made sure I could touch nothing. Cummings, his man of business, refuses to talk to me." He clenched his fists. "Father paid my debts that first time, then kept me confined for six months. When he finally let me go, he vowed I would never again receive a penny more than my allowance despite that I'm his heir."

"How much is your allowance?"

"A paltry five hundred a year." He grimaced.

Alex shook his head. "At the moment, you owe Harris ten thousand, plus another twelve to me. With an income of five hundred a year, it would take you forty-four years to pay us even if you spend nothing on food, shelter, or clothing. Gaming will not produce a windfall. It will only increase your debts."

Harold groaned.

"Is there any way to wring more from your father's estate?"

"No. It's small and located in a rocky part of Yorkshire. He's studied agriculture and animal care until he's cross-eyed, but nothing more can be done."

"His mind may be gone, but he is unlikely to die soon, so you have no access to his investments."

Harold nodded.

Why hadn't Harold killed his father instead of trying to kill him? Few would have questioned the death of a failing man. But that was one question he refused to ask. All he could do was make sure Harold couldn't attack either of them in the future.

"I will loan you enough to pay Harris." The game had likely been Harold's desperate bid to amass his own funds now that Alex's return removed access to the estate accounts. "Beyond that, you have four choices. The most obvious is to turn you over to the magistrate and wash my hands of you. Disclosing your crimes will not tarnish the family. People will applaud that I removed the bad apple before it spoiled the rest of the basket or emptied the family coffers."

Harold's protest died as Alex undercut his argument.

"Your second choice is to marry an heiress. An industrialist's daughter might be willing to wed you in return for access to Society. If you choose that route, I will expect repayment of the entire twenty-two thousand on your wedding day. You will write the debt into the marriage settlement, so no one is surprised to discover it."

"How the devil can I find an heiress?"

"Ask Grandmother or the Dowager Lady Ingleside. Between them, they know everyone in and out of Society."

"Devil take you," grumbled Harold. "A Cit's father would be worse than mine, demanding that I account for every shilling I spent."

"Probably, and I can guarantee he would keep you away from cards. Your third option is to return to your father's estate and stay there. Do your best to keep it running smoothly and prove to Cummings that you've turned over a new leaf. At least it would put a roof over your head and food in your mouth. I would expect fifty pounds per quarter toward your debt and payment in full once you inherit."

Harold's grimace spoke volumes. Alex suspected he had alienated the entire staff during his incarceration, and the neighbors as well.

"Option four is buying colors in a regiment posted to India. If you survive war, heat, and the local diseases, you would have a decent chance to make a fortune, though not by gaming."

"I am not a soldier."

"True, though I've seen far worse. A good sergeant could teach you enough to keep you alive."

"I can't bear the thought."

"So you've reduced your choices to the magistrate or marriage. Which will it be?"

"What if I leave and never return?"

"It won't help you, Harold. Either take your medicine like a man, or I will see that everyone in England knows you for a thief and a fortune hunter. There isn't a household in the country that would welcome you. All you could do is hide on your father's estate and pray he dies before you precipitate a duel or worse."

"If I talk to Lady Ingleside, everyone will know me for a fortune hunter within the hour. She is a consummate gossip."

"Then talk to Grandmother. For the sake of the family, she will keep your secrets. But I expect an answer by morning, so don't dawdle."

Alex shook his head as Harold left the room. He ought to just turn him in and be done with it, but Harold was family and his heir for now. A night of contemplation had convinced him that he still loved Sarah. Forever. He couldn't imagine wedding anyone else, so if she refused him, Harold would someday inherit the viscountcy. Persuading a gamester to reform was difficult, but for the sake of the estate tenants, he had to try.

Chapter Six

By the time the party set out to gather the Christmas greenery, batted eyelashes and insincere smiles had pushed Alex's temper to the breaking point. Michael was right about disinterest presenting a challenge. Despite his antipathy, three girls were plotting to lure him away so they could push for an offer. Their efforts would fail, of course, for Northcote Manor maintained a dedicated grove to provide decorations. There would be no wandering off in search of material.

Alex dispersed the girls by assigning one to cut evergreens with Edward, another to harvest holly with Michael, and the rest to strip ivy from the remains of an ancient wall. His cousin Derrick was already up the oak tree dropping balls of mistletoe into eager hands.

With everyone properly occupied, he joined Sarah. It was time he met her daughters.

"Need a hand?" he asked.

Sarah jumped. "We are fine, my lord."

"As is obvious, but I owe you for this morning's information."

"Unnecessary. Anyone would have done the same."

"But you are the one who detected Harold's plot. That information likely saved my life." He glanced at the girls clinging to her skirts, estimating their ages as approaching three and five. Heflin must have got her with child immediately. Imagining the man forcing himself on her ignited new fury, but he kept his face pleasant. "Would you introduce me?"

Sarah sensed his anger, hesitating before she turned them to face him. "This is Lord Northcote, girls. My daughters Alice" —she nodded to the elder— "and Emily."

Alex bowed. "Good morning. Are you finding good branches?"

Alice peeped through her lashes, then shook her head. "The good ones are all too high."

Sarah seemed mortified, but Alex laughed. "That is usually the case, but I can fix that."

"How?"

"Shoulders." He swept her onto his, drawing a squeal. A glance verified that it rose from delight, not terror, so he moved closer to a tree. That the girls did not fear men proved Sarah had protected them from Heflin, reducing the fences he had to clear to win her.

"Look, Mama! I can reach!" Alice grabbed a high branch and giggled.

"You don't need—"

He cut off Sarah's protest. "You help Emily," he suggested, edging farther into the fir. He waited until she'd accepted his presence, then added, "Do you recall the year it snowed so hard we could barely see?"

She smiled, as he'd intended. "How could I forget? Papa was shocked to discover that we'd wandered into your grove instead of our own." The two groves adjoined each other where the estates touched.

"Not that we could object. I suspect we gathered as much from your trees as you got from ours." He glanced across the boundary. "I'm surprised Norbert isn't out by now."

"He won't come. Despite Caroline's demands, he refused to host a house party—proof of how grim he's grown. We did no decorating last year, either."

Conscious of Alice taking in every word, he dropped the subject. Perhaps Norbert deserved Caroline. "What a fun treat, then," he said to Alice, boosting her higher. "I missed Christmas while I was away. Spain has different traditions."

"How different?"

"The center is a hot, dusty plain, so no snow, of course. I wish we had some this year. Nothing compares to sledding."

"Even when you can't steer straight?" Sarah giggled, sending warmth down his spine. "How many times did you land us in a drift?"

Often, and deliberately. He grinned. "Are you maligning my skill?"

"That would be rude."

"Not as rude as tricking me out of the sleigh, then driving off without me."

Sarah blushed.

Alex turned his attention to Alice. "Can you reach that branch with the two cones?"

"Oof!" She struggled with the shears. "Got it!"

"Good job, sweetheart. Shall we try some holly? The branches are easier to cut, but the thorns can scratch."

"Yes, please."

He moved a dozen yards away, leaving Sarah to decide whether to follow or to trust him with her daughter. He could feel her eyes on his back as he adjusted his gloves over Alice's hands.

Sarah compromised by tackling an adjacent tree, wrapping her hands around Emily's. Alex smiled. Heflin's family apparently didn't want the girls, which was good. He enjoyed children, and hers were delightful.

Alice rapidly lost all shyness. She bounced on his shoulder when she spotted a bird's nest and joined in the singing when someone began a carol.

Sarah remained wary, though he could feel memories of past Christmases parading through her mind. Reminding her of their shared experiences was easing her fears. He could see no evidence that the essential Sarah had changed, so she would make an excellent wife once she relearned trust. Proving that her girls were safe with him was a good start.

As the piles of greenery grew, Sarah relaxed enough to help haul them to the wagon a hundred feet away, leaving Alice behind. And when he moved out of sight around the holly tree to find better clumps of berries, she didn't immediately follow, bringing a glow to his heart.

"How's the view from up there?" he asked Alice.

"Annie has mud on her bonnet." She giggled.

He glanced at the nearest girl. "You have good eyes."

"And William isn't helping," she added, pointing to a ten-year-old who was poking a stick into a pile of leaves.

"But you are doing a wonderful job. Can you reach that branch with three clumps of berries?"

"Uh-huh. Look, Mama!" She leaned forward as Sarah rounded the tree. "I got it!"

"Careful!" When the branch landed on his head, Sarah gasped, then stifled another giggle.

"No harm done." Alex refrained from rubbing the scratches as he untangled the branch from his hair. He'd suffered worse injuries, and anything that made Sarah smile was worth it.

Sarah finally accepted that Alex intended to stay with her—and who could blame him, with girls like Miss Field lurking nearby. The crowd was turning boisterous, with squeals and laughter rippling through the grove. Bits of mistletoe made the rounds. More than one couple emerged from behind trees wearing expressions of sly satisfaction.

What did surprise her was Alice's response to his attention. His fierce appearance didn't bother the girl at all.

She had to admit that working with him felt quite like old times. They had shared many holiday festivities. Despite that unexplained burst of anger when he'd joined them, he seemed softer today. This was the youthful Alex. Kind. Caring. Focused on others rather than himself, just as he'd been with Harbaugh. Perhaps war hadn't changed him entirely.

The nostalgic warmth accompanied her back indoors, where the ladies gathered to turn the mountain of greens into ropes, swags, and kissing boughs. The dowager was determined to decorate the entire house and had enough helpers to accomplish her goal.

Songs, stories, laughter, and the scent of freshly cut pine recalled the Christmases of Sarah's childhood. Alex had figured strongly in those celebrations, for Manor events included the entire neighborhood. For the first time, she admitted how much she'd missed those days. After Alex left, the Manor had turned gloomy, casting a pall across the entire area. Heflin never celebrated anything, adding to the dreariness of those years. And Norbert wasn't much better, having espoused even more rectitude and parsimony than their father. But Alex was finally home, and Christmas again burst with good cheer.

Her heart whispered that his attentions meant she could embrace the love she'd locked away, but she could not afford to listen. Never again would she place her happiness or the girls' safety in the hands of another. Men displayed different façades in public than they did in private. Even Heflin could be charming when he chose. And Alex was often selfish, especially the summer before he'd bought colors. Despite his vow to cherish her forever, he'd left the next morning for a series of house parties. Then he'd run off to play soldier, leaving her at the mercy of scoundrels like Heflin. So she could trust only herself.

Alex's Uncle Henry interrupted her memories. "Good job, Miss Sarah," he said, patting the rope she'd just finished.

"Mrs. Heflin," she corrected automatically.

"No need to use that name. The man was a rotter, begging your pardon. Why remind people you once had a connection to him?"

She looked him in the eye. "My children carry that name."

He shrugged. "It doesn't matter. You needn't pay for his mistakes. Your guidance will keep the girls on the right path."

An attractive thought, but it meant little. "Will you be staying with your brother for a time?" she asked in a blatant change of topic. "He is still occasionally lucid."

He frowned. "No. Much as I cared for Charles, he is no longer with us. Even his supposed lucidity is a sham, for he thinks we remain in the schoolroom. Sometimes the mind dies before the body. He could pass on tomorrow or linger for years. There is no point in ignoring my own affairs."

Proving that selfishness was a family trait. "True. But losing two brothers so close together must be sad."

"Very, but it's been six months. Time to concentrate on the living. Grace seems remarkably better," he added, naming Alex's mother. "Where will you go next?"

"I am considering possibilities."

"Excellent! Someone mentioned a post in the Lake District with a sweet lady who loves children. I'll let you know if it remains open." He rose, collecting the rope. "Time to return to work. This goes on the main stairs."

She started a new rope, though her mind was no longer tranquil. Henry might acquit her of Heflin's crimes, but he did not want Heflin's widow under his nephew's roof, especially after Alex had ignored duty all morning to dance attendance on a childhood playmate. She was now a companion, barred from rejoining the society she had only briefly entered. And her station had been far below his to begin with.

Alex's attention had revived old dreams, she admitted. But the past was dead. She should never have accepted him, for he had been far too young to settle down—as her father had repeatedly pointed out on that trip home. To protect her heart from further damage, she had to avoid him. Selfish men rarely looked beyond the desire of the moment, so succumbing to nostalgia could trap her in another intolerable marriage. And it would endanger the girls. He might smile on them now, but how would he treat them once he produced children of his own blood?

The need to escape became even more urgent when the dowager began sending guests to ask Sarah about the decorating. Should they put a kissing bough in the morning room? What should be installed in the dining room? Should they hang ropes on the terrace outside the ballroom?

The dowager wanted Alex wed, the sooner the better. She must have interpreted his attentions to Alice as a renewed interest in Sarah, just as Henry had. But unlike the worldly Henry, the dowager would accept anyone to cut out Harold, so her support meant nothing.

Thus it remained imperative for Sarah to leave, yet she couldn't return to Potter House. Norbert believed her presence kept memories of their father's suicide in the forefront of his neighbors' minds. Caroline was increasing, which seemed to intensify her antagonism. Sarah couldn't count on Henry's nebulous post, which might well be filled by now, so her best option was to throw herself on the mercy of her Great-aunt Beatrice.

In the meantime, she would make the girls' Christmas as happy as possible.

Squeals marked the raising of a kissing bough. Laughter followed the testing of another. Smiling at youthful innocence, Sarah returned to work.

Sarah retired from the revelries as soon as Alex lit the Yule log, refusing to stay for wassail. For years, she had dreamed of standing beside him at gatherings like this. The pain of losing those dreams made watching impossible. This wasn't a night when sleep would come easily, so she headed for the library to find a book.

She was debating between *Marmion* and *Waverly* when Alex and Harold entered. She automatically slipped behind a screen to prevent discovery, then cursed herself. Alex would never object if she borrowed his books, but revealing herself after she'd hidden would be embarrassing for everyone.

"Have you made a decision?" Alex asked.

Sarah peered through a crack in the screen.

His back to the room, Harold stared into the inky night. "There is a fifth alternative. Father owns a small plantation in Jamaica that has never made a shilling in profit. He tried to sell it several times, but with its financial history, no one in England wants it. Someone needs to investigate its problems, so why not me? Perhaps I can make something of it, or maybe a neighbor will buy the land to expand his own operation."

"The voyage will be expensive. Since Cummings refuses to speak with you, how do you plan to finance it?"

They must be discussing Harold's punishment, Sarah realized, frowning. Heflin would have already settled the matter with fists or worse, but Alex sounded accommodating.

Harold sighed. "I believe he will advance me passage money once I've explained my purpose. He and Father agreed last spring that the steward's reports are suspicious. At the very least, I can find out what the place is worth."

"I can read your thoughts well enough." Temper threaded Alex's voice. "Instead of avoiding cards, you hope that leaving the country will mask your activities. Selling the estate will provide a stake to finance new games. And if you remain away until your father dies, you expect to escape any penalty."

Harold swung around. "Why not? Cummings insists that Father will recover, so he refuses to discuss anything with me, even though it will all be mine soon. You know Father can barely swallow what his nurse pokes into his mouth. He can't last much longer."

"He could linger for years. Inactivity does not require much sustenance. And I will not forget your crimes no matter where you go. Your only hope of a decent future is to reform. If you continue down this path you will lose every penny of your inheritance within a year of your father's death, landing you in the Marshalsea. Then what will you do?"

Harold stared stonily ahead.

"Reform requires effort," Alex continued. "Determined effort. The first step is to admit that your obsession will not disappear. Ever. You must stay away from gaming permanently. It is a habit that returns in force the minute you indulge. Even a friendly game of loo with penny stakes would send you into an orgy of betting. Especially if you combine it with wine."

Harold paled.

"Exactly. Do not convince yourself otherwise. I've seen enough gamesters in the military to know how insidious the obsession can be. Do you have the determination to succeed?"

"I—" He coughed. "I believe so."

"Time will tell. It might be easier to pursue that heiress, for her father would help keep you away from cards." He shook his head. "But I will agree to your option on two conditions. First, Cummings must confirm his willingness to appoint you as your father's representative. He may well refuse."

Harold nodded.

"Taking my own man of business with you when you visit his office will assure that he at least listens to your proposal."

Another nod, accompanied by a flash of irritation. Sarah could almost hear Alex's thoughts. If Harold had planned to forge the confirmation letter, he was not yet committed to reform.

"Second, you will sign two papers before you leave this house. The first is a promissory note for the full amount you owe me—not a gaming vowel, but a note enforceable under law that I can present to your father's executors after his death. The debt will be paid before his estate goes to you. The second is a full confession to theft and attempted murder. If you fail to change your ways, I will turn it over to a magistrate, along with all proofs. There will be no second chance."

Another flash of irritation, followed by slumping shoulders. "I understand."

"Very well. And in case you think to indulge in cards in Jamaica or sell the estate without informing Cummings, I have friends there who will be watching. I will hear how you go on."

Sarah remained long after the men left. Alex's compassion stunned her. She could understand his gentleness with Harbaugh, who was both cousin and valued employee, but Harold? A thief and would-be killer? A man who had hated Alex since childhood? Alex truly wanted to help Harold defeat his vices.

Her heart soared.

Chapter Seven

Alex paused outside the door of Sarah's daughters' room, uncertain of his welcome. He'd already spent time with his mother and grandmother this Christmas morning. Then he'd dug through an attic, unearthing a doll and a wheeled wooden duck. Now he had to convince Sarah to accept his gifts. He rapped sharply.

"Enter."

"Happy Christmas." He slipped the toys behind a chair just inside the door.

"And to you, my lord," said Sarah.

He turned to Alice. "Are you enjoying this lovely morning?"

"Uh-huh. Mama gave me a book!" She held up the volume. "She is teaching me to read it all by myself."

"A very useful skill. What did she give you, Emily?"

She held up a picture book, then shyly ducked her head.

"Is one of the pictures a dog?" He squatted to bring his eyes to her level.

"Dog?" Emily frowned, turning pages. Alice moved to help her.

Alex leaned close to Sarah, whispering in her ear. "I brought gifts for the girls, if you will permit it." When she raised a hand in protest, he continued. "They have been in an attic since my aunt was a child. I would be delighted if someone could enjoy them."

She finally nodded. "Very well. But I am merely a companion, so don't confuse them."

"You have been a dear friend since we were children. Your present occupation does not change that." He straightened as Emily laughed.

"Doggie," she exclaimed, holding up the print. Then she frowned. "But it doesn't look like Timothy."

Alex laughed. "That's because Timothy was a scrappy little terrier." He met Sarah's eyes, recalling the dog she'd rescued at age eight. They'd shared many adventures over the years. He tapped the page. "This one is a hound. He chases foxes away so they don't steal chickens."

"What this?" she demanded, pointing to a print of an arrogant goose.

Alex sat, lifting her into his lap so they could enjoy the book together. Alice crowded closer as he named each animal, then described its use. Pangs smote his heart, for these should have been his children. They would have been his if he had not fled that last battle with his father.

He concocted a tale about the cat with a mouse hanging from its jaw, drawing giggles. His story of how the spotted pony rescued a sheep from a flooded river made Sarah giggle, too, raising his spirits.

When the book was finished, he hugged both girls, then rose to fetch his gifts.

"For me?" Alice's eyes nearly popped from her head. "Are you sure?"

"Very sure."

"Thank you, sir." She curtsied, then ran to show her mother.

Emily stretched a finger to touch the duck. He handed her the string. "Pull gently."

The wheels were not quite round, so the duck wobbled as it moved across the floor, making a clacking sound similar to a quack.

Emily laughed. "Funny duckie." She pulled it again, then ran in a circle. "Look, Mama!"

Sarah smiled. "It waddles."

The girls raced around the room, quacking. Sarah turned to Alex. "Thank you for thinking of them."

"They are wonderful children, Sarah. A testament to you."

"Thank you."

"I will expect them at the children's party this afternoon."

"That might not—"

"Everyone in the neighborhood is invited, including tenants and the innkeeper's son. Surely your girls should join them."

"Very well."

He pulled a package from his pocket and laid it in her hand. "For you." When she would have pulled away, he gripped her fingers. "For you. You remain special, my dear. Happy Christmas."

Sarah stiffened, fighting the heat that radiated from his hand—neither wore gloves, so his touch was incendiary. If only terror would return to banish the feeling, but she trusted his decency despite the horrors he must have experienced. He still cared for others, still paid attention to even the least of those around him. It made remaining aloof harder. But she must.

Retrieving her hand, she opened the gift. Half a dozen handkerchiefs embroidered with an S nestled in the wrapping. How had he found something so quickly?

"They are beautiful." She couldn't keep the amazement out of her voice.

"So I hoped. I bought them in London that last summer, intending to present them on your eighteenth birthday. But in my haste to escape Father's wrath, I left them behind. So, I am delighted that I can finally put them in your hand."

She raised her eyes to his, then became trapped in his gaze. There was heat, but no hint of cruelty. Gray eyes twinkled, their iciness gone. Did he still care?

She lightly touched his arm in a gesture from before, fighting to ignore the heat. "Thank you, Alex. I will treasure them." Tucking them into a pocket, she turned to watch the girls. "Thank you for everything," she added. "We will enjoy the children's party."

"And you will attend the ball this evening?"

"I will consider it."

Sarah led a laughing Alice and Emily to one of the snapdragon tables. Nearly fifty children had come to celebrate Christmas. It was the largest children's party in a generation.

Alex had helped with many of the games, from three-legged races for the older children to hopping contests for the younger ones, but he'd spent more time with Alice's group than any other. Sarah strengthened the walls around her heart. Her imminent departure made the party bittersweet.

A shout rose as an army of footmen entered carrying snapdragon bowls already aflame. Raisins, prunes, and other dried fruits glistened.

"Be quick," she reminded Alice, then demonstrated the technique by snapping up a raisin for Emily. A quick pinch put out the fire, leaving a juicy treat. "Take only the small fruits," she added. "Your hand is little, so snapping up a prune will burn your fingers." A wail from one of the boys proved her words.

Alice hesitated, watching the other children. But the fruit was disappearing fast. She finally inhaled, then snatched a raisin.

"I did it!" She bounced in her seat.

"So you did," said Alex from behind her. He snatched another for Emily. "Try a cherry."

Alice's hand again dove into the flames, this time emerging with a cherry. "Mmm. Good."

Sarah grabbed another raisin for Emily, then shook her head as Alex stuffed a prune into his mouth. "This is a children's party," she reminded him. "Do not eat their treats."

"That rule needs to change." But he gave the next prune to Alice.

"There are few enough activities for the children. We cannot usurp them."

"You are right, of course." Giving the last prune to Emily, he moved on to speak with a neighbor.

Sarah thanked the dowager for including them, then shepherded the girls upstairs to collect their wraps for ice skating. The afternoon was the happiest she'd enjoyed since Alex left. The laughter drove dark spirits into hiding. And watching the girls abandon their shyness infused her with warmth. The skating party would be another delight.

Not so the ball. A companion would be the lowest ranking person present. And she had no wish to confront Caroline and Norbert, for neither would condone her presence. Caroline would create an embarrassing scene. But she would not spoil the skating by worrying about the evening.

The day had gone well so far, decided Alex. Sarah's girls were delightful.

But unease engulfed him as he scanned the crowd filling the skating cove. Since he'd had no hand in sending the invitations, he hadn't realized how many neighbors were included. Even many who had skipped the children's party were present—more than a hundred, counting the guests. Cards and indoor games might have been better, for it had only been truly freezing for a week and a stream ran through the lake, keeping the ice thin in too many places.

He had already ordered grooms to pull the boundary markers farther from the current. Three men had grumbled, but he refused to relent. Despite a long absence, he still knew where the ice would be dangerous for a crowd of this size. And there remained plenty of space even if the skating cove did now resemble a sausage more than a circle.

The other preparations were excellent. There was a fire where a kitchen maid was making chocolate, benches and chairs for observers, and enough skates for everyone.

His feet itched to try the ice, but there were people he'd yet to greet and his grandmother's protégées to avoid. He'd paired the most flirtatious with young cousins.

Sarah was instructing her girls in the art of skating. Other children slipped and slid nearby, marking that end as a beginner's area. He longed to join her. If he helped Alice, Sarah could concentrate on

Emily. But duty called.

As the new viscount, he spent the next hour renewing acquaintance with neighbors he'd last seen in his youth. They presented new spouses, related births and deaths, and filled his head with area gossip. Even incidents reported in his mother's letters seemed different when described by participants.

He kept one eye on the crowd to make sure no one courted danger. Thus he saw the collision that knocked Miss Billington to the ice, triggering hysteria over a ripped gown. Irritation crossed most faces, changing to relief when her mother hustled her back to the house.

Miss Harper flirted with his cousin Nigel, who seemed more than a little interested—they'd gathered greens together, too.

His cousin Derrick was entertaining several dazzled ladies with fancy leaps and spins, having honed his already excellent skill during Alex's absence. Even Miss Norton seemed intrigued. After verifying that Derrick was inside the boundary markers, Alex turned to the next arrivals—Norbert and Caroline.

"Welcome to Northcote Manor." He extended a hand to Norbert, then bowed to Caroline, who backed a pace.

"Huge party this year," said Norbert.

"A convenient way to announce my return."

Caroline glared toward Sarah. "You should be careful about who you include. Some people don't know their place. We have a duty to maintain proper boundaries between the classes."

"To whom do you refer?" Ice coated his voice. If she was so concerned about boundaries, why had she married a man with far better breeding than her own?

"As if you didn't know. Her own husband disclosed her reprehensible behavior. He had to lock her up to control her proclivities. An honorable officer would cleanse his house of contamination." Her voice grew shrill as indignation conquered social sense.

"Caroline," hissed Norbert. "Remember where you are."

"How could I forget?" She scowled at Alex. "You must accept the truth. That woman is a pariah and must be driven away."

Alex kept his voice soft, but employed the tone he'd used to instill terror into hardened soldiers. "It is you who are becoming a pariah, madam."

She blanched.

"That woman, as you call her, has done nothing to draw censure. I know her story, as you obviously do not. If you believe lies spread by a villain to hide his own villainy, then you are more reprehensible than you think her. You will keep your tongue between your teeth while you are a guest on my land, and if you attack her elsewhere, I will see you drummed out of local society. Permanently. Is that clear?"

"But—"

"No buts. I am told that you are a dour, judgmental woman, which your own vitriol confirms. You married well above your station, so citing class boundaries is absurd. If you wish to be accepted by those you try to emulate, then sweeten your ways. Start by seeking three good things about everyone you meet. And the next time you meet them, look for three more."

Turning away in a deliberate cut, he skated in Sarah's direction, determined to demonstrate that she was welcome in his house. But he'd barely traveled twenty feet when her voice pierced the crowd's chatter.

"I said no! I am tending my children and have no desire to skate with others."

"No need to play coy. One turn around the lake will do you good. Someone else can watch your brats."

"No!"

Alex emerged from the crowd as a hulking man grabbed her arm. Sarah blanched.

"The lady said no," Alex growled, removing the hand, then swinging him around so they faced each other.

"Who the devil are you?" he demanded. "If you want a turn, you can wait until I'm done with her."

"You are done now." A glance confirmed that Sarah's color was returning. "Who is this lout?"

"George Parkins, the miller's son."

George was obviously foxed. "In case you haven't figured it out, I am your host. I don't countenance anyone annoying my guests."

"She's no guest. She's a whore who cozzened folks into accepting her as a servant."

Sarah gasped.

"I can hear Mrs. Potter swearing just that, but you are both wrong." Alex shook him. "Mrs. Heflin is a lady and a guest in my home. You are not welcome and will leave. Now. This is no place for drunken cads."

Alex's tone closed George's mouth on another protest. Perhaps he was less drunk than he appeared. His belligerence drained as he trudged toward shore. Alex signaled a groom to make sure he kept going, then turned back to Sarah.

"My apologies for his impertinence. Are you all right?"

"Of course." She stopped rubbing her arm when he glanced at it. "I am not his first victim, though he is rarely this bad."

"Has he accosted you before?"

"Not recently. He was annoying the innkeeper's daughter the last I heard. And the chandler's wife before that. Everyone in the village despises him." She sighed. "Thank you for sending him away."

"I must protect the district from further distress." He wondered how George would enjoy the navy. "How do the girls like skating?"

She relaxed. "They love it. This is the first time they've been on ice. It is something they will remember for a long time."

"They are welcome to skate anytime. The ice will likely be here for weeks."

"But—"

Emily fell with a loud "Ooomph," diverting her attention. She was unharmed, but—

Sarah twisted in a circle. "Alice? Alice! Where are you?"

A child's scream rent the air.

Shouts followed.

Scooping Emily into his arms, Alex took off toward the sounds.

Sarah could barely breathe through her terror, but she stayed with Alex. They broke through the crowd gathered at a boundary marker to see a hole in the ice twenty feet beyond. Alice's head bobbed in the water.

"Alice!" She sprang forward.

Alex grabbed her, thrusting Emily into her arms. "Pull yourself together, Sarah."

Air shuddered from her lungs.

"Everyone off the ice. Now!" Alex's order sent the guests scurrying to shore. "Derrick, stay," he added, tearing off his greatcoat.

"What—"

"I'll get her, Sarah. You and Emily stay with Derrick. We can't risk too much weight out there."

She nodded.

Alice's screams changed to sobs.

"Catch the edge of the ice with your hand, Alice," Alex crooned as he crept forward. She was bobbing next to the hole's edge, partially supported by an angled slab. If she slipped off . . .

"C-can't."

"Yes, you can." He lay on the ice, arms and legs spread to distribute his weight across more surface, then inched closer. "Grab the edge and hang on. It's closer than that fat branch you cut yesterday, and it will keep you from sinking."

His reassurance worked. Alice grasped a point on the uneven edge, keeping hold even as her bare hand tried to flinch away from the cold.

Sarah bit her tongue to stay silent. Where was Alice's mitten?

"Good girl," crooned Alex. "You are floating now, just like a duck." He quacked, drawing a feeble smile. "Now stretch your free hand toward mine." He reached forward.

"T-too c-cold."

"Do it, darling. Remember this morning's story? I'm the spotted pony, and you are the sheep—except I promise I won't use my teeth."

She laughed.

"Good girl. Grip the ice hard, then stretch toward me." He moved another inch, pausing when the ice groaned.

Sarah held her breath, fighting the urge to order Alice to obey. Distracting her could prove fatal. Distracting Alex could dump him in the water, too.

"Almost, Alice, dear. Can you move your feet?"

She nodded.

"Good. I can't come closer, but if you kick hard, you will reach me."

"C-can't."

"You can. The sheep had to help the pony. Remember? We'll work together. Now! Kick!" His voice lashed the air.

Alice lunged upward a few inches. He stretched far enough to grab her hand. Even with the added weight of her drenched coat and skirts, he whipped her from the lake without catching her feet on the slab that bobbed up with her, then twisted her against his side and tried to push himself back.

The ice moaned. A crack appeared at the edge of the hole, arrowing toward Alex. He pulled his hands back to lessen the stress on the ice, but without leverage, he could not move.

"I'll get them," said Derrick.

Sarah grabbed him. "You're too heavy." She pushed Emily into his arms then stepped over the board.

Keeping Alex between her and the steadily growing crack, she crept closer, then eased onto her stomach and stretched until she could reach his boot—

—and tugged.

He moved a few inches, but the crack grew a foot, reaching greedy fingers toward its target.

"Got you," said Derrick, hauling on Sarah's foot to drag them all to safety. He'd given Emily to Nigel on shore.

"Are you all right?" she demanded the moment Alex rose.

"We both are, but we need warmth." He wrapped his greatcoat around Alice, whose teeth chattered hard behind blue lips. Water from her dripping clothes drenched his service uniform.

Sarah scooped up Emily, then followed him to the house, cursing. That Alex would risk his life for another proved he hadn't changed. Love flooded her, warming her with memories.

Pain quickly followed, for she *had* changed. She could not risk another marriage. If anything went wrong, the girls would suffer. And disaster was all too likely. Alex must produce an heir. She'd birthed only girls. Heflin's fury at each failure had exploded into violent beatings, the second one nearly killing her. She didn't think Alex was violent, but what if he favored his own children over hers? Even a subtle withdrawal of affection could prove devastating. To protect them all, she must write to Beatrice immediately, then follow the letter and pray Beatrice would welcome them.

A tub of hot water waited near the kitchen. Alex thrust Alice in, clothes and all.

"She all right?" asked Emily, eyes wide as she watched her sister.

"Of course." He smiled. "She is cold and wet and must remain in bed with a hot brick for the rest of the day, but she will be fine. If you go with Nancy" —he nodded at a maid— "you can watch them prepare Alice's bed. She will be up shortly."

Emily left.

Sarah removed Alice's sodden coat, then halted before attacking her gown. "You also need to change, Alex. Thank you for rescuing her. I've no idea how she got out there."

"Two active children rarely stay side by side. With you distracted by George, it is no surprise that you didn't notice her wander off. I'm grateful she suffered no worse." He shuddered. "I've seen men drown when they fell into cold water. But she wasn't in long enough to suffer permanent damage."

"In North America?"

"Spain. The running battle last winter crossed mountains, with all the attendant snow and ice. It was not a pleasant time." He headed for the door.

Sarah was curious about his experiences, but her immediate concern was Alice. Once the girl was warm and dry, she carried her to the nursery to find a dry Alex waiting.

"Thank you, again, Alex. I will never forget the fast action that saved Alice's life."

"It was nothing."

"It was, but I won't belabor the point. Everything is under control here, so you can return to your guests."

"I have already spoken to everyone necessary." His glare stopped further objections.

Sarah turned to Alice. "What do you say to Lord Northcote?"

"Thank you, my lord."

"How did you get way out there?" she asked, keeping her voice merely curious.

"Someone bumped me, but I stayed on my feet." She smiled, pleased with this accomplishment. "Then I saw a pretty bird. I tried to creep closer without scaring it."

"Did you see the boundary markers?" asked Alex, also keeping his voice light.

"What's a marker?"

"Boards. They mark the edge of the safe ice."

Alice frowned. "There was one by the stream, but I didn't go that way. Mama told me to stay close."

"Did you?"

She tucked her chin against her chest so her eyes no longer met his. "No, sir. When I saw the bird, I forgot."

"Do you understand why you must always remember?" asked Sarah.

"Yes, Mama. That was awful cold."

Alex tucked her new doll into bed with her, then rose. "Leave her for now," he murmured when Sarah started to take his seat. "Nancy will watch them. We need to talk."

She followed him to the library.

"I owe you another apology," he began, wandering to the window to peer outside. The last skaters were straggling back to the house. "I should have marked the boundaries better."

"Hardly. The safe ice was clear. It is not your fault she wandered off. I should have kept a closer eye on her."

He sighed. "You did nothing wrong, Sarah. Perhaps we should

accept that accidents happen. At least no one was badly injured."

"You mentioned a running battle. What happened to raise that note of horror when you spoke of it?"

He bit off what he was going to say, then took the chair behind the desk. His sigh broke the silence. "The mountains between Spain and France are high enough to attract snow and ice. There are no real roads, just occasional paths. And lots of streams. Most of them were shallow enough to cross safely, but one was deeper than expected. A horse broke through the ice, dumping his rider in the water. Within moments three others suffered similar fates. The current was so fast that two of the men were sucked downstream. We never found their bodies. We managed to fish out the other two, but one died of exposure. Two horses also died. It was not a pleasant day."

"I can imagine. War is not just occasional battles, is it."

"No. We could never relax. A French patrol might be waiting around any corner. And we were always outnumbered. Only Wellington's genius brought us through victorious. The American conflict lacks that advantage. I greatly fear we will lose that one."

"It is beyond your control, Alex," she said, laying her hand on his in comfort. "Whatever happens in America, your life now lies here."

"True." He squeezed her fingers.

Heat spread up her arm. Knowing her love was futile, she gently retrieved her hand and headed for the door. "I need to check on Alice."

"You will attend the ball?"

"It depends." So saying, she slipped up the servant stairs to avoid encountering other guests. Memories of the afternoon swirled confusion through her head. George's touch had incited the usual terror, made worse because the girls were at hand to witness whatever he chose to do. But Alex's prompt intervention brought relief. And she'd hardly noticed Derrick grabbing her foot. Terror for Alice and Alex had driven other fears away.

You know who is safe, whispered Temptation.

"No." She could not pursue a course that might harm her girls, no matter how promising it might appear to her.

Chapter Eight

Sarah stayed in the nursery for the rest of the day, helping Alice sound out the words in her book and laughing at Emily's antics. Alex had been right that Alice had taken no harm, but she felt better staying with her.

She had just finished tucking her in for the night when Norbert summoned her.

What the devil does he want?

She was in no position to deny him. As head of the family, he could order Great-aunt Beatrice to refuse her request. So she followed the footman to the morning room, which was empty of all but Norbert.

"What did Caroline do to you now?" he demanded before she even closed the door.

She stared. "What are you talking about? I haven't spoken to Caroline in months."

"She must have done something to drive you from dinner. I know you were invited."

"Norbert!" She glared. "I stayed with the girls, of course. Surely you know about Alice's accident."

"Of course. But that's what servants are for. Spending every waking moment with those brats is vulgar behavior that shames the family."

Sarah drew in several deep breaths. He had always been overbearing, but his rigidity now surpassed their father's. When she could speak without throttling him, she settled into a chair, forcing him to do the same. "The point in keeping the girls with me is to spend time with them." When he tried to protest, she cut him off. "Also, I am a companion, so duty makes its own demands." She refused to mention that Lady Northcote had excused her from those duties for Christmas.

"Caroline is right. I should never have allowed you to take a servant's post," he spat. "It tarnishes the entire family. I'm still paying for Papa's crimes. Your behavior convinces people that I can't support you."

"Only because you invite such conclusions by moaning over my choices and Papa's death to everyone you meet to distract them from recalling how Caroline trapped you."

"Leave my marriage out of this. It is you who keep scandal alive.

Everyone knows your actions killed Papa."

Norbert's anger wasn't unexpected, though he'd never laid his hatred out so clearly.

"Argument is useless," she said calmly. Especially with someone whose mind was nailed shut. "But you can relax, for I will be leaving soon. Lady Northcote has recovered from the debilitating grief she suffered immediately after her husband's death, so it is time I move on. But I also need the girls to remain with me, so—"

"Heflin's family should look after them."

"Never." Heflin was actually one of the better members of that family. His cousin the baron was far worse.

"We will discuss this later," Norbert decided. "I will be delighted to see the last of you, but if you leave before it is clear that Caroline did not drive you off, Northcote will drum us out of society."

They argued for another quarter hour, but Norbert remained adamant. He wanted her gone, but Alex's threats meant she had to stay.

By the time she headed for her room, Sarah was as furious at Alex as she was at Norbert. He had actually threatened her family with social censure. Not that they didn't deserve it, but their behavior was not his business. The power of his title was going to his head, making her departure even more urgent. No matter how much she wanted to trust Alex—no matter how much she *did* trust him—he was still a man capable of high-handed, controlling behavior when in a temper. A man whose title gave him the power to impose his will on others with impunity. Her daughters deserved better.

Alex avoided the protégées by passing the first hour of the ball with neighbors who had not attended the afternoon activities. But Sarah still wasn't there when he ran out of obligatory greetings.

He could understand her dining with the girls. She was an attentive mother. But they would be asleep by now. There was no reason to skip the ball, too. But she apparently was. Every time he thought he was making progress, she erected a new barricade.

Taking advantage of Miss Billington's hysteria over a torn flounce, he slipped away without drawing notice. The girl was occasionally useful.

The girls' room contained two slumbering forms but no Sarah. He doubted that she would be with his mother.

He found her in her room, writing a letter.

"What are you doing here?" he demanded. "You are supposed to be downstairs."

She shrugged. "I have nothing suitable to wear and don't wish to attend, in any case." She turned the letter face down, but not before he'd read enough to know that she was planning to leave.

Fury engulfed him so fast he couldn't control it. And fear. He slammed a fist onto the letter. "You cannot leave. I won't allow it!"

Sarah cringed, but instead of retreating, she held her ground. "I am not your slave, sir. Nor am I your dependent. I work for your mother, but she no longer needs me. Your safe return has lifted much of her remaining melancholia. While she will remain in mourning for some months, she can function perfectly well on her own. It is time I moved on."

"No."

"Yes." She glared. "You may be a lord, but you are not responsible for everyone in Staffordshire. It was arrogant of you to threaten Caroline with censure just because she disparaged me."

"How do you know about that?"

"Norbert is so terrified of both of you that he rang a peal over my head when he discovered my plans. You are both being ridiculous."

"You didn't hear what she said."

"I don't need to. I expect she repeated the lies Heflin used to keep my prudish family from checking on me. But acting the self-righteous prig hurts her far more than me, for everyone knows she criticizes me to make herself seem purer. She will mellow only when she feels secure in her position—perhaps after producing an heir. But she is not your problem. Your threats are as childish and pointless as hers, and they give her a valid grievance. She will be bashing you for years, and your long absence means many will believe her. They no longer know you."

He sighed. "You are right. I should not have threatened her. I never meant to follow through. I just wanted to give her something to ponder in hopes she would become a little more tolerant."

"But that is not the effect you achieved. Enough, Alex. Go back to your guests. I will be gone next week."

Fear choked him. "Don't go. I need you here."

"Your mother—"

"Not to keep my mother company. *I* need you. Nothing has changed. You are still the only one I can envision as my wife." He held his breath, hoping he wasn't playing that card too soon.

"My course is set, as is yours. Yes, you must wed, for only an heir will control Harold. So go downstairs and consider your options. If none of those girls suits, then spend the Season in London. I am no longer available."

"Nor am I. My heart remains yours, Sarah. You've held it since you were fifteen."

She backed away, shaking her head. "No, Alex." She sounded weary rather than afraid, which gave him hope. "You love your memory of me, but that girl died years ago."

"You may have buried her, but she still lives. Neither of us has changed at the core." He pointed at his scarred face. "The world may have battered me and made you wary, but our essence remains the same."

"Don't torture me like this." She put the bed between them.

Torture? "Love is not torture, Sarah."

"It can be."

"No. A love that tortures is false. Do you still care?"

"I can't."

"That makes no sense. You cannot control love."

"But love is not enough."

His heart soared, for she had to still love him.

"I swore I would never again place myself at the mercy of a man. Any man. I swore to protect my daughters, no matter what it took. I will not break those vows."

"Men have treated you badly," he agreed, feeling his way through this new maze. "In a childish rage, I left you unprotected. Your father's weakness forced you into a distasteful marriage. Your brother is even weaker, falling prey to a harpy. And your husband was a brute. But do not confuse me with Heflin. I will never hurt you or your daughters. Protecting them will be easier if we work together."

"So you say, but soldiers must employ brutality and deceit. Even non-soldiers nourish deceit. I've watched men lie and cheat to achieve even insignificant goals."

"Heflin's relatives, I'd wager. If he kept you in the country, you wouldn't see anyone else."

She bit her lip in sudden indecision.

He pressed his advantage. "Surely you met honorable men in London."

"So they seemed, but so Heflin seemed in Town."

He ran his fingers through his hair in frustration. "Open your mind, Sarah. You've always been good at sensing the reality beyond social façades," he reminded her.

"Not really," she protested. "With people I know well, perhaps.

But London's social masks are too solid, hiding both character and interests. The only reason I found Heflin uncomfortable was his incessant compliments."

Years under Heflin's thumb would have eroded her confidence, he reminded himself. "Did anyone else make you nervous?"

She frowned, shaking her head. "No, but—"

"No buts. You knew the others were safe despite their social masks. And I'd wager you also donned a mask in Town. Did you reveal your fine mind or your sense of humor?" She could make any situation seem hilarious.

She shook her head.

"Did you reveal how you rescued injured animals or taught tenants to read or harangued my father because he refused to subsidize a decent doctor, leaving people at the mercy of Masters?"

"No, but—"

"No buts," he repeated, sensing that he was making progress but unwilling to let her thoughts stray. "The London marriage mart—which I have visited more than once—rarely allows serious discussion. Stimulating conversation that reveals character exists, but not in venues your father would have condoned."

"True." She grimaced. "My grandmother often criticized his restrictions."

"You were not in Town long enough to accept that your instincts work there, too. All men are not alike. Just as you are different from Caroline, I am different from Heflin."

"But I can't wed anyone. It is too risky."

"Certainly you can." He stifled a sigh at her continued intransigence. "Marriage is not a prison. Nor is it brutal, despite that Heflin hurt you."

"How—"

"Like poor Timothy, you remain skittish, proving mistreatment. But a real marriage does not encompass pain."

She shook her head. "You need an heir, Alex. There is no evidence that I can supply one."

"Nonsense. You are a good mother to two wonderful daughters. Many ladies birth girls first. It does not preclude also birthing boys. Do you trust me?"

She hesitated, wanting so much to believe him, yet fearful of grabbing a dream only to find it again turning to dust. She bit her lip as the battle raged in her head, but finally nodded.

"Then prove it. Kiss me."

"I can't."

"You can. Christmas is a time for renewing old ties and forming new ones, a season that offers a chance to right old wrongs. Don't we deserve that chance?"

She slowly moved to the foot of the bed, raising both hands to protect her mouth.

"You will do all the work, my dear. I won't touch you unless you ask. But I believe a kiss will prove that we are the same people inside. I still love you. You still love me. With that as a foundation, we can address any other problems and resolve them together."

She moved closer, stopping before her body touched his. He could see the courage that brought her this close, so he remained absolutely still, his hands clasped behind him so they couldn't reach out. Despite that she'd voluntarily touched him several times, a kiss was much more intimate and thus harder.

Another eternity passed before she dropped her hands to her neck, leaned in and touched her lips to his.

Sarah expected a wave of terror, but it didn't come. Instead, she tasted Alex. Just Alex. Their first kiss had been much like this—a dare she couldn't refuse, not that she'd wanted to in those days. She'd already loved him. Now memories of him with her daughters— spinning tales to Emily, pulling Alice from the lake—paraded through her mind. And the children's party. She'd chided him for misbehaving, and he had admitted she was right . . . without temper.

She could trust him. Could trust the girls to him.

Closing her eyes, she turned a hand to touch his shoulder. He shuddered, but kept his hands behind him. Bolder, she settled against him, circling his neck with both arms. This was the Alex she had dreamed of so often during her marriage.

Excitement bubbled through her veins.

His lips moved over hers, inviting her deeper into the kiss. Heat radiated from his mouth, cascading down her back and making her all too aware of her breasts. But in a good way. Alex would not grab and twist until she was screaming in pain.

Her nipples stiffened, knifing pleasure to her core. So like her dreams . . .

"Hold me," she pleaded, snuggling closer.

When his arms closed around her, she stiffened, but only for a moment. This was Alex. She was safe.

"I've missed you so much," he managed against her lips, stroking her hair with one hand. For the first time in years he felt whole. This was where he belonged. "Even when I thought you'd betrayed me, I missed you and longed for you. I cannot live without you."

"I missed you, too," she admitted, burrowing against his shoulder. "I tried not to because it made enduring Heflin even harder, but I couldn't control the dreams."

"Will you marry me, Sarah? I can guarantee that lovemaking will be a pleasure. Heflin was an evil, brutal man who abused everyone who caught his eye. But—"

"—that is not you." She reveled in the arms that felt so safe, the kiss that felt so good, his innate gentleness that raised heat and excitement with every touch. Under Alex's care, the girls would grow into confident young ladies. Never again would they have to hide in corners to avoid notice. Nor would she.

The realization shattered the walls protecting her soul. Memories of every brutality she'd endured since Alex left burst free, overwhelming her senses.

She burst into tears.

"Sarah?"

She pressed against his shoulder as gulping sobs wracked her body. Every horror she'd suffered rose up now that she was finally safe. The beatings. The tauntings. The day she'd locked herself and the newborn Alice in an attic while Heflin destroyed the nursery—the one desire he could not fulfill by force was an heir. The night he'd crammed her in a trunk for correcting his misstatement, or the afternoon he'd vowed to sell Alice and Emily to a brothel if there was no heir within the year. He'd died a week later. She had grabbed the girls and fled.

Alex didn't know what was wrong, but Sarah was clinging to him as to a lifeline, so he lifted her into his arms, settling into a chair where he stroked her hair and murmured soothing sounds. More than half an hour passed before her anguish eased into hiccups.

"Have you cried at all since wedding Heflin?" he asked quietly.

She shook her head.

"Then this was long overdue." And it proved her trust, he realized in relief. He continued holding her, saying nothing while her senses settled. Another half hour passed before she pulled away.

"Thank you, Alex." She rose to splash water on her face.

"You are welcome." He joined her, meeting her gaze in the washstand mirror. "Now, will you marry me, my love?"

"Very well, but you must be patient. I cannot forget the past just because we both want to. This won't be the last time something triggers a breakdown. I will not burden you with tales of those years, but they remain in my mind."

He turned her to face him, understanding her new fear. "The past will fade in time. And should you share it with me, I will never hold it against you. I love you."

She kissed him again, with more assurance, but soon pulled back. "That's enough for now, Alex. It's more than I thought possible. I need time to adjust." She cupped his cheek. "I do love you."

"We have plenty of time. The wedding should wait until Mother emerges from mourning. But will you help me distribute Boxing Day gifts tomorrow?" He tossed her letter on the fire.

"I would love to help." She led him to the door.

"One last kiss," he suggested. "Then I must thank Grandmother. I suspect she plotted this reunion. She always knew how close we were."

Sarah laughed. "It sounds like her." And it explained why the closest friends she'd made during her Season had turned up at this gathering. "Thank her for me."

"Thank her yourself. She was planning to retire at midnight." A clock was chiming in the hall. "She will be delighted if we join her."

She considered the idea, then smiled. "Let's go. Your Christmas homecoming has fulfilled her fondest dreams. And ours. It is something to celebrate."

HOME FOR CHRISTMAS

Alicia Rasley

Chapter One

Near Plymouth, December 22, 1818

"Captain Randall?" The ostler blinked up at him in the predawn dusk, then bent down again to tend to the chestnut's hoof. A stone had lodged under her shoe, in the first mile of road she had run in three months, poor girl. "Of Rose Cottage? Captain Randall's been at sea this past year or more. The Indies. Or whaling. Something. Never met him, I ain't. Sorry, sir."

Disappointment stabbed him, sharp as anger. The notice had appeared in last week's *Exeter Mail,* and yet the man who had placed it, by this account, had been gone for months. He pulled the crumpled piece of paper from the pocket of his greatcoat, stared again at the precise description of the dagger, and remembered the sense of destiny that had struck him when he first saw it. Someone had placed this notice, just for him. "He has family?"

"A wife. Pretty little thing, aren't you?" This last was apparently meant for the mare, not her rider or the wife of the missing Captain Randall. The ostler rose, stroking the mare's nose, tugging at her ear, smiling at her. Absorbed in his flirtation, he added absently, "Leastways, she calls herself Mrs. Randall. Out past Kingsand, on the coast road. Rose Cottage. You'll see it. Covered in—"

Roses. It was a pretty trick of the sheltered Cornish coast that roses bloomed in December, long after the trees had lost their leaves. The cottage was twined in roses, pink and cream and golden, profligate as on Midsummer Day. The sun was just rising, though it was eight o'clock by his watch. He had chosen one of the shortest days of the year to buy back his past.

He tied his mare up on the road beside the cottage, well out of range of the team hitched to a post chaise in the yard. A driver sprawled on the box, his peg leg stuck out before him and his stick beside him on the bench. His posture proclaimed that a poor cripple could not be expected to load baggage as well as drive.

He must have won his argument. A red-cloaked young woman came out of the cottage, her arms full of luggage. With her hood pushed back in the early sunlight, she glowed pink and cream and gold like her roses. She was small but lithe, tossing a portmanteau into the chaise with the ease of a longshoreman, then gathering up her blue woolen skirts in one hand and dashing back through the open door of the cottage. She emerged a moment later with a bag in each hand and a pink baby blanket thrown over her shoulder. It must be Captain Randall's wife or his daughter, on her way somewhere else.

He intercepted her on yet another trip back into the house. "Miss Randall?"

She turned in the doorway, startled, ready to run, her long, dark braid whipping 'round to fall over her shoulder and onto her breast. But he was a gentleman, at least as far as appearance went, and her tense posture relaxed a bit. Still, she did not come off the step to meet him.

Her words came out in a cloud in the frosty air. "I am Mrs. Randall."

"I saw a notice in the *Mail*. For a dagger . . . "

"The Lionheart?"

Now she came to him, eager and bright like a bride on her wedding day, her bare hands held out in welcome. For a moment he could not breathe, then he realized her hands were seeking not him but the dagger. "I don't have it."

She stopped a few feet short, the expression on her face flashing from pleasure to loss to anger. "You don't have it?" she echoed. "Then why are you here?"

It was a moment before he could recall the quixotic impulse that had brought him back to these rocky shores after so many years away. "The notice said the dagger was one of a pair, and you wanted to match the one you have. I thought you might sell if you couldn't buy."

"Well, I can't sell it. I don't have it." Crossly, she slammed the carriage door shut. "I wanted to buy the second to give as a gift, to make up the pair again."

Another fruitless quest. A fool's journey, this meeting with his past. Better that he leave it behind again, sail off, and forget it. He glanced back across the road to the pewter-gray Channel, wishing he could see his *Carrara*. But she was moored several coves away and invisible to him, as well as to the revenue agents. An hour ashore, he was, and already longing to leave.

Something held him there, though. Perhaps it was this young

woman, with her bright eyes and her welcoming arms and her disappointment as apparent as his own. And then he took a breath and held it, thinking of what she had said, the description in the notice, and what he knew of this pair of daggers. "You wanted to purchase the second as a gift. You knew precisely what it looked like, for you had it described in the notice."

"I wrote it myself," she said, with a tilt of her chin.

"Then you've seen the first of the pair. You know, don't you, where at least one of them is?"

"I might. Why do you want to know?"

Just his luck to need information from that rarity, a woman who knew when to keep her mouth shut. He got a grip on his patience and replied softly, "I thought you understood. I want to purchase one—just one—of the daggers. I'm willing to pay one thousand pounds."

She took a quick breath, then released it, her face enigmatic and wary. "Then if you find it, you will doubtlessly win it. You must know I can't afford that sum. You must"—she looked down at the hands she had clasped at her chest, as if in supplication—"you must want it very badly."

"I want it enough."

She had changed, suddenly. He sensed no more despair, only a cunning she was trying to conceal by bending her head so he couldn't see her eyes.

"Tell me where I can find it."

Then she raised her head and studied him, this time letting him see the calculating expression on her face, the appraisal that narrowed her dark eyes. She was a young wife, if wife she was, he thought, remembering the ostler's cryptic comment. Still, she looked too innocent for a courtesan or whatever the ostler thought her to be, with that spray of freckles over her nose and cheeks flushed bright from her exertions in the cold.

That gaze she aimed at him, however, was all woman—assessing, aware, apprehending. Not so innocent after all.

His disappointment drifted off, leaving in its wake a slight tingling sense of anticipation. He was no more superstitious than the next sailor, but he knew an omen when he felt one. Destiny flickered in this elfin girl with the innocent face and bold looks. His destiny. She would lead him to the dagger and that would lead him home.

"If you want it," now her voice was only a whisper, throaty and enticing, "you must follow my lead. Starting right now. Tie your horse on the back of the carriage. It's only a short journey, so she'll be fine."

He was not used to being ordered about, much less by a woman who barely topped his shoulder. But he reminded himself of destiny and did as she bade.

Then she grabbed his hand and, still considering his destiny, he followed her toward the coach door.

"You are a sailor, aren't you?"

It was no more than a good guess sailors were everywhere on this coast, few of them Navy and thus few in uniform. "Why do you say that?"

"Your hand."

She stroked it between her small, cold hands, teasing the hard spots on the palm, the jagged scar along the back, with gentle brushes of her thumbs. Then she released him to pull open the door. No, she was not innocent at all.

"Callused, but not by reins. By rope. And you are so tanned and yet so blond. Like a Viking. Like Eric the Red."

He didn't like being so easily identified, but he knew that his fifteen years at sea had left their mark on his body as well as his spirit. And she was, of course, a sailor's wife. She wore a gold band on that teasing hand. She had already known a sailor's touch. Annoyed, he halted there, refusing to get into the coach. "When can I see the dagger?"

"You shan't ever see it if you don't follow my lead." She smiled reassuringly at him and called back to the cottage, "Lucy! We're ready to leave!"

"Where are we going?" he demanded.

"Don't talk that way, sir. You'll frighten the baby."

Before he could respond, that baby was before them, swaddled like a parcel and held in the arms of a nurse whose disapproval was etched in every line on her careworn face. "Mrs. Randall, are you sure—"

"Of course, I'm sure," the girl said gaily, taking the parcel, hoisting it up, cooing at it, and then handing it to him. It was the size and heft of a rolled-up jibsail, but no jibsail squirmed and uttered inarticulate sounds of rebellion. He was too busy juggling it to protest, until he heard Mrs. Randall tell the nurse, "You see, Captain Randall has made it home after all! He will be escorting me to Porthallow, so you may visit your sister now in good conscience, without the slightest worry for Beth and me. For you may be sure, my husband will keep us safe!"

Lucy was gazing suspiciously at him, as well she might. His incomprehension at being identified as her husband must be plain to see. Then some childhood edict against calling a lady a liar made him assume a neutral mask. He didn't even flinch when the madwoman took his arm and smiled up at him possessively.

"I am so happy to see you again, darling! And just in time. Another minute and you would have missed us! Now you go on into the coach with Beth, and I'll just get the hot bricks for our feet."

She disappeared back into the cottage, leaving him to look down at the wriggling bundle in his arms and wonder if destiny was worth the trouble.

"Baby's getting cold," Lucy said, her voice tight with reserved judgment. "Shouldn't be out in the chill."

During his years at sea, he had survived hurricanes with his ship intact by accepting that events were more or less out of his control, that he had to go with the storm to get out of the storm. Now he saw another storm coming toward him, her face alight, her arms full of flannel-covered bricks, and shoving the parcel under his arm, he climbed into the coach.

It was just a job-coach, but a well-appointed one and quite clean, fit for the most respectable matron. Mrs. Randall's unostentatious traveling garments were also entirely proper, the bonnet she loosened and the leather gloves she removed being of the finest quality. It was incredible that this perfect lady had flat-out abducted him—incredible, that is, 'til he saw the impish, excited glitter in her eyes whenever she stole a glance at him.

But there seemed to be no escape, no awakening from this strangely realistic dream. As the carriage lurched into the road, Mrs. Randall arranged the hot bricks artistically on the floor, spread the baby blanket over her lap, and held out her arms for the parcel. He was glad to be relieved of it but angry at her blithe manner, and he didn't allow her crooning to the child to divert him. "What was *that* about?"

Mrs. Randall laid the parcel on the seat beside her and gently unswaddled it. Eventually, a little face emerged, red and pugnacious. "Oh, Lucy has been combing my hair with a three-legged stool, telling me I shouldn't take Beth on a journey by myself. So now she will be happy. Won't she, sweeting?" This last she crooned to the child, who regarded her quite as warily as he did himself. "We're just going to your Grandpapa's home, aren't we? And that's not even a day's journey." She looked up at him with that radiant smile he was learning boded trouble. "Do you know Porthallow, sir?"

Grudgingly, he nodded. He'd grown up not far from here and had been a privateer half his life. He knew every hidden cove in Cornwall.

"It's on Talland Bay. But I have no desire to go there."

"Of course you do. Otherwise, you will never see that dagger you want so much. And as you are escorting us, Lucy will have no fear for our safety, for how could we be in any danger when my husband is along?"

He hated pointing out the obvious, but with this woman nothing was really obvious. "I am not your husband."

"No," she said thoughtfully, to his immense relief, for he had been infected by her madness and for just an instant wondered if on some drunken night in Plymouth a couple years ago he might have somehow debauched and married this woman and then forgotten all about it.

"No," she said again, adding, "But you might be." She opened her cloak and unfastened the top of her blue dress, and before he could explore exactly what he wanted her to do next, she withdrew a necklace from her bodice and awkwardly with one hand pulled it over her head. "Look and see."

One long, dark hair—hers—was caught on the chain. He twined it around his finger as he opened the locket. There was more hair inside, but this time blond, a wisp of curl about the size of his thumbnail.

"See?" she said triumphantly. "Almost precisely the color of yours."

He nearly retorted that any blond sailor ended up with hair that sun-bleached shade, hair that moreover resisted any comb applied to it and curled mostly because it was deeply imbued with salt. "Is this Captain Randall's?"

"No." She tugged the knit cap off the baby's head, revealing hair as golden and soft as a sunbeam. "Her father's. She got her curls from him."

He took a deep breath, counted to ten, then said as unaccusingly as he could, "Captain Randall is not the child's father?"

"Her father was only a lieutenant." She seemed to think this sufficed as an explanation and went back to unwrapping her daughter. "Lucy always bundles her up like this. I think children need fresh air, and I always unbundle her. It's rather amusing, but poor Beth has never gotten used to being trussed up and hates it." Revealed, Beth turned out to be a child rather older than he had thought, old enough to sit on her mother's lap and put her thumb in her mouth and stare suspiciously at him.

"Don't worry about me, child," he told her, unnerved by her big unblinking eyes and the vigor with which she sucked her thumb. "I'm not the lunatic in this carriage."

Mrs. Randall looked startled and then laughed. It was a pretty sound, low and husky, and when she replied her voice still shimmered with amusement. "Do I confuse you? I always do that. But I am not a lunatic. I just don't explain things well."

"That I believe." He looked back down at the locket, at the blond curl that could have been his own, and marshaled his thoughts. "Answer my questions and only my questions," he said sternly, as if he were talking to an errant cabin boy.

She settled her child into a more comfortable perch on her lap, the head resting against her breast, and said meekly, "I will."

"Where do you mean to take me?"

"To my father's house."

"In Porthallow?"

"Yes." She started to say something else, then remembered her promise and pressed her lips together ostentatiously.

"He has the dagger?"

"One of them. He's always wanted to complete the pair, but he could never locate the other one. I thought it might have come on the market since he quit looking. And I wanted to buy it to give to him at Christmas. I thought that the gift might make him more likely to—Oh, I forgot, I was only to answer your questions."

"More likely to what?"

She bent her head, kissing the child's golden locks. Her voice came muffled. She no longer sounded so blithe. "More likely to accept Beth. I was supposed to bring my husband with me on this visit, so Father could meet him. But I couldn't. So I hoped the dagger would—might—appease him."

He shook his head, as if that might dislodge the cobwebs. "I don't understand. If Captain Randall is in the Indies, how can your father expect him to escort you on a Christmas visit?"

She cast him a sidelong glance. "My father isn't quite convinced that Captain Randall exists."

This took a moment to absorb. "Why?"

Mrs. Randall looked around, as if afraid that she might be overheard. Then she covered her daughter's ears, and while the child removed her thumb from her mouth to protest, she whispered, "Because he doesn't."

Suddenly, he understood. There was no captain, but there was a lieutenant. No husband, but a lover. The advertisement in the *Mail*, the Rose Cottage, the child, were all attributed to the name of a mythical man. "Where is the lieutenant?"

"Dead." She held out her hand for the locket, and when he gave it to her, she closed her fingers around it. He saw her knuckles go white before she loosed her grip and pushed the necklace into her pocket. "I thought it best not to let his family know about her. They—they had been unkind to him, and I'd no reason to think they would treat Beth any better. So I needed a husband with a different name. Captain Randall came along, then."

He knew she had left a lot out, but he couldn't decipher what. "You mean you invented him?"

Her eyes shone with relief at his understanding. He must be going mad, to understand one like this. "Precisely. Eric Randall. It sounds rather seafaring, don't you think? And a captain of a merchant vessel has some standing in the community, even if he is merely the son of a third son of a noble family. I wanted Beth to have a bit of an entree, at least. Perhaps she'll do better with it than I did."

Captain Randall, he sensed, was rather better known to his wife than most real husbands were. She had invented a history as well as a name. And he understood why well enough. A young lady known to have run off with her lover, left with only the one token of his affection, would never be accepted. He couldn't condemn her, really, but he couldn't trust her, either. And what her plans were for him he didn't like to imagine. "How have you supported yourself?"

"Oh, I inherited a bit from my mother, and I give lessons in drawing and music and Italian to local girls. They would never be allowed to come to me, you understand, if there weren't a Captain Randall."

"And he's been in the Indies?"

"Since we came here, when Beth was but a babe. Once I made a trip to Portsmouth to meet him, but I've never brought him here."

It was disorienting, the way she spoke of this husband as if he really existed, only a moment after admitting she had made him up. But he understood, in a way. He had done much the same fifteen years ago, taking a new name and a new role and almost coming to believe that it was true. He had to believe it was true, or he wouldn't have been able to make it work. And because he knew how many adjustments maintaining this role required, he anticipated her answer to his question before he asked it. "What need have you of me?"

Again she cast him that sidelong glance, not sly, precisely, but knowing. Somehow she had sized him up and decided he was just the man she needed.

"You must take the place of my husband. Just for this one visit. Just until after Christmas. Not even a week. So my father will no longer wonder if Beth is a—" The word hesitated on her lips, then was swallowed back, and she tightened her arms around the child. "My father is the only family we have. I would like him to accept my daughter."

He wondered what it was like to be as close as this mother and child, Beth nestling into the curve of her mother's arm, warm and secure as if nothing in the world could touch her now. But there were limits to the security a young mother could provide, and he feared they had already been tested. Life for a bastard child—a girl, and the bastard of some undistinguished lieutenant, no less—would be bleak. Mrs. Randall's blithe way with deception made him wary, but he could not fault her maternal love. There was little enough of that in the world, in his experience.

But he did not trust her. She seemed harmless, but her cheerful manner masked a tigress's ruthlessness. "What do I get in return for playing this part?"

She looked disappointed. Perhaps she thought mere gallantry would be all the incentive he needed. But then she smiled, as if in recognition of their essential likeness. They were neither of them the gallant sort. "The dagger."

"But you haven't got it."

"My father does."

"I can't think what good that will do, since you admit yourself that he is displeased with you." His voice was hard, but to his surprise she took no offense.

"That is nothing new." She laughed again. This time it wasn't such a pretty sound. "I have ever found it easy to displease him. My natural state, I think, is displeasing to him. But—" she paused, then added firmly, as if she meant to persuade herself as well as him, "but I am grown now, and he is old, and Beth is his grandchild—the only one he is likely to have. And he can't help being pleased with her, don't you think? Even if she's not a boy."

He spared a glance at the child, who had been lulled to sleep by the rocking of the carriage. She was angelic enough, at least as she slept, especially when her mother gently tugged her thumb out and her bow mouth went on sucking. But the angel's effect on her grandfather was none of his concern.

"What is to keep me from approaching him on my own?"

Judging from the frown that creased her forehead, it appeared

Mrs. Randall hadn't thought of that. But then she laughed with a childlike triumph. "You don't know who he is!"

"He's your father. In Porthallow."

"But you only know me as Mrs. Randall. My father's name is quite unknown to you."

"I could find it out. There can't be that many collectors of martial antiquities in Porthallow."

"He does not live in Porthallow. Nearby. And his collection is not generally known. My father, you see"—with an innocent air she bent to kiss her daughter on the head—"is usually quite scrupulous in checking the provenance of his acquisitions. But with this dagger, his methods might have been a bit . . . unorthodox."

"A family trait, it must be, unorthodoxy." He could not doubt what she said was true. Fifteen years ago, at least, her father must have had dealings with a broker no scrupulous collector would know, one who hadn't blinked at buying the Lionheart dagger from a desperate fourteen-year-old boy. "If he is such a collector, why do you think he would sell it to me?"

She busied herself arranging the folds of her cloak over her sleeping child, even as she arranged her answer. "You'll have no chance at all without me. But *with* me, as my husband, you might persuade him." She looked away, out the window, at the misty landscape passing by. "That dagger has given him little joy all these years. He wanted so to complete the pair, but he could not advertise openly without calling attention to himself. It's almost been a reproach to him, for acquiring it in such a havey-cavey manner. And a thousand pounds . . . that will buy him many more antique arms." She shrugged, a concession that she had no more arguments to marshal. "If you want it so badly, you must take the chance. It is only for a week, after all."

"And then?"

"And then what?"

"What happens when he wants to see you and your husband again? What then?"

"Then you will die."

Her voice was low, pleasant, matter-of-fact. She had been planning that all along. Eventually, of course, Captain Randall would have to die. Even a sea captain's absence would be remarked after a few years. And the pretense of a widow would be less a strain than the pretense of a wife.

And yet it chilled him, the casualness with which she disposed of him—no, not him, but that Captain Randall he hadn't yet agreed to be.

"What about a grave? A stone? A—a body?"

He didn't really think her capable of—of whatever strange notion had glimmered in his mind when she had said, so matter-of-factly, "You will die." But she was so unknown to him, this woman who invented men. Something lightened in him when she said, "No stone. No grave. Sailors die at sea, and their bodies are committed to the deep. 'My soul fleeth onto the Lord—'"

Before the morning watch, I say, before the morning watch. Silently, he finished the prayer she began. He knew it well, having heard it spoken and spoken it himself over the bodies of shipmates dozens of times. It seemed almost as if they were pronouncing Captain Randall dead. But that was nonsense, of course. This odd young woman was disorienting him, that was all. Captain Randall hadn't even come to life yet.

The child murmured in her sleep, and Mrs. Randall bent and whispered something to her, making tiny adjustments in her position to make her daughter more secure.

"Her father died at sea, I take it."

Mrs. Randall glanced up. "Yes." For an instant there was bleak memory in her eyes, then she looked back down at her daughter and tried to smile. Her voice, when it came again, was determinedly bright. "She isn't usually this good, I must tell you. She's been awake for hours as we prepared to go, and so she needed a bit of a nap. But usually she has much more to say and do."

"What part will she play in this—this charade?"

"What part?" She looked blank for a moment. "It's *for* her, don't you see? So that her grandfather will accept her. Sponsor her. I wouldn't care so much except that . . . I could die."

The genuine surprise in her voice as she spoke of her own mortality almost made him smile. He had been surprised, too, when he first conceived death as an inevitability. And it was hard to imagine this mercurial woman dead, her bright spirit extinguished, her child orphaned and alone.

He wondered if she were exaggerating for effect, to persuade him into compassion. Her father was hardly one to cast the first stone, judging from his collecting techniques. But then again, fathers were like that, weren't they? Righteous. Self-righteous.

"Is your father truly so harsh?"

She frowned. He sensed her trying to be fair, objective.

"I don't know. We were never close. We never knew how to speak to each other. He seemed to be happy to cast me off. Good riddance, he said. And didn't answer my letters 'til the last one. And even then it was just to challenge me. He wants to meet this husband of mine, that is how he wrote it: 'This supposed husband of yours.'"

"What about your mother?" Mothers were more merciful, or so he once believed.

"She died when I was seven. There is only my father." She met his eyes then, but all the boldness was gone. "When I saw you and you looked so very like the man I described, you seemed almost a gift from Fate. As Beth is a gift. I could not refuse it."

She was a tenacious creature, for all her swift changes. She always came back to that point . . . that he must come with her. Somewhere he had lost that initial objection, the one about the child. Oh, yes. "But you want me to pretend to be the child's father?"

"Oh!" She smiled, as if relieved it wasn't more than that. "Oh, you needn't worry that I will thrust her upon you. I shan't require any help with her. And my father would never expect you to pay any mind to a child. Not a girl-child, anyway. You've been at sea most of her life, after all."

It seemed so easy. He could have a chance at the dagger, his only chance, and the payment was merely pretending to be another man for a week. He need not be bothered by the child or consigned to support them for the future. He needn't even see them ever again once Christmas was over. "What have you told your father about Captain Randall?"

She had won, she knew it, but she concealed her triumph courteously, only her shining eyes betraying her. "Not much. He was in the Royal Navy until '12, then joined a merchant fleet as a first officer, and recently got his own command on the East Indies route. The *Tescador* is his ship."

"Wouldn't your father have made inquiries with the East India Company if he doubted your word?"

She flushed, as if confessing a fault. "Captain Randall's not with the Company. Too many officers wanted those posts. So he's with a new group. An informal arrangement. Not yet incorporated."

The story was plausible enough, and his respect for her ingenuity went up a notch. There were plenty of such merchant fleets on the seas since the war, scavenging off the remains left by the East India Company. His own fleet had begun the same way, with a few privateers agreeing to sail together for mutual protection. "What does he ship?"

"The usual. Spices, silk." She met his gaze levelly. "I have done my research, sir. I know the customary sea route and the ones that aren't so customary. I know how much he can expect to make from a voyage, after his crew and the ship owner get their portions. I had all sorts of emergencies that would explain his delay this holiday, but I shan't have to use them, shall I?"

He didn't answer her directly, looking away instead out the window. They were approaching the cove that hid his ship. "We'll have to stop here."

"Stop?" Her bright look dimmed. She thought he was refusing.

Gently, he asked, "Do you have a few sets of clothes for Captain Randall? Or did you expect me to wear this one for a week?"

Mrs. Randall must not have considered that problem at all. She frowned, but her relief broke through and curved her mouth into the smile he had already become accustomed to. "You have a thousand pounds, don't you? I thought you could buy whatever you pleased in Porthallow."

"I do not buy my clothing in Porthallow," he replied. "God forbid." As they rounded the curve, he tapped on the wall against the driver's box. The carriage clattered to a halt. He rose and stretched and opened the door.

It was full daylight now, and the *Carrara* could no longer be hidden in her anchorage off the cape. But she needn't be hidden any longer, he reminded himself as he called down the hill for his boatman. She was as respectable as an Indiaman now, her crew all peaceable sorts, her cargo entirely legal, her captain released by the fall of Bonaparte from sinister missions. It was only habit that anchored her here instead of at the Plymouth docks—and her captain's superstition about the ghosts of the past.

Mrs. Randall—he couldn't help thinking of her as that—had left the child in the coach and come up to stand beside him. "Oh, what a pretty ship she is. Is she really yours?"

"Yes." One of three, he almost added, but the coxswain had clambered up the hill and was waiting for his orders. Within a few minutes, he had dealt with the mare and his baggage, and his first officer was waiting for orders, his speculations about the captain's companion written all over his young face.

A week, at least, away from the ship. "Take her into Plymouth and let the crew have leave—a week, except for a couple to guard the ship. You and they will get leave when I return. If you need to reach me, I'll be at—" He turned to Mrs. Randall, waiting.

She set her lips tight, as if torture wouldn't force her to divulge the address.

"As you wish." He turned back to his officer. "Belay those last orders. I'll be rejoining you after all."

"Morrell Hall. South of Porthallow." Mrs. Randall spun on her heel and climbed back into the carriage, yanking the door shut behind her.

She was over her pique by the time he rejoined her on their journey. She greeted him with a smile and the news that the angel had awakened and was feeling rather demonic. That he could observe for himself. Little Beth was engaged in the annoying game of dropping her mitten and whimpering until her mother picked it up. Mrs. Randall, ever cheerful, ever resourceful, eventually pulled a ribbon off her braid, loosing a cloud of dark curls, and tied it to the mitten's thumb so she could retrieve it without bending over.

Once it was easy for her mother to play, however, Beth tired of the game, taking again to sucking her thumb and staring at him balefully. It challenged him, that suspicious stare from an innocent child, as if she had no confidence at all that he could do the job he had been hired to do. She would think differently, he thought, matching her stare for stare, if she knew him better.

Fortunately for the future of their relations, he found in his pocket a marble one of the ship's boys had left on the deck. It had nearly cost its owner his young life when it got under the heel of the boatswain. He rolled it in his fingers until the child dropped her unblinking gaze to the green glass ball then, tantalizingly, he dropped it. The carriage obligingly hit a pothole and the marble rolled loudly down the floor, ricocheting off the warming bricks. Beth scrambled out of her mother's arms and chased after it on her hands and knees, batting it back up the incline and crowing when it rolled back.

Beyond sternly warning the child not to put that in her mouth, Mrs. Randall voiced no objection to Beth's new game. "How very inventive of you," she added, sounding surprised. If she knew him better, she would not be so surprised. Inventiveness had ever been his besetting sin. It was something else they had in common.

These last miles along the coastal road, past tumbledown cottages and fishing shacks, were all too familiar to him. At Downderry, he thought he recognized a cassocked man who raised his hand in blessing as they clattered past the tiny old church. Werton, that was his name, had been a curate back then, picking up spare silver tutoring bored young lordlings in Latin. But though the vicar smiled benignly as they passed, he could not have recognized the man in the coach as the worst of his Latin pupils—not after so long, not now that he was grown taller and stronger than anyone then would have guessed. He was safe enough, in yet another identity—his third or fourth, perhaps—since he had last read Latin.

This was all familiar to her, too, he realized. She was peering out the window, her forehead pressed against the glass, one hand trailing down to clutch Beth's petticoats. It was strange to think they had grown up within a dozen miles of each other, only to meet under these incongruous circumstances.

"Do you know," he remarked, watching a clutch of schoolboys erupt from the little dame school, "I don't think we have ever been formally introduced."

She had stolen the marble from Beth and was holding it up to her eye to survey her daughter. "Beth, sweeting, you are all green! No, sir, we haven't been." She gave the child back her toy and added, "Though I feel I have known you quite well for a long time!"

She had, it was true, behaved with a familiarity beyond what their short acquaintance would warrant, abducting him and extorting him and smiling at him as if he were a willing conspirator in this scheme of hers. He could not find it in his heart, somehow, to resent this. She had such a roguish smile, after all, which produced a deep dimple in one cheek and glints of laughter in her dark eyes.

"Not so long nor so well. You don't even know my name."

"No! Don't tell me!" In a more reasonable tone, she explained, "I mean, if I know your real name, I might accidentally call you by that instead of Eric or Captain Randall. It would make my father suspicious."

He smiled, but with an edge to his voice, remarked, "Perhaps then you should call me only darling, as you did when your nurse was about."

That made her shy, or at least pretend to be shy. She ducked her head and applied herself to spit-polishing Beth's smudged cheeks. "Lucy is a romantic. Father, I'm certain, is not."

"Tell me your name at least. He will be quite suspicious if I don't know that."

"My given name?" She held her protesting daughter between her knees and rubbed the cheek dry, then dropped a kiss there. Then she released the child and smiled to herself. "My name is Verity."

"Verity." Truth. "How appropriate."

Chapter Two

Morrell Hall's only concession to the holiday season was an evergreen bough tacked onto the great oak door. Otherwise, it stood as stern as ever on the windswept bluff. I'll soon see to that, Verity thought as she knelt on the flagstone walk to tidy Beth's apparel.

"We'll put up holly and ivy and candles in every window," she promised, straightening the little pink bow in Beth's golden hair. "And a Yule log and plum pudding . . . a real country house Christmas, just as we had when I was a little girl. My own mama used to let me stir the plum pudding, and so I shall let you."

She rose and looked back to see Captain Randall paying off the coachman, just as a real husband would have done. She felt in her pocket for her purse, reminding herself to keep an accounting of his expenditures on her behalf. Of course, a man who thought nothing of spending one thousand pounds on an antique dagger probably didn't worry about a couple sovereigns here and there. Still, she had been saving her pennies, hoping to come home, and she needn't get herself any more obligated to this man than she already was.

He was, she thought as he directed the groom to take care of their baggage, very good at this pretense. She could not have asked for a better conspirator had she had the prescience to plan this scheme ahead of time. He had agreed almost straight off, though he obviously thought her half-mad, and raised no tiresome objections about sin and crime and fraud. He even looked the part of the successful sailor. Indeed, he was well used to that role, judging from his pretty frigate. He was of the right class—or seemed to be, anyway—with his cool, unaccented speech and expensive dress—a bit too expensive, she thought. Weston must have tailored that well-fitting gray coat, and few sailors could afford Weston. She would have to tell her father that the last voyage had been a rousing success and all their financial worries solved. That would pave the way for the moment when this half-pay sailor offered one thousand pounds for an old dagger.

He came up now and offered her a quick smile, meant, she supposed, to reassure her. She smiled back. He was rather kind, in his oblique way. As she bent to pick up Beth, she gave last instructions in an undertone, "Remember, my father is Sir William Morrell. He's originally of Hampshire but didn't like the crowding. I have said that your people are from Dorset but that they are all dead."

"Yes, dead relations are so much more convenient, aren't they?"

That made her chuckle, and so it was a merry face she presented when the door opened and the elderly butler beckoned them in. She kept the smile bright, though merely entering the shadowy entry hall had the effect of depressing her spirits. She had forgotten how magisterial, how dark this house was, with the suit of armor guarding the entry and the pairs of crossed lances all the way up the stairwell wall. How had she ever managed to grow up here?

But she remembered her part and forced herself into it. It must be a pleasing family portrait that greeted her father coming down the great staircase—the tall handsome husband, the happy wife holding the pretty child, outlined artistically in a shaft of weak sunlight. No prodigal daughter repentant and returned in this picture, no supplicant grandchild begging for crumbs of recognition.

She felt her smile waver as her father stopped halfway down the steps, the shadow lines from the leaded window above emphasizing his frown. It was characteristic of him to remain above, apart from her, too far to touch, too silent to address. She had never in her life known what to say to him, and though she had been rehearsing her lines for thirty miles, the words rang in her head now, tinny and revealing.

Captain Randall—Eric—must have sensed her momentary weakness. He took Beth from her arms, murmuring an answer to her instinctive protest. "Come, Beth," he told the child, "you must meet your grandfather. He owns this house and that set of armor you are admiring. Perhaps if you are very good, he will let you go a bit closer to it."

He wasn't an experienced parent, and he held Beth as if she were some slippery fish hauled up from the deep and eager to jump back in. But Beth was an experienced child. She gripped him with her knees— he had a boyishly slender waist for a tall man—and leaned perilously out, stretching her hands toward the knight's armor. "Pretty." That was her universal word for approbation, applied to dolls as well as armor.

That did not make Sir William happy, Verity knew as his frown deepened, the prospect of a child roaming through his antiquities. He would likely have them thrown out. She was seized by the urge to hand him the gifts she had brought, bid him a Happy Christmas, then turn around and go back to the little cottage that seemed suddenly so much more of a home. That would be reconciliation enough, with no chance for additional angry confrontations.

But Captain Randall was braver than she. "Don't worry, sir," he reassured the silent figure above. "We shall keep Beth out of mischief.

Verity mentioned a sun porch, I believe . . . "

She hadn't, but it was an easy guess, as most houses in this area were built to take advantage of the gentle breezes and sea vistas. He would know that, she thought, for it was apparent he was familiar with this coastline. He secured Beth's scrabbling hand in a gentle grasp. "We'll confine her to that area when she is not outside or abed. Isn't that right, darling?"

Only Verity heard the slight emphasis on that last word, and despite her anxiety she felt a spark of amusement. She had taken him by surprise this morning, calling him darling, calling him husband. And some of the dawn's optimism rose again in her. He had decided, for whatever reason, that he would do his part. She had only to match his performance and hold her breath for a week or so, and they would come right about.

So as a clean-conscienced daughter might, she came to the bottom of the stairs and held out her hand to the man above. "Father, dear, come meet Eric and our little Beth. I am so glad we can all finally be together, as a family should."

Likely it wasn't the sentimental words that wooed him, but rather the presence of the butler at the door watching the proceedings with an interested air. "Verity," her father said, taking her hand for a moment, then releasing it.

What had she expected, after all? A kiss? A "Welcome home"? No matter. She didn't need him for herself but for Beth. And no one, *no one*, could know Beth long without loving her. It was a settled truth, just as Christmas followed the Winter Solstice, love followed Beth. She turned to the man holding her child.

"This is—" the faintest of pauses, then it came easily to her tongue, "my husband, Eric Randall."

He shifted Beth to the crook of his left arm and reached to take her father's hand. "Sir William."

"And this is Beth. Elizabeth." Verity's voice stopped working right, taking on that pleading note she hated. "After Mother."

Her father cast a cursory glance at Beth. "She hasn't the look of your mother."

When Verity could not answer, Eric said with a smile, "No. She is her father's daughter, I'm afraid. Look how well she clings to the rigging." Experimentally, he withdrew his hand from Beth's back. She grabbed his expensive coat and hung on, laughing.

She's so funny, Verity thought, stealing a glance at her father to see if he appreciated this. But Sir William was asking Eric about his voyage, and Eric was replying with just enough technical detail to sound convincing without giving much away.

At least he hasn't denounced us as impostors and slammed the door behind us, Verity thought as her father turned to order their luggage taken away. He meant for them to stay. As they followed him up the stairs to the drawing room, Eric reached out to take her hand. It was an unnecessary gesture—her father was ahead and couldn't see— but his firm, rough clasp reminded her that, for the first time, she wasn't alone in her father's house. She had Beth, and she had this enigmatic man and his temporary support—and her own not inconsiderable resources.

Sir William could be a good host when he wanted to, and he provided a light repast of tea and bread and butter in the formal drawing room. Beth ate only a few bites of her mother's bread, then demanded to be set down on the floor. Verity glanced warily at Sir William but could not read his expression. So she let Beth slip to the floor, and Eric proved himself yet again to be a quick study. In a marvelously authoritative father-voice, he told the child to stay between him and her mother.

So Beth crawled back and forth the short distance between their legs, rolling the green marble ahead of her. Verity took up her tea with a silent sigh of relief. That marble diverted Beth far more than the familiar doll that Verity had stuffed in her reticule.

There was an awkward silence, broken only by Beth's murmurs to the marble. Verity was usually at ease in a social setting, but with her father sitting in his wingchair like a judge at the bench, she couldn't manage more than a few questions about the house and the village, before she took up her teacup again. Her father kept glancing down at Beth, as if worried she would become sick on his Axminster carpet.

Just to break the tension, Verity gestured to the portrait over the hearth. "That's me at Beth's age. With my mother."

Eric studied the painting as if it really mattered to him. "I don't see much of Beth there—except that smile. You look as if you were contemplating running away from your mother and engaging in some mischief. You haven't changed very much, have you?"

It was true. She had been a mischievous child, with an excess of high spirits, too much for her gentle mother. A hot flush rose in her cheeks. Eric grinned at her, as if this discovery amused him.

But her father only harrumphed and asked, "How old is she, the child?"

Verity answered quickly, in case Eric had forgotten any of the facts she had coached him on as they journeyed. "She'll be two on Twelfth Night." She added proudly, "She speaks very well for her age. Fifty-seven words and more each week."

Sir William's lips moved in silent calculation. "Two at Twelfth Night. That means . . . when were you wed?"

The abruptness, indeed the rudeness, of his question did not unnerve Verity. She had been expecting this and had already worked out a plausible wedding date, somewhere between the time she had run away from her aunt's house in Plymouth and the night Beth was conceived. "February 22."

"1816," Eric added helpfully. "It was a fortunate accident. We'd never have met if my ship hadn't been damaged from the big Christmas gale in the Bay of Biscay. I brought her in for overhaul and saw Verity." He gave Verity a fond husbandly smile. "Hard to believe it's been near three years we've been married. Sometimes it seems as if we have only just met."

Verity glanced quickly at her father, but he had never been sensitive to tone and had not heard that sardonic note. Why, Eric was enjoying this! No wonder he was so adept at masquerade. He had to be a pretender at heart. He only grinned as she frowned warningly.

"That's because you have been gone most of the time we have been married. It is a difficult life, married to a sailor."

"But such rewards there are!" He reached over to take her hand and raised it to his lips. There was the surprising heat of his mouth on her skin, then a playful nip before he let their clasped hands rest on the arm of his chair. She resisted the urge to snatch her hand back to see if he had left a burn mark or the imprint of teeth. "Especially after a voyage to the Indies! Wait 'til you see what I brought you for Christmas."

His kiss was so casual, his warmth so believable, that even Verity, who knew better, felt a connection between them, something warm and taut and strong. And Beth, looking up from her marble at that moment, rose to her feet and tottered over to put her hand on top of theirs, as if ratifying this union.

It was the perfect picture, the three of them together, and for just a moment Verity let the warmth of his hand on hers warm her all the way through. Then she glanced up to see the ironic glint in his gray eyes and gave herself an inward shake. It wasn't true, and just as well. She and Beth were fine alone. She just had to make sure she didn't start believing the drama they were performing so well.

Her father wasn't as persuadable. He leaned back in his chair, eyeing their pretty tableau skeptically, until Beth drew back and climbed into the safety of her mother's lap. "You don't wear a wedding ring," he said to Eric, accusation plain in his voice.

Verity was about to remind him that he never had, either, that few men did. But Eric beat her to it. "I did, in the beginning. Verity insisted. Said she wanted the women to be alerted." He gave her that quick, boyish grin. "I don't know why she's worried. I might as well have *tamed* written on my forehead."

He made it sound as if he were almost proud to have a possessive wife. Now that had to be an act. If a man like this had such a wife, he'd never come back from the Indies. She knew little of him, but she knew that much. Shackling would drive him mad.

But now he was talking to her father with that easy man-to-man air, inventing what she hadn't thought to coach him to say. "Then it caught on a nail forty feet up the mizzenmast, and I almost twisted the finger off. They had to cut the ring off, with my finger so swollen." He detached his left hand from hers and held it up, displaying a ring finger that was indeed bent a little at the knuckle, as if it had been broken. That whole hand was battered, in fact, with the long scar along the back and a black blood-bruise on the thumbnail. A sailor's hand, it was, capable but inelegant. She dropped her gaze to her own hands, now holding Beth still, and recalled how firm and warm his grasp had been only moments before.

But her father hadn't ceased his interrogation. "I don't imagine you have your marriage lines, do you?"

Even the imperturbable Eric was silenced by so blatant an insult. She suddenly recalled she had never described the wedding to him. He was just saying, "Well, you can't expect us to travel with them," when she broke in.

"But, darling, I don't think we ever *got* marriage lines." She turned to her father with a light laugh. "We were married at sea, you know. It seemed rather havey-cavey to me, but Eric assured me it was entirely legal."

"It is." Eric answered his cue immediately, in a tone that suggested they had had this discussion too many times already. "A captain is king and judge and bishop on his ship and may marry passengers as long as he is outside British waters. We were halfway to France, you'll recall. And no, he didn't give us marriage lines, come to think of it. No doubt he recorded the marriage in his log book. At the time, I recollect, you thought it all vastly romantic. It's only since that you have decided the wedding was insufficiently respectable."

His aggrieved expression was so consummate that Verity almost believed he was annoyed with her. And her father surrendered, though he made one last broadside. "This captain who married you. He still exists, does he?"

"Still exists? Unless he's had some accident in the last few days. I passed him Saturday coming round Ushant into the Channel. Captain Bering, of the *Myland*." To Verity, he said, "Asked to give you his regards, in fact. At least, I think it was his regards. His signal flagman isn't much of a speller."

To her very great relief, Sir William apparently decided to accept this man, this marriage. He rose and crossed the room to pull the bell-rope. "I'm sure you'll want to get settled. I've put you in the guest suite in the north wing. I'll assign a maid to help with the child."

The gesture was a considerate one, and as Verity rose with Beth in her arms, she felt relief and happiness fill her. He was going to recognize them. He wouldn't turn them away after all.

Indeed, he even nodded toward Eric, almost genially. "I expect I should welcome you into the family. After you've settled in, perhaps I could show you around Morrell Hall. As a military man, you might appreciate my collection of antique armaments."

She saw the leap of interest in Eric's eyes and hoped that, after he had done so much to help her, he would not be disappointed in his own quest. But he showed no untoward eagerness as he replied, "I should like that, sir. In an hour, shall we say?"

A few moments later, she understood how successful their imposture had been. "Look!" she told her conspirator, spinning around in the middle of the blue bedroom, gesturing to their bags heaped on the floor. "You did wonderfully well. You've convinced him entirely!"

"What do you mean?"

Verity smiled at him, grateful now for that instinct that had made her trust her fate to him this morning. "Don't you see? If he doubted our marriage, he would never have put us in a single bedroom!"

Chapter Three

Eric's thorough exploration proved Verity correct. A small sitting room was accessible through a connecting door, and Beth was settled by the maid in a room just across the little hallway. But there was only one assigned bedroom and, more to the point, only one assigned bed. As he stood in the sitting room doorway, Eric's gaze was drawn magnetically to that bed, heaped high with pillows and half concealed with draperies, large enough for two. Indeed, cozy to the extreme.

He glanced appraisingly at his companion, who was singing softly as she put a stack of nightgowns away in a drawer. She had loosed her dark curls again, and they danced around her pretty face as she rose and shut the cupboard. With quick grace, she crossed to the hall door and looked out, as if wary of eavesdroppers. But they were quite, quite alone in their marital quarters.

A thought had glimmered in his mind since she had first come toward him, eyes alight, hands outstretched, and now it crystallized. This radiant girl, with her songs and laughter and inventiveness, would be lovely in bed.

"I know what you're thinking," she said, closing the door securely behind her.

"You do?" He was glad for the deep tan that hid his hot flush, glad that he was grown and his voice no longer broke when he was startled.

"You're thinking that my father wasn't really very welcoming."

Disappointment struggled with relief and won. She hadn't been thinking about the bed at all. He'd have to be the one to bring that up. But not yet. Better wait 'til evening, when the soft moon was rising and the child was fast asleep.

"Well, he didn't kill the fatted calf. But I think we were let off easily." Odd, how easily the *we* came to him. With luck, she would feel just as familiar come nighttime. "From what you had told me, I was expecting moral outrage personified."

She slanted him an amused look, one that made her dark eyes glint with irony. "I am sorry to disappoint you. He does moral outrage very well. But the important thing is, we have persuaded him that we are indeed man and wife! You were wonderful, truly! You behaved just as I would expect a husband to behave. When you chided me—oh! I almost felt sullen, as if you were forever taking me to task that way! However did you manage the pose so well?"

"Just the way you did. I invented Captain Randall."

"You must have a vivid imagination, sir. For you have imagined him better than I ever did."

She dropped onto the bed, kicking off her slippers and drawing her feet up under her skirt. It was a casual pose, unself-conscious, and his pulse quickened. Already they dealt so well, anticipating each other's responses, as if their roles had become so believable that they almost fooled themselves, too. But it had ever been too fertile, this imagination of his. As she sat cross-legged, her hands busy rolling a pile of cotton stockings into neat spheres, he almost imagined he knew her as well as he pretended to, as if he had shared many bedrooms, many days, many nights with her. He remembered the way her hand had stroked his and could almost feel it again.

He had been too long without a woman, that was all. If he had taken the time when they docked to visit a house of pleasure, his mind wouldn't be reveling so with plans for this pretend-wife of his. At the very least, however, he could wait until nightfall. A sailor learned restraint early on—and he would need every ounce of it, if this Mrs. Randall insisted on looking quite so fetching on the marital bed.

He turned away from her bright face, her slender form, her adept hands, and began pulling shirts out of his seabag. "Tell me more about how your father got the dagger."

She was silent for a moment. He looked back over his shoulder to see that her hands had stilled in her lap. The bright light had gone out of her eyes. She shook her head, as if dispelling cobwebs, and looked down at the white cotton stocking wrapped around her hands. "I don't know. He brought it home from Plymouth one Christmastide. I remember that he showed it to me and told me that he was giving it to my mother. She loved to read stories of Richard the Lionheart."

It was true, then. This was no fool's errand, his venture into Morrell Hall. The Lionheart dagger—the second of the pair—was here. "When was that?"

"Christmas. I don't recall the year. Oh, wait." Slowly, she wound up her stocking, took another from the pile, studied it abstractly, then put it aside for darning. "It was the Christmas before she died. My mother, I mean. I must have been seven. So it's been fifteen years."

"Did he buy anything else from that broker?"

"Oh, I don't think so. He was so furtive about this purchase, I shouldn't think he'd be likely to do that again. He must have wanted the dagger very badly." She added, with an innocence that didn't fool him for a moment, "Just as you do."

He refused to satisfy her curiosity. It was none of her affair why he would go to such lengths for a bit of military history. She would find that he was more reluctant than she to involve others in his past.

He halted his irritated searching through his sea bag and stood up straight to take a deep breath. His annoyance with her was due less to her inquisitiveness than to his own frustrated desire, and it was unfair to let that affect his behavior toward her. Impolitic, too. She couldn't help the radiance that made him want to kiss her every time she smiled, or the quick, graceful movements that made his imagination run riot. And besides, there was no reason to alienate her, not with the night still ahead.

So he tamped his irritation and his desire alike, and pulling out his watch, said, "It's time for me to attend your father. Where should I go?"

She jumped down from the bed, scattering all her stockings on the counterpane. "Oh, I will take you."

"No!" His objection came out more emphatically than he intended, and he saw the flash of hurt, quickly extinguished, in her dark eyes. But the last thing he wanted was her escort. He could hardly go to meet this woman's father with his thoughts still running rampant. Deliberately, he gentled his voice. "No, thank you. I'm a sailor, you see, and I shan't feel right 'til I navigate my own way through my surroundings. Just point me in the right direction. And you needn't fear," he added, "that I shall make a mistake that will ruin your plans. I am not given to making mistakes." Not in the last decade, at least, he concluded silently.

"Oh, I shan't worry about that at all," she exclaimed. "Why, you have already proved far better than I could have hoped." She glanced quickly at his face and then away. "But if he should agree to sell you the dagger, you will stay, won't you? I mean to say, you *should* stay, just through Christmas. Or . . ." Her voice trailed off, then with a determined brightness, she added, "Or if you must leave, I hope you will pretend you have received some urgent summons from your ship, perhaps that the shipment has been confiscated by the excise authorities or that your first officer has been injured in a dockside brawl. Something my father will believe."

There was a quaint courage in the way she kept improvising, as if she had learned to expect trouble and to scramble to deal with it. Watching her eyes, Eric said dryly, "I take it he hasn't many illusions about the decorum of sailors in port. But you needn't worry. I have signed on to your command until after Christmas, and you can trust me to keep my word."

Her eyes flashed her relief, and she declared, "Oh, I knew from the first that I could trust you!"

And on that disconcerting pledge of faith, she flung open the door for him, giving him one of those radiant smiles in lieu of the conjugal kiss he half expected and fully craved.

If Eric had any last doubts about the dagger, they were dispelled when Sir William led him into the armaments room hidden behind the library. The very surreptitious nature of Sir William's posture was enough of an alert. First he showed Eric the tournament lances, the old maces, the fearsome crossbow, hung on the half-timbered wall. He lingered by the glass-cased Saracen swords and British longbows, explaining the history of each in detail. He even pointed out the Algonquin tomahawk. Finally, after circling the large room twice, Sir William stopped in front of a teak cabinet and regarded him rather belligerently.

"Know you anything of blades?"

The particular blade in question Eric knew all too well, but he only shrugged. "I've used cutlasses and sabres, a machete or two. Daggers, of course. They are useful in close combat."

"Come see this one then. But . . . " Sir William glanced around him and, in a conspiratorial voice, added, "I don't show this to very many visitors. But as you're part of the family now—"

He took a key from his pocket and opened the front of the cabinet. It must have been specially made, because behind the wooden door was another door, this one made of glass. A hidden display case. Paradoxical, but suitable for the object within. This was a weapon of war, but inappropriately ceremonial, a meld of the primitive and the ornate. The blade was rough-hammered, with a vicious-looking but impractical serrated edge. The hilt was elaborately worked in gold and silver, mounted with an emerald, featuring the head of a lion with rubies for eyes.

"The Lionheart dagger." Sir William's tone was reverent, proud. "Brought back from the Holy Land by Richard Plantagenet himself in 1190. I was fortunate enough to find it a decade or so ago and bring it here to Morrell Hall."

Sardonically, Eric noted that this account was silent on the whereabouts of the dagger in the intervening six centuries. "May I hold it?"

Sir William hesitated, then nodded and opened the case. Eric took the dagger from its black velvet setting and closed his hand around it.

The last time he had gripped this dagger his hand was so small that the emerald had cut into his wrist. But this was a man's weapon, and he had become a man in the interim. The hilt now fit easily into his hand, the jewel scarcely noticeable against his callused palm.

He held the blade up to the light from the nearby barred window. It gleamed silver, the grain of the hammer strikes reflecting curves of light against the cabinet. He waited for the memories to flood him and they did, as if the last fifteen years had been merely a moment. But instead of the triumph he expected, he felt only emptiness, the emptiness of completing a voyage that had claimed half the crew.

He replaced the dagger in its case. "A fine piece, that one." He forced casualness into his voice. "I have always admired Richard the First, and I would like above anything to start collecting items of his. Would you—" he took a deep breath, then went on, "would you consider selling this to me, to become the center of my collection?"

Sir William was shaking his head even before Eric had completed his sentence. "No. No. Not for any price." He closed the glass door, then the wooden door, and locked it up.

"Why not?"

"I don't sell my pieces. Especially not this one."

Eric could not mistake the other man's adamancy, and for a moment he let the despair fill him. But then he gathered up what remained of his resolve. A week ago, he had never thought he would see the dagger, much less touch it again. He would be here for several days, and that gave him time to be persuasive or, if necessary, more innovative.

"I did well on this last voyage, you know. I can afford to pay you far more than you must have paid for it."

Sir William led him back down the hall, as if removing him from the room would remove him from temptation. "I am sorry, but I cannot sell it. I am pleased you recognize its value. But there is no price that can be placed on it. It's the centerpiece of *my* collection, you see."

"Then why don't you display it openly?" They were back out in the entry hall, and Eric gestured at the suit of armor. "That's Norman, isn't it? It must be worth more than the dagger, and yet you don't keep it hidden."

"You know your armaments, I'll give you that." Sir William touched the handle of the Norman mace with the gentleness most men reserved for their lovers. "This is a valuable piece. But the Lionheart—there's another, do you know? I learned that investigating its history.

The pair got broken up at some point, and—and I acquired this one. The other dagger's owner might be willing to sell to you, and then"—a gleam appeared in his eyes—"then both of the pair will be in the family."

Wonderful idea, Eric thought. "Why haven't you tried to buy the other, then?"

"I don't want to call attention to my ownership of this one." Sir William shot a wary glance at him. "These artifacts sometimes come with uncertain provenance. That's the reason it can't be displayed openly. And why I would be beholden if you kept it to yourself."

Eric shrugged, deciding to let it go for the moment. "As you wish. But if you should decide it's not worth the trouble, remember my offer."

That was the way his luck went on this first evening at Morrell Hall. After a light supper was served in their suite—Sir William said he knew they would be too tired to dress for dinner—and Beth was put down for the night, Eric entered the bedroom to find Verity with an armful of bedlinens. She flashed him a smile and moved past him to the sitting room door.

"What are you doing?"

"I am making up the couch in the sitting room."

Eric put out a hand to stop her. Holding her arm firmly, he said, "You don't have to do that."

"Oh, but you are too tall to be comfortable there. I shan't mind a bit, I promise you."

"I meant—" He took a deep breath to slow down his racing pulse. "I meant that we can share the bed. It looks big enough for two."

She still had the smile, but it wavered uncertainly. "I—I don't think that will be necessary. Father won't come seeking us. We need only make it seem as if nothing is untoward for the maids, and I have already made it clear to them to stay away unless we ring for them."

It was another lost cause, but he gave it a final try. Eric slid his hand up her arm to cup her shoulder, and he felt her tremble through the thin muslin. "I could sleep atop the blankets, you know."

She broke away from his hand. "Oh, but then you would get a chill. The nights are cold here, you know."

"I know." He sighed and gave in to inevitability. "I will take the couch." Her pretty mouth opened in protest but he cut her off ruthlessly. "No arguments. This is your home and you should be comfortable. And I—" he swallowed back a sigh, "I am used to narrow berths. I don't know if I could sleep in a real bed."

Not with her next to him, at least.

And not with her in the next room, either, it turned out. The moon had long set over the harbor before Eric found a comfortable position on the couch and his brain became too weary to imagine which of the angels the lady next door resembled in her sleep.

Chapter Four

December 23

No boots. Verity checked under the bed, under the chair, inside her portmanteau. But her sturdy walking boots were missing.

"Mama, hurry!" Beth cried imperiously. She at least was fully outfitted for a morning's tramp in the woods, in two petticoats, woolen pullover and leggings, and sturdy stockings and boots. Actually, Verity thought with a smile, Beth looked rather like a hedgehog, so roundly and warmly wrapped up was she.

"Just a moment, sweeting. Mama can't find her boots."

On a hunch, she went to the sitting room door and tapped lightly. When she got no answer, she slipped in. Only a sliver of early light pierced the drawn drapes, and she could hardly make out the blanket-wrapped form on the couch. Poor man, she thought, sparing him a glance as she located her carriage bag under a chair. His gallantry must have given him a very restless night, but he was certainly fast asleep now. Only the back of his golden head was visible, that and the outline of a slim but strong form under the blankets.

She found her boots and drew them out of the bag, careful not to make a sound. But it was all for naught. From behind her Verity heard the peal of a child's laughter, and she turned to see Beth in the doorway, pointing at the shaft of light on the floor. "Sun, Mama!"

Verity grabbed up her boots and her daughter's hand and went back through the door. But she wasn't quick enough. "Don't bother, I'm awake," came the resigned voice from the couch.

Guiltily, Verity retraced her steps. "I am sorry, sir. I've promised her a walk in the woods, and she's a bit impatient."

"Just as well. I should be rising, anyway." He sat up, keeping the blankets tight around him. It was too dark to make out his expression, but she saw that his hair was ruffled by sleep, and she imagined he had that drowsy, vulnerable look that even a grown man must get when awakened too soon. "Where are you going?" he asked.

Beth was tugging at her hand and whispering "Mama," so Verity replied quickly, "We're looking for holly and evergreens. My father has not had the staff decorate, you must have noticed. So Beth and I are going out to gather some, and I hope we will be able to bring a little holiday cheer back with us."

Her voice sounded foolishly bright in her own ears, as foolish perhaps as her hope that she could brighten this dark house with holly and pine boughs. But he shook his head as if to shake away the remaining drowsiness. "If you will wait a bit, I'll come with you. I expect it would be more persuasive to your father to see us all tramp out into the woods."

"You needn't really," she said, but he waved her away. And indeed, as she left him to dress, she felt a warmth steal through her that had nothing to do with the merino wool pelisse she donned. It was kind of him to keep up the appearance of a happy family, even if her father was already persuaded. Just as well, a little voice inside said, that Sir William hadn't been willing to sell the dagger. Now she needn't worry that Eric would accomplish his own mission and vanish before she accomplished hers. As long as he was set on gaining her father's goodwill, both their purposes would be furthered.

Her father was in the breakfast room, bent over the newspaper with that absolute concentration that she remembered from a thousand breakfasts in the past. And as she had finally learned to do, she said no more than "good morning" and gently hushed Beth's exuberant gurgling. Gathering up apples and scones and crumpets into a napkin, she urged Beth back out the door to the hall.

"Where are you off to?"

Startled, she almost dropped the napkin full of breakfast. She put on a smile before turning back to her father. "Eric and Beth and I are going to take our breakfast to the woods. We mean to gather up some greens as decoration for the Hall. Then I must go into the village for some wool—I've just a few more gifts to knit. And then—"

Her father's gaze had returned to his newspaper, as if he had already forgotten that his daughter and granddaughter were standing before him. That annoyed Verity so much that she made the request she had earlier decided not to make. "Father, Dolly told me that Isabelle is visiting her parents for the holidays. I'd like to invite them to dinner tonight, if you don't mind."

The Revlings lived a quarter mile down the road, and she and Isabelle had spent their childhoods trading dolls and having spats and making up, only to fight again. They hadn't seen each other in more than three years, since Isabelle's wedding to a wealthy Sussex baron. But Verity knew if her conscience had been entirely clear and her marriage entirely authentic, she would not have hesitated to introduce her husband to these neighbors and friends. It was only lingering shame that made her anxious about the prospect—shame that she needed no more, now that Eric was here.

Her father rumbled negatively, but Verity pretended not to hear. "Oh, good! I'll just send a note over to Lady Revling and speak to the cook, also. You needn't worry about anything, Father, for I will take care of it all. Come, Beth, we must hurry now."

"Just a minute. If you will, tell your husband that I am going to ride around the estate later and that he's welcome to come along. After all"—her father shrugged and went back to his paper—"it will all be his eventually, and if he's the man I think he is, he'll want to know how best to administer it."

All his eventually. Verity took Beth's hand and went back to speak to the cook. Even later, as she sent off a note to the Revlings, she felt a bitter amusement. How very fitting that her father had finally found something to approve of in her—her choice of a husband. And that was the one thing about her that was entirely false.

But she could hardly blame Eric for the sharp sense of injustice that stabbed her. He was only doing the job she had asked him to do . . . and very well at that. She was glad her father liked him and she was not surprised, either, Verity decided as Eric joined them on the terrace. She liked him, too, for he had been nothing less than exemplary since that first moment she had come up with her scheme. A lesser man might have dismissed her outright or failed miserably at pretending to be a husband. And a more venal man might have taken this pose of husband too literally. But Eric—or whatever his name was—greeted her this morning with a light comment, as if he had never for a moment imagined that they might share the bed assigned to them jointly.

She was glad he had taken no offense. Still, she glanced covertly at him as he slung over his shoulder the bag of tools he had acquired. Perhaps he was sorry he had come, since he had so far gotten neither dagger nor bedmate from this effort. At least he seemed resigned to it, striking out into the forest in the direction she indicated.

The sun was brighter than it had been in weeks, as if to proclaim that winter had not arrived, contrary to the calendar. So even in the depths of the home woods, it was light and not very cold. The brisk walk brought a flush to Verity's cheeks and must have warmed Eric, too, for he started whistling "Heart of Oak" softly in time to his strides.

Beth had decided that she liked him, too, and Verity was amused to see that he didn't quite know what to do about it. The little girl trotted along beside him, pointing at every bird and plant and keeping up a steady stream of chatter.

"Am I supposed to understand what she is saying?"

Verity laughed at his puzzled look. "No. Oh, she does speak some English words, you've surely noticed. But she makes up her own more often. Oh, there's a likely tree. Let's take a few of the lower branches."

He pulled out a handsaw and began trimming the branches she pointed out. "Beth *sounds* as if she is speaking full sentences, but I don't recognize any of the languages I know in there. It's disconcerting, for she obviously knows what she's talking about."

"It won't last." Verity gathered up the boughs that fell from his saw and tossed them onto the sheet she had spread out in the clearing. "Soon she will speak only English—and not very well—and she shan't remember a word of this language she's devised."

"It sounds a bit like Mandarin, now that I think of it." Eric paused in his work and studied Beth, who was sitting on the ground arduously stripping the needles from a twig. "Rather a singsong."

"Do you know Mandarin?"

He laughed and moved to another tree. "No. But I've heard it often enough. Two of my best foretopmen are from Peking, and when they get excited, they sound very much like Beth."

With a bit of coaxing, he told her how he had come to employ these Mandarins, then about other exotic seamen he had known over the years. As they finished with the evergreens and started collecting holly, she asked more about his crew, intrigued by his spare explanations of why Malays made the best watchmen and Danes were best at the helm. This led to more questions about his many voyages, as they prowled the woods with Beth in tow. Finally, they emerged onto the bluff overlooking the bay, and Eric walked to the brow and looked out east, as if he might see the ship he had left thirty miles away.

Holding tight to Beth's hand, Verity joined him at the edge of the cliff. Sixty feet below the sea was choppy, though there was only a light breeze. Beth pointed to a large ship bound for Plymouth, laboring a couple miles offshore. "Boat."

"Ship. A boat's not so big," Eric corrected. "Here, I'll show you."

Verity bit back a protest as he effortlessly lifted Beth to his shoulder. No longer was he tentative about how to hold her. Just hoist her up and let her hold on seemed to be his attitude. And Beth loved it, crowing with delight and waving to the ship with one hand, while grasping his arm with the other.

"One of His Majesty's ships of the line. A triple-decker, do you see? Seventy-two guns. You can't see them, Beth, but there are more than five hundred men on that ship."

"Did you serve on a ship like that?"

It was a harmless enough question, but as soon as the words were out of her mouth, Verity regretted them. His eyes had been alight with pleasure at the pretty ship, but just like that they clouded over. "No." He set the protesting Beth on the ground and picked up the knotted sheet that held their morning's haul. "If I'm to ride out with your father, we'd best get back."

Verity, trailing a bit behind with Beth, cursed herself for ruining their amity. He'd already made it clear that he didn't want to talk about his past. And yet she couldn't still her curious mind. He was an enigma, and she hated to let him go unsolved.

But he was also her fellow conspirator, and she needed him. She would be stupid to alienate him by asking questions he didn't want to answer.

Verity spent the afternoon making gifts and decorating the drawing room and the front hall, even festooning the suit of armor with a sprig of holly. But she couldn't keep her mind on her work. Her thoughts were following Eric around the estate, speculating on what he might be saying to her father. I should have gone along, she told herself. But her father would have thought that very odd, indeed, and might have refused outright.

No, she just had to trust Eric not to betray her. And he wouldn't. She might know nothing else about him, but she knew that much. He had promised to see this holiday week through, no matter what.

So when he returned from the ride, she greeted him affably. As her father went up the stairs, Eric pretended to wipe his brow in relief, then grinned at her. "Your secret is safe," he said in a stage whisper, and ran up the stairs two at a time to dress for dinner.

Verity had been looking forward to seeing her old friends again and introducing them to Eric. But when the Revlings arrived, Isabelle had a bright, hard smile on her face, one Verity recognized with a sinking heart. Even as a little girl, Isabelle had looked just that way whenever she decided to regard her best friend as a rival.

It was a silly competition, for they weren't much alike. Isabelle had always been an acclaimed beauty, the only daughter of adoring parents, the county's leading belle. And Verity had never been more than pretty, lacking the toys and gowns that an indulgent father might have given her, and popular more because of her skill at devising games than because of her looks. She was too willful, however, to stay in Isabelle's shadow, and the older they got, the more they argued.

Even now, Verity couldn't help noticing that Isabelle's lilac gown was in the height of fashion, while she knew from her friend's sharp glance that her own second-best dress wasn't. "You haven't been up to London lately, have you?" Isabelle asked with a pitying air as they gathered around the roaring fire in the drawing room. "You should go, you know. Do remind me to give you the name of my dressmaker. She could work miracles for you."

So she couldn't help a spurt of glee that Isabelle was accompanied only by her parents, her husband having elected to remain in Sussex for the holiday. Perhaps he preferred his own company. Perhaps they weren't happy together. Perhaps Isabelle was being so catty because she was even now envying Verity this man who was so undeniably *here*.

Verity slanted a look at the man standing next to her and, for the first time, saw him the way a woman might see him, a woman who didn't need him but might want him anyway. Yes, she decided, a woman would want him—if she liked a bit of mystery. He was tall and lean and impeccably dressed, yet somehow dangerous, with his golden curls haloed by the firelight and his face half in shadow. The perfect corsair, Verity thought, and slipped a wifely hand into the crook of his arm.

After the slightest hesitation, he covered her hand with his own and smiled down at her. To Isabelle and her parents, this probably looked like a fond husband's smile Only Verity could see the ironic glint in his eyes that said both that he knew what she was about and that he understood. Simultaneously annoyed and pleased with his assumption of camaraderie, she told Isabelle, "My husband is just back from the Indies. Isn't it fortunate that he arrived in time for the holidays?"

A slight pressure on her hand told her that Eric at least had heard the edge in her artless comment. A glance up at him told her that he liked that show of spirit—he was a rogue, she told herself, and shouldn't be encouraging her. But it warmed her to think that he was so obviously on her side. She wasn't used to having allies.

It was only when Beth was brought in that Verity wondered if the battle were worthy of her. Prompted by her nursemaid, the child came over to sit on Verity's lap. She was already dressed for bed in a pretty flannel nightdress, her blond curls peeping out from under a lacy cap. With her drowsy eyes and quiet murmurs, she appeared the perfect angel, and if Verity—and now Eric—recalled the mischief she could get into, they knew better than to say so. No one would believe them, anyway, with Beth cuddling against her mother and sucking contemplatively at her thumb.

Lady Revling exclaimed at Beth's sweetness, adding archly, "Well, she certainly takes after her papa, doesn't she, Captain? Such lovely golden hair . . . and those big eyes."

Verity heard Eric's indrawn breath, and she hoped that he would understand. Ladies always liked to attribute a child's looks to one parent or the other, so Verity had always been a great disappointment, being dark-haired and dark-eyed. It meant nothing, really. But after a moment's pause, Eric replied just as he ought. She liked to think that his quick responses were the result of military training. He was never at a loss for long, she thought admiringly.

As Eric listened gravely to Lady Revling's further comparisons between daughter and father, Verity turned to draw Isabelle into the conversation. But then she saw the longing expression in the other woman's eyes and remembered that Isabelle, three years married, was still childless.

Her petty sense of rivalry now seemed mean-spirited. Impulsively, she said, "Would you like to hold her? She's quite good at cuddling, especially when she's sleepy."

Isabelle hesitated, then held out her arms, and Verity gently deposited the child into her care. Beth, as she usually did in a new situation, gazed up suspiciously at Isabelle's face. But then she withdrew her thumb from her mouth and reached to touch Isabelle's diamond necklace. "Pretty," she said, nodding approvingly. "Pretty."

"Careful," Eric broke in. "She'll be persuading you to give it to her if you're not careful. She's got her mother's charm, and she isn't above exploiting it."

"Oh, she's a darling." Isabelle took the plump little hand and kissed it, then reluctantly released the child to her nurse.

Verity felt warmed, as if she were the one being praised She was always more proud of Beth than she was of her own accomplishments. She felt Eric's hand on hers and knew he understood. It wasn't that silly competition with Isabelle anymore, one that she no longer really cared to win. It just made her happy to see her daughter appreciated.

But the peace couldn't last. As soon as Beth was taken off to bed and they adjourned to the dining room, Isabelle recalled that they were rivals. She dipped her spoon into the chestnut soup and inquired sweetly, "Are you in the Royal Navy, Captain Randall?"

"No longer. I am with a merchant fleet now."

"Oh, a *merchant* fleet." After her slighting tone elicited no more than a grin from Eric, Isabelle turned to Verity. "I imagine you have a lovely manor overlooking the Channel, so you can watch for your husband's ship."

Verity gritted her teeth, but following Eric's example, she showed no offense. "Well, it's on the Channel and I like to think it's lovely, but it's no manor. Just a cottage near Plymouth. Tell me about your home, won't you? I collect it's near Brighton?"

And on it went, with Verity deflecting each of Isabelle's little barbs with a smile that grew more and more fixed as time went on. She received no help from her father, who was deep into a political discussion with Lord Revling. And Eric was occupied with Lady Revling, who had taken quite a liking to him and wanted to hear all about his voyages.

So Verity could only nod and smile and wonder why she had thought she wanted to see Isabelle again. No, she didn't have a large staff, only a maid and a nurse. No, she hadn't seen the Regent's Oriental renovation of the Brighton Pavilion. No, she hadn't yet ordered a ruby and lacquer bracelet that was all the rage in London.

Verity had to remind herself that generally she liked her life, liked taking care of her little home, liked giving lessons to the local girls, even liked making her own clothes. She had coped the best she could, and longing for a life more like Isabelle's was shortsighted and frivolous. Just once, her resolve wavered, when Isabelle spoke of her travels. That was something Verity had always dreamed of—travel, adventure, distant lands. And that was something a solitary young woman with a small child could not expect to attain.

But as it turned out, the only road Isabelle wanted to take was the one that went to London. She spoke archly of the balls and routs and theater parties that awaited her. "Surely you will be in Town this season, Verity?"

Unexpectedly, Eric broke off his conversation with Lady Revling. "This season? No, I think not. I mean to take Verity abroad this spring. Paris, perhaps, then, if she likes, Italy and Greece. You haven't ever been to Greece, have you, darling?"

The casual, slightly ironic endearment, the suggestion that Greece was one of the few places she hadn't visited, made Verity look down at her mutton with a secret smile. "No, I haven't," she replied innocently. "Though you've said it's very lovely. I do so long to see the sights you've described, darling."

Their exchange of amused glances was interrupted by Isabelle. She closed her hand on her diamond necklace and sighed almost as if she meant it. "Well, I shall miss you. What fun we had our season after the war ended. Do you remember, Verity? Of course," she added after a tiny pause, "I don't know that you will recall those weeks with quite as much fondness as I do. I vow, I felt as if I were in a whirlwind of pleasure—all the invitations to the *best* parties, all those lovely dresses, all the beaus . . . Sometimes I thought I would dance my feet right off, and yet even after a whole night without sitting out a single dance, I rose happy as a lark to see my morning callers. But I don't know that you had *quite as* lovely a time as I did."

Verity couldn't help herself. With a light laugh, she admitted, "No, I didn't! Why, that season wasn't by any means the zenith of my existence. In fact, my life has done nothing but improve ever since, and I'm so glad I can look back and see how much happier I am now."

It was unforgivable, really, but with a start, Verity realized it was true. No doubt Isabelle's happiness had peaked those few months in London. But Verity, always the optimist, had a strong sense that her own life would only get better, at least now that she could be welcomed back home with Beth.

Fortunately for her future relations with her old friends, Lord Revling sniffed rain in the night air and determined to return home before the clouds broke. Isabelle's manner was a bit chill as they took their leave, but Verity told herself it didn't matter. She was doing this for Beth, to secure her future. And all that was necessary for that was the assumption of respectability and a grandfather's sponsorship.

Sir William grunted with relief when the door closed behind his guests. "Thank God that's over. Revling thought he could convert me to the Whigs if he had another quarter hour. He's bored me so, I'm ready to retire early." He started up the stairs, then looked back over his shoulder at Eric. "Lady Revling certainly had a lot to say to you, didn't she? Prettiest girl in the country when she was young. Still a handsome woman—and still with an eye for the good-looking young Navy officer."

Verity thought her companion might be flushing, and she wondered if he were so unused to observations like that—or if it was the reference to the Navy that unnerved him. Surely Lady Revling wasn't the only woman to find him compellingly attractive. Isabelle's gaze had lingered on his bronzed face so frequently that Verity was almost annoyed. But here Eric was, disconcerted enough that she was led in sympathy to change the subject.

"I'm not tired, are you? Perhaps we can do a bit more with the greenery," she suggested, leading the way back to their suite. "With so little time left 'til Christmas, I hate to lose a moment. Isabelle made me realize how much I have yet to do—the evergreen ropes, the holly wreaths, the berry sprigs."

She had left a heap of evergreen and her sewing supplies on the couch, and here they tacitly decided to remain, next to the fire that had already warmed the sitting room. Verity was uneasy, sitting on the couch where he would be sleeping in a couple hours. It made her heart quicken to look across at his lean form and remember it blanket-wrapped on this couch. She could almost imagine that the leather against her was still warm from his body.

But she forced such visions away. There was no evidence that this had served as a bed, for neat as all sailors must be, he had stowed away the linens, and it looked quite as innocent as any other couch in the house.

He made it easier on her by taking a seat at the desk as soon as she settled on the couch amidst the boughs of pine. He had instructions to send to his first officer, he said, and shipping contracts to review. He remained a dozen feet away, and as long as he did, she could pretend they were sedate married folk, too long acquainted for any sudden acceleration of the senses.

Chapter Five

His correspondence completed, Eric stood at the window, hearing, if he could not see, the great waves battering this battered coast. Isabelle, that little bitch, had been chagrined to find her girlhood friend married, if only to an inconsequential sea captain. Her catty comments about a London season had rankled Eric rather more than they should have, with their implication that Verity had been a failure as a girl and perhaps just as much so as a woman.

He recalled, from another life, the year his sister had gone off to London to make her debut. He never saw her again He went off to sea a month later, when he turned twelve, and she married a Scotsman and moved to Edinburgh. But he recalled the breathless anticipation, the extensive preparations, and could envision Verity at that age in alt, in her element, preparing for a month-long party.

He glanced back over his shoulder at Verity, her head bent low over yet another rope of evergreen, the candlelight gilding her dark hair and the sweet curve of her neck. "So you had a season in London?"

She looked up from her work and studied him for a moment before answering, "Not a regular one. I was supposed to come out in the spring of Fifteen, but Bonaparte had escaped and everyone was in a quiz. So I attended the Little Season that fall, after Waterloo."

"Did you enjoy it?"

She wrinkled up her nose, an ambivalent expression from a usually positive woman. "Oh, I had a deal of fun. But I didn't take, you know. That's what Isabelle was saying, in her nasty little way."

"You didn't take?" It was hard to believe, looking at her now, with the shawl half dangling from her slender arms, a full lip caught in her teeth as she rethreaded the needle. "Were all the bucks blind that year?"

A quick smile, a quick shake of her head, then she went back to her wreath. "Oh, they liked me well enough. As a bosom beau, that is. I was always the one chosen to help them rehearse the proposals they were making to Isabelle." She sewed on a berry sprig and automatically tied off the thread before adding wryly, "It was because I was ever the organizer of our entertainments. While I was making sure the picnic was going off without a hitch, she or some other girl would slip off into the woods with my favorite. I just couldn't learn to be less capable." She smiled, shook her head, and bent to bite through the thread. Whatever pain she had felt then had softened into mere rueful remembrance.

"Is that—?" He broke off, annoyed with himself, annoyed with her for coming to him so complete, with a past he wasn't part of no matter what he pretended. He wondered what had become of that locket she had showed him, the one with the blond curl The square-necked gown was bare of adornment, not that the gentle swell of her breasts wasn't enough. "Is that when you met Beth's father?"

Verity glanced around, startled, and only when she had listened hard, head cocked, to make sure they were quite alone did she answer. And even then she spoke so quietly he had to come back and sit near her to hear.

"No. I met him just after Christmas." The wistfulness in her eyes did not escape him. She was remembering that Christmas three years ago, when her life had changed.

"Not in London."

"No. I was staying with my aunt in Plymouth."

"And it being winter, you hadn't any picnics to organize when he came into port. So he ruined you instead."

She drew back at the hardness of his voice, but he didn't care. He didn't care for that other sailor, either, the one with the same light hair and lighter morals, who had taken such advantage of this lonely, laughing girl.

"It wasn't really as you are thinking," she said, her equanimity regained, her hands busy again with the pine branches.

"How do you know what I'm thinking?"

"I can tell. Your jaw is clenched tight as a fist." Boldly now, as she might have done with that other sailor, she reached over and drew her fingers lightly against his jaw. He closed his eyes for a second, breathing in the piney scent of her hands. Then the scent, the touch, was gone, and he opened his eyes to find her looking down at her wreath, her mouth curved in a smile.

"What is so amusing?"

She shook her head. "Oh, just the thought of Billy as a vile seducer."

Billy. A stupid name. He took the crooked end of her long rope and twisted it backward to straighten it out. "Wasn't he?"

"Not at all. He was only a boy. Only eighteen—two months older than I. He'd never been in love before. Neither had I."

The springy branch broke in his hands. Murmuring admonitions under her breath, Verity took it from him and began the laborious process of putting the rope back together.

He watched her hands weaving the thread around the greenery and saw them moving so deftly over the buttons of a man's shirt, undoing them . . . " What else did he tell you?"

"What do you mean?"

"Did he promise to marry you?"

Her hands stilled their activity, and when she spoke there was no laughter in her voice. "He did. We meant to marry. But we were underage and had no funds with which to bribe a parson. He did try, though . . . "

"You believed him."

For the first time ever he felt her anger, hot and sudden, flashing toward him like a flame. "Yes, I believed him. I *knew* him. He wasn't— he wasn't some hardened rake. He'd never had anyone before, no one who loved him. All he ever wanted was a wife and a family. And if he hadn't been called back to his ship, we would have gone to Scotland and married. Don't you try to tell me any differently, for you didn't know him. He loved me and he would not have hurt me for the world."

She rose, spilling the evergreen rope to the floor. Her eyes in the candlelight were dark and fierce, but then her dark lashes swept down to hide them and she crossed to the door. His anger melted in the heat of hers. This is what she needed to believe, and what harm was there in it, after all? Perhaps it was even true. She would be a great temptation for a lonely man, that much was clear.

Before she could leave, he said, "I'm sorry. You are right. I did not know him."

Slowly, she turned and retraced her steps. When she was back at her chair she didn't sit down, but only knelt on the floor and began to wind up her evergreen rope. "It is only what most people would think. I know that. They would think the worst. That is why—why I thought of Captain Randall."

He went back to the window and looked out, so that he wouldn't have to look at her kneeling there, her arms full of evergreen and her eyes full of hurt. "Do I look like him?" When she made a questioning sound, as if she didn't understand, he added, "Lady Revling said that Beth certainly had her father's looks. She meant that Beth looked like me."

"I think she just meant Beth doesn't look like me. Oh, I suppose there's a resemblance. But—but he was a boy. You're grown. I can't tell He wasn't so tall. And he hadn't your air of command. I always wondered if he was different at sea, if he grew into his role. Because with me he was . . . just Billy."

That wasn't really what he wanted to hear, that he was an older and not so endearing replica of her dead love. But then, "just Billy" didn't seem as formidable a rival after all—if rival he was. He was just a boy, and this woman wasn't just a girl anymore.

So he could afford to be more generous now. "We judge others by our own behavior, I suppose. The wicked among us impart wicked motives to everyone else."

He heard her laughing and turned unbelievingly to see. The wretched girl was incapable of maintaining anger or sadness or any serious emotion for more than a moment or so.

"Well, I am wicked as can be, aren't I?" she said gaily, rising with evergreen trailing like a scarf over her shoulder. "And I impart wicked motives only to the wicked."

"How would you know the wicked from the well-meaning?"

"I am a good judge of character. I am, you know," she said, serious again, for the moment. "I had to learn to read expressions very early, to know if my father was amenable to being approached. For if he weren't, I'd never get what I asked. I developed a sixth sense about people." She went to the door, and juggling her greenery a bit, managed to turn the handle. Just before she closed the door behind her, she looked back.

"For instance, I knew that I could trust you to be my husband. As soon as I saw you, I knew that we would be safe with you. And I was right, wasn't I?"

No. But he didn't say it aloud, and she was gone at any rate, through that door to her bed. No. She couldn't trust him to be her husband. If he were, she wouldn't be sleeping alone.

No. Then she would be sleeping with a man who had no claim on the name she claimed, nor his own name, either. And a woman like her deserved better than that.

Chapter Six

December 24

The whole house was redolent with holly and evergreen, and Eric was congratulating them both on a good morning's work and speaking longingly of lunch. But Verity wasn't done yet with her holiday decorating. The entry hall might be filled with Yuletide spirit, even the suit of armor sporting a bit of holly in his visor, but the front door was still unwelcoming.

As Verity inched the library stepladder along the marble floor to the threshold, Eric eyed it dubiously. "Why don't we get one of the footmen to put up the rest of the greens?"

In a low, reproving voice meant to reach only him and not the footmen, whose feelings might be hurt, she said, "There isn't a footman in the house younger than fifty, and this would doubtless bring on an apoplexy."

She wrestled the ladder out onto the front steps, then stood there hugging herself and shivering as the chill worked its way through her wool crepe gown. The sun was trying bravely to pierce through the clouds, but all that was emerging was a weak ray that glanced off the copper hinge on the ladder. "Eric, let's hurry. It's cold out here."

Eric sighed deeply and emerged. Despite the chill, he stripped off his coat and draped it over her shoulders, then stood beside her in his white waistcoat and shirt, appraising the ladder as if it led all the way to the sky instead of just to the top of the door frame. "If I break my neck, it will be on your head."

She pulled his coat tighter around her It was still warm from his body. The thought of his neck on her head made her chuckle, but she sobered when he made no move toward the ladder. "For pity's sake, Eric, and you call yourself a sailor? Oh, I'd forgotten. You get others to climb the rigging for you. You are a *captain*." She invested that dignified term with the scorn due something like *poltroon*, and predictably he rose to the bait.

"I'll have you know, my girl, that before I was captain of a ship, I was captain of the foretop and spent most of my youth aloft."

"A time long past, I take it, and fortunately so."

He was a good man to tease He scowled deliciously and reached out a hand as if to cuff her. Laughing, she danced out of the way and down one step, so she could see the whole door frame. "Come, now,

Captain, your manhood is at stake here. You have climbed a mast, surely, if you were a foretopman?"

"A thousand times. But—" He took hold of the old ladder and shook it, and it creaked in answer. "But a foremast, even in a gale, is sturdier than this contraption. Come here and hold it for me."

"Let me get the rope first." She dashed back into the house to get the evergreen rope she had made the previous night, then made a great show of wrapping it around him. She let one end dangle over his shoulder, then wound the rope round his chest, under his arms, and again around his slim waist.

He stood quite still, one hand on the top step of the ladder as if he needed that for balance. He made no comment as she tied him up in Christmas greenery. But every time she looked up, she saw the ironic quirk of his smile. They were friends again, for all that she had lost her temper with him the previous night.

As she came to the end of the evergreen rope, she let her hand linger on the smooth fabric of his waistcoat, only a few layers of fabric from the taut muscles of his side. It had been a lifetime—Beth's lifetime—since she had been so close to a man that she could touch him like this. And so for a moment she let herself enjoy this contact, her hand, bare but for a simple gold band, curved around the curve of his waist, warming where it touched his warmth.

She stole a glance up at his face and found all the irony gone. In his eyes instead was pure silver flame, desire so naked she felt naked herself, felt against her hand the tightening that meant he was holding his breath. This was no pretense, no husbandly pose. He wanted her, and he waited only for her to raise her hand to his face to tell him she wanted him, too, wanted his kiss, his caress.

I don't even know who you are, she thought, and his eyes, his desire, answered back, Does it matter?

Once it might not have. Once she would have moved closer to him, breathed in the piney scent of the evergreen, trailed her hand up his chest, lifted her face for his kiss, been as wild and wicked as only she knew how to be. But not now. Not with a man who could only pretend permanence, however real his passion.

She dropped her hand, stepped back, managed a smile. "Now you are properly rigged out for Christmas, Captain."

He turned swiftly away, but not before she saw the anger, the disappointment on his face. It was a moment before he looked back with that ironic expression. "I think I prefer to tack it above the door as we'd planned. You hold the ladder and hand me the tacks. They're in the pocket of my coat there."

At least he isn't pressing me, she told herself. He's a gentleman at heart, whatever else his life has made him. So she held the ladder steady with one foot on the bottom rung and one hand on the side near his booted calf, and with the other hand she passed the tacks up to him. He must not have wanted to prolong this painful proximity any more than she did, because he took only the time necessary to tack the rope around the door frame and then, with an impatient hand, waved her away so he could climb down. "We are done finally, I hope?"

Verity felt in her pocket for the last bit of greenery There was still the mistletoe to be hung. But suddenly a kissing bough seemed too dangerous a temptation. "All done," she replied brightly, and then, as he started pulling the ladder back through the door, she added, "Except for the Yule log, of course."

He wasn't angry He was just cool and remote, the way he had been those first few moments she had known him. "After lunch, I hope."

"Of course, we'll eat lunch first. Beth isn't finished helping the cook with the plum pudding, anyway." She followed him through the door and called to the footman to take the ladder back to the library.

Eric held out his hand for his coat, and she felt a premonition of loss. The cheer they had been tacking up all morning had no effect on the chill in this hall. But she shrugged off the coat and gave it to him, then located her gray wool shawl trailing from a chair. Tying the ends into a bow over her chemisette, she realized the futility of all her pretense—pretending that this house could be a holiday home, pretending she had a family, pretending this man was her husband when he wasn't hers at all.

Subdued, she started back toward the dining room. "You needn't come with us into the woods. My father's in Port-hallow, so he won't be there to see us, anyway. And half the staff will be along to help out. I think even our antique footmen can wield a hatchet. And if they can't, I can."

Eric gave her a sharp look as he held open the door. But he waited 'til they were seated and served before he replied, "Verity with an axe. I shouldn't miss it for the world. I shall be sure to stay out of range, of course."

Her momentary sadness dissipated when he kept up the same teasing attitude as, booted and cloaked, they marched out into the woods, trailing a troop of servants. She studied him as he directed one group of footmen along one path, another to the copse. He looked every inch the commander, even in his riding clothes, even with Beth perched on his shoulder, her hands securely tangled in his hair. The brisk weather had put a flush into his bronzed cheeks and a sparkle into his eyes She could imagine him just like this, steering his ship on some winter voyage through the Strait of Magellan.

Of course, this was a simple country excursion, not the great adventure he was used to. But after that single moment of resistance, he had joined in the fun as if it had been his idea all along. Verity couldn't help being touched by his kindness, especially since she must be a great disappointment to him. He had come expecting to acquire the dagger and, perhaps, to bed her—a reasonable enough assumption on his part considering what she had told him of her past. Last night she had tried to explain that, wild as she was, she had never been wanton, that Billy was special, and that she would not do that again. But he was a man, and perhaps he did not appreciate such distinctions. No matter He was not holding her belated chastity against her, nor her father's reluctance to sell the dagger.

It took most of the afternoon to find just the right log for the Yule fire, for Verity was an exacting mistress of Christmas celebrations. But no one complained, though the more arthritic footmen spent most of the time huddled around the small campfire Eric built with the logs Verity disdained.

The weak winter sun was low in the sky when the youngest of the footmen, a mere stripling of fifty or so, found a log smooth enough to pass her test, a long, thick branch broken from a birch tree in a recent storm. He signaled to Eric to bring Beth over, and after some quiet prompting, she sat down plump on the log and cried out, "Mama! Look! I find it!"

True to his word, Eric let Verity chop off the smaller branches, but then he took the hatchet from her hand to trim the ends of the log. Three of the footmen vied for the right to drag it home, one holding the single length of rope obstinately against his meager chest, the other two arguing seniority or superior strength.

In the end, Eric rigged up a three-part harness of rope, so that each volunteer could tug without too much fear of his heart giving out. As they started back, Eric hoisted Beth onto his shoulder, warning, "If you pull my hair again, little one, I shall set you right down again."

They had gotten far ahead of the servants and were just emerging from the woods when the maid Dolly started singing an ancient carol. Her voice was thin but pretty, and when the men joined in, it carried through the crystalline air. It was a country song, translated from the old Cornish tongue, and Verity had learned it at her nurse's knee.

> *"Mary had a baby,*
> *A sweet baby boy.*
> *And that babe of Mary's*
> *He brought the world joy.*
> *"Joy in the morning,*
> *God's sun comes to rise.*
> *Joy in the evening,*
> *And in the baby's eyes."*

Eric paused for a moment, his head cocked to the side. Verity saw the memory dawn in his eyes, and she realized that once someone had sung this song to him, years and years ago, before he had left his childhood home. She reached out and took his hand, and even through two layers of glove she felt the tingle as he pressed her palm.

But then Beth, excited by the song, took a handful of Eric's thick hair. "You little wretch," he cried in mock anger, and letting go of Verity's hand, he swung the child down in a great swoop. She shrieked in delight as he cradled her in his strong arms and pretended to toss her into a bush.

"She's terrified of me," he assured Verity, and Beth begged him to do it again. By the time they found their way back to the house, the child had laughed herself weary and fell asleep while Verity and Dolly were giving her a bath.

She'll sleep 'til midnight, Verity thought, miss all the Christmas Eve fun, and wake up ready to play. But it was useless to try to wake a sleeping child, and she resigned herself to a sleepless night. That would be nothing new. She thought back to other Christmas Eves, when her mother was alive and her father still enjoyed the festivities. She was always too excited to sleep on those nights before Christmas, when the carolers came and the staff worked late and merrily, preparing for the next day's dinner.

Verity wandered around the house, a bit at loose ends. There was nothing left to do for Christmas, really, except to celebrate it. All her packages were wrapped in the colored paper she had been saving the whole year, and all the decorations were hanging jauntily in their places. Now she had an entire evening yet to get through with no activities to fill her time.

She found Eric in the armaments room, standing in front of the glass case that held the jeweled dagger. He turned when she came in, and for just an instant she saw despair in his eyes before he smiled and asked about Beth. She kept forgetting that he was here not only to help her, but also because he wanted that stupid dagger. And even as she explained about Beth nodding off in the middle of her bath, she determined to help his cause as much as he had helped hers.

As soon as her father returned from Porthallow, she asked him to join her for tea. They had spent little time alone these last two days She wanted him to come to know Beth better, so she usually brought her along. Now she was annoyed to find her hand shaking a bit as she poured his tea, but she nerved herself to ask him for that which she had no reason to expect.

She knew her light manner annoyed him, so she schooled her features into a somber expression as she handed him the cup.

"Here you are, Father. We are nearly ready for the holiday tomorrow, I think. I have wrapped gifts for everyone on the staff. Eric sent back to his ship for a whole casket of tea, and I divided it up into little packets. And of course I have stockings for the maids and new hats and gloves for the men."

Her father only nodded, and she swallowed a frustrated sigh. Had he always been so taciturn? No, it was his isolation here on this remote coast, in this gloomy old house, she decided, that made him so unreachable. But she persevered. "Did you go to Porthallow to purchase a few gifts?"

"And to consult my attorney." He drank his tea and set his cup down on the table, then fixed her with an assessing stare. "I got the child a top."

"She'll like that." *Her name is Beth*, she wanted to add, but held her tongue.

"What would you like?"

Although this was exactly the opening she wanted, his question was so unexpected that she could not answer immediately. It was a measure of their distant relationship that she wasn't sure he really wanted to know. Perhaps it was some sort of trick. But she had little to lose, after all. "Oh, do you know, I've been away from home for so long, I sometimes wish I had something to remind me of Morrell Hall, some memento."

Sir William glanced around the drawing room, no doubt surprised that she would feel nostalgic about this place. But then he shrugged. "You will inherit it all eventually, anyway, you and Captain Randall. If you want something particular, you might as well take it."

Verity took a deep breath. It couldn't be so simple, not with her father. "The Lionheart dagger. It—it is a lovely object. And"—the falsehood stuck in her throat, but she forced it out—"I've always admired it."

"The dagger?" He drew back, his expression wary, dismayed. "Why that?"

"I remember that—that you gave it to my mother for Christmas, when I was just a girl."

For a moment, a smile flickered on his face, and Verity was too surprised to go on. Sir William was not one to laugh, especially about her mother.

"Come, my dear, do you really think I purchased it for her?"

Verity shook her head in confusion. "But, Father, I recall distinctly when she opened it. You said that you knew Richard the Lionheart was one of her heroes and that he had held this very dagger in his hands. She was very pleased." Slowly, she poured another cup of tea, reviewing that vivid scene in her mind. "I know you think I am dreadfully fanciful, but I assure you I did not make that up. It was our last Christmas with Mother."

"Yes."

She must have been mistaken about the smile, for now he was somber, almost angry, the father she best remembered. He rose and went to stir up the fire. "Perhaps she did like it, as she pretended. Do you think?"

Verity stared at his implacable back, wondering if her father were really asking for her reassurance. It was so unlikely, and yet, reassurance was one of those gifts that she was used to giving. And so, warmly, she said, "Of course she liked it, Father. Don't you remember how she sewed a velvet lining for the case?"

The fire was burning merrily again, but still he did not turn around. "Perhaps you are right. I have often wondered since then if I should have gotten her something else . . . a diamond necklace, perhaps. Most women would have preferred that."

"Mother was not most women." Verity nodded for additional firmness, though he could not see it. "She shared your interests, I think."

"So she always said. I never questioned that while she lived." Incredibly, there was a catch in his voice as he went on. "She was so good. I fear I thought that her goodness would make up for the way I acquired the dagger. That if she touched it, it would be clean again . . . " He gave the fire a last stab, then turned to Verity with a forced laugh. "It is not unknown for husbands to give wives what they most want for themselves. Hasn't Captain Randall ever done that?"

She was too unused to the role of her father's confidant to invent some reassuring story of such a husbandly trick. "No. But—but perhaps when we have been married longer he will do that."

And then her father smiled at her, for the first time, really, since she had come home, the first time in years. "Probably not. He seems remarkably considerate of your feelings, that husband of yours."

Filled with confusion, very near tears, Verity returned a tremulous smile, then excused herself and fled from her father's presence. It was only when she was back in her own room that she remembered that her father had not promised her the dagger. No matter, she told herself, rubbing away a few treacherous tears. That he would confide in her that way meant—meant what? That he was glad she remembered those days when they were a family? That he had accepted her with her husband and child as his new family? That he would grant her request?

She heard the door open in the next room, heard Eric moving about getting dressed for dinner. "He seems remarkably considerate of your feelings, that husband of yours," her father had said, almost as if he approved. That was not so strange, was it? Sir William, distrustful of his daughter's judgment, had probably expected the worst of her chosen husband. And Eric, confident, considerate, must have seemed, in comparison, an ideal addition to the family.

But how fragile it was, this new family. It rested entirely on a man who didn't exist and yet had become so essential to them all.

She worried that her father would make up for his unusual candor by being aloof again at dinner. But he was obviously trying to assume the holiday mood. And Eric showed yet again how adept he was at the art of conversation, asking about the local Christmas customs, describing a holiday he had passed in Hawaii, when the missionaries staged a nativity play with a native Mary in a grass skirt.

After dinner, he suggested a walk, and as he was settling Verity's heavy cloak on her shoulders, he said, "You were very quiet."

She pulled her hair out from under the cloak and shook it free. Glancing back to make sure her father had retired to his sanctuary, she replied, "I don't want to alienate him, when there's still your dagger to be bought. I've finally learned that keeping still works best with my father. Children should be seen and not heard, even when they are adults."

He bent close to fasten the cloak at her neck, and so his words were low and gentle, almost a caress. "I'm glad you didn't learn that early enough to silence you. And I hope you unlearn it very soon."

As they emerged into the night, Verity slanted a glance at him. "But you are very good with him. I think he truly likes to converse with you."

She saw a flash of white in the darkness and knew he was amused. "And you can't imagine how a rough sailor learned to be so civil? Well, sweeting, more than navigation, a captain must learn conversational adroitness."

They started down the long lane to the coastal road, and just as she would have were they truly man and wife, she took a companionable hold on his arm. "Why do you need conversation?"

"You would be surprised—or perhaps you wouldn't—at how tense relations get between people confined on a ship for months at a time." He covered her hand on his arm and drew her nearer, so that their bodies touched in several places with every step. He appeared not to notice this distracting connection, however, and continued casually, "The officers have dinner together every afternoon. Every afternoon. Conversation wears thin about three months out, and little irritations become matters of great import. This last voyage, I spent most of my time smoothing over the difficulty between my first officer and the ship's surgeon. We were off the coast of Brazil when they fell into disputing which horse had won the Derby in Aught Eight. The ship's company was soon broken into two camps, and mess groups were challenging each other to fights over the issue." He sighed, though his voice was tinged with amusement. "If we hadn't come upon a squadron of pirates, which brought the crew back together, I might well have had to leave half of them in Rio."

"Who was right? About the Derby winner?"

His chuckle sounded quiet in the stillness of the night. "Neither, of course. It was another horse entirely. And I've learned my lesson. I am taking lists of all the winners of the major races with me next time."

It was a glimpse of sea life she had not imagined—a captain as much politician as leader. *No wonder we do so well together,* she thought, studying him covertly. *We are both used to keeping the peace, not to starting fights.*

And perhaps her father was right, that this was a man who gave unusual consideration to those around him. She wished she knew what terrible hurt had made him so sensitive to the hurts of others.

He has a past, she told herself, *that I know nothing about. He could be a murderer or—or even married.*

No. He was too kind to be a murderer and too alone to be a husband.

She gently withdrew her arm from his when they reached the juncture with the coastal road. The Channel spread out below them, mysterious and majestic in the velvet darkness.

"Come, let's see if we can see Plymouth."

Then, picking up her skirts, she ran across to one of the great boulders that some primeval tidal wave had left all along this coast.

"King Arthur stones." Eric vaulted up onto it as nimbly if he were in his own rigging.

"Yes," she said, surprised. This had been Arthur's kingdom, and these stones were so like the one that once held Excalibur that they were forever assigned to him by the Cornish. Few outside this county knew that. But then, Eric was a seafarer, a privateer, perhaps even a smuggler. He knew more than he ought about many things, she thought as she took his hand and found her footing on the smooth stone.

The night around them was crystalline, so clear that the brighter stars cast faint reflections in the dark Channel, so chill that the mist felt like little shards of ice on her face. The sea was calm, the surf only a whisper against the stillness of the air. It was all so very fragile, like a winter scene kept under glass, that she was afraid to speak for fear it would all shatter.

But Eric was beside her, warm and vital and solid, and he didn't have such womanly fears. He pointed out the faint lights of Plymouth, visible only in the clearest weather. "Even you, I am afraid, cannot conjure up a white Christmas for us."

The night didn't shatter, so she took courage from him and replied. "We never get snow in Cornwall, especially so early in the winter."

"I know. I was sixteen before I first saw snow, and that was in the Atlantic off Halifax. A foot of it fell on the deck in a few hours." He jumped down and held out his arms to her. "I found I hadn't missed anything after all."

She slid down into his arms, remaining there for just a moment even after her feet were on solid ground. Then, sensibly, reluctantly, she drew away before that light, silver as starlight, came into his eyes again. To distract him, she asked, "You were born near here, weren't you?"

The question was simple enough, but they both knew it violated some tacit contract between them. In the arrested expression on his face, she saw indecision, then a deliberate choice.

"Yes. About six leagues from here, in fact. But I left when I was a child, to go to sea. I didn't come onto land very much, though I got to know the coast here quite well."

As if he regretted even this much of a disclosure, he strode down the road without waiting for her to catch up. She quickened her pace, knowing now that her suppositions about him were correct. Only a smuggler would know this coast well, for the Navy had no use for the little inlets and coves that the Channel had carved out of Cornwall. And he was as native as she. A black sheep of some illustrious family, no doubt His quiet, elegant accent was surely left over from some other, gentler life.

She was busy counting off the noble families within twenty miles when he stopped and let her catch up. The look on his face—regretful, restrained—made her cut her list short. It was none of her business, after all. He must have his reasons for hiding his past. And just because she had confided to him every piece of folly she had ever committed didn't mean that he need be similarly open. The look she had sometimes seen in his cloudy eyes told her that his secrets were far darker than her own. Just because she longed to share them, just because she longed to banish that despair, didn't mean she had any right to plague him.

So she ordered her wayward thoughts back into line, rejoining him with the comment, "Listen! I hear carolers!"

And over the rumble of the surf came the gay strains of a Christmas melody sung by a medley of voices. The singers came marching in cadence around the bend of the road, with the vicar in front keeping time with a wooden pointer.

Instinctively, she drew nearer to Eric. The vicar and the churchwomen behind him she had known all her life, and the dozen children she knew from teaching in the parish school years before. There must have been a deal of gossip over her absence these past three years and would be much more if the truth were known.

Eric must have sensed her tension. He nudged her as the vicar and his singers came to a halt near them. "Introduce me."

"Mr. Polton!" She slipped back into her usual friendly manner, reminding herself that they had already fooled her far more suspicious father. "May I make my husband known to you? Captain Randall. And, Eric, these are ladies of the church, Mrs. Tregenny, Mrs. Peverell, and Mrs. Watkins."

There were bows and smiles all around, and not the slightest edge to any of it. Verity let the warmth of the welcome cheer her. And this was a most cheery group for a cold night. A couple of the older boys, made merry by eggnog and the lateness of the hour, were singing snatches of carols, practicing, the vicar said gravely, for their next performance on the steps of Morrell Hall.

Wistfully, Verity heard one of the boys whistling her favorite carol, a gentle one about the shepherds and the angel's tiding.

"What fun you must be having! Please, do come up to the house. My father's retired, I think, but some of the staff is still up, and we can provide something to warm you. It's a long walk to Lord Revling's!"

Unexpectedly, Eric said, "Well, let's go with them, sweetheart. You know you want to."

It was too true to deny, so Verity didn't try. She squeezed Eric's hand gratefully as the group arranged itself around the steps of Morrell Hall

He smiled down at her and said, "Just wait 'til the butler sees us among this motley crew!"

The butler was so surprised, in fact, that he called to those of the staff still awake to come see. After serving out cider, the servants added their voices to the mix, and the song swelled up as if the night sky were a cathedral and they a heavenly chorus. But of all the voices, Verity heard mostly Eric's clear baritone, hesitant at first, as if the song wasn't quite familiar, then stronger when memory brought the words back.

> *"When shepherds watched their flocks by night,*
> *All seated on the ground,*
> *The angel of the Lord came down,*
> *And glory shone around."*

It was indeed a night for small pleasures. A startled Isabelle, hair already braided for the night, coming out to kiss her Happy Christmas. A particularly rousing round of "God Rest You Merry Gentlemen" outside the Royal Oak tavern. The Justice of the Peace pressing a sixpence into her hand as if she were one of the children.

Eric whispering, "I wish Beth could be with us."

So it was hours before Verity went to bed with the Christmas melodies and Eric's voice still echoing in her ears. Drowsily, she thought that perhaps she should come back here to live, oh, not in Morrell Hall, but perhaps in a cottage on the grounds. The villagers would accept Beth now that they had met her father, accept her and treat her well. They could be happy here, a loving little family. . .

Only they weren't a family. That thought chased away the drowsy peace, and she realized with the clarity of insomnia how close she had come to believing the pretense that had fooled everyone else. It was Christmas Eve. In two days he would be gone, leaving her to invent some eventual story of a death at sea. And the man she called Eric would be . . . where? Somewhere else, somewhere far away, and just as alone as she would be.

She had just settled into a troubled sleep when Beth's cries woke her anew. She lay there for a few minutes, waiting to see if Beth would go back to sleep as she usually did. Indeed, the cries muted and soon quieted, but something about the quality of the new silence made her wonder if Beth had managed to crawl from her crib and out of the room. She rose and pulled on a robe, then went across the hall.

As she had feared, the door was standing open. But the room wasn't dark and empty. In fact, it glowed with the faint light of a candle. Verity stopped silently in the doorway when she saw Beth safe in her crib, with Eric sitting Indian-style on the floor beside her. He was still dressed. Perhaps he, too, had suffered insomnia and had been awake to hear Beth call out.

At any rate, he had the child's full attention. She lay on her side, her thumb in her mouth, her other hand stroking the satin lining of the blanket. Beth was to get her caroling after all. Eric began to sing softly—not a Christmas song, but a song of his own devising. A lullaby.

Verity held her breath, careful not to alert him. She recognized the melody, anyone would. It was the Navy anthem, "Heart of Oak," only with words he was making up specially for Beth.

"Come cheer up, my lass, 'tis to morning we steer.

To bring something new to Christmas so near.

To sleep I will rock you, on—on something—something wave,

For who is so fair as sweet Beth is brave?"

The gentle song worked its magic. Before his deep voice faded from the air, Beth's eyes had closed, and Eric rose and picked up his candle. He bent to kiss the child's forehead. For just that moment, in the flickering light, their heads glowed the same pale golden shade.

Then with a quiet, "Night, angel," he left the room.

Slipping away before she could be discovered, Verity leaned against her closed door and listened to him enter the sitting room. Just for tonight, she let herself imagine him with them always, with his quiet voice and generous smiles, with his warm heart and his adventurous spirit. Just for tonight she gave in to the dangerous illusion that he was really her creation, and that she alone could make him real.

Chapter Seven

December 25

Eric sat with his back straight against the hard pew, trying to look like the perfect *paterfamilias* instead of a sailor who hadn't been in a church since Napoleon escaped from Elba. At least the service was a bit familiar, with the stately old organ music and the Christmas reading from the Gospel of St. Luke. He remembered that much from childhood.

He also remembered the restlessness that beset children during a Christmas service, when a hearty dinner and heaps of gifts were to follow. Even if he could have forgotten, there was Beth to remind him, bouncing in her seat, talking to herself, tugging at his arm and her mother's bonnet ribbons. Every now and again Verity would produce some diversion from her reticule, but the effect wore off rapidly, and Eric had taken to bribing the child with pennies. No fool she, Beth preferred the shiny silver sixpences, and he silently urged the vicar to hurry before bankruptcy threatened.

Fortunately, the little church was damp despite the roaring stove fire, and the vicar Mr. Polton wrapped up his Christmas sermon quickly. "Christmas is a warm moment in a cold season, the warmth of a mother holding her child, of friends bearing gifts, of families coming home. As we gather over our Christmas dinners today, let us not forget that our Savior's birth and sacrifice made this warmth possible."

Beth, her hand full of coins, stood up on the pew beside her mother, with one hand on Eric's shoulder for balance. She regarded the vicar's exit from the pulpit with a gravity that indicated she was trying to understand this move. Finally, in a voice that carried through the still church, she asked Eric, "We go? We have oranges?"

In answer, he pulled out the bag of oranges from under the seat and put his finger to his lips. Amazingly, Sir William was looking amused rather than annoyed with his granddaughter. Finally, the accumulated spirit of child and holiday was affecting the old man. He even nodded with magisterial grace to the other churchgoers as the organ postlude swelled and they exited the little sanctuary.

Outside the greetings rang clear in the crisp air. Eric was glad to see that the caroling ladies welcomed Verity in the daylight, too, beckoning and exclaiming over Beth in her little embroidered petticoat and cap. As one bent to examine Beth's handful of pennies, Verity caught Eric's eye and smiled. It was a grateful smile, which said clearly that this was his doing. She and Beth would not be accepted without the respectability his presence lent them.

Verity's gratitude. It wasn't the prize he had come here to get. But it might have to be enough. Sir William wasn't responding to any of his hints about the dagger, and he could hardly steal it now that he'd made the mistake of showing his interest. Verity would be the nearest target for her father's wrath, once her supposed husband disappeared with the Lionheart, and . . .

It didn't bear contemplating. Best to abandon the quest, quit Cornwall, and go back to his ship, counting this holiday as another wrong turn in a directionless life.

At least, as a result of this visit, Verity and her daughter would be reestablished in her home village. He needn't worry about them being lost and alone because now she could count on her father's acceptance if not affection.

It wasn't fair, he thought, handing an orange to Beth, that all this acceptance had to be based on a lie. Verity and Beth shouldn't have to pretend respectability to be welcomed back home—they deserved cherishing no matter what. But that was life, arbitrary, often harsh. Verity had only her ingenuity and charm to forge her own way, but she had those in abundance, at least.

If it weren't Christmas, if it weren't alien to Captain Randall, he thought he might tell these respectable churchgoers exactly what he thought of their hypocrisy. They should realize how fortunate they were to know Verity, with her sunny smiles and her sweet daughter, that in rejecting her they would lose part of the magic in life. . .

But he was Captain Randall, and Captain Randall didn't berate his wife's friends for their inconsistency. Instead, he just kept handing oranges to Beth, who distributed the fruit, along with a burst of nonsensical greeting, to the children who circled around them. When she ran out of oranges, she gave away her coins, and by the time those were gone Beth had become the most popular girl in Porthallow.

Eric and Verity exchanged a glance of wry pride as they stowed the little philanthropist in the carriage.

"We have such a generous child. She would be taking off her shoes next," Verity remarked as Eric pulled the door closed, cutting off the plea of a boy who'd gotten only two oranges and one penny.

"She's got the Christmas spirit, that's all," Sir William put in unexpectedly. "Come here, child. Your papa will help you down."

After a bit of parental urging, Beth slid down from beside Eric and toddled across to the other seat. Still holding Verity's hand for balance, she stood before her grandfather, regarding him warily as he pulled his purse from his pocket.

Sounding almost genial, Sir William said, "Here's a penny for you to keep for yourself, child."

Still suspicious, Beth took the coin and examined it as if it might be counterfeit. Finally, she nodded and, with the dignity of a dowager, said, "Fank you." She tottered back and let Eric hoist her into her seat. Then, in a stage whisper, she said, "Take it, Papa," and pushed the penny into his pocket.

Sir William started chuckling—a dry sound that indicated long disuse. He waved a hand at the stunned Verity. "You were like that, Verity. You used to love to give away your treasures. But not as graciously as Beth. You'd cry when you realized they were gone for good."

Verity looked almost ready to cry now, though there hardly seemed provocation in Sir William's reminiscence. She pinned her lower lip with her teeth to keep it from trembling and turned her face to the window. Eric reached across the child to take Verity's hand, rubbing her knuckles with his thumb as if that might transfuse some strength into her.

It seemed to work. Her voice was steady as she replied to her father, "I suppose I never realized what I had 'til I gave it away. A common failing of children."

"And of adults." Eric addressed this last at Sir William, but the carriage was coming to a halt outside of Morrell Hall and his point probably went astray.

There was but a cold collation for lunch, as the kitchen staff was occupied with the preparations for the elaborate dinner later in the day. As always, Verity kept herself busy, shuttling between the drawing room where the gifts were to be opened later, and the kitchen where the goose was roasting and the pudding boiling. So Eric liberated Beth from the dour nursemaid and took her exploring through the parts of the old house he hadn't yet seen. The little girl kept up a constant stream of chatter as they opened closed doors and climbed up hidden stairwells. Enough of Beth's talk was intelligible for him to have to pay attention and answer occasionally. But even that effort couldn't distract him from the prospect that dropped like an abyss before him.

Tomorrow they would leave this house, the three of them together, and start back along the road they had come down less than a week before. In a few hours they would have traveled full circle to their original starting point, the little cottage covered with roses. And there two of them would stay and one would go off again, alone.

The marble floor in the conservatory glowed like sun-struck ice, and Beth stooped carefully to touch it.

"Wet."

She was speaking figuratively, Eric thought proudly. She is a poetic child. But her comment reminded him of his own childhood forays onto freshly waxed floors, and he let the memory lull away worries about the future.

"Come here, Beth. Let's take off your shoes."

He pulled off his own boots, setting them near the door next to Beth's little slippers. She had to reach up to take his hand, but like the small trooper she was, she didn't hesitate when he explained what was going to happen. Perhaps she didn't understand anything beyond, "We run," which was what she echoed. Then, gripping her tiny hand securely, he walked a bit faster than usual while she skipped along beside him.

"Stop!" he said, and she stopped, and they slid a few feet down the floor.

This tame pleasure had her laughing with delight and begging for more. All the way to the wall of windows they ran and slid, ran and slid, and had gotten most of the way back through the potted orange trees when Verity found them.

When he saw her with the sunlight gilding her dark curls, he halted, waiting for his breath to return, for his heart to slow its pounding. It was only that her coming up so quietly had startled him, or that he felt guilty for teaching Beth this hazardous game, that caused such an excessive response. Nonetheless, he couldn't find the oxygen necessary to explain.

She was good enough to glance at Beth's once-white stockings and say only, "It's nearly four. Time to dress for our Christmas dinner. If you are very good and quiet, Beth, you may sit at the table with us."

Dinner was a quiet meal, with Beth on her best behavior and Verity subdued as she so often was in her father's presence. Judging from the bursts of laughter that emanated from the kitchen area, Eric thought the servants were having a better time of it than their employers. But at least Sir William was unwontedly expansive, recounting how the Lionheart dagger had come to England from the Holy Land. Eric already knew the story but made a pretense of attending. He wondered what all this was leading up to, but Sir William was probably just trying to be a good host, turning the conversation to something he thought would interest Eric. He didn't realize that the subject of the dagger was more irritating than involving, since he had turned down Eric's purchase offer.

That dagger had never been much more than a symbol to Eric, anyway, and now it took on the additional significance of reminding him of the consequences of this impulsive holiday. He would leave this house without the dagger, but with memories that would torment him even longer than the ones the dagger held.

He responded automatically to something Sir William said, but his attention was on Verity, across the table beside Beth. The child was sitting on a chair heightened by several books, but still her chin hardly topped the table, and Verity had to bend her head to murmur instructions and encouragement. Verity's dark hair was sleek now, pulled back into a twist that showed off the elegant curve of her neck above her silvered gown. He ached to kiss her there, to feel her shiver as he knew she would as he traced the curve all the way to her cheek. . .

"Do you think she heard the cook talking about g—o—o—s—e?"

He transferred his gaze from her lips to her eyes, deciding that Verity must be addressing Beth's reluctance to eat the poultry in question. Corralling his thoughts, he sent a stern glance to Beth, but she only stuck her chin out and pushed her plate away.

"She did get rather friendly with some of the g—e—e—s—e yesterday when we walked through the yard," he allowed. "But I don't know if she's old enough to connect them with this." The headless, featherless carcass on the table in front of them, he hoped, could not be identified by a not-yet-two-year-old as the same creature that had once waddled across the lawn. "Let me try."

He took Beth's plate, spooned some brown sauce over the bites of meat, and arranged three peas in a shamrock pattern on top. "There you go. Eat every bite, and I will have a special treat for you this evening."

Beth's mouth made a round O of surprise, and Verity took advantage of this to spoon in a bit of the concoction.

When the whole plate was clean and Beth began asking about the treat, Eric remarked, "You are the most indulged child in the three kingdoms, I have no doubt. You will get your treat when the sun is gone and the Star of Bethlehem has arisen."

The Star—Mars, really, which glowed conveniently to the east of the drawing room window—was well up in the night sky before all the little gifts and *douceurs* had been distributed to the staff. With the servants Verity was in her element, bestowing gifts and warm words of thanks and good wishes, and she had cast off her quiet by the time the last maid had filed out, clutching her booty of tea and stockings and lacy caps.

Verity joined him at the window, and they stood together, looking out into the night.

"Are you thinking about your crew?"

No, he answered silently. About you. "They will have a happier Christmas without me, no doubt. Most of them should be back at their own homes by now. The ones who stayed aboard will make merry enough, I imagine. I sent some funds to the first officer to purchase a party. I hope the ship survives."

"Well," she said, gazing out into the darkness instead of at him, "you'll find out tomorrow when you return."

He couldn't speak, couldn't even identify the ambivalent emotion that coursed through him when she stood so close to him and spoke so casually of their parting. The casualness was a pose, he knew that. He knew her well enough to recognize the effort she was putting into her blithe manner. He reached out and touched her straight back, felt the tension there, traced the warmth of her body from the silken fabric to the silken skin of her shoulders. Wordlessly, she turned to him, her hand going to cover his.

But from his chair near the fire, Sir William cleared his throat. "Time enough for that later, you two. The little one has already ripped one package open."

Beth's impatience provided reason enough to go on with the ceremony, hollow as it suddenly seemed. But Eric found himself caught up in the gift exchange, anyway, if only because Beth so enjoyed ripping the paper and exposing gifts. Even those meant for another.

She accepted with a squeal of glee Eric's explanation that the cork balls, big as her fist, were really marbles. "She won't be able to eat them," he told Verity. "And if they break, they won't cut her."

She even made her grandfather demonstrate on the brick hearth how her new top worked, and Eric, watching the old man guide her hand around the toy, thought that perhaps there was hope for him yet.

Verity, too, wasted no time opening her packages. Eric had sent back to his ship for some of the Indian treasures he had planned to sell in London, and so his gifts were appropriately husbandly. She exclaimed over the bolt of embroidered rose silk, suitable for a ball gown, and blushed prettily at the half-dozen pairs of stockings.

If I were really her husband, he thought, I'd whisper something to make her blush even more. But instead, he held his tongue and opened the gift she had given him—a dark blue cashmere scarf, delicately picked out with silver threads. That must have been what had kept her up late those nights after they arrived—could it have been just three days ago?

Sir William was watching all this with a benign expression. The hot mulled wine had achieved a miracle, Eric thought cynically. The old man even kissed Beth in thanks for the paper of cigars she brought him, then gestured to Verity. "Go on, young lady. Open that box there."

The box was flat, about a foot long, and Eric could see her hands trembling as she opened it. She gazed down into it for a moment, then, with a tiny sigh, drew out a silver-backed mirror. "Thank you, Father. It was Mother's, wasn't it? I remember she kept it on her dressing table."

Verity made a good show of gratitude, holding the mirror up to the lamplight and calling Beth over to look at their twinned reflection. And Sir William smiled and said he knew that she would like something of her mother's, and that every lady needed a silver mirror.

If Sir William didn't notice any disappointment, Eric did, and he wondered at it. It was a sign of some paternal affection, if of a condescending sort, that he now thought Verity worthy of her mother's possessions. But Verity's smile, though wide, wasn't warm enough, not as it had been when she blushed over the silk stockings Eric had given her.

Impatiently, Sir William cut through his speculations. "There's still yours to open, Captain. Best hurry, the child's starting to yawn."

Eric's gift was in the same sort of flat box. He picked it up from the table and felt something heavy slide inside. The dagger. He knew it without looking. But it was too incredible, so he pulled off the lid to see the lamplight winking off the big emerald in the hilt.

"The Lionheart dagger. I—I don't know what to say. Thank you."

Sir William looked away in gruff embarrassment. "Well, it will all come to you eventually, you and Verity. I thought if you liked it so well, better you have it sooner than later. As long as you understand . . . it's not for public display. Because—because it's best in a private collection. You understand." He nodded at the portrait over the fireplace, a woman in formal dress holding a pretty dark-eyed baby in her lap. "It's always been a reminder to me of Verity's mother, but I've got little need for mementos, really, with memories all over the house."

"How kind of you, Father." Verity had recovered her composure and rose, gathering her gifts into a neat pile. "I know Eric admires the piece. Beth, dearest, it's time for bed. Bring me your top and your marbles. You may take the new doll to bed with you."

"No. Marbles," Beth replied with drowsy finality.

As she picked Beth up, Verity exchanged a laughing glance with Eric. "Then you may take the marbles to bed with you. Say good night, now, and thank you."

It was a half hour later that Eric realized Verity wasn't coming back. He excused himself for the night and went up to the suite they shared. She was not in the sitting room, so he knocked on the connecting door and entered.

The room was dark and cold, with only a few coals smoldering in the hearth. He could hardly make out her small figure curled up in a chair near the fire.

"Sweetheart, what are you doing sitting here in the dark?"

She straightened, untucking her feet and rearranging her skirts. "I was just too lazy to get up and light a candle."

He heard the constraint in her voice and was immediately suspicious. But first he stirred up the fire and added another log, then pulled the comforter from the bed and brought it to wrap around her.

"Idiot. You don't need a white Christmas to freeze in these damp old houses, you know."

She let him tuck the comforter around her and didn't protest when he sat on the arm of her chair. "Thank you."

"Have you been crying?"

"I never cry."

"Never?"

"Never. Not for years. Stupid business, crying. I can't breathe afterwards, and my nose gets very red."

"Laughing is better, you think."

"Yes, always."

But there was no laughter in her voice, not even the slight lilt that meant she was smiling. Instead, as if seeking a little comfort, she leaned against his side, her head resting on his arm. He wanted to pull her closer, but something told him to let her find her own way to him. She must be feeling particularly fragile tonight, for if she never cried, she sounded very close to tears.

Softly, he said, "What was wrong with your father's gift to you?"

She shook her head. "Nothing. It was lovely. It just—it just wasn't what I had asked for."

"What had you asked for?"

"Your gift. The dagger. I told him I wanted it."

He didn't know what that meant . . . that she wanted what he had come here to get. He stripped the accusation out of his voice, keeping his posture un-rigid so she wouldn't pull away. "Why? Did you see it as some test of his love?"

Her sigh stirred against his arm. "I guess that is what it was. I asked him to give it to me, and I thought perhaps he would. Then I would know . . . oh, that he held me in some value, to give me his prize."

"But he gave it to me."

"Yes. It's so stupid of me." She shook her head as if impatient with herself. "I didn't even want the silly thing. Just some show of preference. And instead, he gave it to you. Well," she added with a slight edge of bitterness, "he always did want a son to inherit his worldly goods. A son-in-law is substitute enough, I suppose."

"What would you have done with it?"

And then, as she turned her face up to him in surprise, he realized the answer. How foolish to have imagined anything else from this generous woman.

"I meant to give it to you, of course. I could be the angel, then, don't you see?" She laughed finally, and the familiar sound reassured him. "I expect I thought it would be lovely to make you happy and that you would be very grateful to me."

"I am grateful anyway. For I'd never have gotten it without your intervention. And," he added, "this means that we have two gifts of significance between us, not just one."

"You know, I wonder if . . ." She stroked his sleeve absently, slipping her fingers under the cuff to touch his wrist. "Perhaps he meant it for the best."

"What do you mean?"

"He told me yesterday that he had always felt guilty because he pretended he wanted the dagger as a gift for my mother, when all along he wanted it for himself."

Eric wasn't very experienced at being a husband, but he thought this was taking the concept of oneness too far. "Did he really think she would want an old dagger?"

"Well, apparently he's regretted it ever since. She died not long after that, and he never got a chance to make it up to her. Perhaps . . . "

"Perhaps what?"

"Oh, I don't know. Perhaps he thought I was asking for the dagger because I knew you wanted it. That I was pretending to want it, just as my mother did, to make you happy. And he didn't want me to have to go without just to be unselfish."

"Very considerate of him, I'd say."

"If it's true."

She tried to circle his wrist with her fingers, failed, and went back to stroking instead. That was indication enough of her intentions. Kiss her, his desire told him. No, his conscience broke in, she can't be yours, even if she wants to be. He took a deep breath and tried to remember what they had been talking about. "You could ask him."

"I couldn't put the words together. And he would just deny it. We—we just don't seem to understand each other."

"Then you might as well believe it is true, as it's for the good of you both."

The brightness in her eyes as she looked up at him might have been tears, but he thought it was just the glitter of her smile. "Eric, you keep this up, and you will end up a hopeless optimist despite yourself."

"I hope so. If you have taught me anything, it is that it never hurts to hope for the best."

"I taught you that? I hope you don't curse me for it next time you are disappointed."

He rose and pulled her to her feet, then gathered her close so that her head rested against his chest. With his cheek on her hair he could breathe in the delicate scent of her soap and feel the faintest of pulses at her temple. It was true, hope was the most ambivalent of gifts. He had given it up many years ago and didn't know if he wanted it back. But he couldn't refuse anything she might give him, however temporary it must be. He hadn't anything of like value to give her, however, except . . .

Under his hands her body was warm from the fire, the silky fabric of her dress slipping over her body where he touched her. He closed his eyes, caressed her cheek, envisioning her smile when his thumb slipped into the deep dimple. She was still beneath his exploration, until he traced the sweet curve of her mouth. Then her lips parted, and he caught his breath as he felt the dart of her tongue. His hand dropped. She raised her head, and he bent to kiss where his fingers had traced, there, that generous mouth, clinging, opening under his.

She drew away slightly, not far, for his hands were firm on her arms. Far enough that he had to listen to hear her whisper, "Open your eyes."

He shook his head. "No. I know how these dreams work. If I do, you'll disappear."

There was laughter in her throaty voice. "I shan't disappear. I promise. Open your eyes."

Instead, he kissed her again, letting his imagination tell him that the radiance of her eyes was softening, becoming opaque, that she no more than he wished to see the dream vanish. We could stay like this forever, he thought. Then his hands had slipped to her waist, the gentle sweep of her hips, reminding him how much more there was to this pleasure, more even than the sweet pleasure of her mouth tender under his, of her hands seeking to memorize his face.

But he hadn't time to remember what else there was, for she turned her face away, so that his kiss fell harmless on her cheek. He trailed along to her soft ear and nipped it gently.

She moaned low, then, in a whisper, said, "I can't, Eric. Not with Beth in the next room."

He tasted the nape of her neck with his tongue, felt her shiver and drew her closer. "You don't suppose," he murmured, "she could be persuaded to move down the hall."

But he knew he had lost her. She found his hands, took them in her own, brought them up between them. Reluctantly, he opened his eyes. She was still there, his bright Verity, but the dream had vanished, just as he always expected.

"I wish I could. But I can't make that mistake again," she said, gazing down at their clasped hands. "Not that—not that I regret what I did back then." She glanced up at him, that quick glance, seeking his understanding. "Beth isn't a mistake. And Billy deserved a bit of happiness. . ."

So do I. But he never spoke that fierce thought It wouldn't be fair. "Aye," he said instead, withdrawing his hands from hers. "It would be a mistake. I would be a mistake."

As he wrenched open the door, she said, "Eric . . . "

He halted there, watching his knuckles whiten as his grip tightened on the doorknob. "My name is Jason. Jason Brock."

When she said nothing more, he left her alone.

Chapter Eight

The silence was so resonant she couldn't sleep. She sat up in bed, gazing at the door into the dressing room. She was too conscious of him there, quiet and close. He must be lying on that uncomfortable couch, staring into the dark, cursing fate, just as she had been doing for the last hour.

But when, driven by some inexplicable need, she lit her candle and crept through that door, she found him sleeping. She laughed softly, wryly, thinking how easily he breathed, how gracefully he surrendered to slumber, just like a child. She raised the candle and stood over him, so that the light fell on him like a halo. He wasn't any angel, of course, though he was golden enough, and his face in sleep was bereft of the irony she knew so well.

It was an invasion for her to be here, watching him sleep. But he would never know. And when he was gone, back to that dark life she had interrupted, she would still have this image of him, fair and unworried, like the boy he once had been.

He stirred, half roused, murmured, then turned away from the light. The sheet fell off his shoulder, baring his arm. He *would* sleep nude, she thought, wondering how she was ever going to sleep now. Not for him a sedate nightshirt, even in the chill of winter. No, he must needs be a rogue, even in sleep.

There was something on his upper arm, on the hard swell of muscle—a tattoo. Billy had had one of those, too. It was the fashion among navy midshipmen during the war to be tattooed with the image of their first ship. Easier to identify the body that way, Billy had explained casually.

Gently, so as not to wake him, she touched the tiny frigate on Eric's shoulder. The sails must have been white once, but now, in the faint glow of the candle, they were scarce lighter than his tanned skin. She drew her fingers lightly down along the curve of the mainsail, following the curve of muscle. His skin was warm and surprisingly smooth, except . . . She felt a hard ridge of scar tissue and brought the candle closer. Below the tattoo, where the ship's name should be, she saw an angry slash of white—a burn scar, a perfect rectangle like a brand.

She drew in a silent breath and held it. He had tried to burn it off. Had he heated a knife blade in a fire then held it sizzling against his flesh? Once it must have been as wide as a knife blade, but now it had receded, fading so that it was hardly noticeable.

But now, shrunken, it was no longer as concealing. She bent closer, so close she could feel the warmth of him on her face, and saw the faint outline of ink on and above the shiny white ridge. There was a *C,* and a *U,* and farther down *IER.*

He had tried to burn it off.

It came to her then, the name of the ship that he had tried so painfully to conceal. The *Currier.* A famous name, or infamous really, usually spoken in a whisper and paired with the name *Bounty.*

As she withdrew the candle, it tipped and a bit of hot wax dropped on his shoulder. She held her breath, but he roused, rubbing his shoulder as he opened his eyes. He looked more confused than pained, his eyes cloudy with sleep, his brow furrowed in a frown. "Verity."

He sat up, bunching the pillow behind him then reaching out his hand to her. "I was just dreaming this very moment. You came to my bed to beg me to make mad, passionate love to you."

"Yes?" The word was only a breath.

He pulled her down next to him. He radiated a drowsy warmth, and she touched his bare chest, the golden hair tangled in sleep. "Is that why you are here?"

"I don't know." She spread her fingers on his hot skin, through the wiry curls, feeling the thud of his heart under his palm. I've no right to ask, she thought, no right to know.

She lifted her gaze to see the puzzlement in his eyes. But then he smiled, a sleepy, rueful smile.

"Not with Beth so near. You probably only wanted me to hold you."

"Yes," she said again, and he took the candle, blew it out, and set it on the side table. Then he gathered her close, wrapping the blanket around them both and resting his cheek on the top of her head. He was warm from his sleep, his naked skin against her a comfort and a rebuke.

"Only for a moment," he murmured. "And tomorrow I'll remember, but I'll tell myself it was a dream."

"Eric . . . " she started, then amended, "Jason." It was a moment before she knew what she wanted to say, and even then she took her characteristically roundabout way. "I have my faults, you know."

"So I've noticed. Dozens of them, I've counted so far."

His voice, vibrating in his chest next to her cheek, was too laugh-filled to give offense. Whatever these faults he had noticed were apparently not so terrible after all. "The worst is—"

"The worst, my darling, is that you wear altogether too many clothes."

His hands were seeking bare skin, but found none through the flannel night rail and woolen bed jacket. Just as well, she thought. In the darkness, his bare skin, warm and sweet next to her, was quite enough distraction. She caught his roaming hand in hers and held it tight against her chest, which soothed him enough to allow her to continue.

"My worst flaw is curiosity."

"Really?" He pondered this a moment. "No, I'd say your worst flaw is your—"

"Curiosity. Do be still, Eric, and let me confess. I—" she took a deep breath and continued, "I know I shouldn't ask about your past. I know it's none of my affair. And I didn't mean to pry, really. I just wanted to see you. But—but I saw something else." She loosed a hand and slid it up his arm, touching the tattoo and tracing the hard ridge of scar.

He went utterly still. Finally, he said, "You disapprove of tattoos? That's rather a problem for a sailor's wife. We've all got 'em."

"No. It's fine. but—but I could read the ship's name. Through the scar. The *Currier.*"

For a moment, she felt the strength leave him, just seep out like blood from a wound. Instinctively, she lifted her hand to his face, pulled him close, kissed him hard. "I don't care," she whispered against his mouth. "I don't care."

He made a bitter sound but didn't pull away. "What don't you care about?"

"That mutiny. I don't care if you were there. It was years ago, before Trafalgar. You were just a boy. It doesn't matter."

Eric shook his head, his rough cheek rubbing against her lips. "I don't know how you guessed. What a magpie mind you have, Verity, to remember all that." Finally, he withdrew, pushing her gently off his lap onto the couch. "It does matter." As if he regretted pushing her away, he pulled the blanket around her shoulders so they still shared the warm darkness. "It matters to the Navy. There's a death warrant out for me . . . oh, not for me in particular. For all of us."

The night chill crept into her. She shivered and pulled the blanket closer. "But it's been so long. They can't still care."

"The captain still cares. He survived, you know. A month in a tiny boat. No one ever faulted his sailing skills . . . his humanity, perhaps.

But he's made sure it's become a moral crusade for the Admiralty. Can't have companies, especially officers, turning against the symbol of God and King, and getting away with it."

He gripped her hand so tight it almost hurt, then loosened his hold. "Just last year they found the boatswain in a taverna in Piraeus. Gathered the whole fleet and court-martialed him. Hanged him at sunset." He stopped, and the silence was so deep she could hear the blood thudding in her ears. "He went to his death singing 'God Save the King.' It wasn't God or the King we hated."

"But—" The thought that he could be in danger this very moment shot through her, leaving a trembling in its wake. "Then why are you here? You—you told me you had a ship. That you go to London. How can you risk that?"

He shrugged. "I was thirteen. It's been fifteen years."

She had left a lamp burning in the bedroom, and in the sliver of its light his teeth flashed white in a grin. "I was . . . oh, about as high as the ship's rail. Weighed five stone soaking wet. And had freckles all over my face. Might still, for all I know, under the tan." He smiled again, this time with less real humor. "My own mother wouldn't recognize me. And no one else ever has, even though it's a small world for a sailor. A couple years ago in Calcutta, I came face to face with another *Currier* midshipman. We'd shared a berth for months. We were best friends. And he looked straight at me and never blinked. Didn't notice me at all."

"Perhaps he did but feared you'd betray him, too."

"No. He's got nothing to fear. He went with the captain." He added flatly, "If he'd known who I was, he would have had his marines take me right then."

After a moment, he laughed softly. "So you see, I also have nothing to fear. Except from sharp-eyed inquisitive little magpies like you."

She studied his face in the dimness, trying to decide how ironic that last comment was. But his face was nothing but shadow and unreadable dark eyes. "Surely you don't think I would betray you."

"You could. There's a reward."

Paradoxically, the thought of turning Eric in to the Admiralty to claim a reward struck her as humorous. "But—but then what would you do? You'd probably betray all *my* crimes, too! And they'd hang us side by side!"

"You're right. I have too much on you to worry about your betrayal."

"I wouldn't, anyway," she added. "You know that. Tell me about it. How it came to be."

He rubbed hard at his temples with the heels of his hands, rocking slowly as he spoke, as if the memories hurt him. "He was a bad man. A bad captain. He liked to flog. We were out in the middle of the Pacific and couldn't transfer or jump ship or do anything but hate him."

"Can they flog officers?" It was absurd to think of a thirteen-year-old boy as an officer, but that was what midshipmen were.

"No. But the captain can cane them. And he did." His face was still concealed by the darkness and his hands, but she could hear his voice go hard with anger. "One of us would get a summons to his cabin, and we'd all go weak. He thought I had the devil in me, so he beat me the most. Once I thought he'd broken my back, because I couldn't feel my legs afterwards. . . But a week later I got the feeling back. Just a bruised spine, I guess." He laughed softly. "And he was a fool as well as brutal. He used to hold back the rations for mess groups he was displeased with, so the men would sit there at mess and watch the others eat. And he'd flog anyone who saved scraps to feed the hungry ones. Interfering with a disciplinary action, he called it. Then he stopped the grog. For the whole crew. You want to incite mutiny, cut off the grog. Especially at the equator, when the water's gone bad and tastes like poison." Abruptly, he finished, "So the first lieutenant and the third opened up the armaments cabinet and took over the ship. Three marines were killed. The captain and his loyalists were put into a boat and shoved off."

"What did you do?"

"Watched, mostly. The first lieutenant . . . he was always good to me. He shoved me down a hatch and told me to stay out of the way. But at one point he was fighting with the sergeant of the Marines and dropped his sword. I ran out and picked it up and gave it to him, and tripped the marine for good measure. So I can't say I was just a spectator." He raked his fingers down his forehead, as if he might be able to excise the ache. "After that, I couldn't have joined the captain if I wanted to, and I didn't want to. I didn't want to die, first off, and I didn't want to die with him. I should have known Clayton was too self-righteous to die. He thought the Lord had given him a new mission, to bring us all to justice."

"What happened after that?"

"Oh, you've probably heard. It's a famous story, isn't it? They set up on some island near the Marquesas, after they'd dropped some of us off in Hawaii. Clayton took a man-o'-war up to their colony a few years later and got a dozen of them."

"And you?"

He dropped his hands from his face and sat up straight. "I got on a Greek merchant ship and worked my way home. They didn't ask any questions."

He was staring out into the darkness. She touched his mouth gently, felt his breath on her fingers. "And when you got home?"

"I got taken up by some smugglers. They'd hire anyone with a guilty conscience and the ability to hand, reef, and steer. When I made enough money, I bought my own ship."

She sensed that he had left a great deal out, but she didn't press him. "Did you smuggle?"

"Some." With sudden fierceness, he added, "I didn't sit the war out. I had a new name, and a new ship, and a letter of marque from the Foreign Office. That meant I could take French ships, and I did. And other things, too. Whatever the Foreign Office needed done and wouldn't ask the Navy to do. And that letter of marque kept me from being taken up by the press gangs and gave me—gave me some purpose. Some pride."

And then, before she could speak, before she could offer the comfort she wanted so to give him, he rose, leaving the blankets in an untidy heap on the floor. He wasn't naked after all, some remote part of her brain noted, but wore the loose, faded cotton trousers of a common seaman. He walked into the bedroom, and she heard him pouring a drink of water.

As if he regretted confiding in her, he remained apart, silhouetted in the doorway. "At any rate, you needn't worry. I am known as Jason Brock. I am not at risk and not in exile. No one will ever know."

"Unless they take a good look at that tattoo." She made her voice as hard as his. "I doubt I'll be the last woman to wonder at it."

He twisted to look at the traitorous arm, but in the darkness it was in vain. He shrugged. "No one else has ever mentioned it. I haven't thought of it in years. I don't even look at it in the mirror. . . I reckon I'll have to burn it again."

She couldn't maintain that harsh distance, not with him so near and in pain. She stood up, crossing over to him and wrapping her arms around his slender waist. "Don't you dare. Don't. It will hurt too much."

Just for a moment, he rested his forehead on her hair and tightened his arms around her. Then he let her go and stepped back. "I told you not to worry. And you won't have to, will you, after tomorrow? I will take you back to your home, and you won't have to worry about me again. I shan't be your husband anymore. And you'll be lucky of it, to be rid of the likes of Jason Brock as soon as you can."

She started to protest that whatever he called himself, whatever he had been, she was fortunate to know him. But he refused to listen. He urged her gently back into her bedroom and closed the door behind her. She stood there in the lamplight, hand on the doorknob, but then let it go. She understood. He regretted his impulsive confidence, regretted the growing intimacy that had prompted it, regretted her. She had started him feeling again, and all he felt was pain.

There is still tomorrow, she told herself, creeping back into her bed. One more day with him. One more day.

Chapter Nine

December 26

The next morning, in the sunlit carriage yard, Eric was seeing to the stowing of the luggage when he heard Beth cry out—that sharp, frightened sort of cry that meant she was hurt and not just angry. I shouldn't have brought her out here, he thought, pushing the driver aside and running out from behind the carriage. The little girl was sitting on the graveled drive, cushioned by her thick woolens, holding one hand in the other, her wail diminished to sobs and, by the time he reached her, to whimpers.

Wordlessly, she held out her hand as he knelt on the gravel. The knuckles were scraped raw, and one was beginning to ooze blood. As her hand rested small and vulnerable in his own, he carefully picked bits of gravel from the wound, murmuring comforting words to ease the pain. Then he found his handkerchief and used it to dry the tears from her cheeks. The now-wet handkerchief he applied to the scrapes, gently as he could. But even that didn't make her cry out again. She had already forgotten her hurt and was pointing at the anchor embroidered on the corner of the cloth.

"Papa," she said.

"Yes, sweeting, Papa will fix it. What a brave girl you are. I would still be moaning if I hurt my hand like that." He used the handkerchief as a bandage, tying it over the palm with a split-end knot that left the anchor emblem dancing jauntily. He glanced up from his work as the front door opened and Verity came out, dressed for their journey. "There's your mama. Go show her your prize."

He rose and watched as Beth ran to meet her mother at the bottom of the granite steps. "See, Mama, Papa fix."

Fix. That was a new word. Sixty-three words, and she wasn't two yet. And a four-word sentence.

Papa. That was a new word, too, new this week. He wondered if Verity had noticed that and thought she probably had. She kept track of things like that.

And when Verity returned later with Beth in her arms proudly displaying her hand washed and re-bandaged with gauze, he shook his head at the proffered handkerchief. "No. She likes the anchor. Let her keep it."

Verity put her chin up then, a sure sign that she meant to make some provocative comment. But Sir William emerged from the house at that moment, and they could not exchange the angry words Eric thought were a breath away. Later, he told himself, in the carriage. We shall fight and end up glad to part.

But Beth would be in the carriage with them. Shouldn't fight in front of the child, he told himself. He watched Verity assemble her usual smiling face—she could hide her emotions well, at least with her father—and knew she would wait until Beth had fallen asleep. But then they'd have to be quiet, or they would wake Beth up.

It would be all right. He didn't need a shouting fight to let Verity go. He was long-practiced at letting go.

As Sir William approached, Eric silently took Beth from her, freeing her for the farewell. But her father didn't seem to take the hint. He shook hands with Eric and nodded at Beth, then bade his daughter a gruff Godspeed.

Verity took little visible notice of his brusque manner. "Say goodbye to your grandfather, Beth." Almost absently then, Verity went up on her tiptoes to kiss the old man's cheek, and when this made him falter in his directions for a shortcut around Porthallow, she broke in, "Eric knows the way, Father. And you know where we live. Come visit sometime. Thank you for having us." And just as briskly she climbed into the coach, leaving Eric to make a more polite farewell.

She avoided his curious glance for the first half mile or so, getting herself and Beth settled on the wide leather seat. But she looked up when he finally spoke his thoughts. "Good for you."

She produced a sweet biscuit from her pocket and unwrapped it before giving it to Beth. "What do you mean?"

"You let him know he had to make the next move. That you weren't going to beg for his attention."

Her nose wrinkled as she considered this. "Is that what I was doing? I just wanted to be gone."

He couldn't help himself, couldn't hide the longing that filled him, the regret. "Was this such a difficult week?"

She busied herself brushing the crumbs from Beth's face and coat into her hand then opened the window slightly to dispose of them. And even when she answered, she didn't answer. "Not—not so difficult. But you're right. I shan't beg again. And I did get weary of pretending." She sighed and closed the window on the chill sea air. "A week is a long time to pretend, especially with him waiting for one of us to make a mistake. But we never did, did we?"

"Not as far as he knows, anyway."

She didn't ask him to translate that bitter statement, and it was probably for the best. He didn't know what it meant himself. That this longing was a mistake? Or that she should be assuring him it wasn't, that it was meant to happen? That she was glad it had happened? But she was still busy with Beth, braiding her doll's yarn hair into a dozen plaits, softly crooning a rhyme about boys and girls and golden curls.

She was long-practiced, too, at letting go.

Beth, tired of the doll, came over to him with a sly grin and slipped her hand into the pocket of his greatcoat, lying next to him across the seat. He had lately taken to keeping peppermints there, always making a great show of not noticing her little hand inching in and snatching one.

Too late he remembered the Lionheart dagger.

Beth pulled it from his pocket with a triumphant cry. "Pretty!"— her all-purpose term of approval.

"No!" Eric grabbed it back from the child, scarcely restraining himself from slapping her hand. He looked up from the dagger to see Beth's big eyes filling with tears and Verity reaching out to take her.

"Dearest, you mustn't touch. It's dangerous. Nasty. Come here and sit by me."

"No." With an effort, he swallowed back the dread that had gripped him when he saw Beth's little hand on the weapon. She wasn't strong enough to have pulled it loose from the scabbard, of course, but somehow he thought it might defile her, his pretty Beth, to touch that jeweled temptation that had been so long the object of greed and desire.

He hoisted Beth up onto the seat behind him and held the dagger out, hilt first. "See, Beth, this lion?" He took her hand and let her trace the gold lion stamped into the silver metal. "That is the symbol for Richard the Lionheart, one of our great warrior kings. He led the Crusades against the heathens who held Jerusalem."

Beth didn't understand, of course. But as he told her the story of the dagger and the great warrior Lawrence of Broderick, he heard himself using the same words, the same lofty phrases, that he and his brother had heard from his father so many times, so many years before.

And it was simple fate that he looked out then and saw his father's house, high on a bluff across a little cove from Downderry. The sea mist made it nearly as insubstantial as his childhood dreams of glory, but there it was, a half mile away. He could leave the carriage now, walk up the long avenue, open the front door . . .

But Beth was the harshest of drama critics. His performance of the Lionheart story had impressed her so little that she had fallen asleep, warm and weighty against his arm. If he moved, she would slip down against the door and wake herself. Best that he see them both to their home and then come back to his past.

He glanced up to meet Verity's challenging gaze. It made him angry, such a challenge from her. She had dragged him into this, after all, with her teasing laughter and outrageous expectations, dragged him into the life of a man who didn't exist. And now his other life seemed just as illusory and far less fitting—and yet it was his.

"It wasn't meant to be like this." His whisper cut sharp against the rumble of the wheels on the road. "Beth wasn't supposed to be a part of this."

Verity did not pretend to misunderstand. "I told you that you needn't pay her any mind. Father wouldn't have expected it of you. I wouldn't have expected it."

"She calls me Papa." *You call me darling.*

It was so unfair, so tantalizing, and Verity was so ruthless in her realism, intent on forcing the truth on him. "She's naught but a babe."

"You mean she will forget me."

"Would you rather she remembered?"

And there it was, the barren truth. Better that she forget, as she surely would, than to long forever for the papa who would not return.

But Verity would remember, and though she did not speak it, that was the hardest truth of all. He tried to recall why it would be better for her to forget him, though *he* would never forget *her*. But now, seeing her expressive face so still and proud, he found the silent arguments that had convinced him last night—that he was an outlaw and that a link with him would bring her only pain—echoed emptily in his head. This was pain, pain for them both, and it wouldn't ever end.

I'll get myself free and come back again, he promised silently. But how he could free himself from the chains of such a past, he didn't know.

They traveled the last few miles in silence, and too soon the coach had pulled to a halt outside the little rose-covered cottage. He felt a traitorous desire for the place. It felt like home, though he had never set foot over the threshold.

"We're home, darling." Verity gently shook Beth awake and led her by the hand out the carriage door. The nurse Lucy was already there, emerging from the cottage to bob a curtsy at Eric, holding out her arms for Beth. But Verity just stood there, still holding Beth, waiting for him to say goodbye. She would not beg him to stay. She was done with begging. She had told him just a few hours ago. But she would not help him by walking away.

He still had the Lionheart dagger in his pocket. He gripped it until the jewels in the hilt cut painfully into his palm. "Goodbye, Beth," he said finally.

Beth, still sleepy, echoed uncomprehendingly, "Goodbye, Papa?"

"He is leaving," Verity said.

Her harsh voice, or perhaps just her words, made Beth understand, as much as a child could. He turned away from her tears and started to walk back to the coach.

But Verity stopped him. "She wants to know if you'll come back to visit on her birthday."

It was a far too complex thought for Beth, with her sixty-three words, to express. Verity was just speaking in her usual roundabout code, which he had learned this past week to translate.

She was giving him a last chance.

He turned back, holding out his hand, and felt Verity's clasp, warm and secure. He put his arms around them both, whispering, "Twelfth Night. I might as well stay, as it's so soon."

"You would be welcome to stay." Verity's voice came muted, her breath warm against his chest.

"But then there will be your birthday, won't there? What day is that?"

"The end of October. All Hallows' Eve."

"I might have guessed." He was suddenly very happy holding Verity, with Beth squirming between them. "And so soon after that it will be Christmas again. Holly and mistletoe. I expect I should stay for that, too."

"And then Beth's birthday again."

"So many occasions you have planned for me. It would take a century to do them right."

He heard her take a deep breath, readying herself to speak, then Beth demanded, "Put me down!"

They let her slip to the ground and run toward Lucy. "Beth would like you to stay that long," Verity said, her head bent so he couldn't see her eyes.

He tilted her chin up and looked into her dark eyes, somber for once. She was frightened, he realized, unwilling to trust fate. "I would like to stay, too. But what would you want, my darling?"

Suddenly, she smiled, standing on tiptoe to kiss him hard on the mouth. "You know what I want, you rogue."

"Tell me anyway."

"I want to make you happy."

"How very unselfish of you." He pulled her tight into his arms, whispering in her ear, "While you are doing that, might I make you happy also?"

Their kiss was interrupted by Lucy's throat-clearing. "I shall take Beth inside out of the cold, Captain Randall. Mrs. Randall."

"Is it cold?" Verity burrowed deeper into his embrace, and he drew his greatcoat around her. "Captain Randall. Is that what you are to be called?"

"Is that what you would like?"

"Well," she said judiciously, "if we are to live here, I don't know that we could introduce a new name. And my father would be quite suspicious. And besides, I don't think I shall ever accustom myself to calling you Jason."

"It's not my real name, anyway. Another new one won't trouble me." He shrugged off the problems this would cause in his business dealings. Jason Brock could be his *nom de mer*, a shipping identity only.

"It doesn't matter, does it?" Her pretty face turned up to him, her dark eyes filled with—odd, that he would recognize this so quickly, having never seen it before—her dark eyes filled with love and understanding and something else that quickened his pulse as well as his heart.

She said with the same wonderment he felt, "It doesn't matter what you are called, because I know you. As no one else ever has."

"What do you know?"

"I know you are . . . oh, an adventurer, a man used to danger, and yet, despite that, as kind and warm as a man can be. I know that you like to laugh but you haven't done it often enough. And I know that you want to love but have never had anyone of your own. But now you do."

"But now I do." Verity was warm and slight against him, a bundle of energy and light in the gathering darkness. He thought of spending a lifetime in her radiant glow, his wild, warm Verity, illuminating and eliminating the shadows of his past. He kissed her temple and felt her shiver. "And as it's Captain Randall's family I'm loving, I shall take his name, too. Usually, when a woman marries a man, she takes his name, not the reverse. But then, my love, we aren't bound by convention, are we?"

"Should we marry? We could always go on as we have—"

"Lord, no. What if Beth should learn the truth? Though it might be hard to arrange, a marriage for a couple supposedly already married."

"There's always that sea captain friend of yours. He could marry us at sea. On our way to a honeymoon in Paris."

"I thought you said that sounded havey-cavey."

"It is. I love havey-cavey things. That's why I love you."

He had never heard those words, at least not as long as he could remember, and he wanted to ask her to repeat them. But there would be time enough for that later. He had to try to save her first . . . save her from herself and from him. "Are you certain this is what you want? I am no prize. I haven't any real name, and there's a price on my head . . . "

"Which no one will ever collect. Especially not now, when you have become a respectable husband and father." Verity laughed up at him, her eyes bright with their shared secrets. "Of course, you must be careful with that tattoo of yours. Oh, you needn't worry about other men. They never notice such things. But we women have sharper eyes and more inquisitiveness."

"I expect I'd better make sure no other woman ever sees it, is that what you are saying? Easy enough. Easy enough, if you are foolhardy enough to truly be mine, despite—despite it all."

She pulled away, leaving his arms empty and his heart bereft. Crossly, she evaded his inquiring hand, withdrawing a bit to stand straight and stern before him. "Eric, if you are to go through our life together being *grateful* to me for loving you, I shan't like it at all. I tell you I don't *care* about your past. If anything, I love you the more for it. I am taking you for my own selfish reasons, I can assure you. No other man would accept me—"

"Any man of sense would."

"No. Not as I am. Not without my pretending every day of my life that I am virtuous and demure and—and ladylike. Another man would be disillusioned if I ever let my real self show. But not you." She came back into his open arms, whispering, "I think you even like me as I am. If only because I am as much a rogue at heart as you are."

"We deserve each other, that is so. Ah, Verity, I do love you. Too much to do what I ought to do and let you get away."

"Good. I don't want to get away. I've known enough of that. Keep me always instead."

But as she slipped her hands under his coat, around his waist, he felt the weight of the Lionheart dagger in his pocket. He wanted to take it out and hurl it across the road into the English Channel, to abandon it as surely as he was abandoning his long solitude.

But he could not abandon what it represented—a family's past glory, his own past shame.

Gently, he let her go. "Will you wait for me one night? I have one more task to complete before I am free to join you."

The light in her eyes dimmed. She didn't trust this happiness yet. Give me a month, he thought fiercely, and I will make you believe in our future. But first I must finish the past.

"What do you mean to do?"

"You remember that dagger your father gave me?"

She shrugged, as if her father's prized possession held no more import for her. "Of course I remember it. We should never have met but for that silly dagger."

"I must take it back."

She shook her head, as if confused. "To my father?"

"No. To mine."

Chapter Ten

It was full dark when they climbed the hill from Downderry, without even a faint moon to light their way along the elm-lined road. Darker than the night sky, the great house rose up ahead of them, a mist rising from its base. Verity shivered as the chill crept under her skirt and up her legs. Even the low, relentless roar of the surf, which had punctuated nearly every moment of her life, seemed to be sounding a warning.

But she knew better than to complain. It had been hard enough to convince Eric that he needed her presence on this expedition. She wasn't about to confess to second thoughts just because Broderick Manor looked exactly like one of Mrs. Radcliffe's Gothic horror-havens.

A pair of great iron gates loomed ahead, as implacable and impermeable as prison doors. But Eric veered off the road then, slanting west along the high wall, trailing his gloved hand across its bramble hedge. Verity ran after him, then followed so close behind that she collided with his back when he stopped abruptly.

"There was a door here," he said in a low voice. She heard the rustling of his hand across the hedge, then the clang of metal. "Here it is. Careful. The hedge has grown over it. You'll have to slip in sideways."

Verity could just make out a low, arched iron door cut into the wall and overgrown with brambles. She ducked her head and hugged her riding cloak close, edging through the gate as the thorns caught at her like little demon fingers. Eric was right behind her, warm and sturdy but silent, as he had been all along on this eerie trip.

The park here was edged with winter-bare trees, like skeletal ghosts holding out their arms. She shivered again and reached out for Eric's hand.

He took hers in a reassuringly firm grip and finally broke his silence with a chuckle. "You are cursed with a fertile imagination, sweeting," he murmured. "But don't worry. The only ghosts at Broderick are still living."

She didn't ask him what he meant, for she thought she knew. This estate belonged to his father. He could not approach it openly in daylight, even to return this dagger. He must have stolen the dagger and been in exile ever since.

She gripped his hand tighter, as if to tell him again that she didn't care about his past and that she was glad he had stolen the dagger, for it had brought him to her. But he was moving swiftly now through the park, and she had to quicken her pace to keep up.

The spongy ground underfoot gave way to a graveled path and the skeletal trees to a formal garden. Eric was sure of his way now, and he led her directly through a maze of sharp-trimmed hedges to the side of the great house. It was an unwelcoming place, without a single light in any of the windows, as they walked softly up the flagstone steps to a terrace.

Eric stopped before the French doors and took a deep breath. He stood a moment, gazing into the deeper darkness of the room beyond the doors. Then he brought out the dagger and unsheathed it, sliding its slender blade under the latch. There was a quiet rub of metal over metal, then the door opened with a slight squeak.

"Let's get this over with," Eric muttered, sheathing the dagger. "Careful," he added unnecessarily as they entered the room. "It's dark."

It was also cold, almost as cold as the outside, and Verity thought longingly of the fire that would be burning in her little cottage. She was all too mindful that a servant might hear them and imagine them housebreakers. And it wouldn't be only imagination, for they had broken in, after all, if only to return, not to take, the family treasure. But if she knew Eric, he'd rather be tortured than admit that he was the long-lost son of the family, and she would have to go along with him or lose all credit as a rogue.

Just leave the dagger on a table and let's go, she wanted to tell him. But he must have made these plans years ago, going over every step in his head on a hundred dark nights, and he wasn't about to be diverted.

The dark room gave way to a long gallery, with a single lamp burning at the other end. It was still dusky enough that Eric ran into a side table, and as he rubbed his knee he muttered under his breath a string of terrible sailor curses. Verity couldn't help laughing at the inventiveness of some of them, and when he stopped to hush her sternly, she collided into him again. It was more deliberate than accidental, and she got her reward when he pulled her up close and kissed her hard.

All in all, they wasted far too much time getting down to the end of the gallery, where a tall walnut display case stood. Verity saw walls lined with family portraits—most of them of stern-faced men in archaic dress. I'm glad Eric knows how to smile, she thought, making a face at one particularly stiff-featured ancestor.

Eric was already using the dagger on the lock of a display case which contained its twin mounted on velvet behind the glass. But the blade was too thick. "Give me a hairpin."

When Verity complied, her casual topknot tumbled down, and Eric reached out to tug at one long curl. "I didn't mean to take your only pin, love," he murmured.

"The bramble bush took the rest, I wager. Eric, there'll be time enough for that later," she whispered, pushing away his inquiring hand. "Let's hurry before we're taken up by a platoon of strapping footmen."

Eric nodded, somber again. She wanted to bring that teasing smile back, but reminded herself of her own sage advice. There would be time enough for that later. She pressed close to him, watching as his hard, square hands with surprising delicacy worked the pin in the lock.

And then, just as he murmured "Got it," a voice came from the other end of the gallery.

"Justin."

Eric stilled against her. Then, calmly, he opened the glass door and removed the straightened pin from the lock. Only then did he turn, and Verity with him, to see the man who had discovered them.

Elderly, he wore a dark dressing gown and held up a lamp but no weapons. "Justin," he said again in an old man's voice, strong but with a bit of a quaver. "I have been expecting you any time this last decade." He nodded toward the display case. "Did you come to take the second one?"

Eric finally spoke. "No. To return the first."

"Who is that with you?"

"My wife."

Perhaps only Verity heard the intense pride, the challenge, in that simple term, but she slipped her hand into his and felt the comforting pressure.

"Have you sons, too?"

"A daughter."

There was pride in that, too, and Verity was suddenly very happy, happier even than when they had confessed their love. Happy even though they were likely to be flung by this vengeful man into the dungeon. She had given Eric that—the pride that he could tell his father he had a life, a family, a love, despite all that had passed so long ago.

The old man moved closer. He was still straight, still handsome, with Eric's chiseled features but none of the ruggedness that meant a life lived outdoors. "You haven't changed much. You look the same."

"The same? No. Not at all."

"Not the same, perhaps. But you always did look like William. And you still do." Then abruptly, "Did you know your sister died in childbed in Thirteen?"

"I heard."

"You didn't come to the funeral."

There was accusation there, and Eric straightened. His grip on Verity's hand tightened, and his voice grew dangerously low. "You said you'd turn me over to the Admiralty if I returned to England. I gave in to your threats for a decade. But when I heard of Maggie's death, I decided I wanted no more of exile. I visited her grave in London." He turned, pulled away from Verity's hand, and laid the dagger on the velvet next to its mate. "Let's go."

But Verity stalled, making a great show of reaching past him to straighten the one dagger and then the other, silently imploring the old man to say something.

"That last time, you broke the glass."

"I've learned a few tricks over the years."

"You left blood everywhere. On the other dagger, on the glass, all the way down the hall."

Involuntarily, Verity glanced down at Eric's hand, remembering the ugly scar across the back, though she could not see it in the dimness.

Eric shrugged and, gently displacing her hand from the pair of daggers, closed the display case. "Fourteen-year-old boys have a gruesome sense of what's fitting. I liked to think of you cleaning the blood off the dagger I'd left behind. I knew you wouldn't trust it to anyone else. Cleaning it and cursing me."

"And now you have returned."

"No. I have returned the dagger. You have back your prize. We are quits."

Verity felt as if she were witnessing a naval standoff, both ships with their guns unhoused and loaded, neither quite ready to fire but neither about to sail away. Relent, she thought hard, hoping Eric would hear. But when she opened her eyes she saw his face just as hard, his jaw just as implacable, and she realized he had come to the same decision she had. No more begging for recognition.

Undaunted, she closed her eyes and aimed her "relent" message at the old man. It was his place, anyway, to welcome back the prodigal.

Lord Broderick was reluctant to relent. But at least he was still speaking, though his voice was edged with accusation. "Care you at all how your mother fares?"

Eric was looking back at the daggers as if regretting the impulse that had brought him back here. "How is she?"

"Well enough. She longs for grandchildren. William—he hasn't much interest in settling down yet. He might do better to emulate you and marry and have a child."

Eric laughed—unbelieving, angry, but it was still laughter. "Emulate me? That is one for the ages. It is surely the first time you have ever suggested *he* might do well to follow *me.*"

"You two always were at daggers drawn, weren't you?"

"Because *you* made us so. Because it pleased you to see us rivals. Little Broderick warriors . . . " Eric shook his head, as if to clear it of the memories. "He helped me, you know. I was holed up in that cave under the cliff. He brought me food and clothing and all the money he had. Sewed up my hand." He drew a ragged breath. "I shouldn't have told you. You'll probably disown him now. God! I thought I was done with this. I am done with this. Verity, let's go."

He strode down the gallery, passing his father with no more than a cold nod. As Verity followed, she gave the stubborn old man a glare. Say something, she mouthed, wishing she could kick him in the shins besides.

They were nearly out to the French doors before he called after them. "Justin. Your mother—"

Eric stopped, hand on the door handle. He tested it, found it worked to open the latch, let it go. "Yes?"

"Your mother will be disappointed to have missed you."

It was an incongruously conventional observation, suggesting a lady reading her visitors' cards over tea, and Verity battled the impulse to laugh. But Eric only replied, "Don't tell her, then."

"But she will want to meet your wife. And your daughter."

Now the quaver was marking the old man's voice. Verity could hear the plea there, if Eric could not, and something in her responded to it.

Before the silence extended to an uncomfortable level, she said, "Perhaps we shall visit when we return from France." She smiled at the figure outlined by the light of the lamp, though she knew he could not see her face. "We never had a honeymoon to speak of, and Eric—Justin—promised to take me to Paris. But we will be back in the spring, and we might visit then."

Eric made no protest, just pushed open the door. Once they were out on the terrace, he took deep breaths of the cold air, then strode away. Verity followed at a safe distance, waiting for whatever emotion was gripping him to dissipate. Finally, when they were almost back to the wall, he stopped and waited for her. When she reached him, he took her in his arms and leaned against the cold stones.

"Verity, I don't want to start with them again."

She nestled against the warmth of him, glad he wasn't angry with her. "He meant that as an apology."

"That? 'Your mother will be disappointed to have missed you'? A poor excuse for it. And I don't care, anyway. I don't need an apology. I just want a bit of peace, with you and Beth." He added resentfully, "He could have the Marines waiting for me, you know."

"He won't. He's an old man. He's lost one child and regrets driving another away. He said he had been waiting for you for years." She raised her head and said coaxingly, "Oh, let's not worry about it. We have more important things to do first."

She felt his sigh in his chest but heard a smile in his voice. "Getting truly married. And here we are, with a child nearly two. We rather anticipated the parson, I think." He was insinuating a hand under her pelisse, up along her side to the bodice of her gown. Where his fingers touched bare skin, they left trails of fire. He bent to whisper in her ear, "Perhaps we might do so again."

"On your father's grounds?"

He looked back to the house, and reluctantly his hand dropped from the fastening of her pelisse. "I suppose not. Back at the cottage, though—"

It sounded very nice, and still warm in his embrace, Verity was too drowsy even to protest that Beth would be in the next room. But when she drew back from his kiss to hide a yawn, he laughed and let her go. "Come, sweeting. We will get you home and into your bed. Alone. I can't think what Lucy will say, me home only a week and sleeping on the couch."

"She will think that, having worn me out, you are considerately keeping yourself out of temptation's range."

"I'd have to be in the East Indies for that. Tomorrow—tomorrow we will find my friend Bering and force him to take us to France. And he can marry us on the way."

"And make it an entry in his 1816 log." Verity touched his face, tracing the line of his jaw to his mouth. He kissed her fingers and she sighed. "It will be very complicated, won't it? You will have different names for work and home. And your family won't be able to acknowledge you—"

"*You* are my family, you and Beth. And the other children we will have." His gesture toward the house was lost in the darkness. "That is just my past. Tonight I have stopped looking back. If it will give them peace, too, I will come see my mother and brother. But my future is with you. And . . . oh, I expect it to be complicated. With a wife like you, what else could it be?"

"You'd be bored otherwise," she countered.

"I'll never be bored with you." He released her so that he could open the door in the wall. "You will no doubt come up with a score of schemes, so that even when I am away at sea, I will be obsessed with you."

"Away at sea? But, darling," she answered with that slight emphasis they always placed on that endearment, "the sea has had you to herself long enough. The next voyage, Beth and I are coming along."

He was still laughing as they emerged from the brambles. "Coming along, are you? Well, I've never had a woman aboard before. Beth especially will make us an entertaining shipmate."

"And I, my love, intend to make you a *very* entertaining cabinmate."

He caught her up and kissed her, and then, hand in hand, never stumbling, they ran down his father's hill into the night.

.

CPSIA information can be obtained at www.ICGtesting.com
Printed in the USA
LVOW060103221211

260621LV00003B/7/P